"No one—*no one*—writes big, chewy space opera like the husband-and-wife team of Doyle and Macdonald!"

—Jane Yolen

Unscheduled Duel

More footsteps came drumming at the hall outside the gallery, and a moment later Delath and Narin skidded over the threshold. Kief plunged through the door a heartbeat behind them, his long hair flying and his staff ablaze.

"Help us out!" Yuvaen shouted at the startled Mages. "Break them apart!"

"There's luck here, Yuva," Garrod said, panting—the web pulled tighter with every exchange of blows, and he found himself hard-pressed. "Strong luck."

"There's luck everywhere," Yuvaen said. He was moving in toward Ty from behind, his staff up to guard against the danger of backstrokes.

"Not like this." Garrod brought his staff against Iulain Vai's in a move that should have ripped the practice weapon out of her hand. Instead, the maneuver drew him into striking range of her counterattack. "This luck is ours—if we can take it. Now!"

"An intricate tale, rich in characters and maneuverings."

—*Analog*

TOR BOOKS BY
Debra Doyle and James D. Macdonald

MAGEWORLDS
The Price of the Stars
Starpilot's Grave
By Honor Betray'd
The Gathering Flame
The Long Hunt
The Stars Asunder

I Need these

DEBRA DOYLE AND JAMES D. MACDONALD

THE STARS ASUNDER

TOR®

A TOM DOHERTY ASSOCIATES BOOK
NEW YORK

This is a work of fiction. All the characters and events portrayed in this book are either products of the author's imagination or are used fictitiously.

THE STARS ASUNDER

Edited by Patrick and Teresa Nielsen Hayden

A Tor Book
Published by Tom Doherty Associates, LLC
175 Fifth Avenue
New York, NY 10010

www.tor.com

Tor® is a registered trademark of Tom Doherty Associates, LLC

ISBN: 0-812-57192-4
Library of Congress Catalogue Card Number: 99-24561

First edition: June 1999
First mass market edition: June 2000

Printed in the United States of America

0 9 8 7 6 5 4 3 2 1

In memory of Vickie Bunnell, Dennis Joos, Les Lord, and Scott Phillips; and with gratitude to Jeff Caulder, John Fifer, Robert Haase, and Wayne Sanders. Lives spent in service, and not forgotten.

Authors' Preface
(for those who have been here before)

I. So There We Were . . .

... **I**N THE Republic of Panamá. It was the mid-eighties. Macdonald was nearing the end of a career in the US Navy and Doyle was teaching freshman composition at the University of Florida extension campus. And new English-language science fiction wasn't easy to find. The tropical sun did something to our brains, and we started writing short stories, mostly for our own amusement. Or, to be more accurate, Doyle started writing them.

One of the stories—a vignette, really—dealt with a young lady named Beka who'd just been given a spaceship by her father. Odd and exciting doings were hinted at. Macdonald enjoyed reading the story (as did our friend Sherwood Smith, a writer in California with whom we shared our manuscripts). Macdonald got to like Beka, and pestered Doyle for the next story about her. Doyle, who was absorbed by that time in another project, said words to the effect of, "If you want another story, write it yourself."

So Beka landed her spaceship, and spent some twenty double-spaced pages working through all the routine of clearing a cargo through customs in a foreign port, before a booted foot slammed unexpectantly into her knee, knocking her to the ground so that an assassin's shot would miss her head. The boot belonged to a mild-mannered, elderly gentleman with a mysterious past. He and Beka went on to have adventures together.

Doyle took the manuscript, cut out the twenty-page meticulously detailed depiction of filling out paperwork in a government office, poured a bottle of bleach over the purple prose, and said, "Well, go on." The first part of the story went off to California, where Sherwood likewise read it and called for more.

Two hundred pages later, we were still calling the piece "the short story" (being at that point still unclear on the concept of "novel-length") and the older gentleman had gained a name. He was the "Professor." The Prof and Beka continued to have adventures, mailed off to California at the rate of one every couple of weeks, with each episode ending with a cliff-hanger. The new episode would go off by mail to California, Sherwood would reply "Arrrgh!" and we'd be off for the next round.

Move forward a few years of real time. Macdonald was out of the Navy, and was living with Doyle in New Hampshire, far removed from the tropics. They had written and published eight young-adult novels. Their method was pretty much the same one that they had developed while working on the "short story." Macdonald would write a first draft/outline, Doyle would put it into English, and then they'd argue about the details. They were both between projects and that collection of pages about Beka and the Professor looked like it could be made into a real novel.

So, as they say, it came to pass. *The Price of the Stars* was published as a paperback original in 1992. By the end of the novel, the Professor was dead.

But you can't keep a good character down. The Prof had a lot of mysterious past to explore. In the third Mageworlds book, *By Honor Betray'd* we finally learned his true name— Arekhon Khreseio sus-Khalgaeth sus-Peledaen—and in the prequel volume, *The Gathering Flame*, we met him as Ser Hafrey, Armsmaster to House Rosselin. His influence extended, in fact, throughout the entire series, so that Doyle eventually asserted that if she ever wrote another Mageworlds book, it would be about the Professor as a young . . . well, as a young whatever he really was, way back then on the other side of the galaxy.

II. The Dark on the Other Side

Which brings us to the present work. When we came to write this volume, we realized that in the course of five Mageworlds novels we had scarcely visited the Mageworlds themselves at all. Beka Rosselin-Metadi and Nyls Jessan touched ground briefly on Raamet and Ninglin and Eraasi; Errec Ransome was held prisoner for a short while on Cracanth; but little more than that.

And our characters, by and large, were not going to give us any sympathy when we felt guilty. From the viewpoint of the civilized galaxy—as the worlds which later became the Republic and its allies liked to think of themselves—the Mageworlds were a menace, home to a faceless enemy.

"The Mageworlds" was not even the raiders' own name for their place of origin. The name they used, most of the time, was simply "the homeworlds." Sometimes they, or the more politically aware among their adversaries, would call themselves "Eraasians," from the dominant planet in their loose confederation.

Even more than the Mageworlds' attempts at conquest, the metaphysical differences between the two cultures set them at odds. In the civilized galaxy, those who worked with and through the power inherent in the universe called themselves Adepts. Their philosophy favored individual action over collective effort, and they believed in riding the natural flow of power in the universe and letting that flow add to their own strengths.

On their own worlds, the Adepts were historically regarded with both distrust and superstitious awe. As a consequence, they became, as a group, inclined toward secrecy and the protection of their own. Tradition set the Adepts apart from formal involvement in political life; during certain periods, however, their informal participation was considerable. The years during and immediately after the First Magewar were especially noteworthy in this regard.

The Mages, as they referred to themselves (their enemies then expanded the term to cover an entire society, and not merely a comparative few of its members), were integrated into the public life of their worlds as the more solitary Adepts never were. Believing in group action and in the combination of forces toward a single effort, the Mages regarded the power resident in the universe as something to be manipulated and worked with directly. For the Adepts, on the other hand, actually making changes in the flow of power, or attempting to impose a pattern on that flow, was regarded as nothing less than an abomination—"sorcery," as Llannat Hyfid describes it when she first feels it in action on Darvell; "Magework and dark sorcery."

Another philosophical dividing point between the two cultures came on the question of luck. The philosophy of the Adepts, in its strictest form, holds that there is no such thing as luck at all, only the natural flow of power in the universe. Those people who are spoken of by others as "lucky" are regarded by the Adepts as having an innate sense of this power flow, of where it goes and of when and how it is about to change. Even among people who believe in luck in its more casual sense, there is no feeling that luck is subject to conscious manipulation.

The Mages, on the other hand, view luck as something real in itself, and inextricably bound up with human life. Grand Admiral sus-Airaalin of the Mageworlds Resurgency speaks of Beka Rosselin-Metadi as a "luck-maker"; something of the same quality, in the Mages' view, also attaches to her father, Jos Metadi, "whose luck two generations of Magelords had tried in vain to break." The forces of life and luck together make up the *eiran*, perceived by working Mages as a network of silver cords. Attempts on a Mage-Circle's part to untangle the *eiran* of a particular place, or to bring them into a more pleasing pattern, are often experienced by Adepts as unnatural changes or damage to the natural flow of power.

In the aftermath of the First Magewar, these philosophical differences—and, of course, the atrocities committed by the Mageworlders on Ilarna and Sapne and Entibor—almost proved fatal to the Eraasian worlds. Driven by a need for security and a desire for revenge, the military forces of the victorious Republic did their best to reduce Eraasian industrial capacity below the level necessary to wage interstellar war. At the same time, Errec Ransome and his Adepts strove to break the Mage-Circles and eliminate their practices from the civilized galaxy. The combined result was not so much a period of occupation and pacification as it was—to quote the Ilarnan scholar Vinhalyn, who observed the process as a young officer with the Republic's Space Force—"the systematic destruction of a culture cognate to ours, yet unimaginably alien."

III. CONCERNING THE SUNDERING OF THE GALAXY

A great expanse of starless space separates the Mageworlds from the rest of the galaxy. In Mageworlds legend, this interstellar gap was the product of the Sundering of the Galaxy, a catastrophic event with theological or metaphysical roots, prior to which the gap did not exist. The story of the Sundering also exists on the other side of the gap, although the versions current in the rest of the galaxy differ considerably in their details.

Whatever the actual cause and origin of the interstellar gap, it looms much larger in Mageworlds thinking than it does in the greater galactic culture. Some scholars conclude therefore that Eraasi and the other Mageworlds suffered more than the rest of the galaxy from the effects of the Sundering, and thus retained more memories, however distant, of the actual event. Others take the opposite position, and assert that the Sundering's effect on the rest of the galaxy was so much greater that on those worlds proportionately more memory of the event was lost.

IV. OTHER CULTURAL CHANGES

The astute reader will notice a number of differences, both small and large, between the Eraasian worlds as they appear at this earlier point in their history and as they became by the time of the First and Second Magewars. The Eraasian language provides an instructive example. Five hundred years, give or take (and depending upon which planet's revolution is used to define the term), separate the events chronicled in this book from those of the later Magewars; Eraasian speech did not go unchanged in the interim. The reader should note especially the tendency toward greater diphthongization over time, as exemplified in *Rayamet* vice the later *Raamet*. Also contrast the family name *sus-Khalgath* with its later spelling (as derived from Ignac' LeSoit's pronunciation) *sus-Khalgaeth*.

Noticeable changes also occurred in Circle garb and procedure during the five-hundred-year gap. Readers will notice the absence, in earlier times, of the *geaerith*, or full-face mask. The Mage-Circles of Llannat Hyfid's and Mael Taleion's day justify the use of the mask as allowing a clearer perception of the *eiran*. More recently gathered historical evidence suggests—in view of the fact that the *geaerith* also provides its wearer with anonymity—that the change had its roots in political developments in the Eraasian hegemony.

Also worth noting are the differing conceptions of the relationship between hyperspace and the Void. In the rest of the civilized galaxy, technology and cosmology draw a careful distinction between hyperspace (as traveled through by starships) and the Void (as visited but mostly steered clear of by Adepts). Eraasians, however, view the two places/phenomena as essentially the same.

Acknowledgments

THE AUTHORS would like to thank Marina and Sherwood and Thyme, for beta-reading the manuscript; Norman and Marian, for letting us hold down a table at the Red Lantern Cafe while we drank coffee and worked on revisions; and Gregory Feeley, for coming up with a title when our minds remained obstinately blank.

Prologue

*T*HIS IS *the story's true beginning. On other worlds and in other places they tell it differently, but nowhere has it been altogether forgotten.*

In the years when the worlds first bore life, the galaxy was all one. The eiran—*the silver cords of life and luck—wound unbroken throughout all the aspects of human existence. They bound life to life, and world to world, and past to future, and the pattern was all of one weaving.*

But the people of the many worlds grew lazy, and failed to tend the eiran *as they should have done, and as had been their task from the beginning. The* eiran *turned wild, and grew and changed until the pattern was no longer of one weaving but of many, and the cords in the many patterns pulled and twisted in all directions.*

"Look," said some of the people, the clear-sighted ones. "The one pattern has been destroyed through our careless inattention, and who can say what the consequences of that may be."

The others never listened. They no longer saw the one pattern even in the many weavings, but each of them saw a single and separate pattern, and tended only the eiran that lay within it.

"See now," the clear-sighted ones told them. "The threads in the one pattern grow tight and tangled, and the strain on the weaving is greater than it can hold. If the pattern is not mended now it will pass away from us."

But still the others would not listen.

And the day came when the threads of the pattern snapped, and the eiran flew wide across the face of the universe like floss on the wind, and the two halves of the galaxy were ripped apart and flung away one from the other, and the people were blinded to the sight of the silver cords that had perished from their lack of tending.

Of those who had been clear-sighted, only a few remained. All of the rest were lost, and their worlds with them.

I: Year 1116 Eraasian Reckoning
Eraasi: Hanilat Starport
Demaizen Old Hall

*R*IBBON-OF-STARLIGHT, FOREMOST guardship in the sus-Peledaen fleet, waited on the landing field at Hanilat like a dark, angular bird. She was the largest family ship that could actually touch the soil of Eraasi. The merchant ships she escorted were bigger—huge constructs, hold-swollen with cargo—but they never left orbit. The shuttles that would bring up the flats and bales and crates of tradeware clustered like nestlings on the burnt ground next to the *Ribbon*'s protective bulk.

Arekhon Khreseio sus-Khalgath sus-Peledaen, riding out to the guardship in the back compartment of an open landhauler, gave the shuttles nothing more than a cursory glance. *Ribbon-of-Starlight*—his home for the remainder of his fleet apprenticeship—claimed the greater part of his attention. She was a new ship, no more than a couple of voyages old, but already known for a lucky one. 'Rekhe squinted at her, trying for the catch and angle of sunlight that would let him see the *eiran* wrapping and weaving around her.

A moment . . . there . . . yes. To the right eyes, *Ribbon-of-Starlight* was rich with luck, hung about with it in lacework so thick it looked like silvery gauze.

Arekhon himself was a slight, dark-haired youth. He'd worked with the fleet Circle in Hanilat since he was first able to count his age in two digits, but now that he was, by everyone's reckoning, old enough to make a full commitment to the Mages, his duty to the family came first. His brother Natelth was the head of the sus-Peledaen family's senior line, and Natelth wanted 'Rekhe to go through his apprenticeship in the fleet . . . so an apprentice, perforce, 'Rekhe would have to be, and the Circles could wait until later.

"Here you are."

'Rekhe blinked, and the luck-lines went away, leaving the *Ribbon* looming stark black as before, only much nearer. A door was open high on one curving side, and a narrow metal ladder led up to it.

"Thank you," he said politely to the driver of the landhauler, collected his duffel, and climbed out of the back compartment onto the ground. The hauler sped off on its next errand. 'Rekhe shouldered his duffel and started climbing.

A young man in a blue work coverall was waiting for him when he reached the top of the ladder. The crimson piping and insignia on the man's coverall told 'Rekhe that he was a clerk-tertiary, not long out of his own training days.

"Arekhon sus-Khalgath?" the clerk said.

"Reporting for instruction, sir." Everyone outranked an apprentice—even when the apprentice came from the family's senior line—and 'Rekhe took pains to keep his voice respectful. Natelth had made it plain that he would not have his younger brother disgracing the family by causing trouble and discontent.

"Come with me." The clerk-tertiary led the way into the coiling three-dimensional labyrinth of the *Ribbon*'s interior, and 'Rekhe followed.

He tried to memorize the route as they went, but in spite of his efforts he knew that he would have to spend time with the ship's map-models later. The ground-based portion of his prentice-training had given him an understanding of the basic principles of ship construction, but each ship had its own set of variations on the common design.

The clerk-tertiary halted before an airtight door like all the others they had passed by, or through, on the way inward.

"Prentice berthing," he said. "Stow your gear and report to the junior wardroom in an hour."

With that, he departed, leaving 'Rekhe to confront the door alone. Fortunately, it was merely closed, rather than dogged down tight. 'Rekhe pulled it open and stepped over the sill.

The compartment held four bunks, stacked two deep on either side of the door. Corresponding lockers filled the rest of the available space along the bulkheads. The bunks were rigged with the cushions and webbing to double as acceleration couches.

A girl sat cross-legged on one of the lower bunks, reading a flatbook and making notes on the margin-pad with a stylus. She wore prentice livery like 'Rekhe's own—more dark blue trimmed with crimson—and her short brown hair curled around her bent head in a loose mop. She looked up as 'Rekhe stepped into the compartment.

"It's first-come, first-served on the bunks," she said. "You might as well take the bottom one on the other side before somebody else does."

"I like the top bunks," said 'Rekhe. "Nobody steps on your face every night and morning."

The girl shrugged. "No accounting for taste. I'm Elaeli Inadi, by the way."

"Arekhon sus-Khalgath," he said, sketching a bow.

And the *eiran* that had hung like cobwebs around *Ribbon-of-Starlight*'s dark metal hull began to weave themselves into a newer pattern.

On the day that the *Ribbon* left Eraasi for her trading voyage to Ildaon and beyond, Serazao Zulemem was at work in the outer office of the Harradi Group, a firm of legalists specializing in the financial affairs of Eraasi's middle and upper nobility. The Demaizen estate was about to pass into the hands of its final inheritor, and Serazao had drawn the work of sorting and filing all the hardcopy that the case had generated during two decades of legal contests.

Serazao's parents, Alescu and Evya, had come to Hanilat from Eraasi's antipodal subcontinent because well-trained legalists—and they were both well-trained—could prosper in the employ of the merchants and star-lords who made the city their base of operations. Her father soon achieved membership in the Harradi Group; her mother, more combative by nature, kept her own office as a court-litigant.

Serazao herself was a quiet, industrious child. From the time she was old enough to make plans for her future and have others take them seriously, she intended to become a legalist like her parents. To that end, as soon as she reached the age of employment, she worked part time—full time during the school intervals—at her father's firm.

The litigation concerning the Demaizen estate had come near to outlasting the family lines that contended for it. Serazao knew from her parents' dinner-table conversation that only the death from old age of one of the parties involved had brought the matter to a conclusion. Now the remaining heir was required to present himself at Harradi's offices to take possession . . . in this case, of a portfolio full of deeds and account-books.

Nobody had bothered to mention that the last of the sus-Demaizen line was also a Mage; or if they had, they'd done it so long ago that Serazao had not been there to hear. From the length of time that the estate had been in the hands of the legalists, she assumed that its ultimate heir would be another one like the deceased claimant, whom she'd had the misfortune once to meet: Elderly, avaricious, ill-tempered, and infirm, with more money already in his possession than any one man could reasonably think to spend.

Garrod syn-Aigal was not what she'd expected at all.

Her first impression, when he came into the outer office, was that he was the heir's driver, or perhaps his bodyguard: A big man, broad in the shoulders and firmly muscled, but with none of the clumsiness that so often came with strength. He wore plain street clothes, of good quality but far from new, with a long weather-coat thrown over them. It was the middle of Hanilat's rainy season—she remembered the date ever afterward, very clearly—and both the coat and the loose-brimmed hat he wore with it shed water in puddles on the office floor.

He paused inside the door, still dripping, and looked about with a searching expression that lightened when he saw her at work behind the office-bar.

"Good morning, Syr—"

"Zulemem," she said, and then, in reply to his unspoken question, "There's a coatrack in the corner behind you."

He smiled, which made his heavy dark eyebrows bristle even more fiercely than they did already. She didn't like men with thick eyebrows—she preferred an elegant antipodal arch, like her father had, or her cousins—but the newcomer's good humor made them, and the roughness of the features around them, surprisingly attractive.

"Ah. So there is. Thank you, Syr Zulemem."

"Serazao," she said, as he pulled off the coat and the hat and hung them up on the polished brass hooks of the coatrack. With the coat out of the way, she caught her first glimpse of the short wooden staff that the man wore clipped to his belt. Seeing it, she frowned.

He was quick; he caught the change in her expression almost before the muscles of her face made their fractional changes to echo the shift within her mind.

"Is there something wrong?"

"No," she said hastily, "nothing wrong. I didn't realize that syn-Aigal had a Mage-Circle on his side, is all."

"He doesn't, not really." He smiled again. "Or *I* don't, at least—and I was Garrod syn-Aigal the last time I looked."

She felt the blood rising in her face. If any of the office partners found out that she had, at least by implication, insulted their client . . . "I'm sorry; I was impertinent."

"You told the truth as you saw it, Syr Zulemem. No impertinence there."

"Maybe not for you," she said. "But I want to work here someday, when my schooling's finished."

His eyebrows went up again. "You don't look like a legalist to me."

"Oh?" Irritation flared; she frowned at him, never minding what the office partners might have to say. He hadn't looked like a man who would pay heavy-handed compliments of that sort, and it was depressing to find out otherwise. "What *do* I look like, then?"

Once again, he surprised her. "A Mage."

"You're joking."

"About that, never."

"I couldn't—"

"There should be a Circle working near your school," he said. "Ask your instructors; one of them will know. And when you've trained in Hanilat long enough, come to Demaizen Old Hall and ask for me. I'll be building a Circle there."

The wet weather that had been merely annoying in Hanilat was chilly and unseasonable in the Wide Hills district several days later. On the road going up past Demaizen Town, the rain slanted down cold and hard in the driving beams of Garrod's heavy six-wheel groundcar. The vehicle bumped along over the muddy track, then turned the corner in a cut braced by stone shoring and began growling up the final slope.

"There it is," Garrod said. He pointed to the massive stone pile that loomed among its outbuildings at the crest of a long hill. "Demaizen Old Hall."

The driver grunted, unimpressed. "I see it."

The main gate stood open in a twist of rusted iron. The groundcar passed slowly through, and kept on until the road ended in front of the heavy bronze doors of the central building. The beams from the groundcar's driving lamps picked up the Hall's blank windows, its moss- and lichen-spattered walls. Everything here was untended and overgrown, even the road itself; weeds poked up knee-high through what had once been the gravel surface of a circular driveway.

The driver switched the engine to neutral, and the sound dropped to a low throb. "Here you are."

"Thanks, Yuva," Garrod said. He pushed open the passenger-side door. The wind took it, smashing it fully open against the front engine cowling. The rain stung like needles and plastered Garrod's hair flat in an instant. He jumped out of the ground-car, his staff swinging from his belt, and ran the ten feet to the doors.

The arched opening gave at least some protection from the wind, but the doors were locked. Garrod frowned. The keys had not been part of the inheritance.

He unclipped his staff. A moment's preparation, a reaching-out and a pulling-in, and the staff began to give off a steady blue-white light. He touched the door and bent his energies toward persuading it to open, but to no avail—the locks were rusted fast, their mechanisms destroyed by more than a generation without maintenance.

Garrod sprinted back to where Yuvaen waited in the groundcar. "Back her up to the doors," he shouted above the howling wind.

"Got it."

The groundcar lurched forward, then swung back and to the left. Its wheels ground and bumped up the shallow steps until the rear towing bar nearly touched the bronze doors.

Garrod opened the cargo compartment and pulled out the tow chain. He threaded it through the handles of the doors, linked it with a clevis bolt to the rings on the towing bar, and stepped aside.

"Yuva! Ahead slow!"

The groundcar sent out a puff of chemical vapor from its upper tubes, and growled forward. Hinges and bolts gave way behind it in a howl of tearing metal, and the bronze doors buckled under the strain.

"Hold up!" Garrod shouted.

The groundcar stopped. Yuvaen shut off the engine and emerged from the driver's side.

"Give us a light," Garrod said. "Let's see how it looks."

"Right." Yuvaen had brought an electric lantern with him from the groundcar. He turned it on and lifted it to shine a yellow light at the doors of the hall—the right-hand one pulled entirely away from the frame, the one on the left tilted crazily and hanging by a single hinge. He cast a gloomy eye over the damage. "It'll cost you a pretty to have those fixed."

"I've got all the money I need," Garrod said. "What I don't have is time. Come on."

The two men entered the Hall. White-sheeted furniture stood ghostlike in the foyer. Dust lay thick, and gnawing creatures had worked on much of the interior woodwork. Garrod pointed through an arch to where a staircase went curling upward.

"There," he said, and started up toward the long gallery on the second floor. Yuvaen followed.

At the entrance to the gallery, both men paused on the threshold. Their rain-soaked clothing clung to their bodies like wet leaves, and the glow from Yuvaen's lantern cast a swaying circle of yellow light on the space within, where the sus-Demaizen kept their tablets of remembrance.

Plaques and memorials covered the walls—ancient slabs of grey slate scratched with names in a language no longer spoken by anyone living, and newer tablets of painted wood and cast metal. On the altars beneath them, long-guttered candles spilled out their wax across carven wood.

Garrod strode into the center of the room, where a small altar stood in front of a freestanding memorial on tripod legs. The candle holders were empty—whoever had last tended the memorial had scraped them clean when the rite was done—and a spray of white flowers, long since dried, lay on the altar between them.

"This is an end and a breaking," Garrod said. With that he picked up the memorial and flung it out through one of the high, west-looking windows in the center of the long wall. The window glass gave way in a jagged, shivering peal, and the memorial went crashing down onto the gravel drive outside.

"Wait!" Yuvaen cried over the noise. "Hasn't there been enough broken already?"

Garrod put his hands against the wooden altar and shoved it toward the broken window. "No," he said. "Not enough by half. Before I am done, I will break our very universe."

The altar smashed against the low sill and tumbled over it to the ground below. Rain poured in through the gap in the window, driven slantwise by the rising wind.

"Your ancestors will curse you," Yuvaen said.

"My ancestors mean nothing to me," Garrod said, "and I mean nothing to them." He pulled another of the tablets from the wall, and the dried wood splintered in his hands. He threw the tablet out onto the gravel with the other wreckage. "I am the last of my line, and what follows after will follow the older days."

"I don't understand."

"The sundering of the galaxy is not just a parable, or an allegory suitable for children and scholars," Garrod said. He was pulling tablet after tablet away from the plastered walls, working now with a fierce, unstoppable intensity. "It is nothing less than the truth. And I intend to bring together that which was split apart."

Yuvaen shook his head. "You're right not to fear your ancestors. It's the gods themselves that you should fear."

Garrod fished in his pocket and pulled out an incendiary, of the kind used by workers in the metal and construction trades. He pulled the igniter and tossed the incendiary down onto the tangle of broken wood on the gravel drive. A brilliant white light blossomed up, mixed shortly after with red as the wood caught fire. The western windows glowed with the color.

Garrod heaved another wooden tablet out of the broken window and into the flames. "I don't have time to fear the gods, Yuva—you'll have to do it for me. Come, help me clean out this space, for here will be our workroom."

"May the gods forgive me, then," Yuvaen said. "Because I'm with you."

The two men embraced, then fell to stripping the walls of their memorials, and clearing the floor of its altars.

II: YEAR 1116 E. R.
ERAASI: WESTERN FISHING GROUNDS
SYN-GREVI ESTATE, NORTHERN TERRITORIES
Ildaon: Ildaon Starport

THE DEEP-WATER fleets from Amisket, Demnag, and Ridkil Point had been having a bad summer. Like most of the coastal settlements in the Veredden Archipelago, the three towns depended for a livelihood on their commercial fisheries, and a poor haul meant a lean year to come. In autumn, the fish migrated to spawning grounds near the equator—too great a distance for the Veredden ships to follow, even if biological changes during the spawn didn't turn the fish sour and spongy—and winter in the northern latitudes was too stormy for surface craft to ply the waters at all. Winter was for spending the long nights snug in harbor, making repairs and hoping that the money from last summer's catch would last until spring.

As First of the Amisket Circle, Narin Iyal took the season's lack of good fishing harder than most, and most were taking it hard. It was her Circle's place to provide fish-luck and weather-luck, and to tell the captains of the fleet where the silver was running. But all she could tell the captains now was that the fish had abandoned their usual grounds, and she had no idea where they might be.

The nets of the deep-sea trawler *Dance-and-be-Joyful* trailed astern, and the lines still had the slack of an empty haul. The crew lounged in the shadow of the deckhouse, playing cards. The engines throbbed ahead slow.

Narin stood on the main deck, staring over the rail at a horizon made dim by haze, and at the rolling blue waters beneath the empty sky. She was a short dark woman with a square snub-nosed face and calloused hands. The sun, just past its zenith, burned down upon her neck and shoulders. Other than the wind of the ship's passage, no breeze ruffled her hair.

Narin looked up at the distant line where sea met sky. A set of masts there, black lines against the paler sky, told where *First-Light-of-Morning* ran, hull down, tracing a parallel course. They'd had no better luck than the *Dance,* she was sure.

"You asked for me?"

The familiar baritone rumble belonged to Big Tam, Second of the Amisket Circle. Tam was a dark-skinned, wide-shouldered man, and in his many-times-laundered work shirt and loose trousers he looked more like the son and grandson of deep-sea fishers—which he also was—than like a ranking Mage. He'd been with the Circle for almost as long as Narin had, and had been her Second since the beginning.

Narin looked back out at the water. The sunlight sparked painfully bright on the blue swells. "Yes," she said. "If we don't want children going hungry in Amisket by year's end, it's time we did something about our luck."

"I agree."

"Good. Call the others to the meditation room. We will have a working."

The meditation room on *Dance-and-be-Joyful* was a cramped space set forward belowdecks. It was far narrower and more confining than such a room should have been, even for a small Circle like Narin's, and its atmosphere was a malodorous slurry of machine oil, fish, and rank sweat. But space for the Circle was carved out of the *Dance*'s cargo hold, and every cubic inch taken away from storage cost the ship's master money when the fish were running.

Narin made her way below, stopping by her cabin to change into her robes and pick up a small-scale chart of the fishing grounds. As First of the Circle, she had her own quarters. The rest of the Amisket Mages shared crew's berthing, though they stood no watches and hauled no lines.

She took the paper chart forward to the meditation room. In spite of the summer heat above decks, the air inside the room was cold, chilled by the heavy-duty cargo refrigeration system in the adjacent compartment, and condensation beaded and ran down the bulkheads in a steady, relentless trickle. A single incandescent light illuminated the white circle painted on the deck.

Laros, the older of the Circle's two unranked Mages, was already there, dressed in formal robes, with his staff clipped to his belt. In a moment, Tam and young Kasaly arrived as well. Narin swung the door to behind them and dogged it shut.

"The time has come," she said, "for a working. To make our own luck, and force the gathering of the fish."

"Past time," Kasaly said. Kas was red-haired and pretty, and a great favorite with the sailors. Her luck-making was among the best, however, and Narin suspected that she had it in her to be First herself someday, provided that she learned enough patience and discipline first.

"Are we all agreed, then?" Narin asked—a formality, mostly, since it was a poor First who couldn't gauge the temper of her own Circle. It was her right, as First, to direct their combined intention, but she wasn't foolish enough to push them where they were determined not to go.

As she'd expected, nobody raised an objection.

"Good." She walked to her usual place in the arc of the white-painted circle closest to the *Dance*'s bow, and knelt on the welded metal deckplates. On that cue, the rest of the Mages took their customary positions: Tam opposite her, Kas to her right, Laros to her left.

"As we are gathered," she said, "so we are one."

She turned away from her physical surroundings and looked inward, searching the three-dimensional world of the sea for the streaky feeling of the fish's lives. She could sense the others searching as well—Tam strong and steady, Laros knife-blade sharp, and Kas like a bright flame of luck in the deep water. Now she had to draw them together like one of the purse seines that the trawlers used, combining all their energies to bring both the fish and luck in taking them into one physical spot.

"Seek them, hold them, bring and bind them," she said. "We are one." The circle pulsed in the depths like a ring of silver, marking the darting presence of the fish. "Find the place. Join them and lock them to a place."

"We need to be stronger," Tam said. His voice seemed to come from far away, outside of the sea-deeps where the minds of the Circle made their search. "To find the place so that the boats can find it."

"I'll give to the working," Narin said. "Who will match me?"

"I will," Tam replied.

He stood, bringing his staff up before him. Narin did the same, and felt the power of the universe surging around her, ready to be taken like the fish she sought. She drew the power into herself and let it flow out again redoubled, making her staff shine with a deep green fire. Blue fire answered from the other side of the tiny space. The same current that flowed through Narin like one of the rolling seas beneath the ship, flowed now through her Second as well.

The two staves met with a crack. Narin saw the luck fly out from them like rainbows, and felt a surge of joy. This would be a good working, a strong working—the congruence of the inner and the outer worlds would guarantee its success.

Again Tam attacked; again she countered, then counter-attacked. They pressed together, striving to create and make manifest the luck of the fleet through the essential contradiction of the universe opposing itself. Sweat rolled down their necks in spite of the physical chill of the space, and their breathing grew hoarse and ragged.

Then, as quickly as the energy had risen, it flared in a last bright dazzle and fell away. Narin stepped back.

"It's done," she said. "I have them."

She reached into her shirt pocket underneath her robe and pulled out a pencil stub and the chart of the fishing grounds. She drew a neat dot on the chart, circled it, and wrote a time beside it. Then she drew more circled dots, and wrote more times. The dots and times, when she had finished, represented where the fish had been, were, and would be. The pattern showed an eastward drift at slow speed.

"So that's why we couldn't find anything," Tam said, watching over her shoulder as she worked. A fisherman and a fishers' Mage for many years, he knew that the location lay well outside the fleet's usual grounds, farther to the west of the island homeports than anyone had expected.

Narin refolded the chart and tucked it back into her shirt pocket.

"Rest," she said to the other Mages. "I'll take this to the Captain. He'll want to inform the fleet."

The sus-Peledaen convoy guarded by *Ribbon-of-Starlight* made its first trading stop at Ildaon. The chief exports of Ildaon were mineral pigments, raw textiles, and exotic furs; in return, the Ildaonese bought second-cut red *uffa* to blend with the harsher native leaf, and luxury-model flyers of Eraasian design. Captain syn-Avran allowed members of the guardship's crew to go on liberty in the port city, as long as they kept out of trouble. Arekhon sus-Khalgath and Elaeli Inadi were in the next-to-last group to go.

They wore their best apprentice livery for the occasion—inconvenient, if someone on Ildaon had it in for traders, but useful if a port official or a fellow crewmember needed to spot them quickly in a crowd. They also wore sus-Peledaen shipcloaks of dark blue lined with crimson. Ildaon's starport was situated on a high northern plateau, and the season was local winter.

A traders' hostel at the edge of the landing field provided lodging for star-travelers, as well as for operators of Ildaonese ground and air transport. Arekhon, Elaeli, and the others in their group stopped there first. A bored-looking desk clerk assigned them rooms and changed their family scrip for local currency.

The rooms were small and bare: A bed, access to sanitary facilities, and a door that locked. 'Rekhe was accustomed to better; even aboard *Ribbon-of-Starlight,* the quarters were crowded but far more up-to-date than these. He didn't protest, however, since he suspected that most of the people with rooms at the hostel would not be using them. There were, or so he had heard, drinking establishments and houses of notorious behavior on Ildaon, and the crew members in this liberty section had until the next local mid-day to amuse themselves however they chose—provided, of course, that they did nothing that might interfere with trade or damage the reputation of the sus-Peledaen.

"Get in trouble with the local authorities," the prentice-master had said, "and there's no guarantee that the family will pull you out. There's not one of you that's worth losing the good will of a whole planet for."

The information board at the traders' hostel gave directions to public transportation. After waiting for several minutes without any luck at the pickup stand, Arekhon and Elaeli turned up the high, lined collars of their cloaks and headed into town on foot. Prentice-master Lanar had insisted that the ship's apprentices do all their exploration and revelry in pairs—in the hope, he said, of thus adding up to one person's complement of good sense. As the two most junior, Arekhon and Elaeli had fallen naturally together.

"Where shall we go first?" 'Rekhe asked. He was shivering a little in spite of the ship-cloak; the weather never got this cold in Hanilat. The sky was a deep and merciless blue, and a dry wind blew without ceasing around steep-roofed buildings of fired brick and grey stone. "Sightseeing?"

"I don't think there's any sights around here to see," Elaeli said. The wind caught at her loose curls and whipped them into a wild tangle. "All the scenic beauty is probably off over the horizon somewhere, and we can't get there and back in a day."

"What, then?"

"Well—there's always shopping."

'Rekhe looked about dubiously at the square, plain buildings of the starport—a small town, really, compared to the sprawling conurbation that was Hanilat. "What have they got here that we couldn't find a better one of back home?"

"I don't know . . . local stuff, I suppose. Souvenirs, knick-knacks—"

"Gloves," said 'Rekhe. The dignity of fleet livery would not allow for hands in the pockets, but surely gloves—of a proper color and good material—would not disgrace the ship or incur the prentice-master's disapproval.

"Right," said Elaeli. "Gloves it is."

The messenger from Hanilat reached syn-Grevi Lodge at twilight, in the long pale gloaming of Eraasi's high northern latitudes, just before the hour of lunar observance. Theledau syn-Grevi was on the stairs leading up to the moon-room when he heard the front door's two-note chime. He paused, one step short of the second-floor landing, and waited.

The Lodge's doorkeeper-*aiketh*—a cylinder of burnished metal half the height of a living man, wrapped around a carefully built and instructed quasi-organic mind—floated up the stairs to meet him. The counterforce unit in its base hummed gently as it rose. Behind the smoky grey plastic housing of its sensorium, a blue light flickered briefly.

"My lord syn-Grevi," it said. The synthesized voice was genderless but pleasing to hear. Like all of the *aiketen* at syn-Grevi Lodge, its instruction-set had it speaking northern dialect, rather than Hanilat-Eraasian. "Iulan Vai has come with news."

"Vai!" said Thel. He glanced automatically at the antique clock on the landing above him, an old-style devotional timepiece whose complex analog interior allowed its multiple dials to show the phases and movements of the moon as well as the current hour. There would be time to speak with Vai and still keep the moonwatch—excellent. "Where is she now?"

"She waits in the reception room, my lord."

"Good. Instruct the kitchen to bring some light refreshment."

"I hear, my lord," said the *aiketh*, and floated off.

Thel hurried back down the stairs to the reception room where Iulan Vai waited. She was a compact, deceptively quiet woman, dressed as usual in a tailored black overtunic and black leggings. When he'd first met Vai, Thel had attributed her taste in clothing to a streak of austerity in her temperament, but over the passage of time he'd decided that she dressed in black mainly because it allowed her to hide better in dark corners.

Iulan Vai was the syn-Grevi family's eyes and ears in Han-

ilat. Thel's father, before he died, had paid for her training
and seen to her placement in that position. Theledau had his
own theories about the reason why. Vai was a decade or so
younger than Thel, but like him—and like, also, the elder syn-
Grevi in his prime—she had fair skin, and hair of a reddish-
brown so dark that in most lights it appeared as a rusty black.
Thel had offered her formal adoption into the syn-Grevi a
number of times since their first meeting, as part of the customary advancement for someone who had served the family
more than well, but Vai had always refused the honor.

When he came into the room, she rose from the chair where
she waited, and knelt.

"My lord sus-Radal," she said.

Thel opened his mouth to correct her, and then thought better of the idea. Iulan Vai dealt with only the latest, most accurate information. If she addressed Theledau syn-Grevi as the
head not of a minor north-country line but of the entire sus-
Radal fleet-family . . . then the unthinkable had happened, and
it was true.

"Don't do that," said Thel. "We're not in somebody's mansion in Hanilat."

Vai rose gracefully to her feet and resumed her chair. "No,
my lord. But you'll get there."

"How did it happen?" he asked. "We were never all that
close to the primary line."

"Close enough for old Jofre to pass over the whole bundle
of senior lines and pick you to succeed him."

"He was mad," said Thel, with conviction.

"Mad as a mortgaunt," Vai agreed. "Disinheriting people
was a hobby of his. Every time he felt his stomach twist or
his bones ache he'd call in the legalists and start scratching
out names. Only this time, he died before he could change his
mind back again. The sus-Radal are yours, my lord."

A kitchen-*aiketh* floated in bearing a tray of spiced wafers
and two glasses of sweetroot cider. Thel waited until Vai had
made her choice, then took the remaining glass. The cider was
cool and tart, with a natural sweetness and a hint of fizz. Thel
had never heard of it being made or sold anywhere outside
the far north country. In the old time, it wouldn't have kept.

in the subtropical temperatures of Hanilat; these days, he supposed there just wasn't a demand for it.

"You're right," he said after a while. "I'm going to have to leave syn-Grevi Lodge and go to Hanilat. The fleet won't accept me otherwise."

"The city's not so bad. You'll get used to it."

"Maybe," he said. He picked up one of the spiced wafers and bit into it, turning the full circle into a crescent with a couple of bites. "Vai . . . I want you to come work for me in Hanilat."

She gave a faint laugh. "I thought I already did."

"You worked for the syn-Grevi," he told her. "I want you to leave the syn-Grevi behind you and work for the head of the sus-Radal."

III: Year 1116 E. R.
Ildaon: Ildaon Starport
Eraasi: Western Fishing Grounds

T HE SEARCH for gloves took longer than 'Rekhe
had expected. The street signs were all in the local
alphabet, presumably because traders from Eraasi came only
once or twice a year, but cargo flyers and trucks arrived daily
from all over Ildaon. Fortunately, most of the signs also had
pictorial symbols, though the meanings were not always what
'Rekhe would have anticipated. After going down a number
of false trails, he and Elaeli came to a three-story building
about a mile from the hostel. Upon inspection, the building
proved to be a roofed-over concourse housing several major-
emporia and a host of smaller shops.

Inside, the building was warm. 'Rekhe unclenched his fists
and let the heat start thawing out his fingers. He and Elaeli
were the only members of the *Ribbon*'s crew inside the concourse. The bright blue and crimson of their garments stood
out in vivid contrast to the drabber colors favored by local
fashion, and the ambient murmur of voices had the unfamiliar
pitch and rhythm of an unknown language. 'Rekhe felt disoriented and conspicuous at first, but realized after a while
that nobody in the big high-ceilinged building was paying him

any particular attention. With relief, he applied himself to the search for a pair of gloves.

His liberty-companion, he discovered, was inclined to be thorough about such things. Left on his own, 'Rekhe would have bought the first non-disgraceful gloves that happened to fit—in this case, a pair made of dull black leather lined with soft fabric, on sale at a small men's-haberdashery kiosk just inside the main door. Elaeli would have none of it. Undeterred by the lack of a common language, she inspected the stock of every merchant in the concourse with a pair of gloves to sell.

The gloves she ultimately bought came from a large emporium on the top level of the concourse. 'Rekhe could distinguish only minor differences between those gloves and the ones he had seen earlier—black fabric instead of grey for the lining, and stitching done with a heavier thread—but when Elaeli professed herself satisfied at last, he shrugged and purchased a similar pair for his own use. The price, when he translated it from local money to fleet scrip, made his eyebrows go up; he hadn't expected something that small to be so costly.

"Don't worry," Elaeli reassured him. "They'll last forever, and that's what's important. Haven't you ever bought gloves before?"

"No," he said. "I grew up in Hanilat, remember? It doesn't get cold like this in Hanilat."

And his sister Isayana—or the *aiketen* she had built and instructed—had always purchased the family's food and clothing anyway. But 'Rekhe didn't intend to pass along that kind of information to Elaeli Inadi. It might cause her, for some reason, to think less of him, and that was something he already knew that he did not want.

"You've done well," said Captain Soba. He and Narin stood on the port wing of the pilothouse, looking back on a deck running with fish guts and salt water. *Dance-and-be-Joyful*'s crew swung the boom inboard with another dripping load and dumped the fish out onto the deck for processing. In the aftermath of the Circle's working, the sun had continued hot and the skies clear every day for a week, while the crews of the fishing fleet labored to bring up the plentiful catch and stow it in the holds below.

"Well ended, when ended," Narin replied formally, to ward off luck-breaking—but she grinned as she said it.

"We'll have full holds by nightfall," Soba told her. "More than a season's catch. And after that it's homeward bound." He clapped Narin on the shoulder. "It's a feat to tell the youngsters about—from a bare beginning to the best year that I can recall, and all in less than a week."

"You can buy me dinner in Amisket after we sell the haul," Narin said. "In the meantime, I'll be below if you need me."

"Bring more of that luck back topside with you," Soba called down to her as she descended the ladder.

"I'll try, Cap'n."

Narin headed aft along the port side of the main deck to the companionway. When she looked away to windward off the port beam, two other fishing ships were visible—miles off, but hull up, plying their nets and lines. All across the broad expanse of ocean the swells were long and low, with wavelets dancing across their surface.

While she paused there, gazing outward, the vista changed. A long dark line appeared on the horizon, a boundary drawn with black ink between the sea and the sky. Within minutes the dark boundary wasn't a line any more, but a solid grey-blue wall, growing higher and racing across the water with frightening speed. A pale streak at the bottom of the wall marked where rain and wind whipped the ocean into foam.

Narin stood, all thought of going below abandoned, and watched the wall of cloud draw closer. In all her years at sea, she had never seen a squall line move so fast. She estimated its speed of advance at forty knots or more.

Other members of the *Dance*'s crew were watching the onrushing squall and not liking it any better than she was. In the pilothouse above and behind her, she heard the Captain giving orders to the helmsman—"Left full rudder. Increase your rudder to left hard. All ahead two thirds."—and farther aft, the chief rigger shouting to the crew—"Get your load on deck! Fuck the winches, cut the burton!"

Narin held onto the gunwale with both hands, her fingers clamped to the wood, as the front came on. The *Dance* was coming left to try and take the blow on the bows, but the trawler had been moving too slowly, her engines only making enough turns to pull the nets; she wasn't going to swing in time.

Then the wall hit them.

The wind slammed into the ship's side like a fist, whistling and tearing at the rigging, and *Dance-and-be-Joyful* heeled to leeward so far that her spar ends touched the water.

Another moment, and the squall was past. The sun shone again. The ship righted itself, rocking in the churned water, while the wall of mist continued on beyond them. The waves were choppy and confused, and patches of foam showed on the side of the swells.

Big Tam emerged from the deckhouse and joined Narin where she stood looking at the wall of mist and whipping wind as it raced away. On this side of the squall the air felt thicker, and the quality of the light had altered. Everything looked sharp-edged and brittle, like painted glass that a touch might shatter.

"What was that?" her Second asked.

Narin shook her head. "I don't know. Some kind of squall line."

"Kas didn't say anything about foul weather-luck."

"Luck can change in a hurry," Narin said. "And so can weather. Let's find Kas and see if she's got anything more to say now."

They didn't have far to look. Kasaly herself was coming up on deck in bare feet and a thin sleep-robe—the squall must have caught her napping.

"That was a bit more wind than we needed," she said. "Are we going to have to do something about it, do you think?"

"I was about to ask you that," Narin said.

"I don't know." Kas frowned at the ocean. "All I can tell you is that this is lucky weather."

By the time 'Rekhe and Elaeli made their way out of the concourse, night had fallen over the starport. Street lamps at the corners of the city blocks threw overlapping circles of yellow light that didn't illuminate the upper levels of the surrounding buildings. At least in this part of town, the Ildaonese didn't believe in illuminated signs. Except for the concourse itself, most of the establishments appeared to have closed at dusk, and one low, square building looked much like its neighbor.

"Are you sure we're going in the right direction?" Elaeli asked after they had walked for several minutes.

'Rekhe thought about saying that he was sure, then thought better of it. "I'm not even certain we left the concourse by the same door we came in," he said truthfully. "Without enough light to pick out the landmarks, it's hard to tell one street from another."

"I think the port is that way," Elaeli said. She pointed with one newly gloved hand toward where the night sky appeared somewhat brighter. "I saw lights around the field that looked like they might be on after dark."

"If that's what we're seeing now." 'Rekhe had a dubious feeling about the skyglow. There was luck attached to it somehow, loose looping strands of good and bad fortune that cried out to be taken in hand and managed properly. The sensation made him uneasy. He wished that he hadn't given in to his brother Natelth's insistence that he serve out an apprentice-voyage first, before leaving for the Circles. "Maybe we shouldn't go there."

"Why not?"

He groped for the right words. "Something will happen if we do."

"Something will happen if we don't, too. Things happen everywhere. And if we stand here much longer, what's going to happen is that we're going to freeze."

He couldn't argue with that. The temperature had dropped markedly with the falling of Ildaon's sun, and the wind had gotten brisker. Even with his new gloves, his hands and feet were cold, and the skin of his face felt numb.

"Toward the light, then," he said. "If worst comes to worst, maybe we'll find someplace open where we can ask for directions."

They continued onward through the deserted shopping district, past buildings with empty, darkened display-windows and in and out of the circles of light from the street lamps. No transit-for-hire vehicles cruised this part of town at night, probably for lack of custom. 'Rekhe saw no other pedestrians, and the few trucks and private groundcars that rumbled past were clearly on their way to business elsewhere. He feared vaguely that, alone as they were, he and Elaeli might offer an attractive target for footpads and hooligans, but no menacing figures slipped out of dark cross-alleys or loomed up from the shadows of a recessed doorway.

After a while the illumination ahead grew brighter. The street they were following opened up into an avenue lined on both sides by street lamps in close-set rows, and by buildings with locked doors. This part of town wasn't as dead as the one they'd wandered into after leaving the shopping concourse, but it didn't appear to be open for business either.

Their footsteps tapped on the sidewalk, and the echoes bounced off the deserted buildings. The exhalations of their breath showed white under the street lamps.

Elaeli moved closer to 'Rekhe. "I guessed wrong, it looks like. This isn't the way to the field."

"No." 'Rekhe's ears caught the low growl of a groundcar's engine. Further up the street, lights flashed white and violet and amber. "If that's a bus, we'll ask the driver how to get to the starport."

Elaeli looked dubious. "We don't speak the language. He may not understand."

"He'll see the fleet colors," 'Rekhe said. "That should be good enough."

Elaeli made a doubtful noise and pulled the collar of her cloak higher around her neck. The engine sounds grew louder in the street behind them, and the white lights drew closer. When the vehicle drew even with them, 'Rekhe saw that it was not a bus, but a private groundcar.

The vehicle slowed, then stopped opposite them. One of the rear doors swung open. 'Rekhe tensed—perhaps this part of town had thugs and criminals after all—but the voice that called out spoke in Hanilat-Eraasian.

"Hey, sus-Peledaen! You going to the port?"

"Yes," 'Rekhe said.

"Then you're going the wrong way—jump in and we'll give you a ride."

* * *

Narin got to the *Dance*'s pilothouse just as Orghe, the vessel's chief rigger, was making his own report on the effects of the squall. She held back and let him speak; the rigger was a master at his own craft, and at the moment he looked worried.

"Cap'n, the starboard vang's torn away."

The Captain frowned. "How long will it take you to make repairs?"

"It'll take us a day to fix it right," Orghe said. "Or I can have something juried for you in an hour, either way you please."

"I want to top the catch and head for port," Captain Soba said. "I've talked with the other skippers of the fleet by wireless, and they agree." He glanced over at Narin. "That is, if our Circle doesn't have any word against it."

Narin shrugged. "Kasaly says this is lucky weather."

"Call up the weather display," Captain Soba said.

The *Dance*'s quartermaster punched the repeater. A map came up on the pilothouse screen displaying the west part of the Veredden Sea. A list of numbers along the right side showed the local data from *Dance-and-Be-Joyful*'s position.

"Nothing out of the ordinary," Soba said. He hit the reload button to bring in the latest data from the weather satellite system. "All clear. It was a fast squall, nothing more."

His words were reassuring, but his face still looked troubled. Something about the weather was bothering him—and that in itself, thought Narin, was significant.

"Captain," she said, "with your permission, I'd like to consult with the First of the Ridkil Point Circle."

"Of course," Soba replied.

He gestured toward the bridge-to-bridge wireless, and Narin made the connection. The First of the Ridkil Point Circle was on a fishing boat around fifty miles to the south, drawing up from another part of the same shoal of greyfish.

"No, we've felt nothing," he said, in answer to Narin's query. "The line squall passed us, but there's nothing out of the ordinary going on with the *eiran* hereabouts."

"Thanks," Narin said. "Keep your feelings open, just the same. This is unchancy, I think."

"I'll do that. You too."

The sound of the wireless carrier wave was drowned out by a sudden exclamation. The quartermaster was staring at the hard-shell barometer on the charthouse bulkhead, looking from the gleaming glass instrument to the weather repeater and back again.

"Cap'n," he said, "something funny's going on here. This box"—he nodded at the weather readout—"says that everything's fine, no trouble anywhere. But *this* one"—he pointed to the mechanical barometer—"says that the pressure's heading for the basement."

"What's the update time on the repeater?" Soba asked.

"Minus fifteen."

"Extrapolated data, then," Soba said. "Next real info in fifteen more."

He stepped over to look at the barometer for himself. Narin, following him, saw that the quartermaster had spoken true: The needle was swinging downward so fast she could see it moving. The recording thermometer, which plotted sea and air temperatures on a scrolling graph—a useful tool for knowing when the fishing would be good and what species to expect—showed a steady rise, and the hygrometer registered humidity at 99%. Outside the pilothouse the wind was dead calm, the waves flattening in the stillness.

Narin felt a trickle of sweat down her spine that wasn't caused by the heat and the damp air. Soba appeared to feel the same way. He pushed the reload button on the weather satellite repeater. The data there didn't change—and it still didn't reflect what the *Dance*'s local instruments were showing. The time-to-next-pass counter clicked from thirteen minutes over to twelve.

Soba walked back over to the wireless and switched it to the general circuit that all the Amisket captains listened to.

"This is Soba on *Dance-and-Be-Joyful*," he said. "Check your local weather instruments. I think satellite weather's giving us a bad readout."

A moment later, a response came back from Murhad, captain of *First-Light-of-Morning*. "Bugger me naked! What are you going to do?"

"Secure for high seas," Soba told him. "Run for port. And ask our Circle for luck."

Narin could recognize a departure cue when she heard one. She left Soba giving orders to the helm and climbed down from the pilothouse to where Kas and Tam were waiting.

On the working deck, some of the *Dance*'s sailors were striking the last catch below, while others hauled the booms inboard and lashed them to cleats. The engines began throbbing with a deeper note, and the smoke coming out of the *Dance*'s funnel turned to black. Shadows chased themselves across the deck as the trawler came about, her wake tracing a white arc in the sea, changing course to run east.

"Get Laros," Narin said. "Robes and staves, everyone. Meet me in the meditation room. We have work to do."

IV: Year 1116 E. R.
Eraasi: Western Fishing Grounds
Ildaon: Ildaon Starport

IN THE *Dance*'s forepeak, where the bulkheads narrowed between the hold and the peak tank, the
Amisket Circle knelt in meditation. The overhead lamp in its
vapor-tight fixture gave them a steady light, but *Dance-and-
Be-Joyful* was pitching heavily—first lifting up at the bow,
then pausing at the crest of each wave and sliding forward into
the trough.

Each time, a brief moment of near-weightlessness would lift
Narin from the deckplates during the downward slide. Then
she would be thrown forward by the heavy impact at the bottom of the trough, while the *Dance* shuddered around her like
an animal and the metal above her head resounded with the
boom of green water over the trawler's bow. In the next instant, she would be pressed down again as the ship tilted bow-
upward at the sky, coming out from beneath tons of streaming
water to ride the next wave's lifting crest before tilting into
another slide.

The lifting and dropping continued without mercy, and the
booming of the waves drowned out all but the strongest and
most focused thought. Narin did the best she could—one hand

gripping her staff, and the other holding onto a stanchion to keep from being tossed into the other members of her Circle while she worked to see where, in this tumult of wind and water, the *eiran* led.

Where the fleet sat, the lines were tangled. Not far off, she could detect the Circles from Demnag and Ridkil Point at their workings: Demnag trying to ease the storm, Ridkil Point trying to predict what would come. Narin herself was seeking only to understand. She thought she could detect a pattern somewhere on the edge of their current location, hidden in the surface randomness, and with knowledge of the pattern would come awareness of what ought to be done.

"Listen," Kasaly said, her voice breaking into Narin's concentration. "Trouble."

Narin listened. Kas was right; something had changed on the ship. Somewhere aft, a heavy clanging started as a bulkhead-mounted piece of gear began to swing from side to side. The ship's roll—the seesaw movement that caused the *Dance* to tilt from side to side at the same time as she was pitching up and down—grew suddenly more precipitous. The overhead bulb in the meditation chamber flickered once, then returned at half strength.

The change in the light brought Tam and Laros out of their meditation as well.

"Dropped the load," Tam said. He looked grave, and with reason. If the *Dance* lost power, she lost steering, and if the trawler lost steering, she could turn broadside to the waves— and if that happened, they were all done for.

"Soba knows enough to put out a sea anchor and head her into the wind," Narin said. "But losing power isn't the only kind of trouble."

"Could you see anything?" Laros asked.

"I saw a pattern," Narin said. "A made pattern—but not our making. Did any of you feel it?"

"Yes," Kas said. "It's the luck."

The high sound of wind howling in the *Dance*'s rigging penetrated even this far down in the belly of the ship. The noise made Narin's teeth hurt and her nerves tingle. She pushed herself to her feet, still grasping the stanchion with her left hand.

"We brought the fish," she said, "and the fish brought us here. This is all our doing."

Kas shook her head. "No. The luck pattern is different; it's not an echo of our working."

"I'm going topside. I need to talk with the captain."

"We'll come with you," Tam said. "Times like this, we need to keep as close together as we can."

Narin opened the water tight door of the Circle's compartment and made her way out into the white-painted passageway leading aft. Outside the meditation chamber, the force of the storm was even more apparent. The metal skin of the ship trembled with the blows of the waves, and as Narin climbed to the main deck the rungs of the ladder alternately pressed hard against her feet and then dropped away as the ship pitched.

The water-tight hatch at the top of the ladder had been dogged down. Narin spun the wheel and pushed the hatch up until it locked. A cascade of salt water, blood warm, splashed over her as she pulled and pushed her way through—the midships passageway was awash, the water coming in through a non-tight door on the next level above and pouring down.

Narin helped Tam, Laros, and Kas clamber through after her, then dropped and dogged the hatch. "Wait for me here," she said. "I'm going up to the pilothouse."

She climbed the internal ladder to the pilothouse. When she reached the top, she paused, appalled.

By the *Dance*'s chronometer the time was still late afternoon, but the sky was nighttime-dark. Lightning came in vivid purple and blue-white strokes, each flash revealing swirling clouds and water lashed to foam. Salt spray blasted against the pilothouse windows. Somebody had been seasick not long before; the acid smell of fresh vomit burned in her nose.

A glance at the barometer showed the needle hard against the leftmost peg. The atmospheric pressure was lower than the instrument had been designed to measure. While Narin stood there, gripping a handhold for support, the *Dance* slid into another trough, burying her bow completely in the water. Then, ponderously, she raised herself again.

Captain Soba sat in his chair on the starboard side. He had strapped himself into place and held onto the chair arms with tight hands. Outside the windows of the pilothouse the lightning flickered, providing almost constant illumination. Thunder roared; wind shrieked in the rigging. The deck ran with water where the spray was forced past the gaskets of the pilothouse windows.

Narin turned to look at the weather readout. It was blank and dark. "Captain," she said.

"Hello, Narin," he replied. "Come to bring me news?"

"Come looking for it," she said. "What happened to the weather repeater?"

"Lost it when we lost the antennae. Lost the wireless and the imaging when we found out the hard way that we had corrosion in the side of the superstructure. A big wave knocked the receiver room out."

"They all look like big waves to me," Narin said. "Anything from the rest of the fleet?"

"General distress call from *First-Light-of-Morning*," the Captain said. "Lost the signal before we could get a position on her. Lost our own communications right after that." He peered through the lightning-flashed, water-running windows. "Not that I have too good an idea where we are ourselves, exactly. If there's anything you and your people can do—"

"Understood, Cap'n," Narin said, and went back down the internal ladder to where her Circle waited in the passageway below. "Things are looking bad topside," she said. "We have to do a working."

"Where?" Tam asked. "Things haven't gotten any better down here, either—word came while you were gone that there's solid flooding below. We aren't getting back into the chamber any time soon."

"Then we'll do it on the weather decks, out on the fantail."

"In these seas?" Kas demanded. "We'll be killed!"

Narin looked at her. "That's the point, isn't it?"

"You heard the First," said Tam. "A storm like this, we won't get away with anything less."

They shuffled aft, bracing themselves with their hands against the bulkheads. "What's our intention?" Tam asked Narin as they went.

"The pattern here is too great for us to break. We have to slip it. Not quell the storm—just bring as many ships and crews home as possible. That much, we can do."

Laros reached the aft door. "As the universe wills," he said, and pulled up the lever.

The door pulled out, sucked by the wind, and slammed against the after bulkhead of the deckhouse. The noise was lost in the clamor of thunder and wind that awaited them.

'Rekhe peered at the inside of the vehicle. In the light from the street lamps, he could make out at least three passengers, all wearing dark green ship's livery piped and faced with dull gold—the colors of the sus-Dariv fleet-family.

He hesitated, uncertain whether to take the sus-Dariv up on their invitation or not. He couldn't see the luck-lines any more. The bright light of the street lamps had dispersed them, or had dazzled his vision so that he couldn't make them out. But Elaeli had a hand on his sleeve and was pulling him forward— she must have found the empty streets more unnerving than she let on, if the mere sound of a Hanilat accent could be so reassuring.

He decided to get into the vehicle first just the same, so that Elaeli wouldn't have to sit next to one of the strangers. Not everyone from Hanilat was a friend, and the sus-Dariv family had no alliance that he knew of with the sus-Peledaen.

The trio in the vehicle were all young, not much past apprentice age. 'Rekhe didn't know enough about the sus-Dariv markings to be certain of their rank, but they seemed friendly. The one sitting in back had an insulated picnic-box on the seat beside him—he took out a couple of cans and handed them to 'Rekhe and Elaeli.

" 'S a cold night," he said. "You look like you could use a warmup."

'Rekhe took the can but didn't open it. "I don't know—"

"What's the matter?" The sus-Dariv's voice took on a faint note of belligerence. "You sus-Peledaen too good to drink with the rest of us?"

"No, no." 'Rekhe unsealed the can and took a tentative swallow. The liquid inside was hot and sweet, with an astringent overtaste and a definite kick going down. It reminded him of the mulled sweetroot cider he'd tasted once on a family trip to Eraasi's northern interior, only quite a bit stronger. After the long walk in the cold and dark, the drink felt good. "What is this? Something local?"

" 'S 'guggle,' " said the sus-Dariv who'd given him the can. "Something like that, anyhow."

" '*Guukl*,' " said the driver. 'Rekhe thought for a moment that the man was hiccuping, and belatedly realized that he must be the linguist in the group. Not a particularly sober linguist, however; he had one hand on the controls of the vehicle and the other wrapped around his own can of *guukl*.

The car speeded up and slewed around a corner onto another, narrower street. 'Rekhe groped for safety webbing, but didn't find any. To cover up his nervousness, he took a long pull of the hot *guukl*.

"That's the way!" said his seatmate. "Here . . . have another."

'Rekhe shook his head, but the gesture went unheeded. Before he could muster a more effective reply, he had a container in each hand, one mostly empty and the other full.

"I'm Macse," said the sus-Dariv who was handing out the cans of drink. "That's Freo and Tuob up front."

"I'm Tuob," the driver said. He tilted back his can of *guukl* and drained it, then swung the vehicle's front door open partway, tossed out the empty, and reached back to get another can from the ever-generous Macse.

"You sure you know where the place is?" asked the second passenger in the front seat—Freo, presumably.

"Yeah, I'm sure," Tuob said. "Gotta be around here somewhere." He speeded up.

"This doesn't look like the way to the spaceport," Elaeli said nervously. The buildings had opened out into a dimly-lit, monochromatic tangle of bridges and overpasses. Other vehicles were moving on the streets in this part of the city, but their lights were a long way away.

"Don' worry," Macse said. "We're dropping by the party first, 's all."

"Party?" Elaeli's question sounded casual, but the back seat of the vehicle was cramped enough that 'Rekhe could feel her tension. "Whose?"

"Some of the guys who've been here before," said Freo.

"They rented a place for the week, so we don't have to stay in the hostel."

"Th' hostel's a pit," Macse explained.

Elaeli giggled. "That's the truth," she said, and 'Rekhe felt her tension easing. He let himself relax as well—the *eiran* were faintly visible again, here in the darkened interior of the vehicle, and he felt strongly that following them was the right thing to do. He drank some more *guukl*.

To his surprise, the first can turned up dry. He put the empty down on the floor between his feet, and popped the seal on his second. The thought occurred to him that not only hadn't he had anything to drink in a long time, he hadn't had anything to eat since breakfast. The *guukl* was hitting him harder than he expected, and he liked the feeling. So did Elaeli, apparently; she was sitting closer beside him than strictly necessary, with her head leaning on his shoulder.

"Over there! Over there!" Freo shouted suddenly.

Tuob leaned forward and squinted out the front window. "Over where?"

"There!"

Tuob cut sharp right into a residential side street, pressing Elaeli even closer to 'Rekhe with the force of the turn. The car pulled over to the curb and shut down.

"Yeah," Tuob said. "I knew it was around here somewhere. Come on!"

He led the way up the steps of one of a block of seemingly identical buildings and knocked on the door, while 'Rekhe and the other occupants of the groundcar clustered behind him. The door opened and a blast of hot air, noise, and music came out. The light inside was deliberately low, its obscurity punctuated by flashes of green and yellow from a light-sculpture in one corner.

"Hey, Strangler—we made it!" Macse said to the sus-Dariv crew member who had opened the door. "We brought some friends along—sus-Peledaen lookin' for a ride to the field."

"Come on in," Strangler said. "The party's just getting started."

V: YEAR 1116 E. R.
Ildaon: Ildaon Starport
Eraasi: Western Fishing Ground

'REKHE AND the other new arrivals walked up the steps of the house, and in. The room was crowded and sweaty-hot, in spite of the cold weather outside, and the music was loud enough that a normal conversation was impossible. 'Rekhe found more *guukl*, in a bottle this time, pressed into his hand as soon as he crossed the threshold.

"What took you so long?" Strangler yelled at Tuob.

"Duty section's finishing the on-load," Tuob shouted back. "The last stuff was delayed, so we didn't have anything more to do. The Chief let us go."

"Great!"

"Two m're days a' liberty, then off t' Rayamet with a hold full of *leind'r*," Macse shouted. "I'm gonna spend both days gettin' drunk and gettin' laid!"

'Rekhe looked around. Not everyone in the room was wearing green-and-gold. A few tough-looking young people—local, rather than Eraasian, by their features—stood around wearing clothes trimmed with scarlet sequins and other gaudy ornaments. When one of the women saw 'Rekhe looking at her, she jerked her head toward a door at the other side of the room. 'Rekhe shook his head in a little "no" gesture and turned away, his face reddening.

He finished his *guukl* and went looking for another. There was a warming-tub in one corner of the crowded room; he pulled out a bottle and twisted off the seal, then took a long swallow. A sus-Dariv spacer walked over and threw an arm over his shoulder.

"Don't care if you're sus-Peledaen," the spacer said, "I say you're all right!" He took a big swallow of his own *guukl* and wandered off again.

'Rekhe looked around for Elaeli. He spotted her in the middle of the room, dancing with another young man in sus-Dariv colors. The dance was a vigorous one—and almost fit the music, which 'Rekhe presumed was Ildaonese—and sweat had dampened Elaeli's curly brown hair so that it clung to the back of her neck. When the music changed, she broke off the dance with a laugh and headed over to 'Rekhe.

She stumbled a bit, falling against him, and he caught her. She hadn't had any more to eat that day than he had, he thought, and not much less to drink. Her arms went around him, and she pressed close. Her head tilted back, right in front of his, and for some reason he thought that kissing her would be a good idea.

He did, and to his surprise, she responded. When they broke for air about two minutes later, Elaeli leaned against him and said, "That was nice. Let's do it again sometime."

"You've had worse ideas," said 'Rekhe. "We need to keep an eye on Tuob, though. When he leaves, we have to go with him."

It turned out that Strangler was the next one going back to the field, with a first watch in engineering on the sus-Dariv tradeship *Path-Lined-with-Flowers* early in the morning. Elaeli and 'Rekhe left with him. The ride back to the port 'Rekhe didn't notice much. He found that leaning back in the seat with his face pointing straight up felt better than looking out a window. He was aware that other bodies were on either side of him, but he didn't pay much attention.

Strangler let 'Rekhe and Elaeli off by the traders' hostel. Wearily, they collected the gear they had left behind in their unused rooms, and trudged back to *Ribbon-of-Starlight* just as dawn was breaking.

The prentice-master, syn-Lanar, met them at the top of the ramp. "Look what the tide washed in," he said, without visible sympathy. "Inadi, sus-Khalgath—are you ready to turn and burn all day?"

'Rekhe struggled against a yawn. There was something he needed to remember—something to do with the luck-lines that had drawn him down the wrong street in the first place. With difficulty, he pulled the memory out of a confused montage of dance music and *guukl* and green and yellow lights.

"I heard something," he said. "That sus-Dariv ship—*Path-something-or-other*—she's taking on a cargo of *leind'r* for Rayamet. Lifting in two days."

syn-Lanar drew a sharp breath and looked at him intently. "Are you sure of that?"

"Heard it from some people in her crew," 'Rekhe said. "What's *leind'r,* anyway?"

"Spun vegetable fiber," said the prentice-master. "On Rayamet they make cloth out of it, or eat it for breakfast, or something like that . . . we'll need to wake up the Captain and let him know what you've found out." syn-Lanar almost never smiled, but he was smiling now. "This may be a profitable voyage after all."

Narin stepped out onto the deck of *Dance-and-Be-Joyful*, and into the full blast of the storm. The humidity was smothering, and the hot wind tore at her hair and stung her cheeks with spray. She clutched a bulkhead-mounted cleat with her right hand to keep her balance.

A wave washed over the deck, parted by the deckhouse and running from the scuppers. The water was no more than ankle-deep by the time it reached her, but it felt like stepping into a bath. Mist and cloud glowed in the *Dance*'s running lights, and lightning shot through the sky. The air was full of a cacophony of sound—howling wind, roaring thunder, the boom of seas breaking on the ship.

"Lights!" she shouted back at Tam. "We'll need lights!"

Her Second opened the cover on the electric switchbox and twisted the watertight rotary switch. The *Dance*'s aft working lights came up, white glaring bright, shot through with the rain and spray like silver cords. The storm was not natural, Narin could see that much already—though she could not imagine for what purpose any Circle would have raised such a ship-killing tempest.

It doesn't matter, she thought. *We didn't ask for the weather, but we've got it.* She remembered her grandmother's stories of the Big Wind of 1034, when three-quarters of the Amisket fleet had been lost at sea despite the Circle's best work to save them, and the town had taken more than a generation to recover from the loss.

Not this time.

"To bring the ships and crews to port!" Narin shouted to the Circle behind her, her words torn by the wind. "Join me!"

She let go her grip on the cleat and staggered toward the center of the working deck. Staff in hand, she planted her feet on the rolling, plunging deck and opened herself to knowledge and understanding. Her staff began to pulse with deep green color in the rain-streaked whiteness of the working lights. Above her, limned in ghostly blue against dark clouds, the *Dance*'s masts and yards glowed in the coronae of electric discharges.

"As the universe wills it," Tam replied. He let go his own grip and braced himself against the wind. He stepped aft from the deckhouse, and raised his staff. "I give of myself to this."

Narin let the double-seeing take her. On one level she saw Tam and the physical reality of the *Dance*'s rain-swept working deck. On another, she perceived the world around her as a network of shining silver touched with color—the lines of life and luck, that she had set her Circle the task of straightening and binding for the sake of the Amisket fleet.

Tam struck at her, and she blocked. The howling wind slowed her arm, but it also ruined his aim. The blow was sloppy, grazing her shoulder rather than striking cleanly—but the pain it brought conveyed in a burst of sparks the line she needed to pull to bring more order to the tangle of lines, confused as a pond when a rock had plunged in.

Double vision became single, and she saw herself at the pond on a sunny day, watching the ripples and the way they crossed and interfered with one another, sometimes gaining strength from the meeting and sometimes damping one another out. The ripples on the pond were coming from the feet of a man of brass who stood on the surface of the pond.

Narin stood up—she had been lying on her belly on a dock extending into the pond, looking down at the water, seeing only the small bit right in front of her face—and stepped onto the surface of the water. Rings of ripples scattered from her feet, adding to the pattern.

The edges of the pond were beyond her sight. The man of brass was a long way away. Narin walked on the surface of the water, and it felt soft beneath her feet. She bobbed up and down on the soft water for a long time, until the sky blazed with green light, and something heavy fell against her, and she looked down.

It was night outside of the brilliant circle of working lights on deck. Tam had slumped against her, falling to the deck, then rolling to the fishrail with the ship's motion, the last of his power given up for the working.

Her left eye was swollen closed, and her head hurt. She turned to Kasaly and pointed at the Circle's luck-seer with her staff.

"Bring home the ships and crews!" she shouted over the noise of the wind and the driving rain.

Kas stepped toward her, mouth open, shouting back, "As the universe wills!"

They crossed staves and continued the working.

Prentice-master syn-Lanar had been right: Captain syn-Avran of the *Ribbon* was more than pleased to hear the word that 'Rekhe and Elaeli had brought back from liberty. The guardship, having seen the sus-Peledaen cargo carriers safely away from Ildaon and into the void, turned back to the planet on business of her own. Shortly afterward, the sus-Dariv tradeship *Path-Lined-with-Flowers* left Ildaon nearspace and commenced the runup for its own entry into the Void.

Ildaon's sun was behind the planet, shining around the edge of the sphere in a diamond-ring dazzle of light. The *Ribbon*—her active sensors doused, not radiating energy into space—lay in the planet's shadow, where reflected light wouldn't give her presence away. The other choice would have been to hang in the sun-flare, where the *Path*'s sensors would be over-loaded. One way or the other, dazzle or shadow, a guardship intending ambush had to choose a place and stay there until its target drew near enough for interception.

'Rekhe and Elaeli waited, sweating and anxious, in *Ribbon-of-Starlight*'s docking bay, drawn up in formal ranks with the rest of the boarding party. All the boarders carried pikes of steel and molded plastic, and wore gauntlets and hardmasks over tunics and trousers in customary drab. The hardmasks provided both safety and, with their featureless black surfaces, a further degree of anonymity, but wearing them was a hot and stuffy ordeal.

It was also, 'Rekhe knew, a distinct honor for the only two apprentices in the group, a reward for their alertness and per-spicacity in bringing word to the ship of a profitable enterprise. The other boarders were crew members of several years' standing, all with good records. The boarding-chief, a veteran crew member chosen for his size and strength and time in service, stood alone in battle armor at the front of the party, his pike held horizontally before him.

'Rekhe glanced up at the fighting bridge, a suspended trac-ery of expanded metal that ran around three sides of the docking bay. The *Ribbon*'s bridge officers were all there in secondary conn—closer to the planned action than the guard-ship's main bridge, the better to maintain contact and control—and the back-and-forth of their voices carried down to the waiting boarders clustered on the deck below.

"She's coming on fast."

"Very well—" that was Captain syn-Avran, sounding cool and decisive "—rotate into pursuit position."

"Rotating. Speed matching, set. Vector designator, set. Grapnels, set."

"Stand by."

"Target in range, request permission to give chase."

"Permission granted. Commence chase run."

Time dragged out. 'Rekhe fancied that he could feel the *Ribbon* straining as her engines put on speed.

Then, from the sensor operator: "*Path-Lined-with-Flowers*, in sight." And, like an echo, the voice of one of the *Ribbon*'s other apprentices, assigned to safety check for the occasion:

"Visual confirm, *Path-Lined-with-Flowers*. On track for assumed entry point."

"Excellent," said the Captain. "Let's take her."

'Rekhe licked his lips. He could feel the sweat beading up on his forehead, and wished he'd thought to tie a band of cloth around his head before putting on the hardmask, as some of the more experienced boarders had done. More trickles of sweat ran down his spine underneath the coarse fabric of the heavy boarding-tunic.

He glanced over at Elaeli. Her face was a blur behind the clear black plastic of her hardmask, and he couldn't tell if she was nervous or not.

Ribbon-of-Starlight shivered a bit as the guardship's lateral jets nudged her into a position closer to *Path-Lined-with-Flowers*. 'Rekhe tried to stand without fidgeting, and without shifting his grip on his pike, as the minutes passed and the ships converged.

This part of the chase, as the two ships maneuvered for position in hard vacuum, was the most delicate and ticklish of all. The *Path* would be racing to make her entry point without changing course—a missed point would mean a fouled transit, and a chance of emerging from the void in uncharted space, or dangerously close to planetary gravity or the heart of a star. *Ribbon-of-Starlight,* at the same time, was trying to match velocities and achieve linkage with an unwilling target. Any misjudgment or failure in shiphandling could result in crippling damage to either vessel, or to both.

"Let go the grapnels," the Captain said.

"Grapnels away."

'Rekhe felt a vibration in the deck as the *Ribbon*'s electromagnetic grapnels came online. Immediately afterward came the grapnel operator's rapid patter: "Contact—energizing—positive lock. Request permission to begin reeling."

Syn-Avran gave a curt, decisive nod. "Reel."

'Rekhe braced himself. The two ships married with a solid, deck-shuddering impact. He wavered slightly, but kept his balance.

"Locks engaged."

"Very well," said Captain syn-Avran. "Away boarders."

VI: YEAR 1116 E. R.
SPACE: SUS-PELEDAEN SHIP RIBBON-OF-STARLIGHT
ERAASI: WESTERN FISHING GROUND

THE *RIBBON's* boarding party stepped up to the lock. The hatch swung open easily under the hand of the boarding-chief—*positive link-up on both ends*, thought 'Rekhe, *that's good*—at the same time as *Path-Lined-with-Flowers* opened up its lock to meet them.

For a moment 'Rekhe struggled with disorientation. The *Path's* local gravity was 180 degrees out from the *Ribbon's*, so that he looked up, not across, at three ranks of troopers in the sus-Dariv house colors of green and gold, drawn up in ranks with their boarding pikes and spears, seemingly hanging by their boots from the overhead. Their chief, large and rugged in his battle armor, carried a pair of attack swords, one in each hand. He raised and crossed them in salute.

The sus-Peledaen boarding-chief raised his pike in honor to his opponent, then leapt forward into the other's boarding bay. Halfway across, the gravity altered on him, so that he appeared to be falling upward. He twisted in mid-leap, landed on his feet and rolled, coming up into a guard position directly in front of the sus-Dariv swordsman.

"Oh, that *was* pretty," someone up on the *Ribbon's* fighting bridge exclaimed.

The swordsman struck out, high and low, looking for a quick kill. The boarding-chief jumped clear and struck the swordsman in the chest with the butt of his pike. The butt wasn't sharpened, so no decompression occurred, but the blow staggered the swordsman and knocked him backward. The boarding-chief followed that up with an over-the-shoulder swing of the pike blade toward his opponent's left clavicle.

The sus-Dariv blocked up and out with his left sword and lunged with his right. The boarding-chief swung his pike around to take the swordsman's right wrist with his pike staff and knock the sword away. The blade landed, clanging, on the deck, and the sus-Dariv gripped his remaining sword in both hands.

The two fighters paused for a moment, taking each other's measure. Then the swordsman advanced, swinging his blade in a horizontal figure-eight ahead of him. The sus-Peledaen boarding-chief blocked, stepped back, and blocked again. But he had the rhythm now. At the next swing, he dove in under the arcing blade and swung his pike out parallel to the deck. The juncture of blade and shaft took the swordsman behind the ankles like a hook and pulled his feet from under him.

The boarding-chief rolled over to kneel astraddle of his fallen foe, produced a small boot knife, and made the ritual nick in the other man's armor, high up on the left sleeve, that released the over-pressured, moisturized air inside. The air escaped in a tiny plume of condensing vapor—signal of a loss, and of a victory.

The boarding-chief got up, helped his former opponent to his feet, and embraced him. Then they both pulled off their helmets and embraced again, while 'Rekhe and Elaeli and the other members of the sus-Peledaen boarding party pounded their pikes on the deck and cheered.

"Well done," said Captain syn-Avran. "Have the crew rig a transfer tunnel. I'd like to go aboard and take their surrender."

At an order from the boarding-chief, the crew members discarded their fighting gear to start rigging the transfer tunnel—a cylindrical lock with a stairway in each side and a railed plank running between them, its knurled surface twisting completely around at the midpoint between the two ships. The captain came down to the lock from the fighting bridge, glancing at 'Rekhe and Elaeli as he passed.

"Inadi, sus-Khalgath—come along and see how the next part's done."

The two apprentices followed the Captain through the transfer tunnel to the other ship's boarding bay, and up the metal stairs to the sus-Dariv fighting bridge. The *Path*'s Captain greeted syn-Avran with a cheerful handshake and a clap on the shoulder.

"Ruje, you old pirate!" He pulled a sheet of folded paper out of his tunic pocket. "Well, here's the manifest. What would you like?"

syn-Avran looked at the printout, running his finger down the rows. "How about all of your *leind'r*?"

"You would pick the lightest, most valuable thing I had . . . we'll log it as 'captured by freebooters.' " The *Path*'s Captain turned to his Pilot-Principal. "Muster all off-watch hands to number three hold to transfer cargo, and set up the food and drink for the boarders' after-party."

Dance-and-Be-Joyful fought against the ongoing storm. The wind howled and cut the tops of the waves off into flying spray. Narin had lost touch with the passage of time; she didn't know whether the Amisket Circle had been working for hours, or for only a handful of minutes. The dark sky beyond the stark whiteness of the work lights could have been either midnight or a storm-black noon—she couldn't tell.

A wave over the *Dance*'s quarter smashed into Narin and drove her down to her knees.

The wind's veering. Or we're coming about. Broad-side to the waves, either way. We can't last long after that.

Streaks of blood swirled in the water that washed over the deck and eddied around her where she knelt. She forced her eyes, bleared with sweat and salt water, to focus on her surroundings and take stock. It wasn't good: Kasaly's body rolled amid the dirty water in the scuppers, her bright red hair floating about her head and her pale eyes staring up at the work lights. Narin didn't remember killing her . . . only the flow of energy channeled into the struggle to bring Amisket's ships and sailors home to port.

This storm is too strong. We should have found a way through it without the need for such a sacrifice.

But Amisket's fleet would live or die as their Circle worked for them, and Narin could not give up. If the trawler sank, there would be no going home anyway.

Narin struggled to her feet. She hurt all over, and her breath came with difficulty. Kas had fought well in the working, after all. Laros was the only one remaining, and he might be the last of the Circle left alive after her own death.

And what is the fleet to do, she thought, *when the one becomes none and no power is left—what besides sink, drown, and be lost?*

We are their Circle. We cannot allow it.

Staggering as the ship rolled, she found her footing on the deck. Laros stood beside the deckhouse, his black robe whipped about him by the wind, with one hand on a vang and the other grasping his staff.

"Come to me!" Narin shouted. Her voice rasped in her throat. She could feel the words, but scarcely hear them. The wind tore them away as soon as they left her mouth. "Finish the working! Bring the fleet home!"

"As the universe wills," Laros said—at least, his mouth moved with what could have been the ritual phrase. The shrieking wind and the *Dance*'s creaking lines swallowed up all sound, leaving nothing but the motion behind. He stepped forward and raised his staff.

Narin waited. She was all but done in; it could have been her lying in the scuppers and not Kas, if one blow or another had gone differently. She had no energy left for a strong assault.

Laros attacked; she blocked. And so the fight began. She let her awareness leave the physical world of the ship and the storm and go out into the network of silvery lines that wove about her. This would be her last effort to pull them in, her last attempt to still their fierce chaotic lashing. Her energy would go to Laros in the end, and the keeping of the Amisket fleet with it.

The *eiran* shone with an eerie and uncommon brightness. She had never seen them glowing with such intensity; from what source they were receiving their energy, she could not tell. She let herself go still further from the physical world, into the world of vision and metaphor that was the heart of the working, and saw herself standing alone in a landscape of frozen mountains and bare rock.

A howling filled her ears, and she turned. The path ahead of her was blocked by a mortgaunt out of legend, a looming reptilian creature all claws and fangs and oily leather hide. She had no need to guess at its true nature. The mortgaunt was the storm, the deadly menace that she needed to subdue. And it was Laros, as well—offering up the energy of his life, for Narin to take and work into ship-luck and harbor-luck to save the fishermen of Amisket.

She knew without looking, as if it were a picture in her memory, that they were all behind her, Captain Soba and the others, a long line of sailors on the seaward cliffs over Amisket, with a sheer rock face on one side of them and a deadly abyss on the other. She was in the lead, and the mortgaunt blocked her.

A rumble of rocks in the vision brought her abruptly out to the real world. The rumble was the sound of the *Dance*'s laboring engine, and the vibration through her boot soles was answered by a humming from the trawler's rigging. Narin had spent most of her adult life at sea; even in the midst of a working, that sound could draw her attention.

The main yard, the one that provided the high attachment point for the trawler's nets, was bending, whipping back and forth in the storm blast, and the wire ropes that held it vibrated like plucked strings.

She cried out involuntarily. An instant later, the yard cracked and fell, and the lines running through its blocks fell with it in a tangle. The whole mass crashed downward and swept aft across the working deck, striking Laros and bearing him outboard.

He arched backwards, his mouth open in a scream—*his back must be broken,* Narin thought—then he, the lines, and the yard vanished together over the side. The *Dance*'s engines seized as the tangled mass hit the screws.

Narin felt the surge of energy from Laros's life flow upward, surrounding the ship, filling her.

"Now!" she shouted; and Laros, dying, shouted with her

mouth. Then she entered the vision completely, grasping the *eiran,* pulling them, using the strength of her body and mind to open a pathway through them. She had all of Laros's energy now, and she used it as recklessly as she did her own, holding nothing back from the desperate effort.

And the *eiran* began at last to answer to her will. The opening was there, a gap in the web of tangled silver. She turned to the line of sailors on the cliff of her mind and beckoned them through—across the shingle and the fallen rock, toward the glowing lights of home so far away.

Path-Lined-with-Flowers set out the boarders' after-party in the empty cargo space that had formerly held bales of *leind'r.* The sus-Dariv crew members put together makeshift tables out of crates and pallets and loaded them down with food and drink—a great deal of drink. Deep bowls of red-wine punch aswim with ice; strong, eye-watering spirits in thick-sided glasses; bottles of cold Eraasian beer and hot Ildaonese *guukl.* Someone from the *Ribbon* brought over a stack of music rings and a dataplayer, and someone else from *Path-Lined-with-Flowers* wired the output into the compartment's main audio. Music—loud music—bounced off the overhead and filled the space with a buzz of echoes. All the light sources had been covered up with red and blue filters that shifted color randomly as the vibrations hit.

'Rekhe felt young and awkward. He hadn't gone to parties like this while he was living at home in the house of his brother, and somehow he'd ended up at two of them within the past three days. His mood wasn't helped by noticing that Elaeli didn't seem to feel awkward at all. She was dancing with Macse from the *Path* under one of the spots of changing light, and laughing at something he'd said.

I wish somebody thought I *was witty.* 'Rekhe thought, and drifted over to the refreshment table. He pulled a bottle of *guukl* from the warmer and popped the lid.

The hot spicy drink went down as easily as it had before. By the time the warmth had spread to his fingers and toes, he was feeling more cheerful. He finished the *guukl* and started another one.

"Hey, sus-Peledaen!" It was another of the sus-Dariv crew

members who'd given him and Elaeli a ride on Ildaon—Tuob, this time. "Anybody traded with you yet?"

'Rekhe shook his head. So far the *guukl* was only making it spin a little. "Nobody's asked me."

"Who needs to ask? Y'just come up to them like this"— Tuob gave 'Rekhe a clap on the shoulder that nearly felled him—"and y'say, 'Hey, got anything?' Go ahead—try it."

'Rekhe took a swallow of *guukl* and tapped at Tuob's upper arm with his fist. "Hey," he said. "Got anything?"

"Sure do. Take a look at this." Tuob reached into his shirt pocket and took out a folding knife. Red and blue light shifted and reflected off the polished metal case, which had the words "sus-Dariv's *Path-Lined-with-Flowers*" engraved on it in flowing script. He pressed it into 'Rekhe's hand. "Family special. Name on it and all. 'S yours."

"It's too good—I can't—"

"Too late," said Tuob. "You got it now. Trade me something back—'s how it's done."

'Rekhe pondered for a moment, his thoughts somewhat hampered by *guukl*-induced fuzziness, then pulled off his quilted red and blue ship-jacket and held it up. "It's got my name on the pocket. Is that all right?"

"It's fantastic," Tuob assured him. "I'll show it to my girl back home, and she'll know I had some real excitement on this run. You got a girl?"

"Ah . . . no."

"What about th' curlyhair you had with you back in port? She isn't your girl?"

'Rekhe shook his head. "Last time I saw Elaeli she was dancing with Macse."

"Macse's already *got* a girl," said Tuob. "Got a couple of girls, in fact. You want to dance with th' curlyhair, you go find her and ask."

"You think she would?"

"Sure she would. Saw her kiss you, back on Ildaon. Some places, girls don't kiss you like that 'til you're married."

'Rekhe finished his *guukl* at one draught. "If you'll excuse me . . ."

He made his way through the press of bodies in the *Path*'s cargo bay to the cleared space that served as a dance floor.

The music changed, and it took him a minute to spot Elaeli standing with Macse at the edge of the crowd. Quickly, before his nerve could give way, he went up to her.

"Do you want to—I mean, may I have the next dance?"

Her smile was even warmer and more dizzying than the *guukl* had been. "Of course."

Taking hands, they stepped into the dance. Elaeli was soft and graceful, and her hair smelled like flowers. 'Rekhe could have danced with her forever, and felt a stab of disappointment when the music ended.

"Let's go back to the *Ribbon*," she said.

"Now?" He tried to think of some excuse to keep her at the party so he could ask her to dance again. "Have you done any trading yet?"

"Macse gave me a sus-Dariv bracelet," she said. "So I gave him my *Ribbon-of-Starlight* keyholder with the thumbprint lock. I think he wanted something else instead, but I didn't feel like giving it to him."

She smiled at 'Rekhe again, and his head spun. "I'd rather go back to prentice berthing and give it to you."

VII: Year 1117 E. R.
Eraasi: Demaizen Old Hall
Arvedan House
Hanilat Starport

WHEN THE fleet steamed back into Amisket, Narin Iyal discovered that she was a hero. The Storm of 1116, product of a massive weather system raised by the Circles of the drought-stricken antipodes, had raged up and down the length of the Veredden Archipelago for three days. The townspeople of Amisket had feared that the fishing ships were lost, taking their families and the town's livelihood with them. The people were grateful—exceedingly grateful. For weeks afterward Narin couldn't pay cash money for as much as a shoelace, and half a dozen children were named after her in the first month alone.

She wanted nothing to do with any of it. Halfway through the second month, she told the town council of Amisket that they would have to find a new Mage to head their Circle for them. Then she took passage to the mainland on the packet-boat that brought the weekly mail, and walked inland from the coast.

She had no clear idea of where she was going—except away from Veredde—and she wandered the by-roads for almost half a year. The Circles she came across would give her hospitality, and invariably wished her well, but none of them offered her a place. Always, after a day or two, or at most a week, she would thank them politely and move on.

On the first warm day of spring, she was in the Wide Hills district, walking beside the highway running out of Demaizen Town. She'd heard rumors, over the past months, of a new Circle forming in the area. Maybe they would have a place for a Mage who understood the work of a First—all the work of a First, down to the bitter last of it—but who didn't want to do it ever again.

Shortly after she'd turned off the highway onto the road leading to the Hall, she heard the sound of a groundcar's engine, and a truck bearing the logo of a prominent medical-services firm overtook her and slowed to a stop.

The driver called out the window, "Is this the road to Demaizen Old Hall?"

"I think so," she said. "Back in town they said to turn at the stone gate, and that was a stone gate back there. So either this is the right road or we're both lost."

"You're going to the Hall? Might as well ride the rest of the way with me. I've got a delivery to make up there."

She climbed into the passenger-side seat. "What are you delivering?" she asked, as the truck began rumbling once again up the long slope.

"Medical *aiketen*," he said. "Top-line trauma units. Not something you install in somebody's basement every day, let me tell you."

"Are they going to the Demaizen Circle?"

"That's right. Complete installation, fully instructed and fully stocked."

Narin was impressed. Medical *aiketen* cost a great deal of money—the Amisket Circle had made do with the fishing fleet's ancient basic-services model, which only worked half the time and was chronically short of supplies. If the Demaizen Circle was equipping itself with a fully functioning infirmary tucked away in the basement, they could push their workings to the limit.

The Hall itself turned out to be large and imposing—big enough to hide a dozen infirmaries and not feel crowded—but Narin was more interested in the Mage who came out to meet the driver of the delivery truck. She waited, standing a little to one side, while the driver identified himself to the Mage as a person authorized by the company to unpack and install its products, and the Mage identified himself as Yuvaen syn-Deriot, Second of the Demaizen Circle. The driver and the Second signed and countersigned half a dozen different papers; when the driver put away his copies and began offloading, Narin came forward.

"They told me in Demaizen Town that there was a Circle forming here," she said. "Is this so, or is there only you?"

"Myself and the First, for now," Yuvaen admitted. "But Garrod has large plans."

Narin looked at the truck full of crates and boxes. "I can see that. Is there a place in your Circle for a working Mage?"

"Are you asking on your own behalf, or a student's?"

"My own," she said. "I'm Narin Iyal, from Veredde—"

His eyes lit with recognition at the name. "The First of the Amisket Circle," he said. "The one who saved the fishing fleet."

"Saved the fleet," she said, "and broke my whole Circle doing it. I won't lie to you, Syr Second-of-Demaizen—"

"Yuvaen."

"—Syr Yuvaen: My luck is not good. Your First may want nothing to do with me."

"For what Garrod has in mind, he needs strong Mages," Yuvaen said. "If you're determined to leave Amisket—"

"I left Amisket half a year ago. I didn't want to live there any more."

"Were the people that ungrateful?" he asked.

"Far from it," said Narin. "They thanked me until I was sick of hearing the words. But I had no Circle-Mages left, and no wish to find more and train them, then spend their lives all over again the next time the sea decided to take them. And nobody in the Islands would come to Amisket and have me as a Mage working under them—they all said it was not right, when I had been First in Amisket for so long."

Yuvaen smiled. "Come inside," he said. "If you are determined to put away rank and join with us, there are things about the Demaizen Circle that you need to know."

* * *

Delath syn-Arvedan was the odd one out, in a family where everybody else's future was settled. There was an older brother, who would who take the greater part of the family lands in the district; and there were sisters both older and younger, the one already married into a well-off local manufacturing family, and the other bound to Hanilat for advanced schooling in the stargazers' disciplines. For him, there remained a few smaller parcels of land—enough to rent out for a modest income, but too scattered to make up a single holding—and funds sufficient to educate him in whatever profession he might find attractive.

The problem was that he had no inclination toward such a life. When he returned to Arvedan at the conclusion of his basic schooling, he wanted nothing more than to stay there. He found himself, after a few weeks, expostulating in vain upon the subject to his brother, who cornered him in the herb garden near the orchard and demanded to know—as one who would someday be the head of the syn-Arvedan line in his turn—when Delath planned to make up his mind about things.

"I don't want to go back to school and spend another six or eight years training for something I don't want to do when I'm finished," Del said. He had his back set firmly against the stone wall enclosing the small garden with its patches of sweet and pungent flowerings. "I like it here."

Inadal gave an exaggerated sigh. "You can't stay here, Del. There isn't anything for you."

"I thought—maybe—I could help you, eventually. With the farms and all. It's a lot of work. . . ."

"No."

His brother's reply came out flat and unadorned by polite qualification. Del looked at him and saw at last—clearly and unmistakably—the thing that he'd been working hard not to see for almost the past ten years. Inadal truly liked his younger brother, and wished him all happiness and prosperity in whatever life Delath should choose, but Inadal would not cede any part of the syn-Arvedan inheritance, once it was his. Even the drudgery of landwork, which Del would have gladly undertaken just for the chance to stay here in the one place which was best-loved to him on all Eraasi, was to be his brother's, and his brother's alone.

"I understand," Del said. The wind across the herb garden shifted as he spoke, bringing with it the ticklish scent of summer tartgrass—ever afterward the smell of it, in a kitchen or a market or even at table with friends, had the power to make him feel a stab of unexpected sorrow. "I'll think of something else, then. But it's my life we're talking about—let me have a little time to decide."

The streets of Hanilat Starport bred their share of orphans and runaways and nobody's-children. The Port Street Foundling Home didn't take in all of them—no single institution could—but for those unfortunates who fell within its geographical bounds, it provided food, clothing, safety, and the rudiments of an education. Most of the youngsters thus rescued were duly grateful, or at least had the good sense to pretend gratitude.

Ty was one of the other ones. He had been not quite a day old when a security guard working for one of the Hanilat shipping firms heard him crying in a trash bin out back of a warehouse. Because it was the middle of the week when he was found, the warden entered him on the Home's master roll simply as Ty—a traditional use-name for children born on that day. Family and family name he had none, and the Home could not give them to him; he therefore gave the Home nothing back in return, least of all respect.

It was purely by good luck that he wasn't in trouble on the afternoon when the Mages came to speak to the middle-grades assembly. He'd been in trouble only the day before, cast out into the hallway for drawing insulting caricatures on sheets of notebook paper, then making them into darts and sailing them—with merciless accuracy—onto the desks of their targets. On this day, however, he was allowed to file in with the rest of his class and take his place on the third bench from the front, in between Gea and Ismat and close under his instructor's watchful eye.

Ty's good behavior was already wearing thin. This assembly promised to be another dull one, like the time the man from Hanilat City Council came and talked for an hour about city government. The bench was hard, and Ismat was so broad in the bottom that he filled a place and a half on it, pushing

Ty over towards Gea, who had sharp elbows and used them vigorously.

Ty was about to retaliate—a move that would undoubtedly have seen him exiled again to the hallway—when the warden came out onto the stage and said, "Good afternoon, students. For today's assembly we have Syr Binea Daros and Syr Dru Chayad of the Three Street Mage-Circle, who've come here to tell us about their work."

The Mages turned out to be a man and a woman in ordinary street clothes. If it hadn't been for the short wooden staves they wore fastened to their belts, they would have been indistinguishable from the great mass of petty shopkeepers and office workers in downtown Hanilat.

Ty found them fascinating.

Not for what they said—they talked about doing luckbindings for the neighborhood association, and about helping the City Guard with searches and investigations, none of which interested Ty very much—but for the way they moved. All the other people he had met so far in his life moved as if they were half-blind to the rest of the world, pushing through the shining interconnected web of things as though no part was real except the tables and chairs and walls of it, leaving tangles and disarray behind them. The Mages moved like people who saw the connections.

At the close of the program the two Mages sparred briefly, and the whole assembly drew breath when the staves began to glow. Ty, watching as if transfixed, saw more. The blows and blocks and countermoves and parries were pulling the web tighter, drawing it up where it had grown loose and mending it where it was broken. He wondered what the purpose of it was, other than the simple beauty of the doing; then it was finished, and he understood.

Nets and webs were made for catching things, and this one had caught him.

The summer had just started. Del had promised his brother that autumn would find him a student again, on his way to a lifetime of doing . . . he didn't yet know what, except that it wasn't what he had always desired to do. The months in between would be the last he'd ever spend at Arvedan as someone who had the right to live there. When he next came back, he would be only another guest.

He was surprised, therefore, to find that staying home was almost unbearable. The knowledge that he would soon have to leave pressed down upon him so strongly that he might as well have already left. He endured two miserable weeks pretending that nothing was wrong; then he gave up. He got out the frame backpack and the pair of stout boots he had used for expeditions with his school's wildlife-observation club, and told his family that he intended to occupy himself for the rest of the summer in exploring the local countryside on foot.

Nobody protested or tried very hard to dissuade him. The roving-trails in the district were long-established and clearly marked, and the area was well-supplied with campgrounds and overnight hostels. Delath would be only one young person among many who had decided to spend the holidays out on the road.

He was strong, and his endurance was good. By the time half the summer was past, he was out of his home district altogether. As he penetrated farther into new territory, the countryside grew wilder and more open, the hills rising and the horizon growing broader as the continent sloped inexorably upward into the northern highlands. The trails were more rugged than the ones that he'd explored closer to home, and the hostels fewer. Most of the campsites provided flat ground and a fire-pit and little more.

Del thought of spending the remainder of his holiday in the Wide Hills district, navigating with map and compass from landmark to landmark, but if he was going to make it back to Arvedan on foot—as he had, somewhat irrationally, promised himself that he would—he didn't have the time. He estimated that he could spend one last night sleeping out in the hills before turning back.

Maybe, he thought, he could explore the Wide Hills roving-trails during next year's holidays. It would give him something to look forward to while he was studying to become a banker or a legalist or a city resources developer.

His last campsite in the district was a small, unimproved patch of level ground high up on a long hillside overlooking a rolling plain. He pitched his tent, and boiled enough water over his pocket-stove to cook a packet of dried noodles and steep a cup of *uffa*. That done, he should have crawled into his sleep-sack and rested for tomorrow—but tonight, for some reason, he was wakeful. He sat cross-legged on the ground next to his extinguished pocket-stove, and looked out at the landscape and the evening sky.

The plain below him was largely empty, marked into fields for crops or grazing, and divided by the darker and lighter lines of paved and unpaved roads. Demaizen Town, which he had hiked through yesterday, lay somewhere just below the horizon to the south and east. The only habitation in view was a stone manor house, identified on his map as the Old Hall, and marked by the symbol for a landmark building in disused or unoccupied condition.

The sun went down and the sky changed from pale slate blue to a purpler velvet, and then to the dark blue-black of early summer night. The stars came out, great shoals and drifts of them—the same stars he'd seen every night during the past few weeks, but more dazzling tonight, somehow, and more numerous. When the silver lines appeared and began to coil and twist among them, he thought at first that he was watching an auroral display, of the sort that he'd read about in school but never seen.

He watched, fascinated, as the display grew brighter and more intense. Then he saw that the lines of silver were not in the sky alone, but curving and looping across the plain below him—a silver tracery, like writing in some ancient and esoteric script. The lines branched and spread and came reaching up the hillside and out toward the horizon, until he sat in the middle of a tangled network of silver.

This, he thought, still dazed by the beauty of it all, *isn't the aurora.*

One of the cords began to shine still more brightly, as if his realization had given it a kind of life. The quality of its glowing substance altered slightly, so that it seemed to shimmer with a rainbow iridescence, and he found that he could pick out its peculiar shifting colors no matter where it went in the pattern of light that now surrounded him.

He was seized by the unshakable conviction that this rainbow line was, in some fashion, *his.* He rose from where he had been sitting, and followed the glowing thread down the long hill and out onto the plain.

It led him onward, wrapped and entwined in silvery light, from dusk almost to midnight, across the open fields and down the deserted roads until he came to the door of the Old Hall. He pulled on the rope for the doorbell, and listened as footsteps came to answer the deep metallic note.

The door of the Hall opened. The stocky, dark-haired woman who stood on the threshold wore a black wooden staff at her belt. For a moment he thought that it was a rover's cudgel, and that she was only a summer vagabond like himself. Then he looked again at the way the silver cords wreathed around her where she stood, and knew that she was a Mage—and that he, who had never come any closer to the Circle in Arvedan than it took to wish them well at Solstice and Year's-end—had followed the *eiran* to Demaizen Old Hall so that he might become a Mage as well.

VIII: YEAR 1118 E. R.
ERAASI: HANILAT STARPORT

IN THE year 1118, Arekhon sus-Khalgath's fleet-apprenticeship came to an end, and he returned to his family's house in Hanilat. After two years living in prentice-berthing on *Ribbon-of-Starlight*, 'Rekhe found the sus-Peledaen town house in Hanilat to be echoing and empty by comparison. The spacious building was occupied in this generation only by his brother Natelth and his sister Isayana—both of them considerably older than he was—and by the *aiketen* that Isayana built and instructed. At the moment, as 'Rekhe stood in the corridor outside of Natelth's study, there wasn't even an *aiketh* to keep him company. He was, for almost the first time in months, completely alone.

He knocked on the door. Natelth's voice, muffled by the thick wood, said, "Come in."

'Rekhe obeyed. The room he entered was furnished in dark, polished wood—everything solid and proper, like Natelth himself. A deep bay window looked out over the streets of Hanilat as they sloped away toward the port.

In times past, the head of the sus-Peledaen could have overseen the landing field from that window, and the shipyard where the fleet-family's star-going vessels took shape within their great metal cradles. These days the office towers of Hanilat's business district blocked the view, and most of the new construction took place in orbital facilities, but Natelth kept the room's arrangements as he had found them, out of respect for tradition.

Two armchairs and an *uffa* table stood in the window alcove, but they were unoccupied and likely to remain that way—for this meeting, Natelth sat behind his desk with a thick folder lying on the desktop in front of him. 'Rekhe suspected that the folder held the hardcopy records of his time with the fleet; Natelth disliked posturing too much for him to be toying with somebody else's papers just for the effect.

"Allow me to commend you," Natelth said formally, "on the successful completion of your prentice-voyage. The family is pleased to have you back with us." He paused and looked at 'Rekhe gravely over the closed folder. "We need to devote some thought to your future career. Prentice-master Lanar of the *Ribbon* speaks highly of you—your voyage was an excellent one by anybody's standards—and Captain syn-Avran states that he would be willing to advance you to Navigator-Tertiary on merit alone, regardless of your family."

"I'm honored," 'Rekhe said.

"You should be. Lanar, in particular, has been quite critical in years past of inner-family scions who turn out, in his words, to be a dead waste of an apprentice billet."

There was a distinct sour note in Natelth's voice on the last phrase. 'Rekhe wondered if, perhaps, his brother had once encountered the rough side of Lanar's tongue himself. Surely not . . . though Lanar *was* old enough. . . .'Rekhe found the possibility amusing, and strove with some difficulty to keep his thoughts from showing on his face.

"It was the Ildaon thing," he said, "with sus-Dariv's *Path-Lined-with-Flowers*. But that was mostly luck."

Natelth shook his head. "I'd call it keen ears and quick thinking, if the report is true, but I won't deny that syn-Avran believes you're a lucky man. Another reason he wants to advance you, in fact."

That was the opening that 'Rekhe had hoped for. "If I'm a

luck-maker, then I belong with the Circles, not on shipboard. Wild luck is dangerous."

Natelth looked resigned. "You haven't changed your mind, then."

"We had an agreement," 'Rekhe pointed out. "Do my duty, make my prentice-voyage, and I could join a Circle with your good will and free permission."

"I'd hoped that the time with the fleet would change your mind on the subject."

"I'm afraid not," 'Rekhe said. "It's not the fault of anybody in the fleet—if I weren't going to the Circles, I'd take Captain syn-Avran's advancement and be happy to do it."

"I understand," said Natelth, though 'Rekhe didn't think he really did. "syn-Avran's loss will have to be the fleet-Circle's gain."

"Ah . . . no. I don't think that would be a good idea." This was going to be the tricky part; 'Rekhe would have to be very careful. "Going to the fleet-Circle, I mean."

Natelth frowned. "Why not? You've trained with them before, and at least that way you'll still be in the family."

"That's the problem," 'Rekhe said. "I *am* in the family. Too much in the family; it wouldn't be fair to the rest of the Circle, having me around."

"Hmph." Natelth shoved the folder aside and looked at 'Rekhe. "Disappointing, but I can see your reasoning. Do you have another Circle in mind, then? Just so long as you don't go to another of the fleet-families . . ."

"You know I wouldn't do that. I'll look around; there are always new Circles forming and old Circles needing to fill a place."

As the oldest child of his family's senior line, Kiefen Diasul was supposed to study trade and manufacturing and the keeping of accounts, the better to oversee his family's mercantile interests. To the delight of his siblings and several cousins, however, Kief had adamantly refused to learn any of those things. He attached himself instead to the Institute of Higher and Extended Schooling in Hanilat, where he worked in the stargazers' disciplines; and he left his family altars for the workings of the Mages.

The Circle he joined was a quiet one, associated with the Hanilat Institute and drawing most of its members from the students and faculty. The school grounds and buildings were quiet, and the local population was more-or-less well behaved. The Institute Circle had not needed to perform a great working for more than a decade, a fact which Kief found reassuring.

It was true that he had the Mage's gift—he could see the *eiran* glowing like silver threads, and could act in concert with the Circle to make the threads weave according to his desire—but he had no urge either toward heroics or toward changing the shape of the universe. He was content to help perform the small rituals that kept the Institute happy and secure, at the same time as he used the school's massive telescope and its equally massive multiple-node house-mind to watch the distant stars.

The stars, in the end, were his undoing.

From his first years with the Institute onward, he had studied the problem of interstellar navigation. The star charts used by the fleet-families, he would admit when forced to be polite, were marvels of practical utility. They combined observed data from known locations with markers left by Void-walking Mages to produce a tool upon which hundreds of spacefarers daily wagered their lives and fortunes. A good enough tool, and safe enough . . . but Kief nevertheless found it, as an intellectual construct, aesthetically displeasing.

"There's no predictability," he complained, not for the first time, to the fellow student who shared his cramped office space at the Institute. "Until some Void-walker makes it there and back, we don't have a marker. And if we don't have a marker, we can't send a ship. And if we can't send a ship, we don't have observed data . . . and if we don't have observed data, then the points on a star chart might as well be random imaging artifacts for all the truth in them."

His office-mate, Ayil syn-Arvedan—whose own field of interest was the less emotionally taxing question of interstellar gas clouds—shook her head. "I'll grant you that it's not elegant—"

"Elegance doesn't come anywhere near it," he cut in. "If logical processes were pieces of string, this one would be a mended bootlace."

"—but it works."

"So does the bootlace, if you don't pull on it too hard."

He pushed his chair back from a desk covered with sheets of printout material, stacks of stiff plastic charts, a combined chart-reader and house-mind interface, and a half-dozen empty paper cups. Kiefen Diasul was tall and gangling, with long, light-brown curls already turning an early grey, and an abundance of nervous energy that expressed itself in quick, jerky motion. The cramped, windowless office didn't give him much room to pace, but he used all the room that he had, moving restlessly from the desk to the bookshelves to the *uffa* pot on its ceramic heater.

He pulled down another paper cup from the dispenser and filled it with the pale yellow liquid. It was lukewarm, as usual. "There should be a way to make the charts give us hard numbers and not just probabilities . . . hard enough numbers that we can use the charts to reach places we haven't yet been."

Ayil looked at him as if he had produced the last piece of an especially intriguing puzzle. "That's the important part for you, isn't it—the 'never been before' thing?"

"Yes," he admitted. "It's hard for some people to understand. You . . . your family is—what?"

"Country," she said. "Land."

"Then they wouldn't know. And the City-professionals . . . they don't know either. But the Diasul are traders and manufacturers, and we come up against it all the time."

"Up against what?"

Kief made an impatient gesture. "How slow it all is," he said. "So many stars—so many *planets,* if we only knew how to reach them! So many worlds waiting for trade. And the fleet-families own them all."

"Not really," she said.

He gave her a scornful glance. "They own the charts and the routes and the ships, which amounts to the same thing. But that's not the worst of it. They own all the Void-walkers, too."

Ayil blinked, startled. "I didn't know that. I thought—"

"—that the Circles did their work for its own sake?" He was pacing in earnest now, his paper cup of *uffa* forgotten on a corner shelf. "Once, maybe, but not any more. The only

Circles that do serious exploration are the ones attached to the fleet-families, and the fleet-families don't want new worlds opening up faster than they have ships to trade with them . . . and nobody designs ships or builds ships or lifts ships except the fleet-families. So it's slow, too slow. Not enough trade, not enough real data coming in to make the charts useful for anybody outside the families. It's like choking to death when you know the room is full of air."

Ayil was undiscouraged by his tirade. "I was going to say, I thought there were still independent Circles doing work like that."

"Name one."

"Demaizen," she said. "My brother Del is working there, and he says that Garrod—"

Kief halted in his pacing. "Garrod."

He'd heard the name before—had, in fact, more than once regretted coming to the Institute too late to talk with the man who bore it. Garrod syn-Aigal had been the Institute Circle's last Void-walker, with a reputation that had not faded in the years since he left the Institute and took the Second of the Circle along with him.

"This Demaizen," Kief demanded. "Where is it?"

"In the country," she said, and added, before he could expostulate further, "I have the address."

'Rekhe met with Elaeli Inadi on the third morning after the end of their prentice-voyage. His first day back in Hanilat had been filled with all the rituals of homecoming: The greetings and exclamations about his increased height and strength and presumable maturity, the dutiful presentation of flowers and incense at the family altars, the welcoming feast. Isayana had instructed the kitchen-*aiketen* in the identity and preparation of all his favorite dishes, and 'Rekhe had been obliged to eat heartily.

On the second day had come the discussion with Natelth. By the time that bit of family business was over, Elaeli had packed up her gear and left *Ribbon-of-Starlight*. It took 'Rekhe most of the afternoon and evening to find her again, and to set up a rendezvous at the sculpture fountain outside the Five Street transit hub.

'Rekhe arrived at the meeting place early, but Elaeli was already there, sitting on a stone bench and watching fresh water rise up from the pool and tumble downward over the fountain's tall abstract shapes of steel and bronze. Unlike 'Rekhe, she still wore the sus-Peledaen blue and crimson, now with the piping and emblems of a Pilot-Tertiary.

He sat down beside her on the bench and put an arm around her. She leaned her head against his shoulder, and they sat that way for several minutes without speaking, while the rented groundcars came and went in the lot across the plaza, and the city busses rumbled up to the curbside, disgorged their passengers, and moved on.

"How did it go?" she said at last.

"Natelth? Better than I'd hoped, actually."

She chuckled, a warm throaty sound. "You weren't really expecting your brother to order you into the fleet, were you?"

"Mmh," 'Rekhe said. "Natelth's stubborn if you hit him wrong. If he'd taken it into his head that I was crossing him outright . . ."

"He couldn't have stopped you."

"No, but I might have had to leave the family altars for real if it came to that."

"But it didn't," she said. "So where are you going?"

"I have a letter of introduction from the fleet-Circle's First to another Circle out in the Wide Hills district."

"That's a long way from Hanilat."

"It's shorter than the far end of a trading voyage," he said. "And I didn't have much choice. Garrod syn-Aigal is the only Void-walker I know of who isn't bound to one of the fleet-families. He was working at the Institute when we left Eraasi on the *Ribbon;* I thought he'd still be there when I came home."

"But he wasn't, so now you're going away to—where in the Wide Hills, exactly?"

"Demaizen."

"Never heard of it . . . you *will* write me a letter once in a while, won't you?"

He smiled and drew her closer. "Only if you promise to write me letters back."

IX: Year 1122 E. R.
Eraasi: Hanilat Starport
Aregil Hiring Hall
Beyond the Farther Edge: An-Jemayne

THE PORT Street Foundling Home kept the children it took in until they reached the age of legal employment; resources did not exist to shelter them further. The warden made every effort to find some kind of work for those who departed, but not all of his efforts were rewarded with success.

In spite of Ty's unpromising origins, nobody expected him to be one of the warden's difficult cases. He came to what would of necessity be his last year at the Home easy in heart about his future path. He would leave the Home and its school for the fellowship of the Three Street Circle.

He had, by that time, worked with the Circle for half a dozen years: From the early days when he had been a wide-eyed youngster coming around once a week to watch the Mages at their staff practice, to the present, when he was spending all of his free time in their company. He had learned how to use the simple visualizations and meditations, and had begun to practice regularly with—though he did not yet own—a short wooden staff. He had not taken the final step that would mark him as a Mage forever, the act of joining his strength and will to the Circle's larger intent, but he knew that the day would come soon.

When the warden called him to the office one afternoon close to the end of the term, Ty felt no particular twinges of unease. He hadn't been a discipline problem—except sporadically, and in the usual proportions—for years, ever since he'd found out that the Mages wouldn't let him study with them on those days when he had fallen from grace. He'd learned to keep up his classwork for the same reason; he never became one of the Home's shining academic lights, but he did well enough to stay out of trouble.

The office was a small, worn room on the first floor of the Home. It had seen a number of different wardens, and a generation or more of such interviews as this. The immaterial dust of all those past conferences lay thick on the cabinets and the chairs and the wide wooden desk; Ty considered saying as much aloud, but after a moment's thought decided not to bother. The warden, who saw the physical world and nothing more, would only want to have someone come around with a dampened rag.

Ty took the plain wooden chair across the desk from the warden, folded his hands, and waited. The warden looked at him for a moment, then pulled a sheet of paper out of a large grey folder.

"It's time we talked about your future," the warden said.

It was his invariable opening line for an end-of-school interview. The Home's dormitory comedians had been doing parodies of it for decades. Ty had learned sense, if not respect, over the course of the past few years, and kept his amusement to himself.

"Yes, sir," he said.

The warden cleared his throat. He seemed ill-at-ease; Ty, noticing this, felt a distant, feathery moment of apprehension, quickly suppressed by a clear conscience.

"We all thought," the warden said, "that once you left, you would be going to join the Three Street Circle."

The moth-like touch of apprehension returned, stronger this time—*thought? would be?*—but Ty said nothing and strove to keep his bearing serene.

"I was hoping to go there," he said. In spite of his best

efforts, his hands tightened. "Is there a problem?"

"Well, yes . . . they say they can't have you.".

The apprehension wasn't a light and far-off thing any longer; it settled in Ty's stomach like a block of lead. For the past six years, ever since the day when he had first comprehended its existence, he had bent himself toward a single goal. Now—if that effort was to be rejected—he wondered if he had accomplished nothing except to make himself unfit for anything else.

He swallowed. His mouth felt dry inside, like paper. "Did they say anything about why?"

"Umm . . . yes." The warden looked again at the sheet of paper he'd taken from the folder. "The First apologizes on behalf of the whole Circle, but he says that they're not brave enough to teach you."

Ty stared at him. "The First says *what?*"

"Listen." The warden read aloud from the paper. " 'We are, honesty compels me to admit, a minor neighborhood Circle with no ambition to become anything more. Your student Ty has already learned those things which we can teach without bringing him completely into fellowship with us; but to take that final step would, I fear, push our Circle onto a path which we do not have the strength to walk all the way to the end.' "

"Where do I go now?" Ty whispered. His eyes burned with the effort of holding back the tears of shock and betrayal. "What can I do?"

For a moment the room darkened and he saw the bright cords of life like arrows piercing him through hands and heart, straight and hard. Then he blinked and the visions vanished, though not the pain they brought with them.

"We'll find a place for you, of course," the warden said, not noticing Ty's words or the blackness. "Here is a letter of introduction for each of the two hiring halls in Aregil. A strong young man willing to work should be able to get by there while seeking other opportunities."

Karil Estisk turned down her lamp. The rainy night outside was only city-dark. The lights of An-Jemayne, her own lamp multiplied a thousand thousands of times, reflected off the bottom of the low-hanging clouds and turned the sky a sullen charcoal color. The street lights along the road outside her apartment building shone upward, patterning her ceiling with the shadows of tree branches outside and lace curtains within.

These days the planetary news was full of stories about heightened tensions and the chance of renewed conflict to come. So far, though, Karil hadn't seen a return to the blackout nights of her early childhood, when she and her family had slept in the bomb shelter more often than not. If she were lucky, she'd be back into space and away before things got that bad again.

Maybe I should close up the apartment for good this time, she thought. *I can always rent another one if I have to.*

She found the idea depressing. She didn't like the thought of becoming like the older spacers, the ones from her parents' generation and before, who did their best to live their lives outside of atmosphere and never went dirtside if they could help it.

Karil turned away from the light and went back to her treadmill. She used the machine whenever the cold or rain made running outside too uncomfortable. A professional spacer needed to keep in shape. In an emergency on shipboard, the strength and reliability of her own body might be the only thing that would prevent disaster. Karil thought about disasters a lot, trying to work through what to do in each event, so if the real thing ever happened she'd be ready.

Her brother told her thinking about things might make them happen . . . or maybe things that were going to happen made people think about them first. When he talked that way, she wasn't always clear on what he meant. She didn't think that he was, either.

A knock sounded at her door. Karil switched the treadmill off. She wasn't expecting a visitor, and this was hardly the hour for a stranger to arrive at anyone's home. She hurried over to the security flatscreen that showed the view outside her main door. The screen showed static snow. The relay still hadn't been repaired. She made a mental note to file another work order with the house management.

The knock sounded again.

"Damn," Karil said, hunting around for a shirt. One of the benefits of living on an upper floor was that no one was likely to be standing outside her window, and she liked to exercise topless for the sake of freedom of movement. She pulled on the first shirt she found—an oversized stretch-knit with the Swift Passage Freight Line's logo screen-printed on the back— then went over to the door and peered out through the vision prism.

Someone was waiting—a tall, fair man dressed in black, carrying a long wooden staff. With an exasperated sigh, Karil opened the door.

"Lenset," she said. "You have some nerve showing up after everything you put Mamma and Dadda through."

"We all choose our own paths."

"Pompous, aren't you? Come on in before somebody sees you. That would be all I need, for the neighbors to know that I get visits from religious fanatics."

"Your rooms are too small," he said. "Let's walk."

"It's cold outside. And wet."

"Not that wet. Let's walk. I have some news."

Karil sighed again. "Oh, well, if you must." She set the thumbprint lock to positive, pulled down a heavy jacket, and followed her brother back out into the hallway. She closed the door behind her and asked, "Where to?"

"Around. Wherever the spirit of the universe wills us."

"Stop talking that way."

"I won't argue it, not tonight," Lenset said. He walked ahead of her along the hallway and down the stairs—the elevator was stuck again—until they came to the street.

"How did you get in?" Karil asked, breaking the silence at last out of curiosity. "The front door's only supposed to admit residents."

"If I explained it to you you'd only get angry," he said. He nodded to the right, where a paved sidewalk bordered the building's outer wall. "That way."

"You haven't changed," Karil said. Her breath steamed in the cool air. She started out walking at a brisk pace, forcing Lenset to lengthen stride to catch up to her, and willed her teeth not to chatter. She'd just gotten warmed up, and this was not her idea of the way to cool down. "Come on."

"I have a job," Lenset said, after they had walked for a while in silence.

The worst thing about him, Karil thought, was that it was impossible to predict what he'd do. She hated that.

"Good," she said aloud. A hoverbus clamored by on their left, its internal lights showing seats full of sleepy passengers, its side panels lit up with advertising slogans. "That means you won't be asking me for money. This time."

"Aren't you going to ask me what kind of job it is?"

"If it isn't dropping fritters in a quick-lunch booth, I can't imagine what it might be." She looked at his staff. "Do you have to carry that thing around with you?"

"It's a symbol," he said.

"So's everything, with you. You're dying to tell me about this job—you came to see me in the middle of the night, you were so damned excited. So talk."

"Councillor Demazze's hired me."

"You're kidding." The richest, the most powerful, the most mysterious and reclusive member of An-Jemayne's entire ruling elite. If Demazze ever left the city, the press didn't report it. Karil didn't think that they would dare. "Does he know about your little hobby?"

"I think it's what got me the job," Lenset said. "Either that, or I got it because you're my sister."

Karil didn't know how to respond. The whole idea of someone like Demazze paying attention to her—of even knowing about her was downright unnerving.

The main road was coming up just ahead, with its twin lines of illuminated signs. Most of them advertised one vice or another, all the way from gluttony to drunkenness and avarice. They were getting near the starport strip now, and away from places where smart people walked alone at night. Karil avoided this area as much as possible; whenever she needed to get from her apartment to the port she used the direct underground shuttle. Lenset, of course, could walk through all sorts of squalor without even noticing it was there. She supposed the staff was protection for him. Not even criminal scum liked to deal with someone who openly proclaimed mental instability.

This part of An-Jemayne was one of the pre-war areas that hadn't been bombed, and the lack of renovation showed. One sign showed a mug tilting back to a man's mouth, over and over. Karil wondered how the illusion of liquid vanishing into his gigantic maw was done. Holos, she supposed, but the picture didn't have the typical holo fuzziness.

So, was this a mechanical? She let her mind travel that way for a bit, in order to avoid thinking about her brother's news. It was bad enough that Len was here at all. To have him bear the news that a member of the shadow government knew of her existence was worse. Most people—those with an average supply of sense, anyway—tried to escape the notice of the powerful.

"Demazze asked a lot of questions about you," Lenset said finally. "And he asked me to do him a favor. To ask you to do it, that is."

"What kind of favor?" Karil felt a shiver that wasn't related to the air temperature run down her back. This sounded like politics, and it sounded like Len had finally done something too stupid for her to get him out of, and had capped it by dragging her in after him.

"He said to do this only if you wouldn't tell anyone where it came from," Lenset began ominously.

"Cut out the drama, would you?"

"I can see your heart, and . . ."

"Cut it *out,* I said."

A rising whine of traffic told Karil that crossing the street would be dangerous if they hesitated. She grabbed her brother by the right arm, being careful not to touch the staff he carried in that hand, and pulled him across to where a lighted alley showed signs for gamblers and usurers. No one was visible out on the street, which was a blessing.

"Oh, all right," Lenset said. "He wants you to take an envelope, and put it in the Captain's safe on your ship."

"The ship doesn't *have* a safe."

"Well, wherever the Captain puts the papers that only the Captain can see."

Karil fought against a sense of relief. It wasn't unknown for crew members to keep their personal papers in the ship's strongbox, since most regular berthing compartments didn't have much by way of secure storage. So Demazze's favor wasn't impossible. She rather wished that it had been; then she would have had a plausible reason for saying no.

"What sort of story am I supposed to tell the Captain?"

"You're the resourceful one," Lenset said. "Make something up."

"To save you the trouble of making it up beforehand?"

"I don't lie."

"No, you ask me to do it for you. What's this envelope got in it, that Demazze wants to hide it away like that?"

"I don't know." Lenset reached into the inner pocket of his black tunic and withdrew a slim yellow rectangle. "Here."

Karil accepted the envelope reluctantly, then stood for a moment turning it over in her hands. The envelope itself could have come from any stationery store; what made it unusual was what had been done to it afterward. Someone—*Demazze himself?* she wondered. *Who knows?*—had marked the yellow paper with a pattern drawn in black ink: A series of marks, some unique, some repeating, with looping swirls and crooked lines throughout.

She tapped the pattern with one finger. "What's this? Second place in the 'design a bad border' contest?"

"If it's so bad, why would it get second place?"

"Because it's *so* bad. Once the envelope's in the Captain's strongbox—assuming that I put it there instead of tossing it into the nearest trash compactor the instant you're out of sight—what then?"

"Then nothing. Forget it even exists. Leave it."

"Right. Leave it. Len, are you doing anything illegal?"

"Nothing that isn't for the greater good of the universe. I can feel the winds of chance. . . ."

"Oh, give it a break," Karil said, cutting him off. "So you don't know whether it's legal or not. Lenset, if you get into trouble from now on, Demazze will have to bail you out himself. I'll hold this envelope for you, and that's it."

"That's good enough."

"I'm going to regret this someday, I know I am . . . what am I supposed to tell the Captain?"

"Councillor Demazze has great confidence in you."

Karil stuffed the envelope under her jacket. "All right, I have it. What else do you want to talk about?"

"Nothing," Lenset said. "I have to go now—Demazze will want to know that everything is in order."

He stepped aside, then seemed to fade away between the circles of light from the streetlamps. Karil looked after him for a moment, then turned back toward her apartment, trying to walk rapidly but confidently, as if she passed through this neighborhood unmolested every night of the year.

Underneath her jacket, the stiff corners of Demazze's envelope poked at her skin like little paper knives.

Aregil was a commercial seaport on the northwestern shore of Eraasi's primary continent—not the largest port along that coast, but not small either, as cities went. Ty had never visited the place, nor did he know anyone who had. At the end of the school term, he packed up his clothing and his few possessions into an issued rolling case, received his ticket of leave from the hall porter, and walked through the main door of the Home for the last time.

His path to the public transit nexus took him past the renovated office building on Three Street where the Mages had their residence and workplace. He passed by without stopping, but a flutter at the back of his neck made him turn. A woman was following him, running: Binea Daros, from the Circle.

"Wait!" she called out after him. "Stop!"

He kept walking, outpacing her easily in the crowded street. "Why should I?"

"You don't understand . . . we have a letter. . . ."

"I have enough letters already," he said, and didn't look back again.

Instead, he hastened onward to the ground-transit depot, where he exchanged some of his school scrip for a one-way ticket to Aregil, with a transfer at Nakkad. He spent the trip, three days on hard seats, looking out the window at the passing scenery: First the city, then trees, then the bare rock of the mountains and more trees. At last, under a violet sunset, he stood on the Long Pier at Aregil, watching the sun fall away from him into the sea.

The hiring halls wouldn't open until morning. The cash that came with his ticket of leave would not last much longer, even with stringent economies, but he needed a place to stay. He found one in a cheap hotel near the waterfront, an establishment that took cash in advance by the day in return for a worn key to a bare room and a narrow bed.

At dawn, under a sky of red and black clouds, he rose and took his things with him to the first of the two Aregilan hiring halls. His letter of introduction gained him admittance, and in the morning light he saw that the hall was crammed with men seeking a day's wages. They packed the wooden benches that ran along the walls, and filled the ranks of molded plastic chairs set up in the center. The walls themselves were a cream color, curdled by age, with brown-painted wainscoting that wouldn't show marks.

From time to time other men—better dressed than those who waited—came in and paid their fees to the clerk. Then they would point at one candidate or another, and the waiting laborer would rise and follow. The process went more rapidly than he would have thought; before long, the sun was up and shining in the front windows, and the hall was all but empty. Nobody was left except for Ty, sitting strictly upright with his case tucked away for safety behind his knees, and a few old men, broken down by drink and age, asleep on the benches.

An hour passed, then two. A fly buzzed, and behind the service window the clerk rustled paper and clicked away at his keyboard. Ty's mouth felt parched, but he was too proud, or too stubborn, to ask where he could find water. The shadows moved across the floor as the sun moved outside. Toward noon the shadows faded as the sun was obscured by gathering clouds, and a rain squall lashed against the windows.

The door of the hall opened and a woman stepped in out of the rain. Foul-weather clothing muffled the lines of her body, and the rainwater dripped from her heavy woolen cloak and made dark spots on the floor. She went straight to the clerk's station and spoke with him briefly, then came to stand in front of Ty.

"Do you want a job?" she asked.

"Yes. I'm just out of school in Hanilat, and I need a job." Then, remembering his manners, he added, "Ma'am."

"I'm afraid I can't offer you work," the woman said. Her hand reached beneath her cloak and emerged holding a short staff of dark wood, bound with silver. "But—on behalf of the Demaizen Circle—I *can* offer you a working. Will you come with me?"

"Yes," he said.

X: Year 1123 E. R.
Ayarat: Beshkip
Eraasi: Demaizen Old Hall

THE OFFICES of the Zealous Endeavor Manufacturing Company occupied a tall building in the industrial city of Beshkip on Ayarat. The tower overlooked a factory complex whose tall stacks sent up columns of white smoke at the level of the upper windows. Far below on the roadway, ranks of heavy delivery trucks waited their turn at the shipping docks. Farther out on the edges of the industrial park, the cooling pools and the generator buildings sent up their characteristic plumes of vapor into the cool morning air.

Nefil Kammen had a suite of rooms high up on the monolith's inward-facing side, as befitted a rising member of the firm's hierarchy. A wide, uncurtained window gave him an unrestricted view of the whole operation. Today, however, all his attention was on Jaf Otnal, and the bad news that Jaf had brought from Ayarat Spaceport.

"The shipper says there's no mind-gel."

Kammen regarded Jaf with a mixture of incredulity and dismay. "What happened to all the stuff we ordered?"

The mind-gel was a vital part of Zealous Endeavor's operations. Without a steady supply of the quasi-organic substance, imported from Eraasi at considerable cost, local production of high-standard house and ship minds would be impossible. Inorganic components, while available on Ayarat, wouldn't function reliably at the level needed to interface with the Eraasian standard.

"I know we ordered it," Kammen went on. "I signed the requisitions myself. So what happened?"

"Pirates." Jaf's voice still held traces of his native Ildaonese, making it hard for Kammen to tell whether or not the younger man believed what the shipper had told him. Jaf's narrow face and grey-green offworlder eyes made reading his expression equally difficult. "The shippers were hit by pirates."

Kammen snorted. "We've all heard that story before."

"It's covered by insurance. And there's plenty of mind-gel for sale right here in Beshkip, if we don't care too much about its pedigree."

"I'll bet my paycheck against yours," Kammen said, "that most of it comes from our own shipments."

"You're probably right. Do you want to get some anyway?"

"The alternative is shutting down the line." Kammen leaned forward across his desk. "I'll bet you again, Jaf, double or nothing, that the pirates who lifted our mind-gel have the same name as the shippers we hired to carry it."

"No bet. As long as we need imported material, we're vulnerable." Jaf's voice and posture changed subtly—the voice dropping in both tone and volume, while Jaf leaned forward, closing the distance between himself and Kammen. "Some of us have been . . . discussing . . . the situation for a while now."

Kammen's own voice dropped in response. "And did you come to a conclusion?"

Jaf said nothing for a moment. Then he rose abruptly, walked over to the window, and looked out.

"The problem," he said, gazing down at the parked trucks outside, "is the star-lords. They don't do anything more for us than our own truck drivers do—they move goods to the market. What would we do if our drivers were stealing some of our loads and selling them on their own?"

"Discharge them," said Kammen at once. "Punish them. And hire new ones more to our liking."

"So we would," agreed Jaf. He turned away from the window and looked at Kammen directly. "Why shouldn't the same hold true in the case of the star-lords?"

Kammen laughed without humor. "It's the 'hire new ones' part that's the problem. We both know the next fleet-family we contract with will be just as bad as the last."

"Then maybe it's time we broke them all.",

"Let's not talk about that in here," Kammen said quietly. "Too many ears. You and I and Riet need to get together one of these days, though, and talk it over. In the meantime—let's buy some mind-gel. Draw the money from the general fund."

"What about the insurance?" Jaf asked. The inflection and posture of intimacy were gone, and everything was business once again.

"Use it to get a new supply shipped in. Let's see if the pirates hit this one, too."

The Circle at the Old Hall bought most of its perishable supplies at the shops in Demaizen Town, but at least once a month somebody had to rise before dawn and take the ground-car over to Bresekt to buy staples in volume. Narin, whose turn it was this month to make the run, had filled the ground-car's rear seat and its cargo compartment with everything from jugs of laundry soap to boxes of dried high-protein noodles. Eight people involved in strenuous mental and physical discipline could run through an amazing amount of both of those commodities, and others as well.

The journey and the shopping put together took up most of an entire day, and as usual it was late afternoon before Narin returned to the Hall. She maneuvered the groundcar into its sheltered place in a converted outbuilding, then cut power and got out.

She picked up a couple of the jugs of soap, those being the nearest things to hand, and entered the Hall by the rear door that led to the kitchen. Yuvaen syn-Deriot was there when she came in, pouring hot water through a leaf-strainer into a blue pottery mug. The sharp scent of pale spring-picked *uffa* rose up from the steaming mug and pricked at her nostrils.

Yuvaen looked up as the kitchen door slammed shut behind her. "How was Bresekt?" he asked.

"Crowded," she said. She set the two jugs of soap down on

the tile floor near the stairs to the laundry room. "Noisy. Like always. Want to come help me unload the rest of the stuff?"

"Of course," he said.

Several minutes later, the groundcar was empty and most of its contents—still in bags and crates—had been transferred to the kitchen's central worktable. From there, Narin and Yuvaen began the task of sorting through the purchases and stowing them in their appointed places.

"Ten cans of sliced *neiath* fruit in heavy syrup," Narin said, removing the items in question from the bag and passing them to Yuvaen one by one. "The third cabinet from the left, under the counter."

"We still have four cans of *neiath* from the last time," Yuvaen observed as he bent to put the fruit away.

"Everybody likes it. And it keeps."

"A good point." Yuvaen straightened, and added, in the same tone as before, "Garrod thinks it might be time to name a Third for the Circle."

Narin didn't look up from the bags on the worktable. "Four bottles of dish soap, two bottles of shampoo . . . those go upstairs. . . . Garrod's probably right."

"I thought it might be a good idea if I talked with you about it first." Yuvaen stashed the dish soap underneath the main sink next to the floor cleanser and set the bottles of shampoo aside on the counter. "What do you think about taking on the rank yourself?"

She shook her head. "I haven't got the luck for it. Or the nerve, at my age."

"There's nothing wrong with your nerve that I can tell. But you know best about your luck." Yuvaen paused. "That leaves us with a choice of Del or 'Rekhe, or maybe Serazao."

"Not 'Zao," Narin said at once. "She's too rigid. She'll keep the workings anchored as long as she's got breath, but she doesn't have enough imagination."

"So it comes down to Delath and Arekhon."

"Unless Garrod's willing to wait for Ty to get quite a bit older," she said. "And if waiting were an option, we wouldn't be having this conversation in the first place, would we?"

"Probably not," Yuvaen admitted. "But since we are having it, how do you read our two possibles?"

He waited, saying nothing, while Narin unpacked an entire crate of breakfast supplies—porridges, fruit jellies, flaked grains, quick-heating baked goods in long-term storage pouches. Finally she said, "Del's steadier, in some ways, but . . ."

"You don't think he's up to it?" Yuvaen sounded a bit surprised, which confirmed Narin's suspicions about which candidate the Second himself favored. "He got his training right here, after all."

"Which means he's a lot like you. *And* like Garrod. If you're serious about bringing in a Third, you'll need someone with enough difference to balance things out."

"That's why we thought maybe you—"

"No."

"I suppose not," Yuvaen said. "But I don't know if Arekhon's strong enough for the job, either."

She abandoned the bags of groceries and faced the Second squarely, her feet set apart as though she braced herself again for balance on the *Dance*'s moving deck. "You asked my opinion, and I'm giving it to you. 'Rekhe isn't a solid rock like you are, or like Garrod is, or like Del. He's the water that goes around the rock, maybe, or the wind that blows across it—and believe me, Yuva, because I know it, wind and water are strong enough to outlast all the rocks in the world."

Jaf Otnal returned to his own office suite in the Zealous Endeavor Building, full of a warm sense of satisfaction with the interview just past. He wasn't surprised to find his friend Riet waiting in the inner office when he arrived. Riet was the firm's chief economic forecaster, and would have heard about the mind-gel problem from his own sources already—and he knew how long Jaf had been waiting for such an opening.

"Do you think Kammen went for it?" he asked as soon as Jaf had shut the door behind him. Riet was Ayaratan by birth, and had little patience with subtlety and indirect maneuvering. He'd wanted to broach the matter of the star-lords to Kammen several months ago, but Jaf had counseled him to be patient.

"I believe he did," Jaf replied. He walked to his desk, picked up a black onyx puzzle-paperweight and started to play with it. The desk toy was both complex and delicate—a good metaphor, he reflected, for any number of things in life. "But we're still talking about a course that might destroy the company. We could wind up selling fruit pies on street corners, or worse."

"Or we could wind up richer than even the star-lords could imagine," Riet said. "But someone, somewhere, has to make a stand—and if we're the ones who lead it, then we'll be running Zealous Endeavor when the star-lords have all gone begging."

Jaf regarded the chief forecaster thoughtfully. "Don't you think the people on the top floor will have something to say about that?"

"I don't think the top floor needs to know too much."

"What are you saying?"

Riet began ostentatiously counting on his fingers. "I'm saying that all our communications pass through satellites owned by the star-lords—all our essential raw materials move from planet to planet through the star-lords—all our finished goods move back to market again through the star-lords—and the star-lords have enough money to hire the very best in traitors and espionage."

Jaf nodded. "You have a point. Several points. I think we can bury our efforts somewhere in your research budget, at least for now."

"Then we'll need to see results in the next two or three quarters." Riet thought for a moment. "I can give you something, I believe."

"Good. Meanwhile, I'm going to take a leave of absence to clear up some family matters—and visit with a few close friends—back on Ildaon."

Riet gave him a dubious look. "Riding with the star-lords?"

"If the star-lords ever find out about this conversation," Jaf pointed out, "riding in my own groundcar won't be safe. Don't worry about me this time, though. By the time the star-lords notice that something unusual is going on, I'll be back."

"Good luck to you, then. Lunch today?"

"The usual place."

Riet left the office. Jaf watched him go, then glanced down at the black onyx puzzle in his hands. At some point in their conversation, he had slid the last piece into place and locked it down.

"So," he mused aloud. "We're doing it."

He looked out the window, away from Beshkip toward the distant mountains obscured by industrial haze. The project was not, he thought, impossible. The star-lords bought their food somewhere, they bought their steel somewhere, they sold their pirated goods somewhere, and they did their banking somewhere. And somewhere—in one of those places, or in another—they would have to be vulnerable.

He set down the puzzle and touched the desktop switch that reactivated the room's voice sensors.

"I need to take extended personal leave," he said to the office-mind. "A matter of family obligation. Get me passage to Ildaon, first available transit. Make reservations for lunch today at the Windflower, two guests. And purchase two hundred Eraasian tons of mind-gel, local spot market price, immediate delivery."

"Return from Ildaon?" the room inquired.

Jaf thought for a moment. "Leave that open."

XI: Year 1123 E. R.
Eraasi: Hanilat Starport

NATELTH SUS-KHALGATH, senior in the sus-
Peledaen line, waited in his study to receive his
last caller of the afternoon. His darkwood armchair, and the
guest chair that complemented it, occupied the bay window at
the front of his study. On the low table between the chairs, a
polished copper pot stood on tripod legs, a lump of solid al-
cohol burning in its lower tray. A pair of crystal glasses waited
for Natelth to fill them with the fresh-brewed drink.

There was a knock at the outer door. Natelth raised his voice
enough to carry through the thick wood. "Come in."

The door swung open, and his brother entered.

Arekhon had changed in the time since he had left the fleet
for the Demaizen Circle. He'd abandoned the family colors
for plain black and white, and wore his dark hair long after
the country fashion. Even the short staff clipped to his belt
was nothing more than a cubit and a half of polished wood,
chastely ornamented with silver wire. Some things remained
the same, however: As usual, 'Rekhe had delayed his courtesy
visit until near the end of the working day, but not past it, a
calibration too precise to be anything but deliberate.

Typical of him, Natelth thought as he gestured his brother into the empty chair. *Squeezing the family into the thinnest possible slip between daylight business and his own pleasure.*

For a moment Natelth considered inviting Arekhon to join the household at dinner, purely for the sake of throwing his sibling's plans for the evening into disarray, but discarded the idea as unworthy of the head of the sus-Peledaen.

"'Rekhe," he said. "We haven't seen you in Hanilat for quite a while. Isayana worries that sus-Demaizen holds you on too short a leash."

"We keep ourselves busy, I'm afraid," Arekhon said. "Isa frets too much." The implied rebuke had not escaped him; Natelth watched the awareness of it show briefly in his eyes like a spark from grey flint, and felt pleased.

Natelth waved a hand toward the copper pot. "Will you join me in a glass of red?"

"Of course." Arekhon's pleasure seemed genuine. "There's never anything but pale at the Hall, for some reason."

"I'll have the kitchen make you up a package of decent leaf before you go."

"I do well enough with the yellow," Arekhon said. He picked up the glass that Natelth had filled for him, and sipped at it. Fragrant steam curled up from the hot liquid; he inhaled it and let out a contented sigh. "But if it makes Isa happy, I'll take some of the house mix back with me to Demaizen."

Again, Natelth raised his voice. "Kitchen, do you hear?"

The voice of the kitchen replied over the household command circuit. "I hear."

"There; it's done." Natelth turned back to his brother. "What brings you into Hanilat this time—more errands for sus-Demaizen?"

"Not precisely." Arekhon was looking pleased about something; pleased and excited. "I had business of my own to set in order."

The phrasing, coupled with his brother's expression, made Natelth uneasy. He frowned. "Is something going on at the Hall?"

Arekhon gave a fractional shrug. "Only the usual." His tone was unconvincing. After a moment's pause, he added, "Garrod's decided to name a Third for the Circle."

"A Third," Natelth said. That would explain much. He turned a sharper eye on his brother. "You?"

"Yes."

"Isayana will be proud."

Their sister would also, Natelth thought, come close to worrying herself sick. Not all Circles with a named Third did dangerous work—sometimes the honor was merely a way to spread out the drudgery of administration—but Garrod syn-Aigal sus-Demaizen had kept his Circle with only a Second for as long as Natelth had known of its existence.

Something momentous, then, was going on at Demaizen Old Hall. Natelth wasn't sure what to think about that. Hard enough to look at Arekhon and see an ordinary Circle-Mage: 'Rekhe was too young, almost a generation younger than Natelth or Isayana, and he possessed not the least vestige of seriousness. To see him as one of the ranking Mages of a Circle, with all that such a name implied, was something that Natelth found almost impossible.

A rush of questions pressed against his closed mouth. He swallowed all of those which it would have been undignified for him to ask, and which Arekhon—being a Mage, and therefore no longer under his family's authority—had no obligation to answer, and said only, "Other than leaf, is there anything you require by way of foodstuffs?"

"We are quite well supplied with all we need," Arekhon said, a bit stiffly, as if sus-Demaizen's ability to provide for his Circle had been called into question—as indeed it had been. "I should be going."

"Sit, sit," Natelth said, half afraid that his brother would rise and depart without further ceremony. The Mages were an odd lot, and not bound by the usual rules of courtesy. He leaned back in his chair and regarded the younger man patiently for a moment before speaking again.

"You know that all of our family's resources lie beneath your hand. Surely there is something?"

"Perhaps one thing," Arekhon said.

"Name it. It is yours."

"The charts. All the stars, all the worlds. I want to take copies back to the Old Hall."

At that moment, Natelth was aware that he had been maneuvered into the offer. Not dishonorably, not by trickery or force, but maneuvered all the same.

He did not allow his face to show any change. "You have them," he said. "And now, come join me for dinner. You must; the family will wish to see you."

At least, Natelth thought, not allowing his lips to curve either up or down, *I have paid him back in small part. Whatever plans he has for the evening are now disrupted.*

Elaeli Inadi paused at the entrance to the Court of Two Colors. Night had fallen outside; within, dozens of lamps on tall wrought-iron poles reflected like stars off the crystal dome of the Court. The waters of the central fountain rose skyward and fell again to their hidden sources, mingling and interlacing in the air above the pool, and throwing back the lamplight in a glitter of refraction.

A discreet scan of the room reassured Elaeli that she had come dressed appropriately for the place and the occasion, in a tailored outer dress over satin leggings, all in dark blue piped and lined with crimson. Not a fleet uniform, but near enough that the garments felt comfortable to somebody who had worn the sus-Peledaen livery since her apprentice days. That the colors also looked well with her fair skin and her loose, light-brown curls was a pleasing bonus.

One of the Court's servitor-constructs glided toward Elaeli across the black and white tiles that gave the establishment its name. The *aiketh*'s counterforce unit kept it hovering a handspan above the floor in spite of its mass. A red light glowed inside its smoky black housing as it spoke.

"Be welcome, honored one. Are you awaited here?"

"Arekhon sus-Khalgath sus-Peledaen," she said. "He reserved a table earlier."

The *aiketh* hummed and flickered—communicating with the Court's main intelligence, Elaeli supposed. The makers of the Court's *aiketen* had done their work well; when this one spoke again, its artificial voice held a carefully-constructed note of polite regret.

"Lord sus-Khalgath begs that you will take your ease at the chosen table and await his coming," it said. "Matters at the house of his brother force him to delay."

Elaeli suppressed a smile. *So Natelth got you for dinner after all. I told you he would.*

"I'll wait," she said.

The *aiketh* led her to a table near the fountain. Clear water, fed by the Court's own spring, fell plashing into the basin and filled the air with a cool mist. Green and blue ferns in tile planters muted the sounds of the Court and gave the illusion of a private grotto.

True privacy could also be had here, for those who desired it, but for now Elaeli had no objection to being seen. Arekhon might have left his family altars—such as they were, Natelth never having struck her as especially pious—and gone off to the Mages, but there was no estrangement. Word would get back to the sus-Peledaen fleet that Pilot-Ancillary Inadi, daughter of a greengrocer and a physician's assistant, nevertheless dined at the Court of Two Colors with a member of the family's senior line, and those who might have opposed her future promotion would speak a bit more civilly to her thereafter.

You're a clever man, 'Rekhe, she thought, *and a good friend to boot. Whatever you've got in mind this time, I'll help you if I can.*

The *aiketh* brought her a crystal goblet of woodflower cordial and a bowl of candied fruit, and she disposed herself to wait. The Court was a pleasant place to wait in, which was fortunate; almost an hour went past before Arekhon sus-Khalgath came into the area beneath the crystal dome. He was dressed as he must have been for the visit to his brother: In plain black and white, with nothing to mark his calling but the staff at his belt, and nothing to mark his rank except his unstated assumption that anyone in Hanilat who needed to know him probably already did.

Elaeli smiled. 'Rekhe had a prideful streak in him, but it was buried deep—far deeper than her own ambition, about which she had no illusions at all.

He smiled back at her as he sat down in the chair opposite. "Ela! I'm glad you waited. Natelth trapped me, exactly like you said he would. I was barely able to snatch a moment free to send word to the Court."

"How could I not wait?" she said. "It's been a long time

since we shared a table—they keep you busy at Demaizen."

"Not that busy." He beckoned to the *aiketh* and continued, "Circle work and ship work keep their own seasons, and the fleet was out-system the last time I came to Hanilat."

The inorganic servitor glided up to the table in response to Arekhon's summons, and took his request for a glass of the woodflower cordial and a platter of hot and cold foresters' delicacies. The bits of game, some fresh off the grill and others preserved in smokes and pickles, would serve two people quite well for dinner if one of them had eaten a full meal already.

They spoke of inconsequential things until the platter arrived. Elaeli regarded its heaped and garnished bounty with admiration for a moment, then speared a curl of shaved meat on the twin tines of her fork. "The fleet mess is nothing like this, let me tell you. . . . I see you survived your dinner with Natelth and Isa."

"Natelth isn't so bad," said Arekhon. He sounded pleased, and Elaeli knew what that meant.

"Put one over on him this time, did you?"

'Rekhe had been contending with his older brother—half in jest and entirely in earnest—for as long as she had known him. Elaeli, who had no siblings of her own, found the relationship both inexplicable and fascinating.

"I came away with what I needed," Arekhon said.

"And that was—?"

"A packet of fresh leaf. Nobody at Demaizen drinks it red besides me."

Elaeli shook her head. "Red leaf. Only you, 'Rekhe . . . only you."

He was laughing now, the mischief sparkling in his grey eyes. "It's true."

"It and what else?"

"Nothing."

"Hah. Get better at lying, 'Rekhe."

"Nothing yet," he amended.

She looked at him over the rim of her glass of cordial, and realized that more than amusement was underlying his current mood. "Is something going on at the Hall?"

"Garrod's named me Third for the Circle."

" 'No profit without risk,' " she said, quoting the *Ribbon*'s old prentice-master to cover her own moment of dismay. "But if it isn't breaking any oaths to speak of the matter to outsiders . . . exactly how profitable are things likely to get?"

"Demaizen isn't the fleet," he said. "We could go for years without seeing any trouble."

"And Garrod went for years without naming a Third, too. 'Rekhe—"

He met her eyes, but didn't answer her question. "That was the other thing. I spoke to the fleet legalist before I paid my duty call at home, and had him put you down on the list for outer-family adoption."

"You had him—" For a moment the news pushed aside even her concern over Arekhon's elevation to Third. *Me . . . Pilot-Ancillary Elaeli Inadi syn-Peledaen!*

By tradition, no one rose to the highest ranks of the sus-Peledaen fleet who wasn't already a member of the family. That made adoption one of the traditional rewards for a promising young officer, as well as a reliable source of new blood for the inner line. Elaeli had hoped to earn such an honor for herself—who wouldn't?—but she'd never expected it to come so soon.

Or to come this way. Arekhon shouldn't have been able to sponsor anyone into the family for another couple of decades, at least. Not unless—

"What else did you speak to the legalist about?"

"You know, Ela, you're a lot harder to distract than Natelth."

" 'Rekhe. What else?"

He sighed. "I had him take my name out of the line for good this time. I can't be a proper Third for Garrod sus-Demaizen if the fleet still has a claim on me. That's where the sponsorship comes in—you're going to be my replacement, if you're willing."

"Of course I'm willing," she said impatiently. "Who wouldn't be, in my position?"

"That's what I mean. You're on Fleet-Captain syn-Evarat's list of possibles already, and probably on a couple of others the legalist didn't tell me about. You might be better off waiting and taking sponsorship from somebody who'll be around to help you afterward."

"I'll take it from you, if you don't mind." She spiked a bit of pickled wood-fungus on her fork, and added, "Besides—a patron in the fleet is good, but getting an early start and not owing favors to anyone over you is even better."

"I thought you'd see it that way."

"Clever man." The pickle was sharp and bitter on her tongue. "I hope I'm not doing you a bad turn by letting you get away with it."

XII: Year 1123 E. R.
Eraasi: Hanilat Starport
Ildaon: Ildaon Starport
Country House of Elek Griat

THELEDAU SYN-GREVI SUS-RADAL kept his town house in Hanilat because such a residence was necessary for the head of the family's pre-eminent line. Given a choice he would never have come to Hanilat at all, but since that was not possible—the sus-Radal were star-lords above all, and no one could rule them who turned his back on the port—he contented himself with making his official residence as much like home as he could. The carpets and wall hangings were thick-piled and patterned with bold north-country geometric designs; all the chairs and tables were made of pale wood carved in clean straight lines; and on the top floor, where otherwise an attic would have been, Thel had put in what might have been the only proper moonroom south of the mountains.

The room was circular, with a bare floor of polished board, and it stood empty of furnishings beneath a vaulted roof of clear glass. At home, on a night like this one, aurorae would ripple across the sky above the moonroom like luminous banners. Hanilat, lying nearer to the equator, provided no such display. The pale moon and the stars shone down to flood the room with grey unwavering light.

Thel spent the customary hour of respect in the room each evening nevertheless. So he had done when he was at home in the northland, where keeping the moonwatch in winter required both real devotion and a quilted jacket, and so he would do now, even if the sky over Hanilat was not the one he had been brought up to honor. Members of the sus-Radal fleet-family whose work brought them to Theledau outside the normal hours of business came to know the moonroom well.

Iulan Vai was one of those people. The town house recognized Agent-Principal Vai as one of those with the right of uncontested access, and let her come and go unchallenged in all the public and semi-private rooms.

Tonight she had come to Theledau halfway through the hour of respect. He didn't think that Vai would have disturbed him for anything trivial, and her first words proved him right

"My lord," she said, kneeling and rising again in one graceful movement. The moonlight threw her shadow onto the polished floor, sharp-edged as a black paper cutout. "One of sus-Demaizen's Circle came into Hanilat this morning, and met with representatives of the sus-Peledaen."

Theledau looked upward at the night beyond the skylight. *Garrod,* he thought. The reclusive master of Demaizen Old Hall was First of a Circle everyone suspected to be pushing at the borders of what was known about space and the Void. He was also touchily independent and famously eccentric— but all things changed with time. *Has the taker of no man's money taken somebody's coin at last?*

"Who was Garrod's Mage?" he asked.

"sus-Khalgath's brother. Arekhon."

"It could have been nothing," said Thel. He remembered the junior sus-Khalgath as a quiet young man, without any of Natelth's forceful, ambitious nature . . . well suited, in fact, for the isolated life of a country Circle. "They're still kin."

Vai shook her head. "He met with the sus-Peledaen legalist first. And one of their pilots after."

"Which one?"

"Inadi. Pilot-Ancillary. Junior, but rising fast. If Garrod's decided to work with the sus-Peledaen after all, she could be his contact in the fleet."

"The sus-Peledaen already control more trade routes than

any other fleet-family on Eraasi," Thel said irritably. "What use have they got for more?"

"Maybe it's not another trade route. Maybe this time Garrod is onto something even bigger."

"Find out what it is. Get it for us."

Vai knelt and rose again. "As my lord commands."

Elek Griat had ordered his driver to take him to the spaceport as soon as the working day ended. Now Ildaon's sun was setting out beyond the western flats, and the chill of night was coming on, but Elek continued to wait. *Wild-Bird-at-Morning,* a passenger craft belonging to the sus-Dariv fleet-family, had reported to Ildaonese authorities upon entering the system, and among the messages transmitted for local recipients was a personal one directed to Elek: Jaf Otnal would be arriving on Ildaon as soon as the *Bird*'s first shuttle made port.

Elek hadn't seen Jaf since the day the younger man left Ildaon for Ayarat and a position with the Zealous Endeavor. At that time Elek had been Jaf's friend and mentor, and—much against the promptings of his own heart, which would just as soon have seen the younger man stay on Ildaon—he had advised in favor of the change. He was happy to learn from the contents of the message that his judgment had proved sound, and equally happy with the prospect of having Jaf's company once again, however briefly.

He didn't know exactly when the *Bird*'s passengers would arrive—the times from in-system to ground were not exact—but Jaf deserved to have someone waiting when he came in and cleared Ildaonese customs. There would be no trouble with the officials; Elek had made sure of that already. A few well-placed words, and the payment of a discreet "vehicular traffic fee," had procured for him the right to park the groundcar at the edge of the landing field nearest to where the shuttle would touch down. It only remained for him to wait.

Shortly after sunset, the shuttle from *Wild-Bird-at-Morning* came down from the orbital docking station. At the same time a wing of supply craft lifted from the hard-packed earth, their bright trails sparkling across the dark blue of the evening sky, bound for the station with food and drink and export goods.

At last, Jaf Otnal emerged from the entry hatch of the grounded shuttle.

Outside the groundcar, Elek's driver held up a placard with "Otnal" written on it in block letters. Jaf spotted it and broke into a smile. Gesturing at the luggage carrier to follow, he hurried over to the parked groundcar. He appeared pleasantly surprised to find his friend waiting for him inside.

"I hadn't expected to see you for another six hours," Jaf said after they had embraced and exchanged greetings. He settled himself across from Elek in the car's rear passenger compartment, where yellow-tinged lamps shed a warm, luxurious glow on plush seats and rosewood paneling. "This is an honor."

"No more than you deserve," said Elek. "I was delighted to learn that you'd come home for a visit."

"And I'm delighted to see you, as well," Jaf replied. "How are things going at the old firm?"

"Prosperously—I'm in the tower now, and well-placed to do even better. And you?"

Jaf glanced modestly downward. "Not quite so elevated yet. But I persevere."

Elek caught his eye, and chuckled. "Judging from the priority treatment the *Bird* gave to your transmission, you've come a long way already."

"I wouldn't be the one to say so. I've done my work and drawn my pay." Jaf paused, and looked up to meet Elek's gaze directly. "But something has come up that has the potential to change everything. It's risky, though. Very risky . . . I'd be grateful for your advice on how to handle it."

"Let's not talk business yet," Elek said, though Jaf's confidence warmed him. "We've got a groundcar ride to the flyer port ahead of us, and more travel after that. We can spend the time catching up on old acquaintance, and discuss weightier matters after a good night's sleep."

When the last of the cordial was gone, Elaeli went back with Arekhon to his room in the Court's guesthouse. She had known since their days together on *Ribbon-of-Starlight* that any dealings she had with him would be like this—but she always forgot, in between times, how much she enjoyed being with him.

"And just as well, too," she concluded some time later, as she lay on the bed in a state of pleasant exhaustion. "Considering the frustration if I had to keep on remembering it for . . . how long has it been this time?"

"Two years," he murmured drowsily. "Plus three months and four days." His head rested on her shoulder, the dark straight hair spreading out like a fan across her breast. He'd let his hair grow since leaving the fleet; in the old days he'd worn it clipped even shorter than her own loose curls.

She laughed under her breath. "I suppose you found a calendar and worked it out."

"That's right." He was two-thirds asleep, and she wondered if he was truly listening to himself any more. He yawned, a warm breath against her sweat-dampened skin, and added, "All your fault."

"*My* fault? How did that happen, 'Rekhe?"

The question seemed to wake him up—or maybe he hadn't been as near to sleep as she'd thought, after all. He propped himself up on one elbow and looked at her.

"I started calculating in earnest after the last time I came into Hanilat on Circle business," he said. "When I found out I'd missed seeing you by half a day."

There was no laughter in his eyes this time. Elaeli stroked his dark hair back from his face by way of apology.

"syn-Evarat took the fleet out of port early," she said. "Somebody slipped him word that the sus-Radal were planning to use our jump-points and take out a convoy ahead of us. I tried to make a voice-call to Demaizen, for a chance to talk with you for a few minutes before we left, but the woman I spoke to said you weren't there."

"I would have been on the road by then."

"I couldn't have waited even if I'd known."

"It's all right," he said. "Did you beat them to the jump? I dreamed of fires and explosions all that night, but I couldn't tell whether it was a true vision or only my disappointment telling lies."

"We had a bit of a chase," she admitted. "syn-Evarat sent a guardship and a couple of scouts up ahead of the convoy to make certain the jump-point was clear. Turned out the sus-Radal had thought of the same thing."

"They do keep on trying, don't they?"

"There's only so much trade to go around," she said. "And it opens up so slowly . . ."

"That could change."

He was smiling again. Elaeli thought about his visit to the sus-Peledaen legalist, and about whatever it was that he'd talked Natelth out of before dinner, and about his new position in the Demaizen Circle. She sat up and looked at him sharply.

"Garrod's working on something big, isn't he?"

Arekhon lay back on the pillow. He looked pleased with himself, Elaeli thought. Hardly fair, considering what holding named rank in Garrod's Circle was likely to entail, but that was 'Rekhe for you.

"Garrod," said Arekhon simply, "thinks that the sundered half of the galaxy may not be barren after all."

"He's not the first one to think that," Elaeli said. She felt cold already—the air circulating in the guesthouse bedroom made the hairs along her arms and spine stir and stand up—but she went ahead and asked the next question anyway. "What makes Garrod's theory different from all the rest of them?"

"Nothing." Now 'Rekhe was looking smug and pleased and excited all at once, and Elaeli would have slapped him for it if she'd thought it would do any good. "But this time Garrod plans to walk there and find out."

The groundcar reached Elek Griat's country house at daybreak, after a long night journey by flyer and a cross-country drive afterward. The land was a former working farm, but the fields and farmhouses had been replaced by new landscaping and structures built to Elek's own design. The high-walled grounds, with their acres of fruit trees watered by swift-running streams, and the sprawling manor house itself, pink-lit with the glow of the rising sun, were all supported by Elek's position at Prosperous Unity Mercantile.

Elek had long wished that he could share his happiness in acquiring such a property with his friend and former protégé, but he'd never had much hope of doing so. Now that the opportunity had arisen, he found himself watching Jaf keenly for his reactions—both to the estate itself and to the not-inconsiderable achievement that it represented. Nor did the younger man disappoint him.

"You *have* done well for yourself since we parted," Jaf said as the groundcar purred up the long driveway. "It surpasses anything I've achieved so far, that's for certain."

"I'm sure Ayarat has any number of places that are equally appealing, or that can be made so. Give yourself a bit more time."

As always when returning home after a long journey, Elek went first to his devotions. Those, too, had changed in outward form—though not in substance—since Jaf had last attended them in his company. The family shrines, that had been so cramped and ill-dignified in their old quarters, now occupied a wing on the ground floor. A spacious, high-windowed gallery held all the plaques and icons, the altars, urns, and boxes, that Elek had gathered together and maintained over the years.

With Jaf following along respectfully, Elek approached the table of the Eldest, and placed on it a single white flower. Then he knelt, bowed his head, and thanked all the old ones for his success, for the visit of his friend, and for his current prosperity. A bit of smugness entered his thoughts at that juncture, but he promptly banished it, and asked instead for continued good fortune.

The ancestors, he hoped, were pleased with their present circumstances. He himself was unlikely to continue the family line—perhaps his sister would—but the luck that the old ones had sent him over the years meant that he was not too far removed from their favor.

At last, his devotions finished for the day, Elek rose and gestured to Jaf—who had knelt likewise, at an outsider's respectful distance—that he should rise also.

"The household *aiketen* will take you to your room," Elek said. "Refresh yourself, and rest for as long as you need to. When you're ready, we can have breakfast—and speak, perhaps, of this matter you mentioned to me earlier."

Iulan Vai left Hanilat at midmorning, not long after Arekhon sus-Khalgath set out on the road to Demaizen in the Hall's well-maintained but elderly groundcar. Vai had passed along the job of keeping an eye on Elaeli Inadi to one of her contacts in the sus-Peledaen fleet. The contact was well placed to see what, if anything, Pilot-Ancillary Inadi brought back to the ship; if it turned out to be nothing more than pleasant memories, at least Vai wouldn't have wasted any of her own time on a false lead.

Arekhon sus-Khalgath, on the other hand, she kept for herself. It was possible, she supposed, that the young Mage's evening engagement at the Court of Two Colors had served no purpose other than a bit of nostalgic pleasure. He and Inadi had served their fleet-apprenticeship together, before he had gone to the Circles, and Vai knew how such an experience could bind people for years afterward.

But there was more than dining and dalliance going on this time, she thought. *I can smell it. Natelth and the fleet legalist both in the same day, and Inadi kept for best-and-last—that's not the schedule of a man with nothing but pleasure on his mind.*

Vai made the journey to Demaizen in a rented high-speed flyer expensed to one of her department's fictional companies. Not surprisingly, she reached the countryside near the Old Hall well in advance of her research subject. She used the extra time to pick out a comfortable vantage point on the brush-covered slopes to the west of the Hall. Her coat and leggings of dappled brown fabric blended into the stone and leaves of the hillside, and—in case she should be noticed in spite of her efforts—she carried a wildlife observer's pocket recognition guide and tally pad.

The observer's clothing also justified the long-range spyglasses through which she had been watching Demaizen Old Hall for the greater part of the afternoon. So far she had seen only normal activity, plus a genuine and duly recorded sighting of a speckled whipworm slithering out of sight between two rocks.

The Hall itself was a broad, sprawling building made out of the buff-colored local stone. Glass windows—three stories' worth, not counting attic and basement—flashed in the afternoon sunlight. According to Vai's research, a few generations ago the Hall had been the social and political center of the entire district, the residence of the main line of the sus-Demaizen family, with nearly a score of permanent residents and a full staff of servants. These days, all the servants were long gone, and so were all the sus-Demaizen family but one.

The purr of an engine on the road below drew Vai's attention, and she raised her spyglasses. It was the Hall groundcar, all right, a battered grey six-wheeler that hadn't been new since Garrod's grandfather's day. It ran with far less choking and sputtering than a vehicle its age had any right to do—*that engine is last year's model at the very oldest*—and even on the winding one-lane track leading up to the Hall it maintained a steady, rapid pace.

The groundcar slid into one of the Hall outbuildings that had been renovated to make a garage. The sound of the engine died, and a minute or two later Arekhon sus-Khalgath came out of the building. He carried no luggage with him into the Hall except a small black satchel. Vai could see it plainly in the slanting afternoon sunlight, along with the ebony rod that hung by a clip from his belt.

She watched his posture and movement as he crossed from the garage to a door at the rear of the main building, and nodded to herself.

Whatever he's got, he doesn't want to let go of it. Getting it away from him isn't going to be easy.

XIII: Year 1123 E. R.
Eraasi: Demaizen Old Hall

DEMAIZEN WAS far enough to the north and west of Hanilat that the autumn air had a sharp bite to it, and the fire that burned on the kitchen hearth was useful as well as ornamental. Arekhon, bringing in his packet of red leaf to store in one of the preserving cupboards, found Kief and Narin making fish stew for dinner. Kief tended greens and stock in the steaming soup kettle, while Narin worked at turning a platter of silverlings into spoon-sized chunks. She apologized to each fish before she made the first cut; at least, Arekhon supposed that the muttered words in her native Veredden were an apology.

The kitchen at Demaizen had been brought up to date more than once since the construction of the Hall itself. The gleaming metal counters with their inset cookstoves and cupboards and cold-storage bins came from the most recent rebuilding, as did the long central worktable, but the great man-tall stone fireplace had been part of the room since the first. The hooks and cranes for open-hearth cookery remained in place—if the Mages of Garrod's Circle ever decided to spit-roast an entire sunbuck, they had the equipment to do it.

Kief looked around from the soup kettle as Arekhon entered. "I see you made it back from Hanilat in one piece."

"Actually, I was waylaid by bandits on the road," said Arekhon. He found an empty jar in the preserving-cupboard and tucked the packet of leaf inside it, then closed the door. "They sliced me into collops and you're talking to my ghost."

"More stew for the rest of us, then," said Narin. Another silverling came apart into neat bits underneath her filleting knife as she spoke. "Did you get what you went for?"

Arekhon hefted the leather satchel he'd carried with him from Hanilat. "It's all in here. Family stuff, so be careful—if any of it turns up with the sus-Radal, Natelth will have an apoplexy."

"We'll be careful," Kief promised him. "Can the Hall read your charts, or are we going to have to find a ship-mind to translate them first?"

"These are all house copies. As long as we've got a working data-reader, there's no problem."

Narin had come to the last of the silverlings. It lay gleaming on the white pottery dish, its dead eyes round and yellow, like buttons. She said something to it in Veredden, then slashed it open and lifted out the bones with a flick of her narrow blade. She glanced up from her work for a moment to ask, "Does Garrod know you're home yet?"

"What . . . oh. No. I came in by the back way." Arekhon had been distracted, briefly, by the smooth economy of her work with the knife. "Will you teach me how to do that sometime?"

"Cut up fish? What for?"

He shrugged. "I might want to do it some day, and I might as well do it right. Where is Garrod, anyhow?"

"In the long gallery," Kief said. The steam from the soup kettle came up in clouds around him as he stirred. "Practicing staff-work with Yuva and the rest of them."

"And he let you two dodge out of it? He must be getting soft-hearted."

"Never fear," said Narin. "He got Kief and me first thing. Beat the pair of us up one side of the gallery and down the other, then sent us off to put salve on our bruises and start cooking dinner. He'll get you, too, as soon as you show up."

"As long as he lets me put down the charts first," Arekhon said. He nodded amiably at the two cooks, then left the kitchen by the inner door and ambled off.

The gallery at Demaizen ran the length of the Hall's upper story. Tall uncurtained windows along one side of the room and at both ends provided ample sunlight. In the late afternoon, minute flaws in the window-glass caught the sunlight and sent it back out in prismatic sparkles onto the empty walls. The floor of the gallery was made of plain wood, once carpeted but now bare; Garrod's Mages used the room for practice with their staves.

As Kief had promised, the rest of the Circle was already at work when Arekhon came into the room: Delath and Serazao and Ty and Yuvaen syn-Deriot, practicing staff-work in pairs under the eye of the Lord of Demaizen himself. Garrod looked away from the fighting for a moment as Arekhon approached. His eyes went at once to the leather satchel and he smiled, making crinkles appear beside his dark eyes and causing his thick, grizzled brows to tilt upward at a reckless angle.

"So you have the charts," he said. "That's good. What did you have to promise Natelth for them?"

"Only my company for dinner, would you believe it?"

"He values you that highly?"

"Probably not," Arekhon said. "But I'd already made plans for the evening, and he knew it. So he got something for his trouble anyway."

Garrod chuckled. "I hope you weren't too disappointed."

"Not really. I expected that Natelth would try something like that, so I set my own appointment accordingly. I was still late . . . but not so late that anything was spoiled by it."

"Clever of you," said Garrod. "Now, if you give me that satchel, you can take your staff and go fight with Yuva for a while. We'll see how clever you are then."

"That's right," Arekhon said. Laughing, he pulled off his outer coat to stand in his shirt and vest, then unclipped his staff from his belt and raised it above his head in a long, elaborate stretch. "Take advantage of a man stiff from sitting in a groundcar all day."

Garrod beckoned to Yuvaen syn-Deriot. "Instruct him,

Yuva. Or let him instruct you, as the case may be."

The Second of the Demaizen Circle had already unclipped his staff. He held it out level in front of him with both hands, twisting his torso from side to side, limbering himself. Then he released the end of the staff in his left hand and made the ebony rod whistle as it spun before him. He looked at Arekhon through the blur of motion.

"You can't fool me, 'Rekhe. Rested up from a long night's sleep in a soft bed, that's what *you* are."

Arekhon thought of Ela, and of how he had fallen asleep in the Two Colors guesthouse with his head lying upon her breast, and smiled in spite of himself. "I can't deny it—my pillow, at least, was very soft."

"This is where you get the lumps to make up for it," Yuvaen said. "Are you ready?"

"Ready."

"Then let us begin."

Yuvaen took the third guard position, with his staff guarding his left side while his upper arm guarded his right. Arekhon also took third, his knees flexed. Yuvaen was taller than he was, but he was used to that—so were Delath and Garrod himself, and Arekhon was accustomed by now to regular sparring with bigger and heavier opponents. It was not size that made Yuvaen syn-Deriot formidable: He had been Garrod's Second since the time the Demaizen Circle was founded.

For a little while neither Arekhon nor Yuvaen moved. Then Yuvaen began to open and close the first of his empty hand, curling and uncurling the fingers in a slow, steady motion. A pale green light stole out along the length of his staff. Except for the regular flexion of his left hand, he remained motionless.

Arekhon didn't move. A slow exhalation, and a violet light began to glow around his staff: Faint, almost invisible, throwing no illumination.

Yuvaen smiled. "Hiding something?"

He slipped the end of his staff underneath Arekhon's and pressed it aside, leaving Arekhon open to a thrusting blow. Or he would have, had not Arekhon, in the same instant, raised his staff and dipped it down again—a click and slide of wood on wood, and a quick, economical blur of motion—leaving them back in the position from which they had begun.

Yuvaen didn't stay there long. He pushed his staff sidewise against Arekhon's, trying to shove it aside and clear the way for a thrust. He had the strength and the physical mass to do it—*but I'm not that much of a fool, Yuva,* Arekhon thought, and made no effort to resist the pressure. A slight change in the position of his hand, instead, and the angle at which he held his staff shifted, sending Yuvaen's weapon sliding away and pulling Yuvaen himself out of guard.

Yuvaen reached to recover, and Arekhon moved. The end of his staff flicked out toward the opening on Yuvaen's left side. Yuvaen twisted and caught Arekhon's staff with his own to block the blow.

The vibration made Arekhon's hand sting—and a second later, he felt Yuvaen's staff slam into his ribs. His mind registered the bruising impact of wood against flesh, but there was no time to dwell on it. Yuvaen had already used the rebound from the blow to clear the way for a strike coming in to Arekhon's ribs from the other side.

Arekhon took a step backward. *Let's make things a bit more even,* he thought, *see if we can unbalance you a bit;* and he brought his staff down in a strike at the pressure point in the upper part of Yuvaen's left arm.

The blow went in cleanly. Arekhon felt his staff shiver with the unmistakable feel of a solid, proper hit. His brief flare of satisfaction died an instant later, when Yuvaen's counterstrike smashed into his wrist and knocked his staff away, and he realized that the Second had taken his disabling blow on purpose, for the sake of the opening it had provided.

"There it is," Yuvaen said. Sweat beaded his forehead, and his left arm was hanging limp, but his staff was in his right hand while Arekhon's lay on the wooden floor. "Thank you for your instruction."

Arekhon cradled his aching wrist in his left hand. He would be spending time with the Hall's medical *aiketh* later, between that and his ribs . . . *well, so will Yuva, so it's not all on one side this time.*

Dinner came at sunset. By custom, the members of the Circle took their meals together in the small dining room—the great room at the heart of the Old Hall served another purpose these days. Garrod was the last of his line, but previous generations at sus-Demaizen must have run to families of considerable size, since the table in the small room easily accommodated all eight of the Hall's current residents.

As the Circle's most junior Mage, Ty from Port Street had the chair at the far end of the table from Garrod and Yuvaen. Kiefen Diasul had occupied the bottom place before him, and if the Circle ever gained a ninth member, Ty would yield to the new arrival in the same way.

Ty was hungry after the afternoon's practice, and the smells of fresh bread and Narin's fish stew made his mouth water. Meals were always good when it was Narin's turn in the kitchen. Ty's own limited cooking skills came out of working refectory detail at the Port Street Foundling Home. He could lay out a platter of cold sliced meat, boil up a pot of breakfast gruel, or—in a pinch—tear up greens for salad, but not much else. Nobody went hungry on the occasions when Ty's name stood at the top of the work roster, but they didn't show up early for dinner, either.

Garrod was silent during dinner—Ty suspected he was already turning over in his mind the best way to use that satchel full of sus-Peledaen charts—but Yuvaen was in good spirits and disposed to be talkative.

"So," he said to Arekhon sus-Khalgath, as cheerfully as if he hadn't come close to breaking the new Third's wrist a little while before. "How did you find the pleasure-palaces of Hanilat?"

"Mostly with a street map," the Third replied. He didn't sound like someone who had been the recipient of one of Yuvaen's bouts of vigorous instruction, either; Ty, whose own welts and bruises still smarted, had to admire his air of unconcern. "Yours, I think . . . at least, I found it in the ground-car, and the notes were in your handwriting. Did you ever settle that bill from the establishment on Five Street?"

Yuvaen had opened his mouth to reply when the doorbell rang. The sound cut off further speech in mid-word. The others at the table, equally startled, also fell silent.

Ty hadn't heard the bell ring since the day he first came to Demaizen from Hanilat. The apparatus was older than Garrod's occupation of the hall, a chain-and-chimes antique with a tone that reverberated throughout the entire lower floor. Nobody who lived at the Hall ever used it, and even the occasional visitors from Demaizen Town knew enough to go around to one of the side doors first.

Garrod looked at Ty without speaking. One of the duties of a Circle's junior Mage was to carry out tasks like answering doorbells. Ty rose and left the room as the bell rang a second time.

The Hall's main entrance was on the building's western side, underneath the long gallery on the floor above. The fan window over the door shone bright red with the glare from the setting sun, and the whole vestibule was full of crimson light. The bell sounded yet again as Ty opened the door.

A woman stood at the top of the short flight of semicircular granite steps. She was about Ty's own middling height, with short, neatly trimmed black hair, and wore a field-coat and leggings of brown and black stippled fabric. She was hung about with bits and pieces of outdoor equipment—a weatherproof logpad, a set of long-range spyglasses, a daypack— and the field-coat sported a patch proclaiming her to be a member of the Wide Hills District Wildlife Protection League. Her expression was one of mild bewilderment.

First time out from the city and she's lost her way, Ty decided instantly. He had already drawn breath to give her instructions for following the Hall road back to the main highway and, presumably, her abandoned groundcar when she spoke.

"Please forgive me if I shouldn't ask . . . but is there a Circle here?" Her glance flicked downward from his face to the staff at his belt, and back up again. "Because if there is . . . then I think I have come to ask for instruction."

XIV: Year 1123 E. R.
Ildaon: Country House of Elek Griat
Eraasi: Demaizen Old Hall

THE GUEST bedroom in Elek's manor house, with its cut flowers and crystal, was everything Jaf had expected from the greeting he had received so far. If the material results spoke truth, his friend and mentor had prospered beyond even Jaf's own hopes of success. The bed was soft and wide, the covers warm, the air pleasantly chill. Jaf slept well.

Some hours after noon—his body was still on ship's time— he awakened feeling rested but hungry. While he'd slept, the household *aiketen* had unpacked his luggage and placed the contents in the wardrobe. The servitors had augmented his personal effects with items from the household stores, including fresh hand towels and a satin-faced dressing robe. Jaf put on shirt and trousers, sandals as befitted a private visit, and the robe, to honor his host. Then he left the room to go exploring.

He heard music playing, somewhere out of sight, and followed its strains down the hall to a sunny conservatory. There he found Elek, also informally attired, playing the contra-cithara in harmony with a recording of the Brightwater String

Consort's performance of "The Turning Year." The sound system, Jaf noted, was excellent.

The conservatory's high windows and solarium ceiling let in the strong rays of the afternoon sun. Elek's back was to the door. His shoulders moved with steady rhythm as he drew his bow across the strings of the contra-cithara, the magnificent music swelled, and Jaf stood rapt.

At last the crescendo peaked, the Solstice theme reasserted itself one last time, and silence replaced the notes of the Brightwater Consort. Jaf stepped forward as Elek laid the contra-cithara on its rest, stood, and threw back his shoulders.

"You never told me you played," Jaf said.

Elek turned, brushing his hair back away from his forehead. "Only for my own pleasure," he said. Perspiration shone on his face. The contra-cithara required vigorous motion.

Jaf stepped toward the older man, even as Elek turned again and walked over to one of the conservatory's tall windows overlooking the grounds. Jaf followed him. They stood there side by side for some time without speaking, until finally Elek let out a quiet sigh.

"I never expected to see you again in the flesh," he said. "Though I sometimes hoped . . . Tell me something, Jaf. Why did you really come?"

Jaf winced; his friend's question stung all the more for the truth behind it. "Does there have to be another reason?"

"If being with me was all that you wanted, you'd never have left Ildaon in the first place." Elek smiled and shook his head. "You don't have to hide your ambitions, Jaf; if they've brought you home for a little while, then I'm grateful for them. Now let me indulge my pride and show you about the estate before dinner."

Jaf was suitably impressed by Elek's house and lands, both of which more than lived up to his initial glimpses at the time of his arrival. The tour ended in the dining room, where one of the *aiketen* waited—a faceless, columnar construct with a dim "inactive" light glowing behind its blank front panel. The shell would be Ildaon-built, to harmonize with local styles and requirements; the interior workings, Jaf knew, would contain more Eraasian imports than native ware.

"I should allow you time to change before the meal," Elek said. "But if you don't mind informality . . ."

"What pleases you pleases me." Jaf allowed himself to be guided to a chair, and the *aiketh* brought in their first course, a chilled sour-fruit soup.

"It's only kitchen-work," said Elek, when Jaf remarked on the dish's excellent flavor. "Assembled by the numbers, no improvising. Employing a professional cook just for myself would be . . . excessive."

"Then my compliments to the kitchen's instructor," Jaf said. He waited until the *aiketh* had brought in the next course, a platter of grilled vegetables drizzled with peppery oil, and said, "Elek, I need your advice."

"Aha—I thought so." To Jaf's relief, Elek looked more flattered than dismayed by the revelation. Perhaps over the past few years he had felt the lack of a protégé as keenly as Jaf had at first felt the lack of his former guide and sponsor. "Bring forth your problem, then, and we'll think about how to handle it."

"The problem is an old one," Jaf said. "But not something I was in a position to worry about before now."

He paused. Having finally come to this point, he felt a considerable reluctance to speak of the matter aloud. Talking mercantile politics with Kammen and Riet had been a thought-exercise, abstract plotting in an artificial vacuum; speaking on the same subject with Elek Griat could set into motion processes that he might not be able to halt.

"The Eraasians are strangling us," he said finally. "There must be a way to stop them. Stop the star-lords, anyway; they're the worst of the lot. I want to do it, Elek—I think that it can be done."

"Have you spoken this way to anyone else?"

"It's come up in conversation a time or two," Jaf admitted. "Among like-minded friends."

Elek's expression became unreadable. "Tell me the truth, Jaf: Are you merely grumbling, or do you and your like-minded friends honestly contemplate something more?"

"We've had talk without action for long enough. That's why we need your help—if this thing is going to be done, we have to get it right the first time or we're lost."

" 'We'?" Elek said. Jaf looked away, accepting the implied rebuke, and said nothing—too much persuasion, at this point, would be worse than too little. Finally his former mentor gave a faint sigh. "Since you've already enrolled me in your conspiracy, you might as well tell me what prompted you to start conspiring in the first place."

"Nothing dramatic, I'm afraid," Jaf said. "Just that over time, I came to realize that I wasn't happy with the idea of living off of the star-lords' leavings."

"Those aren't enough?" Elek said. He gestured at the well-groomed lawn of his estate, stretched out beyond the conservatory windows. "If all the star-lords happened to vanish overnight, what more could I ask for that I don't already have?"

"Freedom?"

"A highly over-rated commodity. It doesn't trade on the Ildaon Exchange."

Jaf shrugged. He had made the effort to win his friend's assistance; becoming importunate would help nothing. "I won't speak of the matter any further, then."

Elek laid a hand on Jaf's arm. "Wait," he said. "You didn't say anything that I haven't thought more than once already. I took my accumulated weeks of holiday-time as soon as your message arrived—you see, my feelings for you have continued—perhaps, in that period, something can be arranged."

On the morning after Arekhon's return to the Hall, the three ranking Mages of the Demaizen Circle came together in Garrod's private study to discuss—among other things—the matter of the sus-Peledaen charts.

Though he would never have admitted it, Arekhon felt somewhat intimidated by the occasion. He had been in the First's study before, and the room and its furnishings were familiar to him: Massive antique bookcases, built in another century to support the weight of heavy, board-bound volumes; an ugly, once-fashionable light fixture a much earlier lord of Demaizen had added to the plaster ceiling when the hall had been converted to electric power; solid wooden chairs with threadbare velvet cushions.

He had sat opposite the First of the Circle more than once, with the wide top of the office table stretching out between them, talking of the group's work-in-hand and his own progress as a Mage. But today marked the first time he had come here as one of those responsible for the welfare of the Circle, and for directing its efforts.

Clear yellow light poured into the room through the eastern windows, and dust motes floated lazily in the warm sunbeams. Garrod was there already; the satchel that held the star charts rested on the table in front of him. He gestured at Arekhon to take a seat. Yuvaen arrived a few seconds later, nodded to Arekhon as if the younger man's presence at the conference was already an accustomed thing, and took the remaining chair.

"Before we get to these"—Garrod nodded at the satchel—"we need to talk about our newest student."

"The wildlife observer," said Yuvaen. He sounded amused, Arekhon thought, and a little skeptical. "Syr Vai's appearance on our doorstep could, I suppose, be a mere accident of time."

"Stranger things have happened," Arekhon said. He wasn't sure why he was taking Iulan Vai's part in the matter, unless it was out of the principle that all sides of a thing bore discussion. "We're lucky we haven't had more people come looking to join us before now."

"Luck is strong here. And there are advantages to isolation." Garrod looked from Arekhon to Yuvaen. "What do the two of you say—shall we take her in?"

"If she was searching for us," Arekhon said, "then we have an obligation to teach her."

"Or to find some other Circle that can," said Yuvaen.

"Granted. But it was us she came to, and not some other Circle. We owe her at least a trial before sending her on."

"And if she isn't what she seems?"

Garrod chuckled. "Peace, Yuva. If the young woman is not, after all, a seeker of instruction, it will become obvious soon enough, and we can deal with the situation as we see fit."

"That's fair, I suppose," Yuvaen said. Arekhon nodded agreement.

"Good—then we're in accord." Garrod paused a moment, waiting for an objection that didn't come, before continuing, "Now we come to the serious business." He pushed the leather satchel across the table toward Arekhon. "Show us what we have in here, 'Rekhe."

Arekhon took the satchel and worked the code on the lock. The mouth of the satchel gaped. He reached inside and started removing the charts—house copies, as he had promised, palm-sized slices of stiff transparent plastic. "We'll need a reader."

"There's one on the shelf behind you," said Garrod. "It's old, but it can talk with the Hall's house-mind and most of the newer ones can't."

The reader didn't look promising. It was almost as big as the satchel the charts had come out of, and its blocky, unornamented lines embodied the aesthetic standards of several generations back. Scrapes and smudges marred its black plastic housing. Arekhon settled its feet into the take-up slots on the office table and waited for the yellow display lights on the reader's side panel to stop blinking and turn to violet.

He wondered, uneasily, how old the hall's house-mind actually was. Newer than the light fixture overhead, certainly . . . maybe . . . he hoped. Older than Garrod, without a doubt.

A fine help to the Circle I'm going to be, he thought, *if it turns out that the family charts are too new for the Hall to cope with.*

The telltales on the side panel stabilized. Violet . . . that was good. Arekhon slid the first chart into the reader's intake port and held his breath.

The scuffed and dusty black box began to glow internally, a crimson light that pulsed like a beating heart. Arekhon let himself exhale, giving thanks for his brother's innate caution and conservatism as he did so. The charts were good.

"You aren't going to get the same level of detail that you would from a more extensive house-mind and a newer reader," he said to Garrod and Yuvaen. "But for what we're planning, this should be clear enough."

"If we have to, we can always get better hardware," Garrod said. "Bring up the first image."

Arekhon laid the flat of his hand on the reader's upper surface. The plastic felt cool and slick against his skin. Inside the box, the crimson light flared twice, checking his palm print against those recorded as having access to the sus-Peledaen charts. The telltales remained violet—his identity was confirmed. He lifted his hand, and the chart began to take form in the air above the reader.

He heard a faint intake of breath from Yuvaen. The Second came from a landowning family, not from the star-lords or those who dealt with them; if he had seen a star chart before, it had never been one like this. It spread out over the tabletop like a floating carpet: The misty grey base layer, the multi-colored sparks and swirls and whorls of star systems, the red and blue streaks that marked off the normal-space routes and the Void-transits of the family's fleet.

"One thing you have to remember," he cautioned the other two Mages, as the *Ribbon*'s prentice-master had cautioned him, "is that all of this is nothing more than a picture to make some things easier to think about. The real chart is a construct that only the ship-mind can see." He paused, remembering his sometime encounters with the raw data of starship navigation. "Curves of probability, mostly, and their solids of rotation."

Garrod gave him a quick, impatient nod. "I understand. But for what we need, the picture will do. Which chart are we looking at now?"

Arekhon didn't need to consult the symbols on the readout panel. "This one shows my family's common routes from Eraasi to the Edge. This marker over here"—he unclipped his staff and used it as a pointer to circle the flashing green dot— "is the homeworld. The routes go out from it—the darker the color, the longer the transit. The family's colonies and trading worlds show up as more dots; the colors for those mostly have to do with what's bought and sold at the port."

"Nothing that concerns us, then," said Garrod.

"Most of them, no. The bright orange dots, though . . . those are known and charted worlds where the fleet never grounds a ship, even in an emergency."

"Why not?" Yuvaen asked.

Arekhon shrugged. "Believe it or not, there are places where the people don't like us. sus-Radal trading partners, some of them; their fleet and ours have been pushing against each other for a while now. Others . . . I don't know all the reasons. There's a lot of strange stuff out there."

"This blank area at the side," said Yuvaen, pointing. "Is that the Edge?"

"It is."

"Why aren't there any worlds marked beyond it? There are

stars on the far side—and if there are stars, then presumably, there are planets, and the stargazers should have a fair idea of their locations."

Arekhon reminded himself again that Yuvaen was one of the planet-bound. "There aren't any worlds marked on the far side of the gap because there's no point in marking them," he said. "No ship can make a transit to a place where no beacon has been set."

Yuvaen snorted. "They're afraid to try it, more likely."

"If my brother asked such a journey of his captains," said Arekhon, a bit stiffly, "they would attempt it. But Natelth isn't a fool, and he's not going to send the family's ships through a transit without a Mage to walk the Void before them and set the markers."

Garrod had been studying the chart in silence while they wrangled. At Arekhon's last words he looked up again, his eyes burning with a familiar purposeful fire.

"The fleet-Circles and the stargazers don't want to think about what lies beyond the Edge," he said. "They make their little explorations for the sake of trade, and whenever they find a new world for their charts they mark it down and never think about what its existence implies. Why is there even one settled world, let alone a hundred?"

He made a circular gesture that took in the whole building. "The foundations of Demaizen Old Hall were laid before the first starships ever left Eraasi. Other worlds have houses equally old, that were already there and waiting when our ships arrived. How did such worlds come to be?"

"The usual answer is that they must have been peopled before the Sundering," Arekhon said. "Or that the inhabitants were all descended from Mages who walked the Void and remained on their new worlds." He shrugged. "Of course, the people who say that are also the ones who insist that the Sundering is a pious allegory."

"I know," said Garrod. "And I threw their writings onto the bonfire with my family shrines. *I* say that the Sundering was a real event, brought about by some physical cause—and if populated worlds survived on this side of the interstellar gap, then others must have survived beyond the Farther Edge. If the fleet-Circles have no interest in finding them, then here is a Circle that will."

XV: YEAR 1123 E. R.
ERAASi: DEMAIZEN Old HALL

ULAN VAI spent the morning in the company of the young Mage who had opened the door for her the night before. It was his job, he said, to make certain that the new pupil knew her way around the Hall and met all its inmates.

Vai had no objection. She had her own reasons for coming to the Hall, and a proper orientation would make a good starting-place for uncovering as much as she could about Garrod sus-Demaizen and all his works. To that end, she had returned her high-speed flyer to the rental agency in Demaizen Town, and sent a message informing the second-in-command of sus-Radal's investigative force that she would be absent indefinitely on House business.

"Did Lord sus-Demaizen train all of you here?" she asked as they made their way up the great staircase.

"Depends on what you mean by training," said the young man. His name, or as much of it as he'd seen fit to give to her, was Ty, and the Hanilat port-slum accent was strong in his voice. Vai would have marked him down as nothing more than an ambitious street urchin with a touch of the Mage's gift—except that this was Garrod's Circle. "We've worked together for quite a while, if that's what you want to know."

"So is your Circle going to"—she paused, as if hunting for the right phrase—"pass me along to somebody who's more accustomed to working with raw beginners?"

"Maybe," said Ty. "Or Garrod may decide that since you came to us, we're the ones who should take you in."

They had come by this time to a long, narrow room on the second story of the hall. There was no furniture other than a couple of low benches and a stack of folded-up exercise mats, and the wooden floor had the scuff-polished look of regular use. The wall on the room's western side was mostly windows; on the other side, the white plaster showed paler oblong patches, regularly spaced, with empty wooden ledges beneath.

A quick glance upward at the ceiling revealed, as Vai had expected, the faint discoloration left by the smoke from years of offerings. The sus-Demaizen line had been an old one, and a long one before Garrod, childless, came to end it; this had been their votive gallery. Vai had never considered herself one of the devout, but she found the room's change of purpose disquieting all the same.

"This is where you practice?"

Ty took one of the battered teaching staves from its rack. It was a piece of plain light wood, not a polished black staff like the one that he himself carried; Vai supposed that the Circle kept the ordinary staves around for training tools, rather than as objects of focus and meditation.

"Here, give this a swing or two," he said. "If you're going to join us, you'll have to get used to it."

Vai took the staff, weighed it, and swung it in a lazy arc before settling back, balanced, with the staff in guard before her.

"You never learned *that* birdwatching," Ty said, watching her. "Which Circle did you train with?"

"I didn't," Vai said. "A woman living alone . . . I took classes. Some of my teachers might have been Circle-trained; I never asked."

"Want to show me what they taught you?"

"Is it all right?"

"It'll be fine," Ty said, taking up a practice staff of his own.

"Quarter speed, nothing to the head or knees. Sound fair?"

"Fair enough," Vai said.

She. wondered what she ought to do about this situation. Deliberately losing might be as dangerous as trouncing the boy. And the prospect of losing from lack of skill did not please her at all . . . *ego,* she thought. *A good operative can't afford one of those.*

Ty took his own stance, smiling. "We spend our lives with bruised ribs at Demaizen Old Hall," he said. "But Garrod's medical *aiketen* are first-rate, and Narin has some salve that works wonders on anything they miss." With that he let his staff swing slowly toward Vai, his right, her left, aiming for wood, not flesh.

Vai brought her staff just as slowly outward, maintaining it in a vertical line, and blocked his blow. When the staves kissed, Ty brought his back as if it were rebounding, while Vai stepped forward and left, and lowered her staff to the horizontal. Her right shoulder pointed at Ty's chest, and she swung outward toward him, inside of his staff, where he could not block, nor bring more than the strength of his wrist into a counter-blow, while all the muscles above her waist were set to slam her staff into his chest.

Ty did the only thing he could. He stepped back, out of range, and recovered his stance.

"Very good," he said. He was still smiling; she thought he was happy to have discovered her unexpected skill. "No need to show you the basics. You have 'em. How do you feel about half-speed?"

Vai stepped back into guard.

"What pleases you," she said, "pleases me."

Arekhon lived on the third floor of the Hall, in what had once been a guest bedroom. The room was smaller than the one he'd had while he was growing up in Hanilat—and which remained, technically, his whenever he chose to visit—but it was larger than the cabin on *Ribbon-of-Starlight* that he'd shared with three other fleet apprentices. In common with most of the other rooms in the Hall, it contained worn-but-good furniture several generations older than Arekhon himself: A bed, a night-table, a wardrobe full of clothing, a desk.

The desk lamp and the reading light on the bedside table answered to a switch plate by the door. Like most of the Hall's other concessions to modernity, they had been less than efficiently fitted into the building's existing features, and had to be activated by hand—the house-mind wasn't sophisticated enough to accept verbal instructions.

The desk, however, said, "You have a message waiting for you from Pilot-Ancillary Inadi," as soon as Arekhon opened the door. He'd made the necessary alterations to the room himself, not long after the last time he'd missed returning one of Ela's calls—first installing the thumbnail-sized scanner where it could watch the door, then linking it to the desk's contact with the house-mind so that it could respond with the appropriate status-change update. The original version, made for his shipboard locker back when he was a fleet apprentice, had said, "Touch my good boots, Meni, and you die horribly," but he'd civilized it a bit since then.

Elaeli Inadi was one of the callers whom the house-mind knew to pull out of a message queue and announce by name at once. There weren't many. He'd lost contact with the other, more casual friends of his apprentice days, and he'd never been that close to his older brother and sister. He entered his recognition code into the desk's message box. It hummed for a moment, then clicked twice. The desk spoke again, this time in Elaeli's voice rather than the synthesized one which Arekhon had provided for it.

" 'Rekhe—looks like I've missed saying goodbye to you again. The fleet's going back out ahead of schedule—syn-Evarat isn't telling anybody where until we link up with the cargo convoy. I think your brother's got him seeing spies under his bunk or something. He says the run this time should be a short one, but for all I know he's making that up to fool whoever Lord Natelth thinks is listening.

"At least we had a chance to talk while you were in town. I'll call you when the fleet comes back. Wish us luck."

The message box clicked again, hummed, and was silent.

Arekhon stood for a moment, gathering his thoughts. A wish for luck was no casual thing to ask of a working Mage, though a friend could ask it of a friend and expect nothing stronger than positive thoughts and maybe an offering to the spirits of the house. Ela had probably meant no more than what was usual—she'd known him before he went to the Circles, and still thought of him, he suspected, as more fleet than Mage. But just because she hadn't counted on anything besides the common intentions of goodwill toward a traveler, was no reason for him to give her only that.

Now was as good a time as any. If he failed to appear for the mid-day meal, the others would assume—truthfully—that he was absorbed in some project of his own and would make an appearance later.

He locked the door against accidental intrusion, and drew the curtains that he normally kept open. The heavy fabric blocked most of the light; only a dim greyness remained. He unclipped his staff from his belt, then settled himself into a kneeling position on the worn carpet, with the staff lying on the floor in front of him. Then—carefully, gently—he let out his breath and began the process he sometimes thought of as taking down the shutters of his mind to gain a better view of the universe.

When he was very young, it had been easier to see the world this way than not: As a web of life-threads and luck-threads overlying physical reality. Growing older had been a matter of learning how to shut out the parts of the universe that others didn't see, in order to move and talk and think like the people around him. The Circles, in turn, had taught him how to go back.

Elaeli Inadi, now as always, was a bright thread running through the weave of his universe. He found her thread and followed it into the complicated pattern of many threads that was the sus-Peledaen fleet.

Luck, he thought, and began sorting through the glowing lines, bringing them together where they threatened to stray apart and making the web stronger where it threatened to wear thin. *Jump luck to make the Void-transits clean and hold the engines steady; fighting luck to keep the family's cargo away from thieves and pirates; trader's luck to bring a profit home.*

And lovers' luck, to bring her safe to me.

Garrod and Yuvaen remained in the study after Arekhon had departed. The First sat musing over the star chart, with one hand under his chin and the other tracing out the lines from Eraasi to the Edge. Each mapped planet would have its beacons for the ships that came after. It would have other beacons as well, non-material ones left as guideposts by the first Mage to reach that world through the Void. Not until after passing the Void-marks for Rayamet, edgemost of the sus-Peledaen trading worlds, would a walker need to strike out into the blank spaces of the interstellar gap.

Yuvaen, meanwhile, had located the textfiles that gave instructions for interpreting the chart, and pulled them up onto the desk's reader. He paged through them, shook his head, and closed the file.

"It's a good thing we've got 'Rekhe to explain this thing," he said. "It's nothing but blinking lights to me."

"I told you he'd do well," said Garrod absently, most of his attention on the chart. "He's young, but so were we, once, and it didn't—"

He stopped, breath catching, and looked up from his contemplation of the starmap. His gaze met Yuvaen's and he knew that his Second had likewise felt the sudden, almost visceral pang: The twisting, stretching sensation of luck-lines being woven into a new design. And this wasn't somebody's personal undertaking done with a stronger-than-usual will— more than one hand lay on the threads and pulled the pattern taut.

"There's a working going on," Garrod said. "Somewhere in the Hall."

"How—?"

"I don't know." Garrod pushed back his chair and stood, leaving the chart to blink and swirl unheeded on the desk-top. "But if this goes out of control—"

The sense of cords weaving and interlacing had grown stronger as he spoke; he could see them, if he let his vision widen to take them in, thick bright cords whose names and purposes he didn't know and had no way to guess. The design they wove pulsed in his view, demanding his care and attention, all but shouting its importance.

"The long gallery," he said to Yuvaen. "And hurry!"

Without looking to see if his Second followed, Garrod ran down the hall outside his private chambers, up the half-stairs, and through the door that led to the second-floor passageway along the edge of the grand staircase. He caught a glimpse of Delath passing by in the hall below, and shouted down to him, "The long gallery—fetch everyone!" without breaking stride.

The sense of urgency that had impelled Garrod from his study had not eased with his decision to take action, but rather drove him faster. Halfway down the hall from the long gallery, he could already hear the sound of cracking staves.

Who could have been so reckless? he demanded of himself as he began to run in earnest. A pounding of footsteps told him that Yuvaen was a pace or two behind him. *None of them are as foolish as that, none of them. . . .*

Garrod took his own staff in his hand as he ran, and let it blaze with blue-white fire. When he reached the door of the long gallery he didn't bother stopping to open it, but burst on through by main force, so that his shoulder tore the bolts away from the antique jamb.

In the middle of the gallery, wreathed in spirals of green and golden fire, Ty and the newcomer fought with staves. Garrod's eruption into the room made no impression upon the pair. Their concentration was wholly on each other, and the sound of fast blows blocked and returned echoed off the high ceiling.

Garrod drew a sharp breath. Full speed and full strength—this was a working, indeed, and a serious one.

But was it intended? Or is there more to Iulan Vai than we thought?

"Break them apart," he commanded. "They can't be allowed to finish—it's a rogue pattern, and no true weaving."

Yuvaen started forward, but Garrod was moving as he spoke, and interposed his own staff between the two combatants. In an instant he found himself on the defensive as they attacked both him and each other, at seeming random but with more than random skill. Garrod fought back, striving to guard himself against injury and against being himself drawn into whatever pattern Vai and Ty had inadvertently—he hoped—begun.

More footsteps came drumming in the hall outside the gallery, and a moment later Delath and Narin skidded over the threshold. Kief plunged through the door a heartbeat behind them, his long hair flying and his staff ablaze.

"Help us out!" Yuvaen shouted at the startled Mages. "Break them apart!"

"There's luck here, Yuva," Garrod said, panting—the web pulled tighter with every exchange of blows, and he found himself hard-pressed. "Strong luck."

"There's luck everywhere," Yuvaen said. He was moving in toward Ty from behind, his staff up to guard against the danger of backstrokes.

"Not like this." Garrod brought his staff against Iulan Vai's in a move that should have ripped the practice weapon out of her hand. Instead, the maneuver drew him into striking range of her counterattack. "This luck is ours—if we can take it. Now!"

Narin had been circling outside the melee. On Garrod's word, she launched herself forward in a rolling dive, slamming into the back of Vai's knees. Vai lost her balance and toppled backward; Kief and Delath grabbed her arms and pinned her almost before she hit the floor. In the same moment Yuvaen dropped his staff and stepped forward to wrap Ty's upper arms in a crushing hug. At once the blaze of colors dimmed. Only Garrod's staff continued to give off light.

He turned slowly, looking from one member of the Circle to the next. Ty and Vai were dripping with sweat, their expressions like those of sleepers pulled from their dreams by a bucket of water. Yuvaen, still gripping Ty closely, was looking, if anything, even more stolid than usual; Garrod, who knew him well, understood from that the depth of his Second's dismay. Kief and Delath looked concerned and—on the part of the former—not a little frightened, but they didn't let go their hold on the unprotesting Iulan Vai. A few feet away, Narin was pulling herself to her feet and saying nothing.

"Where are Arekhon and Serazao?" Garrod demanded after he had scanned the room. "Narin—go and fetch them. I want the entire Circle here for this.".

"No need to send for us, my lord," came a voice from the door—Serazao, sounding worried but not unduly so; she hadn't been part of the brief, fierce melee in the long gallery. "We're here. Del told me to find 'Rekhe, and I did—he was at a working in his room, and didn't hear you call."

"A working, you say?" Garrod pointed his blazing staff at Arekhon as he, too, entered the room. "What kind of working, that twists the patterns so strongly it catches up these two young ones and nearly burns them out altogether?"

Arekhon shook his head. "It was a luck-sending, nothing more," he said. His grey eyes were wide and dark-pupilled, as they would be if he'd been dragged out of deep meditation without warning, but nothing in his bearing spoke of guilt or deliberate wrong. "A private intention, as a favor to a friend."

"This was no private intention," Yuvaen cut in. "It was a working, and nearly a great working. If we hadn't—"

"Peace, Yuva!" Garrod said. "He's telling the truth. Which friend, 'Rekhe?"

"Elaeli Inadi," Arekhon said, after a second's pause. "A pilot with the sus-Peledaen. We were fleet-apprentices together, and kept up our friendship afterward."

"More than friendship," said Garrod, "if the intention was so strong. And for whatever reason, this time the luck you sent traveled no farther than to the Circle. This is world-changer's luck, 'Rekhe, and nothing we dare to waste."

He heard Yuvaen's breath catch, and ignored it.

"Tonight," Garrod said. "Tonight I will walk. The time is now, and we can't afford to wait any longer."

XVI: Year 1123 E. R.
Eraasi: Hanilat Starport
Demaizen Old Hall

I T WAS close to noon in Hanilat. Natelth sus-Khalgath was at the desk in his study, going through the latest set of documents from the family's legalist-in-chief. He came upon the autumn quarter's list of recommendations for outer-family adoption, and raised his eyebrows at the sight of his younger brother's name set down as the sponsor for one of the pilots in the fleet.

What's 'Rekhe up to now? he wondered, and flipped through the files in the reader until he found his brother's name again, this time on a formal letter of severance.

"*. . . craves your permission to withdraw his name permanently from the rolls of the sus-Peledaen fleet, and to be freed from any ties beyond those of natural affection and of proper respect; wherewith he submits to the family in his stead the name of Pilot-Ancillary Elaeli Inadi . . .*"

Natelth frowned. He was tempted to refuse the severance, but 'Rekhe had done everything in order and in the proper form. To turn him down would be capricious, and Natelth loathed caprice in all its manifestations. He scowled, feeling as if his brother had boxed him into taking action yet again, and marked the documents "approved."

The study door opened then, without forewarning. "Isa," Natelth said instantly. "What's the problem?"

His sister Isayana was the only other person whom the house-mind would allow to open those doors set to his personal lock—not surprising, since she had given the house its operating instructions in the first place. Dealing with inorganic and quasi-organic minds was her specialty, and she had been in charge of the sus-Peledaen affairs in that area for almost two decades.

She was a tall woman, at least for the sus-Khalgath line, with greying black hair pulled up into a loose knot. At some point earlier in the morning, she'd thrust a stylus into the knot for safekeeping, or to free her hands for some other task, and then had forgotten about it. It would stay there, Natelth suspected, until the time came to change for dinner.

"No problem," she said. "But I thought you'd like to know—I checked the private logs, and you've got some activity on that set of charts you passed on to 'Rekhe."

"What kind of activity?"

"Standard open-and-display, so far. Nobody's interfaced anything with it besides a reader. They didn't lose any time waiting to do that much, though." She gave him a sharp look. "And they looked at the routes going from Eraasi to the Edge. Exactly what are 'Rekhe and his friends planning to do with those charts, anyhow?"

"He didn't say."

"But Garrod's made him Third, and we all know what that means." Her eyes darkened. "You shouldn't have let him go to Demaizen in the first place—the fleet had more than one Circle willing to take him."

"He was set on working with Garrod," Natelth said. This was not the time, he reflected, to tell his sister about 'Rekhe's letter of severance. She had raised their younger brother as a mother would have, and there was a distinct chance that she would take his formal departure from the family more personally than 'Rekhe had intended it. "You know how he is when he makes up his mind."

She nodded in rueful agreement. "He could give stubborn lessons to a stone."

And slippery lessons to a mudsnake, Natelth added to himself. The matter of 'Rekhe's transfer from the fleet to the De-maizen Circle still rankled; it had not been one of Natelth's more successful moments. That had been long ago, however, and Isa's fears were part of the present. He set himself to allaying them as best he could. "He's only been Garrod's Third for a couple of days now; you probably don't need to worry about him for quite a while."

While Garrod was making himself ready for the evening's working, Yuvaen called the rest of the Demaizen Mages—with the exception of the problematic Iulan Vai—to an infor-mal conference in the long gallery. Arekhon was the last to arrive, after making a circuit of the Hall to see if all was well after the disruptions of the morning. He only wished that the temper of the Circle could be as easily called back into order. The rogue working and Garrod's subsequent decision had set everybody's nerves on edge, and it showed.

Kief and Ty and Serazao, the three youngest in the Circle—in service if not in age—sat close together on one of the pad-ded exercise mats. Delath stood nearby at one of the tall win-dows, and Narin sat on one of the wooden benches a few feet away. Arekhon would have gone to sit on the bench next to her, except that he was no longer one of the unranked Mages, but Third of the Circle. He went, instead, to stand beside Yu-vaen, where the Second waited beside the rack of practice staves.

"Everybody's accounted for," he said quietly. "Garrod's meditating, and Syr Vai is in her room."

"Tactful of her." Yuvaen pushed himself away from the wall. "Whatever else the woman is, she's not a fool."

He had the attention of the others by now. Del turned around from the window, and the three junior Mages, seated together on the mat, looked at the Second expectantly.

"Tonight the First will go out into the Void," Yuvaen said. His voice took on the steadying cadences of a formal speech, and Arekhon felt the tension in the room ease slightly. "And we will anchor him. This working is the one for which he formed our Circle in the beginning. Our practices and our lesser efforts have all been steps toward this end. The time has come a little sooner than we expected, but only a little—if we hadn't been ready, the wild luck would have passed us by. We *are* ready, and all we have to do is settle the practical details."

"What kind of details?" asked Serazao. She had her arms wrapped tightly around her updrawn knees, and her yellow-hazel eyes were bright and intent in her narrow face.

"Iulan Vai," said Del from his place near the window. "She isn't a member of the Circle—so what part does she have in our working?"

There was a silence in the workroom. Del, square and solid and dispassionate, had asked the question that everyone had been worrying about. Arekhon drew breath to give his own opinion on the matter, but at a glance from Yuvaen he let the breath out without speaking.

Finally Kief said, "I think we ought to send her away."

His voice rang harshly against the gallery's high ceiling, and Arekhon saw him flinch at the echo. Kief tugged at his early-greying hair with long, nervous fingers and went on, not quite so loudly, "There are other Circles. If she wants training, we can recommend her to one that will train her. If she's meant to come to this Circle she can return later, when we're done."

Narin shook her head. "I don't know. If Syr Vai brought the wild luck along with her to Demaizen, then we won't help ourselves any if we send her away. Let her stay and make herself useful. In a working as long as this one's going to be, we'll need someone to keep watch and fetch water for the rest of us."

"That's another thing," said Serazao. She turned to Yuvaen. "How long do you expect this working to last?"

"Perhaps as long as a week. Perhaps not."

Serazao continued to look doubtful. "I've never heard of any walk through the Void lasting for more than a day."

"This one goes beyond the bounds of what we know," Yuvaen said. "And once we begin it, there's no stopping."

"That's what worries me," said Delath. "If the working runs into trouble . . . we've lived together in this Circle for years. We know what we're capable of and how we'll react, no matter what the emergency. Iulan Vai, on the other hand, is an unknown quantity."

"We were all unknown quantities once," Narin said. "And the Circle took us in. You've kept quiet so far, 'Rekhe—what do you say?"

Arekhon looked over at Yuvaen, but this time the Second made no gesture for him to keep silent. "I believe that Syr Vai was meant to be here," he said. "When she became part of the accidental working, she became part of our greater design as well."

"But what kind of part?" Delath asked. "Yuva, will Garrod give us a ruling on this?"

"No. His part of the working has already begun."

Narin said, "You're the Second. Give us a ruling in his place."

"So be it," said Yuvaen. "The newcomer stays."

Iulan Vai sat in a straight-backed chair at the window of her room, looking out over the hills of Demaizen. The room was a small one on the third floor, one of several along a central hallway—guest bedrooms once, when the Old Hall was the heart of the district's social life, and now living quarters for the Mages of Garrod's Circle. Of whom she was, apparently, one.

She couldn't remember the moment when her good-natured exploratory sparring with Ty had transformed into something else. Once or twice in her career as a confidential operative, she had found herself in the position of having to fight for her life, and the episode in the long gallery had possessed some of that same intensity. What was missing from the experience, though, was the driving, knife-sharp underpulse of fear. In fear's place had come an ecstatic subsumption into rhythm and movement that made the combat into something closer to dance, or to the act of love.

The combination of the two feelings was one she had not experienced before—but one which she already knew she would do much for, in order to experience it again. The ruse she had employed to gain entry into the Hall had turned out to be truth. Now she had to wonder how much of the idea had been her own, and how much of it the luck of the Circle, drawing her in.

If this was going to happen to me, she thought irritably, *why did it wait until now?*

Footsteps sounded in the hall outside her room, and she turned as the steps halted at the open door. She wasn't surprised to see that the visitor was Arekhon sus-Khalgath, whose private intention for his beloved in the fleet had meshed with the sparring in the long gallery to create that unexpected—and nearly fatal—transcendence. He had come by the room earlier, a brief and preoccupied stop on the way to what Vai had suspected was a conference on how to handle the problem that she presented.

He didn't look preoccupied now; in fact, his grey eyes fixed her with a direct and specific regard. She knew a sudden panic fear that the Circle had decided to send her away, and told herself that the fear sprang out of concern for her mission and for her employer's good.

"What happened this morning—" she began.

Arekhon waved her to silence. "What's done is done. The important thing is that you'll be staying here with us, as you asked. You won't be able to start your instruction right away, though; you'll have to wait a week, maybe more, until after Garrod's latest working is done."

"You're not sending me away?" she said, and then dealt herself a mental slap for the eagerness that crept into the words. *The first rule is never to let them know what you really want.*

She discounted automatically the folk-belief that Mages could read minds. No Mage of her admittedly scant acquaintance had ever made that claim, and her own experience was that no one could do so, else she would have been out of a job long since. And if Arekhon had noticed her reaction, he at least had the courtesy not to show it.

"We're not sending you anywhere," he assured her. He sounded almost apologetic as he went on. "But for the moment you'll be mostly an outsider. Not completely, though; if you like you can help us by taking care of the chores that would normally fall to the junior member of the Circle. Things like fetching water for those who need it, or dealing with accidental disruptions from outside."

"I think I can handle that," she said. "Housebreakers and

lightning-rod salesmen get told to come back later."

He laughed, and the moment of good humor warmed his features in a way that made her unexpectedly aware that Natelth sus-Khalgath's baby brother was, in fact, a very personable young man indeed. "You've got the general idea. It doesn't sound like much, especially if you've been used to holding a lot of responsibility someplace else, but a nonworking watchkeeper is a luxury we hadn't expected to have until you showed up."

"It sounds like a great deal of responsibility to me."

"Some people never see past what's on the surface," Arekhon said. "Fortunately for us, you're not one of them. The working will be starting in a few hours; when the time comes, I'll send Ty up for you."

"What, exactly, *is* the working?" Vai said. It was a reasonable question, one that a newcomer to the Circle could plausibly ask. And as Theledau sus-Radal's Agent-Principal, she could learn as much from what information she wasn't given, as from what she was actually told.

But Arekhon answered her at once, with—as far as she could tell—perfect openness, as one member of the Circle would speak to another. "Garrod is going out into the Void in search of a new world, one with people on it. Beyond the Edge."

"Beyond the Edge," Vai repeated in a whisper.

"If the thought frightens you—"

"No, no," she said. "I just didn't expect to walk into something quite so big."

"You'll do fine," he said. "Rest while you can; I have a few more things to take care of before we start."

He left. Vai waited until his footsteps had receded into the distance of the stairwell at the other end of the hall. Then she put her hand into her jacket pocket and closed her fingers around a small, flat object about the size and shape of a drinking flask or a hiker's posit-finder—neither of which it was, though its appearance, when she pulled it out into the open, did a fair job of mimicking the latter tool.

She flipped the case open to reveal a flatscreen and keys like those of a miniature pocket-scribe. Using the stylus from her wildlife observation log, she carefully picked out a message: BELIEVE SUS-PELEDAEN INTEND TRADE BEYOND EDGE. CONFIDENCE LOW. TAKE NO ACTION AT THIS TIME.

Then she erased the visible text, set the flat object on the floor near one of the power lines that fed into her room, and used the stylus to press another key. Her encrypted message entered the house power system, and went along the backflow toward the district distribution system to be lost in the surge and roar of power's creation.

Long before then, however, the small repeater that Vai had fastened yesterday to the grid between the Old Hall and the nearest substation had already found her intelligence mixed with the carrier. The repeater extracted the message, boosted its strength, and with a tiny camouflaged antenna squirted the information to a fixed satellite belonging to the sus-Radal. From there one copy would go to Vai's files, with a second copy eyes-only to Theledau syn-Grevi in Hanilat.

That done, Vai closed the device and put it back into her pocket. Then she went downstairs to see if there was anything she could do to help the Circle with its preparations.

XVII: Year 1123 E. R.
Eraasi: Demaizen Old Hall
Space: sus-Peledaen ship WIND-ON-THE-MOUNTAIN

DURING HER employment as a confidential operative for the sus-Radal, Iulan Vai had done any number of unlikely things, but until coming to Demaizen, she had made it her practice to leave the internal workings of the Mage-Circles strictly alone. She had thought, when she left her observation post on the hillside, that a rational calculation of risks and benefits had led her to abandon her usual methods in favor of investigating Garrod's Circle from within. Since the episode in the long gallery, however, she was no longer certain that rationality had played any part in her decision.

She sat where Yuvaen had directed her, in a corner of the big downstairs room at the heart of the Hall. The Second had told her to care for those members of the Circle who might need help, and had shown her the part of the room where the materials—the water jugs, the extra candles, the ominous, carefully labeled medical packs—were stowed. For the present, at least, she would obey his commands as if she were here to seek instruction.

Heavy black curtains blocked out light from the outside—

if the room possessed windows at all, which her mental diagram of the Hall's exterior dimensions suggested that it did not—and made the room's size difficult for her to estimate. The only illumination came from fat candles in freestanding holders set around the room's periphery. The white-painted circle in the middle of the black floor was big enough that all of Garrod's Circle could kneel around it without crowding.

Except for Garrod himself, they were kneeling there now. All the Mages, from Yuvaen down to young Ty, had short wooden staves lying on the floor in front of them. Some of them had brought to the working the same staves that they habitually wore at their belts, or others much like them; but one or two had weapons considerably more ornate. Narin Iyal from Veredde, for example, who during the day had carried only a polished brown rod of common wood, had a gleaming black staff wrapped with an intricate lacing of silver wire.

The Mages wore hooded robes of black cloth, with plain cloth belts, as well as—on a prosaic note—sturdy but flexible boots. Arekhon's pair, Vai suspected, had once been part of his sus-Peledaen fleet uniform; they had that look about them. Like the rest of the Mages, he also wore gloves, long and gauntlet-wristed, made of black leather supple enough to let the hand within grasp and move freely.

None of the members of the Circle had moved or spoken since they had taken their places. Vai, in her corner, tried to remain equally still and quiet. She had heard any number of highly colored stories—who had not?—about what could happen during a working. Now she would have the opportunity to learn whether the stories were true.

She heard the door to the room swing open, but no light came in—the wall-enshrouding curtains blocked that source as well. Then she heard the latch click shut. A moment later the yellow candle-flames bent and came straight again as the curtains parted and Garrod stepped through them into the light.

His choice of clothing and equipment for the working startled Vai briefly. Unlike the other Mages, he wasn't wearing a robe at all. Instead, he had chosen to dress in the fashion of a hiker who planned to spend a week or more rambling through the back-country: Sturdy trousers and high lace-up boots; a many-pocketed cloth jacket similar to the one Vai herself had chosen for her role as an ersatz wildlife observer; and a well-furnished metal-frame pack big enough to hold all the necessities for an extended holiday. Even the staff in his hand, if she overlooked the black wood and the silver bindings, could have been taken for a rover's cudgel.

The only things that marred the illusion were the breathing mask that Garrod carried slung across one shoulder, and the sailor's life-vest he wore uninflated over his jacket. Vai was inclined to find those items humorous, until she considered what they meant—that Garrod had no idea what he might encounter at the end of his journey, even to the presence of breathable air or solid ground under his feet.

What will he do, she wondered, *if he comes out of the Void in a place where the gravity can crush him flat, or the heat of the sun broil him between one heartbeat and the next?*

Considered in that light, it was no wonder that the Mages of the fleet-Circles were so reluctant to find new worlds for trade, if the stargazers couldn't at least point them to a less-than-fatal destination first. She watched with a new respect as Garrod entered the painted circle, passing between Ty and Yu-vaen and—without pause or sign—vanishing in mid-stride when he reached the center.

Pilot-Ancillary Elaeli Inadi—*Inadi syn-Peledaen*, the notification of approval for outer-family status having come onto the board as the ship left orbit—eased the waistband of her uniform trousers with her thumb before sealing the front of her tunic and straightening the lower hem. She'd had the new uniform tailored to her measure during her first day in Hanilat on leave from the guardship *Wind-on-the-Mountain.* But that had been over two weeks ago, and the water-bloating that came with the arrival this morning of her monthly courses was making the snug fit of the trousers just tight enough to be annoying.

The mirror on the inside of her locker door annoyed her further by giving back the reflection of a trim young woman who—regardless of how she felt—looked fit and eager for action. Captain syn-Evarat would have no qualms about keeping her hopping well past the end of her watch.

At least my luck is good, she thought. She closed her locker and headed for the bridge. *But I've probably got 'Rekhe to thank for that.*

There were advantages for an unmarried woman in consorting with a Mage and a luck-maker, and not having to worry about the expiration date on her contraceptive pod was one of them. She'd pushed the renewal on her current one somewhat farther than was prudent. With no need for it on the last voyage, she'd forgotten all about the matter until the fleet came back to Eraasi, and then she hadn't wanted to waste her precious port time putting·up with a week or so of new-implant nausea and fatigue.

As soon as we're in the Void, she promised herself. *I'll get the* Wind's *physician to do it then.*

Elaeli, in her rank as Pilot-Ancillary, and now also as part of the family of the sus-Peledaen, had both the right and the obligation to be present on the guardship's bridge during the jump to transit-in-convoy. Fleet Captain syn-Evarat and Pilot-Principal Kuyiva were already waiting on the bridge when she got there; the rest of the *Wind*'s bridge crew followed shortly.

The *Wind* would be going ahead of the convoy, as usual, to clear the path on the way to Ayarat, sister-planet to Ildaon— a short voyage this time, as she'd predicted when she spoke to 'Rekhe's message-taker at the Hall. Ayarat claimed to be the original home of men, and had some fossils that seemed to prove it. Elaeli wasn't certain she believed in Ayarat's fossils. Too many other worlds had something similar. Eraasi even had radio sets, or something like them, mixed into sedimentary deposits laid down before the start of the historic record.

Moreover, Ayarat lacked significant in-system reserves of natural adamant, without which the first Void-capable engines could never have been constructed. In fact, the bulk cargo that *Wind-on-the-Mountain* was guarding on this run consisted mostly of refined adamant for the Ayaratan shipyards, which constructed small short-hop craft under license from the sus-Peledaen. The local builders paid for the license and for the imported materials both, enriching the family considerably in the process.

Unless, of course, somebody decided to attack the convoy and seize the adamant for themselves. The fleet-families weren't above such tactics, though most of them were inclined these days to contest for trade routes and jump-points instead of cargo. The planetary merchants presented a threat as well: Not all of them appreciated the chance to buy pure Eraasian product at the family's established price. Sooner or later somebody on Ayarat was going to figure out a way to outfit a locally-designed short-hopper with guns, and then the guardships would have to fight.

The Pilot-Principal cleared his throat. "Transit briefing," he said, and the faint buzz of conversation among the bridge crew stopped. Elaeli took a step closer to the main chart-reader, not so much to gain a better view as to make a good impression, and looked attentive.

"Flip on chart section one," the Pilot-Principal continued after he had everyone's attention. In response to his words, a projection filled the air above the pilot's station. "Here in-system we'll be flying the markers. I have the path and times highlighted here, in pink. They'll be displayed in pseudocolor out of the ports on approach. Marker One-five-seven is our hop, approach along line Two-two-seven true. We should be lined up two markers before. Jump bearing is One-eight-one true on Marker Four-four-three. Normal transit, no emergence for course changes. The emergence pattern for Ayarat is a standard sphere; our sector is dorsal four, distance eight to twenty, guide on the cargo-haulers. From emergence, if we're in the slot, finding the landing field on Ayarat is their problem. Questions?"

Elaeli shook her head. No one else on the bridge team had any questions either. This was, as the captain had said, a normal run. Half of the guardships would jump before the cargo carriers while the other half watched after the convoy's departure. The advance force would—at least theoretically—emerge from the Void in an open ball formation. After they had swept the globe's interior volume clear of any lurking ambushers, the cargo ships would drop out into the protected area, and the remainder of the guardships would follow to strengthen the enclosing sphere.

"Right, then," Kuyiva said. "Departure is in three hours. Who's handling the out-leg?" He glanced over at syn-Evarat. "Captain?"

The Fleet-Captain shook his head. "The Pilot-Ancillary takes it."

So much for a short watch, thought Elaeli, resigned.

"She'll want to finish her qualifications in a hurry," syn-Evarat continued. "Good news makes a fortunate beginning for a voyage, and we have word today that Pilot-Ancillary Inadi is going on to better things. She's syn-Peledaen now, and after this run she's off to the family yards to work on new construction."

The Fleet-Captain was looking pleased; the new billet must have been his pet project for her advancement, as the adoption had been 'Rekhe's. "Plate-owner of a fresh craft—it was years before I was honored like that. You have luck, Inadi."

"Thank you," said Elaeli, as the bridge crew cheered and applauded and a few of the younger, rowdier ones made a show of tapping at her insignia to see if some of her good luck would rub off on them. What she actually had was cramps—but this didn't seem to be the time to say so.

Arekhon knelt on the painted floorboards and let the clean, waxy smell of burning candles drift around him on the barely moving air. His staff lay on the floor in front of him, a horizontal slash of silver and ebony against the white of the circle. He focused his thoughts and his gaze on that bold design of black and white.

The world around him receded from his awareness, and his mind slid out of the physical universe and into the interior landscape of the working—not a garden, as the Circle's intentions often seemed to him, or a flowing river, but a harsh expanse of broken stone. There was no help here in his vision, and no sustenance, save what he had brought with him.

The *eiran* coiled around him where he knelt on the rough ground, and ran outward again toward the distant parts of the universe. He took the threads into his hands and sorted through them for those he knew best: Yuvaen, steady and dependable; Narin, whose self-effacement could never entirely hide her strength; and Ty, with the undefined boundaries of the mystic—a thread not unlike what little he could perceive of his own.

He followed the lines out to where they intertwined with

the rest of the Circle, and beyond, as the single many-twisted cable of their collective will wound itself around the heavy, pulsing line that was Garrod syn-Aigal sus-Demaizen, walking through the Void. The Circle had tied itself to him, to hold him, to find him again. The rope of their combined intention would not be unwound until his return.

There was another line among the many that stretched across the rocky landscape—this one was rough with luck, in flecks of scarlet and grey amid the silver, and he knew without having to search further that it belonged to the newcomer, Iulan Vai. She was here as she had said she would be, apart from the greater working, an observer only.

Arekhon stood. The sun above him was harsh and burning, in spite of the cold wind that blew across the field of stone. He had made a decision—or had chosen one possible future out of many; here in the landscape of his mind the two were often the same—and it was time to act upon it. Iulan Vai would be a member of the Demaizen Circle.

He reached for the grey and scarlet cord and pulled it toward him, then looped it around the width of Garrod's line. Then he brought another loop of the grey and scarlet to an upthrust spike of rock, and tied it into place.

There. He regarded the result of his efforts with satisfaction. *She is bound to us, and we to her. For the time of this working, and after.*

XVIII: YEAR 1123 E. R.
ERAASI: DEMAIZEN OLD HALL

VAI BEGAN to lose track of how long she had waited in the darkened room. The timepiece on her wrist told her it was the tenth hour of the morning, but without the evidence of the guttering candles—she'd had to replace all of them once already, and she'd soon need to do it again—she wouldn't have known that a day and a night had already passed.

Thinking about it, she discovered she was hungry. Yuvaen hadn't said anything about the observer not leaving the room; she slipped through the opening in the curtains and out the door. In the deserted kitchen, she made herself a quick meal of bread and cold meat, something she could eat out of hand without wasting time, and hurried back to the meditation room.

It occurred to her that with the First of the Circle gone away in the Void and the other Mages intent upon the working, now might be a good time to search the Hall for information of interest to the sus-Radal. She considered the idea for a moment, then put it aside. The search, if she did it thoroughly, would keep her away from the meditation room for several hours, and she might be needed during that time. A genuine student of the Circle, such as she was pretending to be, would never take such a risk. Her brief foray into the kitchen had kept her away long enough.

She made a quick circuit of the downstairs, checking all the locks and finding them in order, then slipped back into the curtained room. Her eyes took a few seconds to adjust to the comparative darkness; when they did, she saw that nothing had changed since she left. The Mages still knelt in their Circle with their staves laid out before them, and neither moved nor spoke.

Vai cleaned the candle stubs out of the holders and put in new ones, then settled back in her corner to wait some more. The candles had not burned for long this time before a faint, hoarse voice broke into the silence.

"Water."

It was Arekhon sus-Khalgath who spoke, and Vai could tell by looking at him that he didn't see any part of his physical surroundings. She filled a metal cup with water from one of the insulated jugs, then brought it to him and wrapped his hands around it. Thus prompted, he drank, without turning his gaze away from whatever inward landscape commanded his awareness.

After a moment's thought, she filled the cup again and offered it to Yuvaen in the same way. When the Second responded, like Arekhon, by emptying the cup, she went on to bring water to the rest of the Circle as well. All of them drank, but none spoke except for Ty, who whispered "more" while looking at infinity with unseeing eyes.

She brought him a second cupful, noting how the working so far had left blue-purple shadows under his eyes and hollows under his cheekbones, and went back to her vigil. How long, she wondered, would it take a man to traverse the interstellar gap from edge to edge? All that she knew about walking through the Void came from popular stories, and made the journey from one place to another sound almost instantaneous, like opening a door and stepping through it into the adjoining room.

She was beginning to understand that the popular stories had lied. Twice more, the candles burnt down and she replaced them; and more than twice she made her circuit of the kneeling

Mages with a mug of water in hand, pressing the rim against parched lips. One of the insulated jugs was already empty.

And still Garrod had not come back. The members of his Circle kept up their vigil, barely speaking and barely moving, and Vai cared for all of them as best she could.

She slept in brief snatches, never longer than a few minutes at a time. At intervals, when she remembered to do so, she went down to the kitchen for food, since there was no point in letting herself become as worn-out and exhausted as the Mages she was tending. None of them had slept, or taken anything but water, since the working began.

As the days wore on, she began to fear for their health. When she left the meditation room, she had to force herself to stay away long enough to feed herself and check on the hall's external security. The thought that something might go wrong in her absence pulled on her like an elastic cord, and the farther from the Circle she went, the stronger the tension became.

Sometime during the fourth day, the young Mage with the curly silver-brown hair—Kief—gave a low moan and collapsed into a crumpled black-robed heap. She hurried over to him, and saw that he'd gone so pale that even his lips seemed bloodless. Drops of sweat gathered on his forehead, and he was shivering.

He needs to be put to bed . . . and maybe turned over to Garrod's medical aiketen *down in the basement first.*

But that wasn't going to be possible. "Nobody leaves the Circle until the working is finished," Yuvaen had cautioned her, days ago now. "We lie where we fall."

A pile of folded blankets lay in the corner with the water jugs. Vai used one of the blankets to make Kief a rough pallet next to his place in the Circle, a second to lift up his feet, and a third to wrap him warmly. Then she settled cross-legged on the floor beside him to wait—and to wonder how many others she would be tending before Garrod returned.

For Arekhon, the realization that failure was near came gradually. He had wandered for a long time in the private places of his mind, chief among them the field of bare stone, where the *eiran* of the Circle combined to hold tightly the single cord that was Garrod. Now and again he let himself return to an awareness of the physical chamber where he and the rest of the Circle knelt. Iulan Vai was there, with water— he saw how the *eiran* twisted around her, and knew that his binding held, true. Always, though, he went back to the place of stone.

He didn't know why the working had chosen to embody itself for him in such an unfamiliar configuration. No place that he'd ever seen on Eraasi looked like this, and no place on any of the worlds that he'd encountered during his apprenticeship with the fleet.

A reflection, he thought, *of how things are.*

Or of how they will be.

He shivered a little. The barren landscape did not attract him, either as an image of some real but unknown locality, or as a metaphor for something internal to himself. Then he felt a pang of guilt for fretting about his own affairs in the midst of a working, and turned back to the cable of twisted silver that was the luck of the Demaizen Circle.

The cable still anchored Garrod's single cord to the rock beneath—but Arekhon saw with dismay that the cord itself was stretching and attenuating, growing thinner at its nearer end. If the knot slipped free, Garrod would be lost.

Arekhon opened his eyes, but held on to the secondary reality of the working, so that he saw with doubled vision—the candle-lit, curtain-shrouded darkness of the meditation chamber, overlaid with the stony expanse of the unknown landscape. He looked across the cracked and streaky whiteness of the painted circle, and saw that Yuvaen had opened his eyes to look across the circle back at him.

"More power," Yuvaen said. The Second's voice was hoarse and rusty. "We need more power, if we want to bring Garrod back across the Void."

Arekhon had seen how the *eiran* of the Circle were slipping away from what they sought to hold; he knew what sort of power would be needed to pull Garrod home. It was for this, after all—not for his family's star charts, and not for his own fleet training, not even for an extra hand in the day-to-day administration of the Circle's business—that Garrod had chosen to name him Third to Yuvaen's Second.

He picked up his staff and rose to his feet. His knees creaked and popped with the motion after kneeling for so long, and his head felt light.

"As the universe wills it," he said, and brought his staff up into guard. "So let it be done."

Vai had given up expecting anyone in the Circle to move—unless, like Kief, their bodily endurance failed them and they collapsed where they knelt. She was no longer certain why she herself maintained her vigil, except that Arekhon sus-Khalgath had asked it of her, and she had agreed.

Then Yuvaen opened his eyes and spoke. "More power. We need more power, if we want to bring Garrod back across the Void."

Across the painted circle from him, Arekhon stood. "As the universe wills it. So let it be done."

Yuvaen rose also, and lifted his staff. He moved stiffly at first, as had Arekhon—nobody could remain motionless for so long and not show the effects—but in short order the awkwardness faded. *Good training,* thought Vai appreciatively, just before the staves began to glow.

She had known from reports and stories that such a thing might happen. She even had a hazy memory of seeing her practice staff burn golden when she sparred with Ty. But the former was all hearsay rather than direct experience, and as for the latter . . . her state of consciousness had not been normal at the time. Neither research nor memory had prepared her for the moment when Yuvaen was no longer holding a cubit and a half of polished wood, but a bar of living flame, red as blood and hot as the inside of a star.

The two men met in the center of the circle. Their staves touched lightly, burning crimson against deep violet, in a contact that was half a formal salute and half a gauge of strength. After that came a few slow moves, almost a dance, as they worked together to stretch muscles and loosen joints.

Then, without warning, the pace and timbre of the combat changed. Arekhon dropped into a low position, his knees bent, and slashed to the right with the tip of his staff. Yuvaen blocked farther to the right—no gentle tapping of staves this time, but a full-strength encounter that rang out like a wooden gong—and stepped in closer to smash his staff across Arekhon's spine and kidneys.

Vai drew a sharp breath. This was not merely sparring at full strength; in her professional career she had seen enough blows delivered with killing intent that she could tell the difference.

Arekhon sus-Khalgath and Yuvaen syn-Deriot were good friends and close colleagues, and this was a fight to the death.

Blazing pain drove Arekhon forward. Yuvaen had struck him a blow meant not to raise welts or leave bruises, but to crush anything in its path. Arekhon went with the motion— diving, rolling, and coming back to his feet again facing the Second. He shifted his grip upward on his staff, to shorten it. If Yuvaen attempted to get inside his reach again, he'd be ready.

Two fast blows came in, overhand, aimed at his head. Yuva wasn't a man for playing the same trick twice, even in practice or the lesser workings. Far less now, in this.

Arekhon blocked, and blocked again. His hand stung with the blows, and the bones of his arm seemed to vibrate from the marrow out, but the voice of the meeting staves shivered through his open and receptive mind like music. What had been inert wood under his hands the moment before, now gave out light against the darkness, weaving lines of deep, intense violet against Yuva's fiery red.

A net fit to draw in all the luck of the universe, Arekhon thought, and beat down Yuvaen's staff to take it out of guard. The lines of red and violet tightened, entangling the floating silver *eiran* and pulling them into accordance with the Circle's will. *But not yet strong enough.*

Not yet.

He thrust toward Yuvaen's belly. Yuva struck the blow aside. Arekhon stepped forward into the opening and smashed his staff butt-end upward against the point of Yuvaen's chin, so that the Second's head snapped backward with the force of the blow. Arekhon had no time to appreciate the changing patterns of colored light and silver thread—an instant later his skull rang and his vision blurred as Yuvaen struck him on the side of his head, beside his left ear.

When his eyes cleared somewhat he saw that he was back in the stony place of his working imagery. There was the great cable of the Circle's bound and unified will, and there was the fading and attenuated cord that was Garrod, slipping away.

Not enough. Still not enough.

Yuvaen was facing him here as well, looming black-clad and indestructible, driving a blow past Arekhon's guard into the ribs on his right side. Arekhon felt bone shatter under the blow, and more pain flared with his next breath from the broken rib-ends grating together, but the cable of the great working shone with renewed light.

Arekhon let out a gasp of satisfaction and struck at Yuvaen in his turn. Bone broke—in Yuvaen's upper arm, this time; Arekhon felt it go. The Second grunted with the pain, but the lines of life and luck grew even brighter, and the barren field seemed warmer than before. Then Arekhon realized that the warmth was his own blood from a lacerated scalp, flowing down over his face.

Yuvaen's foot slipped, turning on a pebble or a shard of loosened rock, and his concentration wavered with the momentary loss of balance. Arekhon saw it—a shift in the pattern, an opening—and his staff slashed forward and took Yuva straight across the eyes, shattering the orbits, crushing the nasal bone, and sending Yuvaen's blood flying outward in a bright spray of red.

The blood was everywhere—even the rocks were covered with it—and Yuvaen's staff took up the color and increased its light tenfold. Arekhon had never seen the like.

Garrod's line was no longer slipping away. The power drawn in by the working was making it stronger, holding it tighter to its homeworld . . . but holding only.

Not enough.

Arekhon didn't know if the thought was his, or Yuvaen's, or if the difference even mattered.

Still not enough.

He slammed his staff forward again, striking at Yuvaen's already shattered face with all his strength.

Yuvaen stood, accepting the destruction. Arekhon felt his friend's skull collapsing inward under the blow, doing damage that could never be repaired. Power was everywhere, flowing outward—

—*still not enough*—

—and Yuvaen lashed out with a blow to Arekhon's injured side that drove fragments of bone deeper into the wound—

—*all we have, if it takes all we have*—

Then, with a blaze of light, Yuvaen fell.

Vai saw the last blows of the combat like explosions of color in the darkened room. *Synesthesia,* her mind told her; *your senses are blurring things together.* But what her mind said didn't matter; she knew that the room was full of a network of silver lines, stretching out over everything and growing steadily brighter.

She shook her head, trying to see past the lights and colors to what she would have thought of, a few days ago, as the only reality. She didn't succeed in banishing her new vision completely, but after considerable effort she was able to push the silvery lacework into the back of her awareness and see instead the room around her.

There was blood inside the painted circle, clots and spatters of it on the white floorboards, and more of it matting 'Rekhe's hair and flying away in droplets as he moved. Yuvaen stepped in a patch of the smeared blood and the sole of his boot slid a few inches before he caught his balance—a second later, he recovered, but it was too late. Arekhon's staff swung round and caught him in the face.

Vai bit her lip. That was a killing blow, even if Yuvaen hadn't yet given in to it, and Arekhon was making ready to strike again. Yuvaen put up no defense; he must have known that there was no point. Instead, he drove in one more bone-crushing assault on Arekhon's injured side. Then Arekhon hit him for the last time, and the silver cords pulled so tight around Vai that she cried out aloud.

The sound of her voice was muffled by the thick black curtains. Arekhon stood alone in the middle of the circle with Yuvaen dead at his feet, and the silver cords were drawing tighter because he held them all in his hands. She felt his strength failing as he pulled against something she couldn't see.

"Narin!" he called. "Help me!"

The woman from Veredde picked up her staff and rose to her feet.

"As the universe wills," she said, and struck at him in the next instant, without pausing to salute or come to guard.

Arekhon blocked the attack—it was a beautiful move, smooth and instinctive despite the injuries he had taken, and Vai marveled at it. His counter-strike nearly did for Narin as he had done for Yuvaen a few seconds earlier, but the islander turned the blow in time. Then, suddenly, she dropped her staff and sank to her knees.

"He's moving!" she shouted. "He's coming near—'Rekhe, help me pull!"

Arekhon threw his staff aside, out of the painted circle, and gripped Narin's shoulders. Vai felt the cords that bound her go taut and shiver with the effort the two Mages were exerting—*something's tied me into this,* she thought; *I don't think I'm ever going to be able to get loose.* The pull drew her up to her feet. Despite her attempts to withstand it she began edging forward, closer to the circle's boundary.

Then she felt the resistance at the far end of the cords give way. Narin collapsed onto her hands and knees, taking Arekhon down with her. At the center of the circle a figure appeared, took a step forward, staggered, and started to fall.

Nobody else was moving; the working had left them spent. Vai sprang forward, caught the man by the shoulders, and eased him to the floor.

It took a moment for her to recognize Garrod syn-Aigal. The First of the Demaizen Circle had not been a young man before he left on his journey, but now he was old. His face was lined and wrinkled, bearded rather than cleanshaven, and his grizzled black hair had gone completely grey. Even his clothes were not the practical garments she had seen before. The fabrics likewise were unfamiliar, either synthetic or derived from natural substances she didn't recognize. Their colors seemed equally strange, garish where she would have expected dull, and muted where they should have been bright.

Garrod's body was jerking spasmodically, his mouth working and his eyelids twitching. He shouted a phrase in a language Vai didn't understand, and lay still.

XIX: Year 1123 E. R.
Eraasi: Demaizen Old Hall
The Void

AREKHON FELT nothing, only a great, echoing emptiness. Blood was everywhere, on his face and on his hands; he knelt in a puddle of it. Yuvaen's blood . . . Yuva was dead, gone in the working.

Somewhere far away over his head, there were voices.

"Bring a stretcher, quickly." Vai, the newcomer, the unfamiliar accent stronger in her voice than before. "We have to get him down to the infirmary."

He heard the shuffling of feet and the whisper of robes . . . not everyone was dead, then; that was good . . . and Serazao's voice choking out a phrase in a language he didn't understand. He heard the distress in it, though, and tried to rise . . . he was the Second, if Yuva was dead, and it was the Second's place to deal with such things . . . but the effort caused his broken ribs to grate together so that his head swam with the pain.

"Help *him,* then." Vai again, her voice sharper than before. Something was wrong . . . not just the end of the working . . . Arekhon tried again to stand up.

This time somebody was beside him, helping him rise and taking most of his weight: Serazao, from the thin, strong hands and the faint odor of spice-flower soap.

"Up you go, 'Rekhe." 'Zao's voice was steadier, but whatever had caused her to cry out in her birth-tongue had not gone away. "Let's get you downstairs."

"Who else . . . ?" His tongue felt thick in his mouth, and he had to struggle to think of the words he needed to say. "The working . . . what happened?"

"It's done," 'Zao said. "Garrod is back."

Her words heartened him, even through the fog of pain. "Then it was enough," he said. "So long as we didn't fail."

Later that night—much later—Iulan Vai came back to the bedroom that had been assigned to her over a week before. She was dead tired, but full of an adrenaline-charged restlessness; she knew from experience that it would be some time before she could relax enough to sleep. The medical *aiketen* in the infirmary belowstairs had labored over the injured members of Garrod's Circle from afternoon until well after dark, mending broken bone and damaged tissue. For Kief, and even for Arekhon, all that remained was a time of rest and nourishment, so that their own bodies could finish the processes already begun.

About Garrod, Vai wasn't so sanguine. The First of the Circle had not regained consciousness under the ministrations of the *aiketen,* and the Mages who had touched him to carry him downstairs were grim and closemouthed about what, if anything, they had sensed from the contact. And Yuvaen . . . tomorrow they would bury Yuvaen.

She'd asked Narin Iyal what should be done about the late Second—thinking that someone, surely, had to be notified about what had happened. The other woman had shaken her head.

"The Circles bury their own," Narin said. "The sus-Demaizen had a family crypt, not far from the hall. Garrod meant for us to use that, if we ever needed to."

"Shouldn't we tell the watch?" In Vai's experience, the district watch had an inconveniently strong interest in knowing who had died within their purview, and for what reasons. Maybe in the countryside it was different, but she didn't think so. "Or his family?"

"Later," said Narin. "Yuva was ours, and it's for us to care for him. There are five of us still on our feet; enough for what needs to be done."

What needs to be done . . .

Vai, remembering, sighed and extracted the signaling device from her pocket, where it had lain forgotten during the whole length of the great working. She sat cross-legged on her bed in the darkened room and contemplated the device's tiny back-lit screen. There were other things that needed to be done as well, and she had to decide how she was going to handle them.

Slowly, with her stylus, she began picking out a message.

DEMAIZEN WORKING FAILED. GARROD INCAPACITATED. AN-TICIPATE CIRCLE BREAKUP WITHIN THREE MONTHS.

She stared at the finished text until the letters lost all significance and became random lines and dots on the pale violet of the messenger's screen. If what she had written was true, her work here for the sus-Radal was done . . . a dead end, no profit, time to go home.

But had she, in fact, written the truth? *Something* had happened during the working, and the Garrod who had returned was not the same as the Garrod who had left. Where had he been, that had aged him decades in the span of a week, and who had given him that unfamiliar clothing?

A jab of her stylus consigned Vai's first report to oblivion. She tried again.

DEMAIZEN WORKING SUCCESSFUL. CONTACT MADE BEYOND THE EDGE.

There. That was right. Time to send it off to her employer and be done.

She didn't move. The pale violet backlighting of the display screen shone at her, unblinking, in the dark. Finally, she erased her second attempt as well.

Entering the third draft of her report took a long time, because her hands were shaking.

ALL QUIET AT DEMAIZEN. NO RESULTS AS YET. CONTINUING SURVEILLANCE.

Quickly, before she could think better of what she had done, she placed the device next to her room's power line and started the message on its way to Hanilat.

* * *

He was Garrod syn-Aigal sus-Demaizen, and the first lesson that he had taught to his Circle was this: In the Void all places and times are one. To seek for a place within the Void, therefore, is to find it, and to make the journey is to arrive. He stepped away from the meditation chamber at Demaizen Old Hall, and began the walk that would take him across the interstellar gap to the still-unknown world that existed—would have to exist, since he had resolved to find it—somewhere on the other side.

The Void itself stretched out around him like an expanse of featureless grey nothing, full of a pale mist that curled about his feet and wrapped in tendrils around his legs and torso. He knew that the mist was not real, that he only saw it as mist because—like the numbers and equations contained in Arekhon's star chart—its true nature was something that a human mind and body had no means of understanding.

He felt a rumbling, a deep vibration coming up through the soles of his feet, as if some immense and unseen thing was causing the nonexistent ground to tremble beneath him. The vibration from below was matched by a sound in the air, a stir in the nothingness, a low growl half-heard, half-sensed.

He turned toward the thing that his mind perceived as a sound, and saw a dark line out at the limit of his vision, something that looked like a vertical stroke of charcoal on a grey background. The mark appeared to grow higher and thicker as he walked toward it, or as it came toward him, and the vibration coming up through his feet became a sharp tingling, like the points of needles.

The black mark took shape and became a solid, three-dimensional object, protruding from the substance of the Void like a rock out of the sea. And like a rock surrounded by angry waves, the darkly glistening object rose up from a swirl of turbulent mist.

As the object drew closer to him, he saw that it was not a rock but a starship, the largest one that he had ever seen. Pale roundels and oblongs marked out windows high above along its curving sides; fleeting shadows within betrayed where officers paced or looked out upon their featureless domain. The mist cut away from the nose of the craft like the bow wave of an ocean-going vessel straining under full sail.

The starship's hull bore no insignia or family colors that Garrod recognized. Neither could he identify the design of the craft, or the yard which had constructed it—and there were few enough builders of starships in the homeworlds that a man with a good eye and a retentive memory could know them all.

It was a ship, then, from beyond the Edge.

The great ship bore down upon him, pushing the Void away before it in a surge of white mist. He let the massive bow wave take him and drive him under, out of the grey nothingness and into the world he had come so far to find.

As she had expected, Vai found herself unable to sleep. After spending so long isolated from the normal rhythms of day and night, napping fitfully when she slept at all, her natural cycles of rest and waking were in complete disarray. The disruption, coupled with the aftereffects of prolonged tension upon her body's chemistry, kept her eyes open and her nerves on edge even after the other inhabitants of Demaizen Old Hall had settled at last into exhausted sleep.

She thought of going back to the basement infirmary and requesting a sedative from the dispenser there, but feared that the unit's resident *aiketh* would not consider mere restlessness a sufficient need. One of the Circle's established members could probably override the unit's prohibitions, but in the haste and confusion of the past week, Vai had never been introduced to the house-mind. She had the talent and knowledge to deal with that obstacle as well, but considered it impolite to do so for a trivial cause. She lay for a while staring at the ceiling of her room, considering various methods of circumventing the dispenser.

None of them appealed to her, and she abandoned the idea. After a while she threw aside the covers and got out of bed. It was for the sake of taking care of the Circle that she'd gotten out of the habit of sleeping; maybe if she checked on the survivors of the working one more time, her mind would relax long enough for her body to give in to exhaustion.

A worn but sturdy night-robe had been lying folded at the foot of her bed since the day she came to the Hall: Somebody's cast-off, presumably, pressed into service as sleeping gear for an unexpected visitor who had arrived with the scantiest of personal effects. Vai, who habitually slept without clothing, had ignored it until now. She belted the robe around her and padded out into the darkened hallway.

No sound came from Garrod's room, where the First of the Circle lay in his unresponsive stupor, with Narin to watch over him. Vai had offered to take her place, since Narin was almost as wrung-out as Kief and Arekhon, but the other woman had said no—better for Garrod to encounter a familiar face upon waking, if he ever woke. Narin herself was nodding in her chair; Vai left that room undisturbed, and continued upon her self-imposed round of inspection.

The carpet in the upstairs hall was old, like so much of Demaizen, and the worn patches scratched at the soles of her bare feet. She checked the other bedrooms each in turn; none of Garrod's Mages bothered to lock their doors at night, and for one of Vai's talents it was easy work to slip into a room and out again unnoticed by a sleeping occupant.

Ty, judging from his regular breathing, was deep in recuperative slumber, as was the gently snoring Delath. Both of them, she thought, would be back to normal—in body, at least—by the time they woke up in the morning. Kief, she estimated after observing him for a short period, would need at least another day in bed to recover, though his sleep, too, was peaceful. Serazao slept also, but uneasily; she had tangled herself in her blankets, and as Vai approached her bedside she flung out an arm and muttered a disjointed phrase before once again lying still.

The last room belonged to Arekhon sus-Khalgath. Vai paused outside the door, struggling against a sudden urge to flee Demaizen Old Hall before the sun came up in the morning. She knew, with a certainty that went beyond reason, that if she stayed with Garrod's Circle nothing would ever be the same again . . . not with her life, and not with far more than her life alone.

She had never been one to rely on hunches and intuitions, preferring instead hard data painstakingly gathered. This new awareness disturbed her; it was tied somehow to whatever had drawn her to the Demaizen Circle, and to what had happened since. She was changing, and she wasn't sure she liked it.

In the end, nothing kept her from running away except the

knowledge that, like it or not, she had already changed. The deliberately misleading report that she had sent earlier was by now a permanent entry in her employer's files.

Silently, she opened Arekhon's door. A pale white night-light blinked on as she stepped across the threshold—someone, probably Arekhon himself, had installed a door scanner. She hadn't known that he was a tinkerer, but the solitary and somewhat finicky hobby was one that fitted with his profile. She paused inside the door, ready to fade back out into the hallway if the light should wake him, but he stirred no more than had the others.

She moved closer to the bed. The pale glow of the night-light illuminated the Third—no, Vai corrected herself, the Second, and possibly before long the First—of the Demaizen Circle as he slept. He lay on his side, his long black hair falling across his face, hiding the square shaven patch where Garrod's *aiketen* had trimmed away enough to do their healing work. Seen thus, he looked incongruously young for what he was, and for what she had seen him do. He *was* young; she'd read his profile and knew his true age, as she knew so much else about him.

She had not anticipated, before coming to Demaizen, that she would find him physically attractive.

Slowly—knowing quite well that she was about to do an incredibly foolish thing, but no more willing to stop herself than she had been willing to remain on the hillside overlooking the Hall—she unbelted her borrowed night-robe and let it drop to the floor. Then she lifted the covers and slid beneath them.

For a moment she did nothing more, only lay there and let herself become accustomed to the warmth of Arekhon's body next to hers, and to the fact that she had put herself into a position from which there would be no going back. *I've gone mad*, she thought dispassionately; comforted by the diagnosis, she took him in her arms and held him.

He turned and embraced her in return. "Friend?" he asked in a sleep-muzzled voice.

"Friend," she replied.

Somewhat surprised by what her own hands were doing, she began to stroke his back. His hand reciprocated, and they drew closer together, so that she felt the hardness of his arousal. He bent his knee, and she parted her thighs enough to take his leg between hers.

She rolled him onto his back—he went unprotestingly, more asleep than awake—then straddled him and took him inside her. Toward the end, he cried out "Elaeli!" Vai was surprised how much that hurt.

Then they were lying side by side, and he was deeply asleep. Vai decided to remain there until morning. Let him wake up beside her. If he turned out to be angry, and she had to leave the Circle . . . well, that would be a solution to at least some of her problems. She could report the episode to her employer as a failed attempt at seduction, and think no more of it.

In the morning, though, she was awakened by a kiss on her cheek, and a whispered, "Vai—I thought I was dreaming." And then they repeated the process, and he knew who she was.

XX: Year 1123 E. R.
Beyond the Farther Edge: Garrod's World
Ildaon: Country House of Elek Griat

AFTER THE grey mist of the Void, the first things Garrod felt were the sunlight beating against his face and the pressure of solid ground beneath his feet. The walk to this world had proved even more strenuous than he had anticipated. Time and space meant nothing in the Void, but the work of finding a hospitable planet in that featureless infinity—an action that was neither searching, nor summoning, nor calling into being, though it contained elements of all three—had left him cold and drained of energy.

The new world to which he had come, however, was pleasant beyond his greatest expectations. The steep-sided hills that rose around him were green with low brush, and the air was sweet and pure. High overhead, a straight-line cloud made a white streak across the vivid blue sky, an effect that could only have been produced by the engines of a high-altitude mechanized flyer.

Seeing it, Garrod smiled. An advanced technological civilization existed on this planet, and such a civilization meant the possibility of trade and cultural exchange. More, it meant that his theories on the Sundering were correct, and those of other philosophers were wrong. Still smiling, he lay down on a patch of sun-warmed stone and let the heat that the Void had sucked from him re-enter his aching bones. He slept.

Later, when he awoke, the sun had changed its position in the sky. He assigned the sunset direction the name "west," then rose and began stretching to bring back flexibility to muscles cramped by sleeping on the bare ground. Stiffness aside, he could move easily. The long walk through the Void had blurred his judgment of how closely the gravity here matched that of Eraasi, but the difference could not be great.

Further investigation meant leaving his current position. A pocket-compass settled its magnetized needle in one direction. Garrod called that direction "north," and decided to proceed on that bearing until he saw something that would make another direction seem more promising.

Perhaps a quarter of an Eraasian hour later, he saw his first artificial structure: A slab-sided tower on a distant hilltop, its featureless sides reflecting the light of the setting sun. Rather than walking toward it, he decided to cast in another direction. Such a large and deliberately impressive structure could have a purpose inimical to his own researches. A guard tower with an unfriendly garrison, a microwave tower with deadly radiation—there were too many possibilities.

He altered his course slightly, so that the tower shifted out of his direct line of sight, and moved on through the alien landscape. Small creatures chirked and rustled amid stands of low, scrubby-looking trees. He noticed an abundance of flying things, both large and small—not birds and insects as he knew them on Eraasi, but apparent functional equivalents for the local ecology. He was not a student of the life-sciences, to analyze things in greater depth; such efforts would come later, when others came in ships along the way that he had marked for them.

So far, what he had seen bore out his idea that the Sundering of the Galaxy was not legend, but truth. If he could find one of the natives, one of the intelligent beings, and see that they were like him—two legs, five fingers on each hand—it would be further proof.

The galaxy had been one. Of that, Garrod was convinced. There had been spaceflight, trading, the intermingling of the seed of worlds. Perhaps the ones making the contact had been Void-walkers like himself; more likely, they had been the spacefarers of an unimaginable past, before truth had been overwritten by legend, and legend by allegory.

"And the sword fell because the people had offended. . . ." The pious tale from his childhood still had the power to fill him with anger and confusion. What could anyone possibly have done, to merit so deep and terrible a blow?

Eventually the shadows grew long and the sun went down behind the western hills. Garrod stopped and made camp for the night. Walking in the dark would bring him nothing more than a twisted ankle. He didn't light a fire, for fear of drawing unwanted attention.

Nevertheless, he had observations to make if the Eraasian fleet-captains were ever to find this world. He removed his instruments from his pack and set them up—his bubble sextant, his star spectrometers, his chronometers—and began to measure the stars that glistened in the night sky.

Later he would find his way to another hemisphere, and make measurements from there as well. He would need to remain on-planet for at least half of the planet's orbit around its star, so that he could make observations through the daylight sector too. All of these things Garrod had done before on other worlds, though none of them so distant as this one. He had earned the name of Explorer before he ever headed a Circle of his own, and he was doing what he had the talent to do.

Jaf Otnal had been some days at Elek's country estate, and had begun to think that he'd made the transit from Ayarat for nothing, when he came downstairs one morning and found three strangers seated around a fully laden breakfast table— one dark man, one fair, and one with the indefinable difference in looks and manner that marked him as an offworlder of some kind, rather than native-born Ildaonese. Jaf stood for a moment in the doorway, uncertain of his welcome, before hearing Elek's voice.

"Ah, Jaf, good morning." The older man entered the morning-room through an interior archway, holding a crystal flask of fruit juice in one hand. He took a seat at the table and gestured for Jaf to take the remaining chair. "I'd like you to meet some associates of mine. Mael Oska"—he indicated the stocky fair-haired man with the thick mustache—"Gath Tinau"—the darker one, a thin, edgy-looking man—"and Felan Diasul, who's come the longest way of all of us to be here. I have to ask you to trust these fellows. I trust them, but unless you trust them, there's nothing that can be done."

"On your word," said Jaf, "I'd trust anyone."

"A dangerous way to live," Elek said. "Not even I trust myself that far. But I trust you—and because my friends here have all had occasion, in the past, to echo your sentiments concerning the fleet-families, I've asked them to trust you as well."

"Such high regard honors me," said Jaf. To cover his self-consciousness, he broke open one of the breakfast-buns and began filling the interior cavity with golden jelly. "I hope I can deserve it."

"Trust and deserving are all very fine," said Oska. He took a long drink of the chilled fruit juice—bits of pulp stayed clinging on his damp mustache—and set the glass down with a thump. "But what are we going to do about the star-lords? It's easy enough to hate them, but let's be honest, they hold all the advantages. They control all our interplanetary communications. They control all our interplanetary trade. And they're loyal to themselves alone."

"All very true," Elek said. "But they have weaknesses."

Tinau laughed harshly. "Name them."

"Since you ask . . . the fleet-families aren't monoliths. Simply because a person is born or adopted into one of their lines doesn't keep him or her from having private goals and failings. And outside of keeping space travel and transport in their own hands, there's no common interest among them. The captains play at raiding and piracy, scoring points off one another with honest people's cargos, while the senior members spy on each other at home. They aren't accustomed to looking for threats from any other quarter."

"What do you intend to do, then?" said Tinau. "Send the families money in an unmarked envelope, and watch them knife each other in the back while they fight to claim it?"

Elek smiled. "That's the general idea. You can help us there, if you want to—"

"Oh, yes." Tinau's dark features had begun to take on an eager light. Here was one, Jaf suspected, whose grudge against the fleet-families went beyond matters of business or politics. There was an interesting story in that probably; a pity he'd never get to hear it. Tinau didn't look like someone who called out his private grievances to the world. "Just tell me where to start."

"You can begin by setting up a front organization or two," Elek told him. "Something high-minded, with 'peace' or 'co-operation' in the title. Then add some cutouts so that our names won't be the first ones that show up when someone takes an interest. That'll be our unmarked envelope."

The man called Felan Diasul spoke up for the first time. He was a lean, bony individual, with light brown hair; his Ildaonese was fluent enough to be colloquial, but his accent was Hanilat-Eraasian. "What about **me**?"

"You're absolutely vital," Elek said. "We can't do this without somebody on Eraasi to keep an eye on things from close up." He poured out more of the fresh juice all around, as calmly as if they were not discussing a complete upheaval in the usual way of things, then continued, "And if you don't mind exploiting your own family connections in a good cause you have a brother who's a Mage, don't you? The next time you talk with him, see if you can ask him to work luck for us, without being too specific as to what you need it for. Trade-luck and work-luck; it's true enough if you look at it the right way, and everything helps."

Jaf, who sat listening in respectful silence, knew that his self-imposed mission to Ildaon had been successful. And there was no way to back out now. Elek might have been reluctant at first—but having made up his mind to join a conspiracy, he would conspire with all the boldness and insight that had so impressed Jaf when he was the older man's student and protégé. The prospect, in all honesty, was a somewhat daunting one.

I wonder, Jaf thought, *in my heart, did I come to Ildaon hoping that Elek would talk me out of this venture before it went too far? I should have known better.*

"We could be starting a civil war," he said aloud. "If anybody has qualms about something like that, now would be a good time to say so."

"Too late for that already," Elek said. "The mere fact that we gathered here at all would be enough to condemn us, if the star-lords ever got word of this meeting. Which they will, in time. All we can do is take precautions and strive to put off the day."

"I'll talk to my brother about the luck," Diasul said. "But it may take me a while to reach him—he's back on Eraasi, working with Garrod syn-Aigal."

"What?" Tinau exploded. He turned to Elek. "Why don't you invite the star-lords to sit in on our discussion in person next time!" To Jaf, he explained, "You're not from Eraasi. You wouldn't know. But Garrod's Circle is in the pockets of the star-lords. Sus-Peledaen's own brother is in that Circle!"

Elek nodded, unfazed by the announcement. "So much the better, if the Circle is above suspicion. From unexpected quarters, the victory will come."

Later that first night on his newly-discovered planet, Garrod slept again, wrapped in the warm coverings he had packed from home.

He started awake, midway through the dark hours, at a sound. Something had passed overhead, making a mechanical whining noise. It was gone before he could come fully awake.

Dawn came, then sunrise. Garrod continued on his way, making observations as before. The sun rose to its zenith and started to sink again. It passed to the north of him when it was highest in the sky, an indication that he was in this world's southern hemisphere.

The mechanical noise returned in mid-afternoon, a whuffling sound more than a whine. This time he was able to locate the source of the noise: A lenticular disk, cruising through the sky. Without knowing the object's size, he couldn't tell its exact distance; but assuming that it was a double arm-span across, it was perhaps five hundred feet overhead. He froze in place, making himself quiet and still after the way of the Circles' discipline.

He had reacted in time, or so he hoped. The disk neither

slowed down nor betrayed any curiosity about his location. Whether the disk itself was an intelligent or quasi-intelligent being, like the *aiketen* at home, or whether it merely served as eyes and ears for a distant observer, Garrod couldn't tell.

The disk continued on to the north—the same direction in which he had been walking. It went between two hills, paused, circled, and turned east, flying in that direction until it passed out of sight.

Garrod reached that line of hills himself in mid-morning of the next day. Beyond the hills lay a valley, and up the middle of the valley, leading from west to east, was a road, or something that had once served as one. Now it was a cracked mass of blackish rocks, laid out on the dry ground like a mosaic, with short narrow blades of dusty green vegetation poking up through the cracks. The sort-of-road had edges, though not distinct ones; the rocks grew farther apart, and the vegetation thicker, until there were no rocks at all.

He contemplated the road for a while. Whatever used it— if anything still did—seemed not to wear down the plants. Maybe it was disused, after all, and fallen into ruin. Or perhaps not. The surface, weed-grown though it was, remained largely clear of dirt and sand, and the weeds themselves grew no taller than the width of his palm.

Garrod determined to make camp for a day or two in the high ground to the south of the road, where he could watch and yet remain concealed. He had a week's supply of water left in his canteens, and the nearby hills made as good a place to stay as any while he waited for this new world's secrets to reveal themselves.

XXI: Year 1123 E. R.
Eraasi: Demaizen Old Hall
Hanilat Starport
Beyond the Farther Edge: Garrod's World

THE SUN slanted golden into the upper room at Demaizen Old Hall, and cast a bright square of light on the juncture between wall and floor. The late-autumn sky outside the windows was a clear, intense blue.

Serazao and Narin finished cleaning up Garrod. They had given him his breakfast—warm cereal mixed with sugar—that Serazao spooned into his mouth while Narin wiped his chin. They had cleaned his mess and changed his clothes, and Narin had talked to him throughout, speaking of the day-to-day activity of the Circle as though he were able to understand. Through it all Garrod did not seem to notice, but rocked back and forth, playing with his fingers and saying nothing at all.

At midmorning Delath arrived to continue the watch, and the two women left the bright room for the gloomy hall beyond. This had been the routine at the Old Hall for nearly a month, the members of the Circle taking it in turns to care for Garrod, in the hope—now flagging—that he would return to himself and speak of what he had seen beyond the Edge.

Narin turned to Serazao. The younger woman was taking this very hard, though she never betrayed any emotion in front of Garrod beyond a steadfast cheerfulness.

"It's time to move on," Narin said. "Will you come with me? I have to talk with 'Rekhe."

"High time. But we'll have to find him first."

It took longer than Narin had anticipated. Arekhon had kept his old room, rather than moving into the larger chamber left empty by Yuvaen's death, but this morning he was not in either one. Kief, in the kitchen, and Ty, in the library, didn't know where he was either. Vai, sweat-covered from solo exercise in the gallery, thought he had left the building. A check in the former stables showed that the groundcar wasn't missing. If he was out, he couldn't have gone far.

"What now?" Serazao asked. The two women stood beside the stable door, looking out across the grounds of the estate.

Narin didn't reply for a few moments. Then she pointed toward a wooded hill that stood off to the southeast. "Let's go that way."

Narin had always been good at finding lost people and things. When the two women had climbed the hill—not a great walk, but strenuous, over steep ground covered by mosses and rounded stones—they found Arekhon sitting under a tree with his staff across his lap. He was looking down at the Old Hall where it stood below them in the distance, its blank windows reflecting the morning sun. Something about his expression made Narin wonder if Yuvaen had been the lucky one in the great working after all.

To give so much, and to have it come to nothing . . . and now we're about to ask him for even more.

But there wasn't any help for it. She moved into his field of vision, deliberately breaking his concentration, and said, "We can't wait any longer. You have to become the First, if the Circle is going to continue."

Arekhon looked up at her. "By Yuva's death I'm Second, nothing more. Garrod is First, while he lives."

"Garrod," said Serazao flatly, "is incapable."

"We need you, 'Rekhe," Narin said in a more reasonable tone. "We're just going through the motions down there. Without guidance, without a controlling hand, it's all going to fall apart. We'll drift off to other Circles, and spend the rest of our lives doing safe, tidy little workings—and what will become of Garrod's vision then?"

Arekhon shook his head. "Garrod is still alive."

"Yes, he's alive. He had a goal, and he came near it. Now he needs you to carry on his work."

"I will not be the First." Arekhon's protest was weaker this time, and Narin saw her opening.

"No," she agreed. "Garrod is First. But you have to lead us in his name until he comes to himself again."

Garrod continued his measurements of the skies. The days on this world were longer than he was used to on Eraasi, but each daylight period was shorter and each dark period was longer now than the one before, as if what might be the equivalent of winter was approaching. From time to time, the flying disks passed by, but he was unable to assign either a schedule or a pattern to their movements.

Two days after his initial sighting of the flying disks, his patience was rewarded.

Just before the sun rose, but while the sky was growing light, he heard a sound coming from the east, a growling noise with a high-pitched whine beneath it. The noise grew louder, and from around a bend came three boxy vehicles, roughly rectangular but with the forward ends sloped sharply downward. The vehicles moved at a walking pace. Ahead and on either side of them, and behind them, loped men.

Or at least, Garrod gave them that name by courtesy. They were bipedal, and progressed with jogging movements. Round heads surmounted their trunks, and they had arms with hands. Their knees bent in the same way that his did. But while similar in their rough outlines to the people of Eraasi and the other worlds on the far side of the interstellar gap, these were crudely misshapen. Their eyes were too large, their bodies too thick and coarse.

The vehicles they escorted had no wheels, but stood above the surface of the road, not touching it. Garrod nodded to himself, understanding now both the road's apparent disuse and the lack of any tall-standing overgrowth. Vehicles here used a method of propulsion similar to the counterforce units used in free-moving *aiketen* on Eraasi.

But these units would have to be much more powerful, Garrod reflected. The tinkerers at home would love to get their hands on one and take it apart for comparison.

Garrod watched the vehicles as they passed from east to west and vanished again around a turn. They had scarcely gone out of sight before a flash of light came from that direction, followed by a column of white smoke. An instant later, the sound came to him: A loud *whump*, muffled by distance.

Three black vee-shaped flying objects—small ones, like the flying disks—came out of the west to dive and circle around the source of the rising smoke. Lines of light shot up from the ground in response. A beam touched one of the flying vees, and it exploded in mid-flight.

More smoke floated upward. The piercing beams stopped. Minutes passed. Three smaller explosions sounded, in rapid but paced cadence.

Garrod watched, and kept still. Then, with a rumble of jets, a winged craft rose vertically from beyond where the smoke had risen. The flyer was painted in a flat, dark color, black against the sky. Its downward-pointing jets swiveled, and with a rising whine it shot away to the west.

The smoke from the encounter drifted away on the wind. The sun continued on its upward course. No sound, no motion, came from the road below. At last Garrod stood, picked up his pack, and walked downhill. He turned west, toward where the smoke had been.

He didn't have far to go. The vehicles, their counterforce units dead, lay smashed and fallen to the surface of the road. Their rear doors hung open, marked with the scorching of explosives. Their interiors were empty.

The men who had accompanied the convoy were here, too. They were all dead, their bodies as torn and broken as the vehicles they had guarded. Garrod could see now that what he had taken for misshapen bodies were in truth only shells, heavy suits containing mechanical aids to their muscles. The young men who had worn the suits looked as human as he did. Any one of them—if he were not bloody, broken, and burned—could have walked unnoticed through downtown Hanilat.

Garrod said the prayers of well-wishing for the dead, and turned away.

* * *

Theledau syn-Grevi contemplated the racks of reports that his agents had brought him, and swiveled in his chair so that the reports lay behind his back.

All the information in the world, he thought, *and not one hard fact in any of it.*

Outside the windows of his office the towers of central Hanilat thrust up against the skyglow. He would be late arriving home tonight; the moon was already rising, and he would have to keep the hour of watch later than was proper. But he would not forego it. He had given up enough of what he valued in order to come to this city he did not like, to labor for the good of the sus-Radal.

As he had done all day, and was still doing. The key to the future, if one existed, had to lie in the mysterious reports he had gotten from Iulan Vai. His Agent-Principal had always shown an uncanny knack for turning up at the center of the real concern while others remained distracted by trivialities—and Iulan Vai had left Hanilat without notice, delegating her investigations in the city entirely to her subordinates. She had gone instead to Demaizen Old Hall, where Garrod syn-Aigal and his hand-picked Circle were doing . . . something.

Thel considered the two cryptic messages he had gotten from Vai since the beginning of her investigation.

BELIEVE SUS-PELEDAEN INTEND TRADE BEYOND EDGE. CONFIDENCE LOW. TAKE NO ACTION AT THIS TIME.

ALL QUIET AT DEMAIZEN. NO RESULTS AS YET. CONTINUING SURVEILLANCE.

He had gone over and over the brief communications, trying to determine what his Agent-Principal had intended to convey. That whatever Garrod had been up to was a failure? If so, then why continue her investigation—and if it was *not* a failure, then why report that there had been no results? He could only trust in Vai's competence and hope that she would enlighten him.

In the meantime, one thing was clear: If the sus-Peledaen meant to trade beyond the Edge, they would need to build more ships. And so would he—ships faster and stronger and farther-ranging than any vessels his rivals might send out on such a journey.

He turned back to his desk to write the appropriate orders.

Narin had been wrong. It wasn't going to work.

Arekhon sat in Garrod's study, at Garrod's desk, toying with the pens and the writing pads. Through the half-drawn curtains, the tall window showed low grey clouds. Late autumn had given way overnight to the chill wind and rain of early winter. The study was dim and gloomy, but Arekhon hadn't bothered to turn on the lights. The cold, clammy day suited his mood.

It was all very well for Narin to say that he should lead the Circle in Garrod's name. Leading required a direction, and he had none. Instead, the Circle was spinning away from him—he could feel it. They had failed, and a path was not clear before him. He could not recover the disaster.

The star charts he had brought from home, that he had opened for Garrod with such pride and enthusiasm, lay in their leather case on a chair against the far wall. He would have to give them back to Natelth the next time he journeyed to Hanilat on Circle business, if he ever had any Circle business to transact.

He was ready to go down to the kitchen—someone would always be in the kitchen—and tell them all to go away. To find other Circles. That this was no place for them. Yuvaen and Garrod had defied the gods, and now they were both gone.

Instead he did nothing but play with the small objects on the desk.

Then a mad feeling seized him, and he swept his arm across the desktop, clearing it of papers and pens and useless, outdated data wafers. He stood. A secret existed, and the universe was concealing it. Perhaps studying the chart would bring new insight, another line of attack, and the Circle would continue, made stronger and bound more tightly by its losses.

Arekhon removed the charts from their case, and took down the reader from the bookshelf where it had been stored. A small voice whispered to him that his real motive in not breaking up the Circle lay in his new-found discovery of a warm and experienced bed-partner, present on a nightly basis, not merely whenever her ship was in, and he was in town, and if no other obligations got in the way.

. He pushed away the thought as unworthy of the meditation—the private meditation—that he intended, and inserted the reader into the desktop. The lights flashed and cycled, and he slid the first chart into the slot. The reader snortled, sounding like the antique that it was, and the lights of the worlds and the shipping lines came up.

There was the dark border, the Edge beyond which nothing existed, nothing was known. And there, in the uncharted space beyond it—Arekhon leaned forward in his chair, feeling his face grow hot with amazement—glowed a single white light.

Alone and isolated.

Impossibly far away.

But real. In a place that had held nothing but darkness the last time he'd seen this chart, there stood now the marker for a world rich in all resources, ready for trade at advantageous bargains.

"Son of a bitch," Arekhon breathed. "Garrod. You left a beacon for us on the other side."

XXII:
Year 1123 E. R.
Eraasi: Hanilat Starport
Ildaon: Country House of Elek Griat
Beyond the Farther Edge: Garrod's World

NATELTH SUS-KHALGATH had been away from home for ten days, making a formal tour of the new starships under construction in the family's orbital yards. He hadn't enjoyed the excursion. Travel beyond the home-world's atmosphere didn't appeal to him, and he had done as little of it as possible after completing his apprentice voyage. But as head of the sus-Peledaen, Natelth was expected to visit new ships—not every vessel that was built, certainly, but any time there was a significant change in the design—and he didn't believe in skimping on family duty out of personal dislike.

The front rooms of the town house were empty when he returned. He surrendered his impedimenta to the entryway *aiketh*, a black-and-silver model that hovered a little above the floor on its pocket-sized counterforce unit. The *aiketh* floated off toward his rooms upstairs, sagging a little under the weight of the luggage—it wasn't really a heavy-labor unit, but an information center that Isayana had retooled for her own amusement several years before.

"Wait," said Natelth as the *aiketh* reached the bottom of the staircase. "Where is Isa?"

Light flashed inside the *aiketh*'s shell as it communicated with the larger house-mind. "Your sister is in the kitchen," it said. "The kitchen reports that an unscheduled meal is under-going consumption."

"Thank you," said Natelth. Politeness was always worth-while, even to quasi-organics.

The *aiketh* continued on its way upstairs, and Natelth went on to the house's spacious and well-appointed kitchen. Isa was there as the house had said, cutting slices off of a fresh loaf of nutgrain bread and spreading them with jam.

Arekhon was with her. Natelth had heard rumors of strange goings-on at Demaizen Old Hall, and looking at 'Rekhe, he believed them. His brother was thinner than he'd been when he came to borrow the star charts—and 'Rekhe had been lean enough already—with something about his eyes that suggested he hadn't been getting enough sleep.

He looked cheerful, though, which filled Natelth with sus-picion. Arekhon didn't come to the house these days unless he needed something from the family.

"'Rekhe," Natelth said. "We haven't seen you in quite some while; if you'd come a day earlier I'd have missed you."

Arekhon finished his slice of bread and wiped the jam off his fingers with a damp towel. "That's why I came today. I wanted to talk with you about something important."

Isa laughed. "Scoundrel. You told me that you came home for some fresh bread."

"I did. Nobody at the Hall makes anything like yours, and the kitchen there isn't teachable—it's strictly cook-it-yourself."

Natelth sat down at the table across from his brother. Arek-hon was excited about something; that much was plain for anyone to see. With luck it wasn't something dangerous, like being named the Third in a Void-walker's Circle. Isa had fret-ted about that appointment for weeks, and worry had troubled Natelth's own sleep as well.

"If it's bread recipes that you came for," Natelth said, "I can't help you. So it must be something else."

"You're right. Do you remember those charts I borrowed?"

"You've brought them back?"

Arekhon shook his head. "They're still at Demaizen."

"Then why—" Natelth began, at the same time as Isa said, in reproving tones, " 'Rekhe, don't tease."

"Because there was a working," Arekhon said, abruptly serious again. "Garrod walked through the Void, out past all the known markers—and he found a world on the other side of the gap beyond the Edge."

"Beyond—" Natelth found himself at a loss for further words. None of the fleet-Circles had ever dared as much. It was common knowledge, or so the sus-Peledaen Mages had always insisted, that making so long a walk would destroy both the Mage who tried it and the Circle that backed him.

"A world," Arekhon said. "Inhabited and fit for trade. Garrod left us the marker for it."

"A new world is all very well," said Isa sharply. "But what has it got to do with your brother, or with the family?"

"Ships," Natelth said at once. In spite of his better judgment, he'd begun to catch some of his younger brother's enthusiasm. There hadn't been a new world opened for trade in almost two decades, and the chance of making the sus-Peledaen the first family in a new part of space was enough to make anyone's heart beat a little faster. "Isn't that it, 'Rekhe? You can't get to Garrod's world without a starship, so you've come back home to ask for one."

Two of the guests at Elek Griat's breakfast meeting, Oska and Tinau, departed that same morning, but Jaf Otnal remained at the country house. So—to his chagrin, for he had hoped to spend the rest of his extended leave of absence enjoying his friend's company in solitude—did the Eraasian conspirator, Diasul. Elek played the contra-cithara for hours at a time, while Diasul and Jaf walked about the grounds during the day and read the information text-channels in the evenings. Diasul talked about his life on Eraasi, his ambitions as head of a flourishing mercantile house, and his desire to influence planetary politics. Jaf found it all exquisitely boring.

One evening he took Elek aside. "Is there some reason why that man is still here? You never speak to him, and the Oldest knows I don't want to."

"Diasul is clearing his mind before he speaks with his brother," Elek replied. "The Mages can't read minds that I know of, but a talented one can tell if you're lying about something—and where family is concerned, even a little talented could be enough. You're also providing a distraction to cover the activities of our two other friends, who've been setting things in motion elsewhere. You've been under daily surveillance, in case you didn't know."

Jaf hadn't. "How?" he asked. He'd thought that the country house was too remote for eavesdroppers—had suspected Elek of choosing it for that reason.

"From above. Anywhere there's a sky, the star-lords can look down to observe and record, if they think they've got a reason. You haven't written anything about this matter and left it lying by a window in daylight, have you?"

"No," said Jaf. Elek was joking, he decided, but there was enough truth in the jest to make him uncomfortable. "There's nothing in writing at all."

Several days later, near the end of Jaf's visit, the conspirator named Oska returned, this time bringing with him another, younger man. Dinner that night—Jaf's last evening at the country house—was a formal affair, at which Oska introduced his companion, Syr Seyo Hannet of the League of Unallied Shippers.

"I must confess," Elek said after a sip of wine, "that I have never heard of the League of Unallied Shippers."

Seyo laughed. "They're my own invention. And empty, at the moment. But I have one family of star-lords who will be the core of the movement, and another who will join. More families will come later, and faults will develop in their cozy system. Suspicion will grow from there until the first atrocity will make everyone call for blood."

Jaf looked at Seyo dubiously. "Who guarantees that we'll get an atrocity when we need one?"

"Such things can be arranged," said Seyo. "I've talked with a fleet-family pensioner or two, and I have all the details of their little games. A ship will vanish, and its crew with it— the work of outlaw raiders, undoubtedly, the sort of rascals that the fleet-families hunt down themselves whenever they get the chance. Another ship, from another family, will arrive shortly after with the missing cargo, and not be able to explain how they got it. The rest—" Seyo shrugged. "It's all in the play of the hand."

"A clever plan," Elek conceded. "But how do you intend to implement it?"

"Two faked cargoes," Seyo explained. "Observe. A family— sus-Peledaen for example—accepts and transports a load. It is all serial-marked material, and a copy of the manifest stays at their offices. But that cargo—manifested, noted, inventoried, and logged though it may be—never actually goes aboard. What does go on that sus-Peledaen ship in those boxes is a bomb, timed to remove that ship without a trace during its transit through the Void."

Elek began to smile. "I see. And I take it that the cargo that should have gone aboard the sus-Peledaen ship is actually aboard the craft of one of the families in your League of Un-allied Shippers?"

"Exactly," said Seyo. "They take off with it, all unknowing. When they arrive at their destination, they have with them the cargo they loaded aboard—but the firm they contracted to deliver it to has gone out of business! They follow customary practice and sell that cargo to the highest bidder, at which time the serial numbers are revealed. The sus-Peledaen find out— how could they not, since we'll be ready to tell them if necessary?—and the Unallied Shipper's logs are examined. They do not bear the signatures for incidents of piracy and boarding. In fact, the ship's captain and crew deny having seen the other craft, far less stealing from them."

"Tricky," said Jaf approvingly.

"It gets better," Seyo assured him. "The fleet-families will have started building warships by then, and they'll be eager to use them. Once one family loses a ship to another—or thinks it does—they'll feel honor-bound to fight."

The vee-craft and the armed flyer had come from the west, or at least had returned in that direction after ambushing the ground vehicles. Garrod considered the possibilities for a while, and turned his footsteps east. He hiked parallel to the road, keeping it in sight but being careful to stay off of it, as the days stretched into a week.

One night, a red glow suffused the sky to the east. To Garrod, it looked like a distant city burning. The road wasn't deserted after that. Vehicles remained few, but there was a steady flow of foot traffic—people, young and old, carrying all that they possessed, walking with a trudging hopelessness, their eyes fixed on the road ahead of them.

Refugees, Garrod thought. Eraasi had not experienced the phenomenon during his lifetime, but he had seen pictures and had read the historical accounts.

He pondered the situation for some time. The way of caution would be to return at once through the Void to Eraasi—he had already made enough observations to prove his point about the existence of living worlds on the far side of the interstellar gap. But he had not yet gained all the information he needed to make return navigation sure. Nor had he broken his family altars in order to be cautious.

That evening after dark, he buried most of his gear beneath a pile of stones a little distance off the road, and approached a small group of refugees. He hoped that in the general confusion his lack of language skills wouldn't work against him. If he approached someone sufficiently downhearted, he would not himself be in great physical danger.

He chose to approach a group of three—a woman carrying an infant child, and an older man, perhaps the woman's father—as they camped, ragged and dirty, beside a stone wall near the roadside. He observed them from a distance first, sizing them up as he waited outside the circle of light from their fire.

He was close enough to hear them talking. He didn't recognize the language, which was unsurprising; nevertheless, he derived a certain gratification from noting that all the sounds they produced fell within the known capabilities of the human vocal apparatus. He was considering how to approach their camp without seeming vulnerable or worth robbing, but at the same time without appearing threatening, when matters moved beyond his control.

A younger man entered the camp from the direction of the road. He wore clean clothing in a single color—livery of some sort, Garrod suspected, like that worn in the fleet-families—and held an object in his right hand that Garrod considered likely to be a weapon. He spoke sharply, in a loud tone of voice, and gestured with the weapon-object.

The young woman screamed, then began to cry softly, cuddling her baby. The older man spoke in reply, hands clasped in front of him, eyes on the ground.

The young man stepped up beside the older one, and placed the weapon against the other's head. He repeated his command, loudly but briefly. The older man began to speak again, a soft, tumbling rush of words. To Garrod it seemed that he was begging for mercy, or perhaps praying to an unseen deity.

There comes a time to observe, Garrod thought, *and another to act.*

He stepped forward and smashed his staff against the young man's back, parallel to the ground, about the level where the fellow's kidneys would be if he were human. The young man flung his arms wide, his head back, and grunted with pain. Garrod put his staff in front of the other's neck, and pulled backward.

The weapon in the man's hand fired a beam of greenish light. Grass and brush smouldered where the line of light touched. Garrod continued to pull. The man went limp. The weapon stopped glowing and dropped from his hand.

Garrod waited another slow count to make sure the man was dead, then released him. The body slumped to the ground. Then Garrod stopped, picked up the weapon, and slid it into his belt. The front end was hot to the touch.

The older man was still standing before him, eyes closed, continuing his prayer. Garrod spoke, in slow, careful Eraasian, putting all the strength of his personality behind the words, so that his intent might carry even if the words did not make sense:

"You are safe," he said. "I am a friend."

The older man stopped talking, and looked up. He saw Garrod standing, staff in hand, and the body on the ground. The man spoke, but Garrod didn't understand him.

The Magelord reached slowly into his pocket and pulled out a stick of trail-candy—the high-energy kind with plenty of nuts and fruit in it. He peeled back the silvery wrapping and broke the stick in half, offering one part to the man. Then he raised his own half to his lips, took a bite, chewed, and swallowed, to show that it was food and not poisonous.

Or I assume not, Garrod thought. *These people are like me. The Sundering divided us, but they have not changed so much since then to look at—how much could they have changed internally, and still not have it show?*

The man tasted Garrod's offering, tentatively. Then his face lit with a smile. He called out softly, one word. Garrod assumed it was the woman's name.

The woman—no more than a girl, really—appeared from the shadows, the child in her arms, and accepted the bar of trail-candy from the older man. She looked down at where their late assailant lay. Then she walked over and spat in his face.

The man turned to Garrod. He spoke. Garrod put on his best puzzled expression and cocked his head to one side, hoping that the man would take his meaning. He said, "I'm sorry, but I don't speak your language."

"Ah," the man said. He made a drinking gesture with his hand, and pantomimed taking a pull from a bottle.

Garrod echoed his gesture. The man took a bottle from his coat pocket and handed it across to Garrod. The Magelord opened it, tilted it back, and drank.

It wasn't water. This was a potent liquor. It burned. Garrod sputtered, his eyes streaming tears, and handed the bottle back. The man laughed, and put an arm around the Mage's shoulders.

"I think," said Garrod, as soon as his head had cleared, "that we've found a basis for communication."

Later that night he helped bury the young man's body in the woods. By morning, the four of them were walking on together, and Garrod was making his first progress at learning their language. He knew their names—the man was called Hujerie and the woman Saral, and the baby answered to the name, or perhaps the endearment, of Minnin—and they knew his, though their pronunciation was odd.

No odder than my pronunciation of theirs, Garrod thought.

They were going to a place called Raske, he learned, and the land around them was called Tulbith.

The world, so he understood the man to say, was called Entibor.

XXIII: Year 1124 E. R.
Eraasian Space: sus-Peledaen ship
RAIN-ON-DARK-WATER
Eraasi: Hanilat

THE GUARDSHIP *Rain-on-Dark-Water* loomed up, mountain-high, in her construction cradle at the sus-Peledaen orbital yard. Elaeli stood on the cradle's embarkation platform, taking in the pleasing sight. She'd been the *Rain*'s Pilot-Principal for almost a month now, since returning to Eraasi with syn-Evarat and *Wind-on-the-Mountain,* and she was eager to see the sleek and powerful vessel come out of the construction phase for good.

Pilot-Principal on a new-built ship was a prize in itself, an assignment that marked her out as one of the family's up-and-comers. She contemplated the long upward slope of the *Rain*'s matte-black side, and allowed herself to imagine her future career.

From Pilot-Principal to Command-Tertiary was a gap that no more than a few in each generation would cross; she could serve the family in her present rank for three decades or more, and be counted among those who'd had a good career in the fleet. But if she ever did achieve that first level of command, then all the others became possible as well: Captain, Convoy-Captain—even, someday, Fleet-Captain, with authority subordinate only to Natelth sus-Peledaen himself.

Natelth's younger brother, to whom she owed her present good fortune, was the reason she was waiting here on the embarkation platform. The lifter-shuttle that climbed like a cog railway up the mountain of the ship's side had delivered two carloads of personnel to the *Rain*'s main hatch already. 'Rekhe was, not surprisingly, late.

The door on the far side of the docking platform slid open. Elaeli turned her head quickly in the direction of the noise. Yes, it was Arekhon, dressed in the plain black and white that he had affected ever since leaving the fleet to join Garrod's Circle.

She saw at once that he had changed since their farewell at the Court of Two Colors. His hair was the same sleek black as it had always been, with no trace yet of the early silver that sometimes came with Magework, but clearly something had happened during her absence. He looked older, and the hint of mischief that had always lurked in his grey eyes was muted.

He smiled when he saw her—the smile was the same, at least—and took both her hands in his.

"Ela," he said. He glanced at her insignia and cocked an eyebrow. "Pilot-Principal . . . that's new."

"It came with my transfer to the *Rain*," she said. "syn-Evarat pushed for it, but I think it was your recommendation for adoption that finished the job."

"syn-Evarat's a good man." Arekhon paused. "What's the *Rain*'s captain like?"

She thought for a moment. "I haven't worked with her for more than a couple of weeks, and we're still in the cradle. But I'd say—steady. I don't know anything more than that."

"Steadiness is what we need," he said.

She glanced at him sharply. "Need for what?"

"That's why I came here. Are your quarters safe to talk in?"

"As far as I can tell."

"Then let's go there," he said.

"And talk?"

Arekhon smiled again, and this time the mischief came back to his eyes. He lifted both her hands to his mouth and kissed them. "That too."

* * *

For Theledau syn-Grevi it was the hour of observance.

He went to the moonroom as usual, but as soon as he stepped through the door he became convinced that he was not alone. He stepped no farther in than the threshold, but reached out and tapped the switch on the wall beside him. A dim silver light began to glow from recessed sources dispersed around the circular room.

He half-expected to find a burglar hiding there, or a spy from one of the fleet-families with reason to dislike the sus-Radal. As befitted half an expectation, he was half right. Iulan Vai was waiting for him, curled up on one of the watching-benches, wearing plain black garments and balancing a stick—no, not a stick, a Mage's staff—across her knees.

"Good evening, my lord." Vai rose to her feet and knelt to him as politely as ever, then resumed her seated posture. "I thought it was time I should report to you in person."

"More than time," Thel said. "You've been running your operations from Demaizen for long enough."

She accepted the implied reproof without changing expression. "My people are well trained. Did you ever lack for anything that they could have supplied?"

"Not that I know of. But if I didn't have it I wouldn't know about it, would I?"

She smiled as if he had made a pleasing joke. "That's the way it always is," she agreed. "It's the things you don't know you're missing that'll get you every time. My lord, I stayed at Demaizen because of one of those things. As I told you at the time, matters were in train there which required my close personal observation."

"And have these matters finally reached some kind of conclusion?"

"Oh, yes." She paused—whether it was for effect, or to marshal her words properly, Thel couldn't say. "Garrod syn-Aigal has found a hospitable world on the far side of the interstellar gap. I anticipate that the sus-Peledaen will be sending out an explorer ship before very long; Lord Arekhon's in town and talking with his brother now."

Thel scowled. "That *is* information you could have given me earlier."

"To what end? Our fleet has no ships capable of making so

long a transit. Better that the sus-Peledaen should take the risk of the first voyage . . . after all, you'll be getting copies of all their data from your agent on board."

"You?" he asked.

She nodded. "Demaizen will provide the ship's Circle, and I'm a part of Demaizen now. You'll have to appoint my current Agent-in-Charge to Agent-Principal in my place, of course."

"Of course," Thel said drily. Vai had always been high-handed where her operations were concerned, and he had tolerated it because she provided him with excellent results. She had not previously been accustomed to use that same high-handedness with Theledau himself. "You do realize, that's not an appointment I can make, then take away again?"

"I know." She lifted the ebony staff briefly from her knees, then balanced it again across them. "I have another place to come back to, if I come back at all."

"I understand," he said with some regret, since Vai's Second, however competent, was not likely to prove her equal. "Satisfy my curiosity, if you would: How in the world did you manage to convince Garrod syn-Aigal—whom nobody has ever called a fool—that you were a Mage?"

Vai's smile had a rueful twist to it. "In the only way I could, as it turned out afterward."

"You've actually become one of them?"

"I have." Her face took on a distant expression. "Like I said, it's the things you don't know you're missing . . . it wasn't a development I anticipated, but it's done. If you want to release me from your employ altogether, I'll make no objection. But speaking as your Agent-Principal, you'd be foolish not to get one of your people onto that sus-Peledaen ship."

She was right, as usual. "Make whatever arrangements you need to for transmitting reports," he said. "And, Syr Vai—"

"My lord?"

"You've done well."

After Vai had left, Thel darkened the moonroom again, and sat in thought for a long time below the clear glass dome. He came to the conclusion that he envied Iulan Vai. If he were younger, and free of the ties that bound him in service to his family, he would be half-tempted to hire on with the sus-

Peledaen as common crew, just for the chance to take part himself in this venture beyond the Edge.

But he was who he was, and nothing about that could be changed. He would do as much as he could through Iulan Vai, and the sus-Radal—as always—would reap the profit.

Arekhon had wanted to speak with Elaeli alone about the news, and not merely for the opportunity to renew their friendship in the sweetest way possible. In a venture as audacious as the one proposed for *Rain-on-Dark-Water,* having the Pilot-Principal's firm backing was essential. If she took against it, or even expressed strong reservations, the always-delicate balance between a ship's Circle and its captain would take on a distinctly fleetward tilt—and such a tilt, when the First of the Circle was not the First at all, but only a jumped-up Second, could prove impossible to overcome.

To his dismay, however, the *Rain*'s captain was waiting for them inside the ship's main hatch. Captain sus-Mevyan was a lean, grey-haired woman with strong bones and a dour expression; Arekhon suspected, from her name, that her family had been far-island nobility before turning starward and throwing in their lot with the sus-Peledaen.

She was not, he decided ruefully, the sort to be impressed by Natelth sus-Khalgath's younger brother.

"Captain," he said politely.

She nodded. "sus-Khalgath. Will you and Pilot-Principal Inadi take *uffa* in my quarters? Lord sus-Peledaen's message bears discussion in private."

I couldn't agree more, Arekhon thought. *Unfortunately, I'm not going to get the chance.*

He said a reluctant mental farewell to the prospect of leisurely discourse with Elaeli, and followed sus-Mevyan through the *Rain*'s interior labyrinth to the captain's cabin, where a polished copper pot was already steaming on its tripod. Three carved wooden folding chairs—one with a back and arms, and two without—waited in conversational arrangement on the heavy carpet. More tapestry panels, in a green and gold far-islands pattern, covered the metal bulkheads. Standard light emplacements studded the overhead, but their output was scaled down to a dim glow.

Arekhon and Elaeli took their seats in the two guest chairs, and waited as sus-Mevyan poured *uffa* into cut-glass cups. The Captain took her leaf pale, Arekhon noted with resignation— no truckling here to inner-family taste by claiming a preference for red.

"Now," said sus-Mevyan, after the first taste of the hot liquid had been respectfully sipped and savored. "sus-Khalgath—tell me about this new world your brother's message spoke of."

Arekhon heard Elaeli's breath catch slightly: She remembered, then, what Garrod's Circle had been working on. He didn't dare take his attention off sus-Mevyan long enough to see if she remembered it with favor or with dismay.

He kept his eyes fixed on the Captain instead, saying, "My brother told you that Garrod syn-Aigal sus-Demaizen has found a new inhabited planet circling a distant star. How much more did he tell you?"

"He told me," sus-Mevyan said, "that the Second of Garrod's Circle would come aboard and convey the details in person. From which I assume that this new planet is something out of the ordinary, if Lord sus-Peledaen feels unable to trust even his own fleet's crypto systems with the full transmission."

"Natelth has a point. The planet Garrod found lies beyond the Farther Edge."

With great care and precision, sus-Mevyan set her cup down on the low table beside the copper pot. "You are quite sure of this?"

"My life on it," said Arekhon.

She took the meaning as he intended. "Demaizen will provide the ship's Circle for this voyage?"

"Yes."

"It's risky . . . very risky." sus-Mevyan turned her icy, penetrating gaze on Elaeli. "Pilot-Principal, what do you say about this venture that Lord sus-Peledaen and his brother have proposed for us?"

Arekhon concentrated on keeping his breathing steady and his expression noncommittal. Elaeli deserved the chance to give an honest answer, and sus-Mevyan didn't need to know how important her Pilot-Principal's opinion was to the acting head of the Demaizen Circle.

"I'll be honest, Captain," Elaeli said. "I think the voyage could kill us all. But if it doesn't kill us"—she grinned suddenly, with a blaze of pure honest ambition that filled Arekhon's senses like a lambent flame—"we'll come back so covered with glory that Natelth sus-Khalgath sus-Peledaen will give us whatever we ask him for."

XXIV: Year 1124 E. R.
Eraasi: Demaizen Old Hall
Beyond the Farther Edge: Entibor

IT'S SETTLED," Arekhon said. "We have a ship, and
the Captain is with us."

The surviving functional members of the Demaizen Circle
sat together in Garrod's—now Arekhon's—study, where the
star-chart projected its illusory topography into the air above
the desktop. The brilliant golden-white dot that marked out
Garrod's new-found world glowed unblinking beyond the dark
line of the Edge.

"A sus-Peledaen ship," said Kief. "And the sus-Peledaen get
the trade, I suppose."

Serazao spoke before Arekhon could form an answer. "The
sus-Peledaen, or somebody else; it doesn't matter. We're doing this for Garrod's sake."

"And we need to think about how we're going to do it,"
Arekhon said. "Since the First is . . . how he is, he can't make
the journey himself. But he *is* the First of our Circle, and it
wouldn't be right to leave him behind in the care of strangers."

"Not to mention what might happen to our luck if we tried,"
said Narin. "Nothing good ever comes from abandoning one
of your own."

Arekhon nodded, grateful for the opening. "Narin is right. Which is why I propose to split the Circle, some to go and some to stay. Those who stay will keep the *eiran* smooth and untangled here at home, and send luck to those who cross the interstellar gap. And Garrod will remain the First at Demaizen, as before."

"How are we going to make the split?" asked Ty. "Draw lots?"

"Nothing quite so random," Arekhon said. "I had in mind meditating together on the question."

"Now?" asked Kief. "Without preparation?"

"It's the best way to find out a true division," said Arekhon. "There's no time for us to be influenced too much by the desires of one person or another."

He stood up, and looked at each of the Circle members in turn—Narin and Delath and Kief, Ty and Serazao and Iulan Vai. "Come."

He left the room without looking back to see if the others followed. He had anticipated a brief stir of conversation and questioning, but heard nothing beside the sounds of scuffing chair legs and footsteps on carpet. That was good; it meant that the rest of the Circle had concurred in his decision without the need for talk.

The group that reassembled in the meditation room was a quiet and sober one. No workings had taken place in the chamber since Garrod's return. All the physical traces of the previous occasion had been cleared away, but the patterns of that time were plainly marked to the inward sight. Arekhon knelt in Yuvaen's old place—Garrod's he left empty—while the others took their places as they had done before.

Iulan Vai hesitated. Arekhon beckoned her into the group as well. Last time she had been an observer; this time, and for the voyage to come, she would be a part of the whole. Ty moved aside, yielding the newest member's position, and Vai knelt with her usual limber grace.

Arekhon nodded, satisfied, and closed his eyes.

The place he came to, when his inner vision cleared, was chaotic. A tumble of ragged, grey-black clouds blocked out the sky overhead. The land itself was shattered stone, like the place Arekhon had seen when the First had gone Void-walking before. But this time the land was divided at Arekhon's feet, stone from air, in a cliff that plunged straight down, a hundred times the height of a man, to a churning lead-grey sea below.

Water smashed, wave on wave, against the foot of the cliff, then withdrew in white foam between jagged teeth of rock. The wind whipped Arekhon's hair around his face, then snatched it back again, as the force of the air pushed him first toward, then away from, the edge of the cliff.

When he looked out across the sea, he saw a boat tossed about on the water. Two figures sat and rowed away from the cliffs; a third stood in the stern. He recognized the rowers as Ty and Narin, pulling hard lest their craft be sucked in amid the breakers and dashed to pieces. The third he recognized as well: Iulan Vai, standing pale and beautiful, her hand raised in salute or farewell.

"Wait!" Arekhon called. "Wait for me!"

The wind tore away his words, and the rowers did not pause. Arekhon launched himself over the edge of the cliff. The sea came closer and closer, the rocks grew large, the waves boomed, and the roaring wind howled about his ears as he fell, and fell. . . .

Arekhon opened his eyes and found himself once more kneeling on the floor of the meditation room, with his Circle gathered around him. For a moment there was silence; then, slowly, the Mages began to speak.

Narin was first, turning to face Ty and saying, "I saw you."

"And I saw you," Ty replied. "You came to help me break down the wall, and Vai did . . . I think we're meant to go together on the ship."

Kief, standing with the other group, met Arekhon's questioning glance and shook his head. "I didn't see you with us at all."

Del and Serazao nodded agreement. What they might have seen, Arekhon did not ask, nor did they volunteer the information.

The Circle had made its division.

In the company of his new friends Hujerie and Saral, Garrod continued his journey through the region of Entibor known as

Tulbith. They traveled by day, walking with greater confidence as no further armed men or fighting machines showed up to impede their progress, but they did not abandon all their old caution. The times, or so Garrod inferred from his companions' half-understood words and fleeting thoughts, were unsettled in the extreme—and his own earlier observations did nothing to contradict that impression.

The refugees avoided buildings and settled areas, living chiefly on fruits and berries found along the wayside, and on small animals that Hujerie proved adept at snaring, augmented by the concentrated rations that Garrod carried in his pack. Every night they camped, and while the others slept, Garrod pulled on the *eiran* to bring good luck to them all.

As the worst dangers of the road receded into the distance behind them, Garrod's spirits and those of his comrades began to lift. The woman Saral smiled more now, and the songs she sang to baby Minnin were cheerful ones.

Hujerie, for his part, talked to Garrod almost constantly, with expansive gestures. Garrod soon realized that the man's flow of conversation was deliberate, a conscious attempt at instruction in the local tongue, and bent his own efforts to the same end. With both men working at it, the process went much faster, and Garrod was soon able to carry on a simple conversation. When he made mistakes, which happened frequently, Hujerie would only laugh, then correct Garrod's errant pronunciation or pantomime an action to supply a missing verb, and carry on.

Eventually Garrod learned enough of the language to piece together the essentials of his friends' story. Hujerie was not Saral's father, as Garrod had first assumed, but her grandfather, and the baby boy Minnin—it was a name after all, and not an endearment—was not her child. Both Saral and Hujerie were in service to another, much more powerful family, of which Minnin was the youngest member. Hujerie, if Garrod understood the abstract ideas correctly, had been some kind of family tutor, but was now officially retired, and Saral was the baby's nursemaid. When the city of Feliset, supposedly a safe haven, was attacked and burned, the two of them were alone in the house with the child. They took the baby and fled, with the goal of bringing Minnin to safety and reuniting him with the rest of his family.

"They must be very worried," Garrod said.

"Worried indeed," Hujerie replied. "But we will repay their trust. And you, too, shall be rewarded."

"I do not seek a reward."

Hujerie clapped him on the back. "Good man," he said. "But we will reward you just the same, for your deserving."

They walked on. As Garrod's vocabulary grew larger, he began to make careful inquiries about the history and the political system of the world through which he traveled. He learned through indirect questioning that Entibor's political divisions were roughly coterminous with its major continental masses, though the exact boundaries—and the exact rulers—of some areas were currently the subject of intense dispute. Garrod accepted the situation without comment, although he felt rather as if he'd slipped backward in time to Eraasi's own remote and disunited past; Hujerie and Saral apparently took him for a wilderness vacationer from one of the smaller regions, stranded a long way from home by the outbreak of open warfare, and he didn't want to disabuse them of the notion.

One day, however, as they were descending from the hills toward a distant sparkling sea, a statement from Hujerie brought Garrod to a stop, and made him doubt his growing fluency in the local dialect.

"It isn't like this on other worlds."

"Other . . . 'worlds'?" Garrod hoped that his expression and inflection betrayed linguistic bewilderment rather than the shock he actually felt. He had not thought that a planet still in the grip of internecine warfare would have access to anything beyond its own immediate space.

" 'World,' yes, that's the word," Hujerie said approvingly. "Miosa, Khesat, those pious bastards from Galcen. And all the rest."

Garrod nodded, and listened, and knew that he held the luck of all Eraasi in his hands.

XXV: Year 1124 E. R.
Eraasi: Demaizen Old Hall
Entibor: Raske-by-the-Sea

ONCE ALL the decisions were made, the days until the *Rain*'s departure slipped by with unnerving speed. Arekhon felt the two halves of the Demaizen Circle, those who would go and those who would stay, beginning to draw apart and take on separate purpose. His own preparations were brief. He packed lightly for a journey to the other side of the galaxy, taking with him little more than his staff and his working robes, and enough changes of regular clothing to see him through a ship's wash cycle.

The other travelers followed Arekhon's example. Narin and Ty had not accumulated large stocks of personal possessions—Narin through lack of inclination and Ty through lack of time and opportunity—and Iulan Vai, as far as Arekhon could tell, had cut the ties to her old life completely when she came to the Circle.

He worried somewhat about that. His own abandonment of the family altars had been mostly a formality—it was his choice of Circle that had, for a while, put a strain on his relations with Natelth and Isa—but making the severance was harder for some people than for others. Vai's reticence argued that she might be one of the unlucky ones, for whom the late discovery of a Mage's calling could prove disastrous to an established and well-ordered life.

In the quiet of the last night at Demaizen, his conscience prompted him to seek her out. She was in her room, shutting down the clasps on the duffel that contained—as far as Arekhon was able to tell—everything that she wanted to claim by way of material goods. He saw a couple of her old Wildlife Protection League patches, their anchoring stitches neatly unpicked, lying on the bedside table in the pool of yellow light from the reading lamp. After he had greeted her, somewhat tentatively, with a kiss, he nodded toward the patches and raised his eyebrows.

"You're not taking those?"

She shook her head. "The gear itself may come in handy, you never know, but the patches seemed like a bad idea. Someone might misinterpret them."

Arekhon paused a moment to admire Vai's practicality; but the admiration carried him back to the same concern that had brought him here in the first place. Someone on Eraasi had been accustomed to enjoying the benefits of Iulan Vai's peculiarly clear and efficient mind, and was enjoying them no longer . . . to the Circle's good, but not necessarily to the good of her own out-questing spirit.

"Iule—" he began.

"Just 'Vai'," she said. "Please. I know it sounds odd, but I'm accustomed to it."

"Vai," he amended—*and was there never,* he wondered silently, *anyone at all before now to call you by the forms of affection?*—"once we're on the road tomorrow, we might as well have left Eraasi behind. So if there's anyone to whom you feel the need or the obligation to say goodbye, this is the time to do it. You're part of the Circle, so the Hall's distance-connections are as much yours as anybody else's."

"That's all right," she said. "There isn't anyone in particular. My old job's gone to someone else by now, and the job"— she shrugged—"was all there was, really. I won't be missed."

"That's no fit life for anyone to lead," said Arekhon, with a shiver for the essential loneliness her words implied. "I'm glad you found us . . . Demaizen and the Circle . . . because *I* would miss you, if the division had made you one of the group to stay."

She smiled at him. "You're a sweet young man, Arekhon, and honest enough to be dangerous." She paused, then asked, with careful lack of emphasis, "How will the Circle be quartered, on this ship of yours?"

"According to the usual custom," he said. "Private cabin for the First—or whoever's in charge—and the rest bunk with the crew."

"And the gossip, I suppose, is perpetual?"

"Never-ending," he agreed. "And memories are long."

"I see." She turned away for a moment to lift her sealed duffel off the bed and set it against the wall by the door, then came back to stand beside him. She lifted one hand and gently touched the corner of his mouth, while with her other hand she worked at undoing the braided loop fasteners of her high-necked tunic, one loop at a time. "Perhaps, then, we should make good use of the time we have."

Serazao Zulemem did not sleep at all on the last night the shipbound Circle members spent at Demaizen. Instead she worked at the desk in Garrod's study, with the star-chart and its display turned off and removed to a shelf, making certain that the Hall's legal status was in order. It would not do for some hitherto unknown, but litigious, offshoot of the sus-Demaizen family to make a sudden appearance while the Circle's acting First was out of touch.

Arekhon had only that afternoon handed over to her the necessary keys and passwords. She'd had a few sharp remarks for the occasion, concerning his dilatory habits and his irrational fondness for keeping secrets well past their useful date. Now she feared that Garrod's files would turn out to hold some disastrous matter which could not be resolved in time, and which would hang like a cloud over the divided Circle all during the long separation.

As the night wore on, however, it became clear that her worries were groundless. Garrod had taken good advice when he came into the sus-Demaizen inheritance, and had made provision in great detail for the Circle's continued welfare in case of his own death or disability. Extending those provisions to cover any problems caused by the absence of Arekhon and the others would not be difficult.

She was not aware of how long she had worked, checking out every detail and rearranging the material into an order more conformable with her own habits and training, until the sky outside the windows began to grow light. She heard a footstep on the stairs, and put aside the stack of data wafers to go see which of her fellow Mages was up so early.

It was Kief, heading down to the kitchen to start the *uffa* brewing for breakfast. "And fresh biscuits," he said. "Since I'm awake anyway."

She fell in beside him. "I'll help—if I go to bed now I'll only have to get right out again."

"You were up all night?"

"I knew I wouldn't be able to sleep," she said. "So I spent the time going over the Hall accounts, just in case."

The kitchen was still dark. Kief turned on the overhead fixture as they entered, filling the long, high-ceilinged space with clear white light reflected off of spotless metal. The brewing urn sat in coppery majesty on the bare counter; Kief rinsed it out and filled it with clean water. Serazao pulled the leaf canister out of storage.

Kief shook his head. "The little packet. In the jar there."

She put back the big canister and took out the smaller one. "Why this stuff?"

"It's 'Rekhe's private stash. He likes it red, and he doesn't get it that way very often. So, for a send-off—" Kief shrugged. "Why not?"

She measured out enough of the curly dark leaf to make a full brewing, and poured it into the filter. Leaving the urn to heat, she turned back to Kief.

"Are you sorry not to be going?" she asked. "I know what holds me on Eraasi, and I can make a guess about Del, but what keeps you?"

"I don't know," Kief said, scooping out biscuit flour from the bin as he spoke. There was a careful quietness to his voice that Serazao found disturbing. "The *eiran*, maybe—when we made the division, they were all I could see, growing over the Hall like vines, with me and you and Delath and Garrod all tangled up in them together. The more I tried to work my way free of them, the tighter they pulled."

"It sounds frightening."

"I've been places I liked more." He took the salt-box down from the shelf, and paused a moment with measuring spoon at the ready to look at her across the kitchen. "I don't suppose you saw anything similar?"

"No," Serazao told him honestly. "I didn't see anything like that at all. Only the Hall and Garrod, and the windows full of light. So I knew that I was to stay."

The journey from Demaizen to Hanilat took most of a day by groundcar, even when the roads were clear. The members of Garrod's Circle who were bound for the sus-Peledaen ship *Rain-on-Dark-Water* left the Hall first thing in the morning, when the sun was coming up and turning the clouds in the east bright red.

They had time for one last round of farewells, with all the Circle members crowded awkwardly into the converted out-building that served as the Hall's garage—quick, silent embraces, after everything to say had been said and said again. Then the four who were going took their places inside the heavy vehicle and closed the doors. The engine grumbled to life and the groundcar pulled away, out of the garage and down the long gravel drive to the road. Narin was steering; Arekhon had yielded the first turn to her in exchange for navigating the vehicle later through the intricacies of downtown Hanilat.

Arekhon resisted the urge to turn his head for a last glimpse of the Hall as the road curved away. He was the Second of the Circle, the First in all but name, and he needed to set an example for the Mages traveling with him—looking forward, not back.

Ty was the first to speak, several minutes later when the Hall was well behind them and the groundcar was purring down the open highway. "The other side of the galaxy."

"Figuratively speaking," Arekhon said. "More like the middle, if you want to be accurate. Still, it's no place we've ever been."

"Unknown waters," said Narin. "And we're the chart."

"You could say that."

Silence descended again for several minutes. Arekhon thought, from the sound of their regular, even breathing, that one or both of the rear-seat passengers had fallen asleep, but Ty surprised him by speaking again.

"I've never been on a spaceship."

"Not even in school?" So Vai hadn't been asleep either. She sounded curious, but not excessively so—a good tone, Arekhon thought, for soothing tight nerves and drawing out confidences from the reticent.

At any rate, it seemed to work for Ty. "We were supposed to go visit one at the port," he said. "But I was in some kind of trouble and didn't get to go."

"Somebody probably told you that you'd be sorry for it one day, too," said Narin. "And you probably didn't believe them."

"I was sorry for it right then. But I wasn't going to tell them so."

Vai chuckled. "Well, I'd say you came out ahead in the long run. You're not just wandering through with a guided tour—you're part of the show."

Arekhon said to her, "You sound like you've been off-planet a time or two yourself."

"To high orbit a few times," she said. "And once to Rayamet. Part of my job."

"Passenger?"

"Mostly. But I've got the emergency qualifications, just in case."

Narin made a skeptical noise. "Interesting work you must have done."

"It paid the bills."

"Good enough," said Arekhon. "But you'll need to report those qualifications to Captain sus-Mevyan once we're aboard—keep the ship's records up to date." He turned slightly in his seat, so that he could look at all three of the others at the same time. "Does anybody else have emergency qualifications like Vai's . . . or anything like them that I ought to know about?"

Ty shook his head, and Vai spread out her empty hands in a gesture that could have meant almost anything. Narin said, "I can repair a marine engine, and find my way on the ocean by the stars and the shape of the waves, and by the smell of the wind in a pinch—but I don't think any of those things are going to do Captain sus-Mevyan any good."

"Report them all anyway," Arekhon told her. "Unknown waters, as you said. You never know what may come in handy."

With half the Circle gone, the Old Hall was full of silence and unexpected shadows. It was the turn of Delath and Serazao to waken Garrod, to clean him and get him ready for the day, a task they would be sharing with Kiefen Diasul for however long it took for the rest of the Circle to make their journey and return.

Kief wasn't surprised that the other two Mages had been part of the half-Circle to remain at Demaizen: 'Zao still cherished the hope that some day she might see the First return to some kind of normal awareness; and whatever Del thought on that matter, he had proved to be as careful and reliable in tending Garrod as he had been in the Circle's workings. Kief was far less certain why he also had been chosen to remain.

He wandered through the empty rooms of the Hall: The dining room, the front entry, the kitchen—the breakfast dishes were stacked on the counter where 'Rekhe had put them before everyone went to the garage, so he moved them into the washer and started it cycling—down into the basement, with its warren of storerooms and the Circle's infirmary and the back way out to the gardens through the old root cellar—then around the Hall on the outside and in through the front.

Only minutes of time spent, and the rest of the Circle would be gone from Demaizen for . . . how long? His stargazer's knowledge let him make an estimate, and the answer was a depressing one. Years . . . years to stay at the Hall with an incapable First and a Second gone away into the Void, and nothing to do except work the luck. He saw himself as he had been in his vision, bound into the Hall by the silver network of the *eiran*, and laughed without humor.

"The luck of the Diasul."

He shivered as his words fell into the unnatural quiet of the Hall. He'd gotten a voice-message from his younger brother just yesterday, another one of Felan's long dull rambles about the family business, matters of buying and selling and who-did-whom-out-of-what that Kief found impossible to keep straight in his head.

He did remember that Felan had asked, as usual, for Kief's luck-intentions in the furtherance of some profit-making enterprise. Kief felt a stirring of anger, that his brother should be thinking about such petty matters in a time when men like Garrod were risking and losing all in an effort to remake the very galaxy.

Still, family was family. He would make the intentions for his brother—and for himself as well. For surely, if luck was needed for anyone involved in *Rain-on-Dark-Water*'s voyage of discovery, it was needed for the ones who stayed behind.

XXVI: Year 1124 E. R.
Entibor: Raske-by-the-Sea
Villa of Mestra Adina
Eraasian Space: sus-Peledaen
Orbital Docks

WHEN THE travelers came at last to Raske-by-the-Sea, Garrod's sense of foreboding deepened. The city—not one of the first importance, from the way his friends spoke of it—was at least twice the size of Hanilat. Everything about it seemed gleaming, new, and filled with wonders, things he had never seen on Eraasi: Fast-moving groundcars that hovered above the earth without touching it, like the armored vehicles he had encountered earlier on the road; immense, delicate-looking buildings that glittered in the sunlight like ice palaces caught in webs of metal; gaudy images in light and sound that unfolded from the pavement or danced across the sides of the impossible buildings.

The spectacle filled Garrod with a terrible fear. This world, clearly, was rich in natural resources, and existed at a higher technological level than any planet on the other side of the interstellar gap. Yet he'd learned from Hujerie's recent comments that Entibor was neither the richest nor the most powerful of the known worlds.

We have found them. What shall we do when they find us?
For a few minutes Garrod considered quietly vanishing, re-

turning to Eraasi and never mentioning this place at all. It would be safer all around—for him personally, and for Eraasi, which this world would snap up like a solstice-cake if the people here ever put their minds to it.

But he was Garrod the Explorer, and leaving a world unsurveyed and uncatalogued would not make it go away. *The danger has always been here,* he reminded himself. *We just didn't know about it until now.*

Neither Hujerie nor Saral paid the wonders around them any heed. Hujerie, in particular, seemed unimpressed by Raske's smooth rainbow-hued pavements, its gleaming towers, its multitude of booths and kiosks selling objects about whose use Garrod tried in vain to speculate. Instead, the former tutor walked through the city streets with a singleness of purpose and a near-quivering anticipation.

They came eventually to yet another kiosk, this one situated next to a broad tree-lined boulevard. Hujerie, looking pleased, placed his hand within a dark opening inside the kiosk, and a moment later turned back to Garrod.

"You have been our savior," he said. "Now it is our turn to show generosity, though it may be less than a hundredth of your own."

Garrod began an awkward speech of demurral—he could understand the spoken language fairly well by now, but constructing a sentence involving abstract concepts like friendship and gratitude still had the ability to slow his tongue. He was saved from having to finish his reply by the appearance of a shadow on the pavement. A moment later, with a scarce-heard whistling, an atmospheric craft descended to hover a few inches above the sidewalk.

The craft looked and sounded nothing like the flyers Garrod was familiar with on Eraasi. It was smooth, almost ovoid in shape, with bubbles like eyes on its forward end. The doors on either side opened upward, winglike, revealing a cozy interior with padded seats. Cool, sweet-smelling air washed out over the grimy and sweat-stained travelers like a friendly welcome.

They entered the craft, the doors swung down and closed, and a moment later pressure beneath his feet told Garrod that the vehicle was rising rapidly. A moment later, they were flying with incredible speed over the ocean. Dazzling sunlight reflected back at them from the waves below, its intensity mollified by the tinting of the flyer's windows.

"Safe at last," Saral said. She hugged Minnin, then held the baby out at arm's length, bouncing him until he crowed with delight. "Your mamma and dadda will be happy to see you again."

Soon enough the ocean was replaced by land, and the flyer came down to a smooth landing. Its doors once again lifted open, and the travelers stepped out onto a hillside covered with soft grass.

Something that looked like a ground vehicle waited nearby. A door on the vehicle's side slid open, and a woman—young and pretty, in a loose gown made of some shimmering fabric that shifted colors as she moved—jumped out. She ran across the grassy hillside to snatch Minnin from Saral's arms and hug him close.

"Come, come," the woman said, somewhat breathlessly—she was still hugging Minnin, and the baby didn't seem to know whether to be happy or distressed about it. "Teng will be so pleased. We scarcely dared hope, when your message came—"

She shooed them into the groundcar. The vehicle rose from the ground and shot forward in a way that made Garrod suspect it contained a counterforce unit of some kind—but one far more powerful than those which gave mobility to the *aik-eten* back home on Eraasi.

"Who is your friend?" the woman asked Hujerie, as soon as she had soothed the restive Minnin into quiet. She talked more rapidly than the older man, and with a different accent, so that Garrod hoped he was understanding her correctly.

"He is called Garrod," the old tutor said. "We owe our survival to him."

The woman turned to Garrod. "Then you are a friend to us as well. What did you do, Friend Garrod, before the war?"

Garrod hesitated a moment before answering. In this strange world—so advanced in some ways, and so primitive in others—it did not strike him as a good idea to announce outright, "I am a Mage."

Instead he told the woman, "I was a scholar"—at least, he

hoped that was what he had said, and the self-description was not completely untrue.

"Ah, Master Scholar Garrod," the woman said. "Welcome to our House."

Natelth sus-Khalgath stood in the observation box overlooking the cradle holding *Rain-on-Dark-Water.* The newly-finished deep-space explorer was ready for her long voyage, and all but the last few crew members had ridden the gondola up her curving side to the open hatch. When the hatch closed, the chamber would seal its air-tight doors and the last phase in the construction cycle would begin.

Family responsibility decreed that Natelth should be present for the occasion, in the company of the director of the sus-Peledaen orbital yard and half a dozen of its most senior ship-builders, all outer-family by adoption at least. And the first departure of a ship like the *Rain*—larger, more advanced in its design, and with a longer range than any of the existing vessels in the sus-Peledaen fleet—required more than Natelth's approving presence. Such a momentous occasion demanded his full participation in the speeches and festivities, all duly broadcast for the benefit of ordinary workers and family members currently enjoying their own, much less formal, celebration.

Natelth had expressed, for the record, the family's gratitude toward all the workers who had made the *Rain* into such an advancement on the fleet's existing design, and the family's unswerving confidence that her crew would find in her a swift journey to luck and glory. The shipyard director had thanked innumerable people without whom the *Rain* would not have reached her current state of perfection, and had enjoined the captain and crew to treat the new ship with the affection and respect which she deserved. Captain sus-Mevyan, speaking over voice-comm from the *Rain*'s bridge, had thanked the family and the shipyard alike for giving the ship into her hands, and had promised to care for the *Rain* like a sister.

Then the shipyard director poured out glasses of red wine all around, as Captain sus-Mevyan would be doing on the ship's bridge. Everyone spilled the ritual drops that would do courtesy to the spirits of the ship and of the orbital yard, as well as to any of the family's dead who might feel a connection with the venture.

All that remained was for the ship's Circle to go abroad. Natelth could see them, far down below on the cradle platform, four small figures in hooded black robes, standing together in an inward-facing huddle. Not much to look at—but without them, and their presence on this first voyage, Garrod's marker for the distant world was useless.

The director of the shipyard keyed on the voice-comm to the construction chamber. "Have you seen the luck of the voyage?"

The question was traditional: The Mages of a ship's Circle, being the last of the crew to go aboard, had a good vantage point from which to see all of the diverse luck-patterns that hung about a vessel. On a new-built ship the lines ought to be clear and untangled . . . but Natelth fancied that there was a moment's pause before Arekhon's voice came back, not loud but quite distinct all the same.

"The voyage is fortunate. We see the lines going forth and coming back again."

"Are you ready to board?"

Another pause. The distant figures on the platform appeared to consult one another briefly. Arekhon's voice came over the speaker again.

"We are ready."

"Board her, then," said the shipyard director; and, a few moments later, "Gondola away."

The gondola began its slow ascent to the open hatch. When it reached the top, the four tiny figures that were Arekhon's half of the Demaizen Circle walked across the hair-thin bridge to the hatch and passed into the ship. The bridge retracted into the belly of the gondola, the hatch closed, and the gondola descended.

"Prepare to evacuate the compartment," said the shipyard director.

The lighting in the construction area began shifting back and forth between its normal spectrum and an intense, disquieting amber, and the long, repeated bellow of an alarm horn penetrated even the heavy glass of the observation booth. The alarm and the flashing lights went on for several minutes—

long enough for anyone caught in the construction area by accident to find an exit and depart.

"Cycle to vacuum," said the director.

More minutes passed as the orbital yard reclaimed its atmosphere from the sealed compartment. The director turned to Natelth.

"My lord, if you would give the words of release . . ."

"I would be honored." Natelth stepped up to the voice-comm. "She is sus-Peledaen's *Rain-on-Dark-Water*. Send her away."

With a heavy, vibrating groan, the walls of the area outside the observation box parted. The *Rain*'s construction cradle fell away in segments like the opening petals of a gigantic metal flower, revealing black space and the stars beyond. Slowly but inexorably, the vast matte-black bulk of the explorer ship fell free of its orbital birthplace, slipping away from Natelth and the other watchers and receding into the emptiness that was her natural home.

Another moment—her engines flared crimson—and she was gone.

Over the course of the next several days, Garrod learned much—through listening and observation—about the state of political affairs on the world he had discovered. The government was fragmented into a number of geopolitical entities, ranging in size from a handful of small islands to the greater part of a continent, caught up in a web of treaties and personal agreements so complex that Garrod made no effort to untangle them. He wasn't certain that the native Entiborans understood them, either; otherwise there wouldn't have been so much argument on the subject.

Apparently nobody had been expecting a tricky diplomatic situation to break out into open and general war—though why it shouldn't have done so was another thing that Garrod didn't try to understand. He took advantage of the confusion to pick out a fictitious homeland for himself, settling on a district half the world away from his current situation, and one that had been overrun twice already by different armies. Most of the public buildings on the Immering coast had already been destroyed, and the records they'd housed were gone along with them. It wouldn't surprise anyone to learn that Master Scholar Garrod's biographical data had also vanished. With luck—and under the circumstances, he would not hesitate to make all the luck for himself that he could—no natives of the area would turn up and start addressing him in a language he didn't understand.

For the moment, at least, his aid to Saral and Hujerie had won him a place in the entourage of Mestra Adina Therras, as baby Minnin's mother was formally known. The Therras family was one of several maneuvering for control of the local government—the entire area involved wasn't as big as the Wide Hills District back on Eraasi, but that didn't seem to have deterred anybody so far—and Mestra Adina welcomed the chance to expand her House's roster of clients and protégées.

"Appearances," Hujerie explained to Garrod, "are everything, especially when the world is so unsettled. For the Mestra to have taken a foreign scholar under her protection is very impressive."

Garrod thought privately that the Mestra and her fellow petty-nobles would have done better to give up impressing each other, and concentrate instead on keeping their pocket-sized state away from destruction. But in the meantime, the Mestra's ambition was providing him with room and board and at least temporary safety—though he kept his pack loaded and ready in case he should have to leave on short notice.

A little over a week, by Garrod's Eraasian reckoning, from the time of his arrival at the Mestra's villa, the Therras family gave a party to celebrate Minnin's safe return. Saral and Hujerie were among the honored guests; and so was the newest member of the Therras household, the distinguished foreigner who had been so helpful to them.

Garrod had attended other parties where the force behind the occasion wasn't pleasure but ambition, and he knew what was expected. His part was to wear the locally made clothing that the Mestra's servants produced for him, and to make labored conversation with her guests in what passed for an Immering accent. It wouldn't fool a genuine Immeringer for a moment, of course . . . but his luck was still holding. There was nobody at the Mestra's party from that far away.

The evening was a tiring one: Too many people in too small a room, speaking too loud and too fast in a language he only imperfectly understood. Garrod felt washed over by waves of data-laden conversation that he would have to record and sort out later. He didn't like the music either, though the trio of instrumentalists were clearly skilled and expensive; the scales they used had too many notes in them, and their alien harmonies put his nerves on edge. He drank Mestra Adina's weak punch and wished he had some of Hujerie's liquor from the road to enliven the bowl.

The liquor was not forthcoming, but Hujerie must have caught something from his expression. The Entiboran scholar came up to him and said, "You have spoken with the Mestra's friends all evening . . . let me bring you someone more to your liking."

The scholar disappeared into the press of people and emerged a few minutes later with a plain-looking man in a tunic and trousers of drab black. The man carried what appeared to be a tall walking-staff of some kind, though he had no hesitation or limp in his gait that would make him need to use one.

"Master Scholar Garrod," said Hujerie, "it gives me pleasure to introduce Master Drey of the Cazdel Guildhouse. Drey's studied on Galcen, but he isn't one of the ones who've forgotten what world they came from in the first place."

Garrod let the unfamiliar concepts go over him like an incoming tide . . . when the water receded, he would see what new information it had left behind.

"Master Drey," he said, after Hujerie had departed. "Are you another ornament for the Mestra's party?"

Drey laughed. "You have good eyes for a foreigner, Master Garrod. We're both decorations, here to give solidity to an ambitious House. Adina likes to think she has the Guild behind her. Or likes others to think so, at least."

"Hujerie said you studied on Galcen."

"For a while, yes," said Drey.

"What was it like? I myself never had the good luck, you understand, to study anywhere but Immering."

"Galcen would go hard with you, then," said Drey. "They never speak of luck there at all, even as a joke, in case speaking about the flow of the universe should pull it out of its true course. A bit extreme, in my opinion, but good for discipline if you don't take it too far."

"We certainly don't want to do that," agreed Garrod. He filled his glass again with the Mestra's punch and drained it off in one long swallow, to disguise the fact that his mind was still struggling to make sense of what Drey had said.

No luck . . . they don't believe in luck. How does their world manage to exist at all, if there's no one willing to work the eiran *for it?*

XXVII: Year 1126 E. R.
Eraasi: Hanilat Starport
The Interstellar Gap: sus-Peledaen
ship RAIN-ON-DARK-WATER

U NLIKE SOME of his rivals in the game of interstellar trade, Theledau syn-Grevi preferred to
make a distinction, whenever such a distinction was possible,
between his home and the working world. The head of the
sus-Radal fleet-family ran its business affairs from a downtown
building, not from the town house he had only reluctantly
consented to occupy.

In the time just before dawn, Hanilat had not yet put on its
mid-day grubbiness, and the tall, many-windowed buildings of
the central metropolis had the appearance of polished crystals
under the slanting light of early morning. The clean, spare
elegance of the deserted urban landscape was one of the reasons Thel preferred coming in at this hour, before the crowds
and traffic claimed the city for another day.

Away to the south the vapor trail of a lifting ship turned
pink as the rising sun caught its passage. That would be
Swiftly-Through-Starlight, carrying house-mind sub-units to
Ruisi in the hopes of trading them for offworld spices and
organic medicinals—a long trip, but a good profit if no mis-
chance intervened. One ship running alone wasn't as safe as

a convoy, but the gain in speed was worth the risk for a perishable cargo.

The desk behind him chimed. "Yes?" he said without turning.

"One comes," said the desk. "A representative of Hanilat and Eraasi, to speak with the head of the sus-Radal."

Thel abandoned the view of the city and faced the office door. Musing on beauty and profit brought no one closer to either. Sooner or later, it was necessary to act.

"Let him enter."

The door opened to admit a stout, well-groomed man in an expensively tailored rambling-jacket. Thel recognized him at once as Kerin Feyal of the Hanilat Feyals. Feyal was dressed for a friendly meeting rather than for an occasion of business; Thel supposed that the early hour would lend verisimilitude to the fiction that one of the city's most active political go-betweens had merely stopped by the sus-Radal office tower on his way to a day in the country.

Not that Thel believed it himself for a moment. "Syr Feyal," he said, after he had waved his guest to a chair beside the window and taken one for himself nearby. "What brings you here on such a fine morning?"

"Lord sus-Radal," Feyal said. His manner was full of warm sincerity with a touch of deference, and Thel didn't believe that for a moment either.

Feyal was a legalist by training, from one of Hanilat's oldest families—too proud of their city roots and long respectability, some said, to feel the need for a noble prefix before their name. Theledau suspected that the Feyals viewed the sus-Radal as upstarts, and Thel's own syn-Grevi line as mere provincial interlopers. "The turning of the seasons reminded me that it had been too long since I'd last had the pleasure of your company. And since I chanced to be passing by your offices when the thought struck me—"

"Get to the point, Ker," said Thel. He wasn't on short-name terms with his visitor, strictly speaking, but it wouldn't hurt to jar Feyal a little. "There's no one here to fool but me, and I know you better than that."

Feyal remained unruffled. "So you do. Let's talk of business, then. The matter that concerns me—that concerns all of us—is the piracy that increasingly disrupts Eraasian commerce on certain trade lines. You have suffered yourself, I believe, from the attacks of these deep-space bandits."

"On occasion," Thel said. Feyal hadn't seen fit to mention what everyone knew: That most of the bandits wore the colors of respectable fleet-families. *Deep space belongs to no one,* or so the proverb ran, and trade went to whoever was bold enough to take it. Thel knew of at least one family that had gotten its start by raiding the established fleets, and he would bet good money that they were among the loudest complainers now. "We all suffer losses now and again."

"True. What would you say, then, to making the sus-Radal part of a coalition of traders and shipowners organized to counter the threat?"

Thel gazed out the window for a moment. The sun was hitting the upper ledges and cornices of the buildings now, where the glass and metal trim glittered like ice. "I might say yes," he said, after a suitable interval had passed. He looked back at Feyal before the man could say anything in reply, and added, "Or I might not. How many people have already joined this coalition of yours?"

"Natelth sus-Khalgath, for one. Also syn-Veru and syn-Kaseget—"

"If the head of the sus-Peledaen wants to stop his share of piracy," Thel said, "all he needs to do is pass the word on to his captains."

Feyal looked amused. "I've heard the same thing from other sources. But the names were different . . . and one of the names was yours."

It was time, Thel decided, to take offense. "I have trouble believing that you showed up at this hour just to play games with me. What do you really want, Ker?"

"Only to speak the truth," said Feyal, all good will and transparent candor. As Thel expected, his next sentence had the hook in it. "They do say, in some quarters, that your captains cross well over the line of what is acceptable. What better way to prove that the raiders aren't yours, than by helping to curb them?"

What better way, indeed? Theledau thought. *I wonder who thought up this scheme—an old family that doesn't need to*

*take cargoes any longer, or a new family that doesn't have
the resources to seize ships and protect them at the same time?*

Aloud, he said, "Such things aren't done by talk alone.
Who's going to command this agency of correction?"

"That," said Feyal, "is something that remains unsettled until we know for certain which of the families have pledged
their support. But even those who mistrust the sus-Radal admit
that your fleet is well-officered."

First the hook, Thel noted without surprise, and then the
bait. "I could say the same in return about half a dozen others,"
he said. "This 'support' that you mentioned . . . what form are
you expecting it to take? My name on a list, my voice in
debate, money—?"

"Ships and crews."

"When?"

"As soon as they can be built for the purpose."

Theledau forced himself to lean back in his chair as if he
were considering an ordinary business proposition, and not a
proposal so radical that its originators—whoever they might
be—had managed to keep its development secret even from
the fleet-families themselves.

Maybe it didn't start with one of us after all, he thought.
*We like things the way they are, mostly; this comes from some-
one whose interest lies in forcing a change.*

"You're talking," he said, after a moment spent in deliberate
contemplation of the sky outside the window, "about starships
designed from the cradle for offensive operations."

"Essentially, yes."

"My ships carry cargo," Theledau said after another long
pause. "Or they protect the ships that carry cargo. A ship built
to do nothing but hunt other ships has no place in a merchant
fleet."

"Then you are unwilling to support the coalition?"

"The last time anybody built warships on Eraasi," Theledau
said, "they sailed on blue water. We should leave the things
of the past where they belong, and not bring them forward
without cause."

Feyal gave a faint sigh, and stood. "I won't make myself
tedious by pressuring you to act against your will. The morning draws on, I'm afraid, and I have an engagement to keep.

Do keep our conversation in mind, however, in case you reconsider your position."

"I certainly shall," Theledau said, rising also.

He escorted Syr Feyal to the door and made the necessary polite farewells. Then, as soon as the door was shut again and Feyal was safely away, he went back to his desk and pressed the button that would summon his primary assistant.

"Summon the family's best designers and engineers," he said as soon as the assistant appeared in the doorway. "Tell them to make us warships. Secretly, but quickly."

Rain-on-Dark-Water had been in the Void for a long time.

First transits were always lengthy ones, as the ship drove through nothingness toward a point that existed only as a Mage's marker in the featureless Void. Arekhon knew that the ship's crew on such a transit looked to the Mages aboard for signals that all was well, and he was glad that the members of his half-Circle remained steady.

Ty was young enough to find the experience of space travel entertaining all by itself, and to form casual friendships among the apprentices and the junior crew. Narin spent most of her time in practice and meditation, and the rest of it in trading stories with the repair crews and the cargo-handlers. And Vai . . . as far as Arekhon could tell, nothing ever knocked Iulan Vai off-center.

Like the rest of the Circle-Mages, Vai bunked with the *Rain*'s regular crew. Arekhon, as the acting First, found his separate cabin to be a lonely one. He understood her reasoning—the crewmembers weren't likely to understand that in the Circles, distinctions of rank meant something other than what they were used to. He'd even been ready, more or less, for Vai's apparent desertion.

He hadn't expected that Elaeli would do the same.

She had explained herself to him, half-apologetically, in the last hour together they had made for themselves before the *Rain*'s departure. He was sus-Peledaen, as well as the acting First of the ship's Circle; she was known to have come into the outer family under his sponsorship. It would not look good—it would look very bad, in fact—if the two of them were seen to be lovers as well.

"On a trading voyage it might not matter," she'd said. "But this is going to be different."

"It's all right," he said untruthfully. "I understand."

His cabin was cold during the night watches, and the transit seemed to go on forever. He worried about the rest of the Circle, back home on Eraasi, and slept uneasily.

When Captain sus-Mevyan sent word that the acting First was wanted for emergence from the Void, Arekhon was ready. The call came during ship's night, when temperatures were lowered and lighting dimmed, and the *Rain* kept a minimal crew on station. On the bridge, the illusory grey mists of the Void swirled beyond the armored windows. Captain sus-Mevyan waited at the nearest, and beckoned for Arekhon to join her.

"It's time," she said. "Now we see if our calculations were any good."

Arekhon nodded. This was always the tricky point on a blind voyage. The distance to a new system couldn't be determined exactly from the marker on a star-chart . . . only inferred, based on comparison with known distances on the same chart, and on the stargazers' uncertain measurements.

"I see no reason we shouldn't drop out," he said.

"Do you want to give the order, for luck?"

"This is your ship, Captain."

"So it is," agreed sus-Mevyan. She didn't change expression, but he could tell that the courtesy pleased her. She turned to where Elaeli stood at the Pilot's station—like the First of the ship's Circle, the ship's Pilot-Principal had been called up because of the solemnity of the moment—and said, "Stand by for dropout."

"Dropout on time," Elaeli said, her face downbent and her eyes on the glowing screen beside her watch station. Letters and numerals shifted from purple to amber and back again, making a play of color against her face. "Stand by, on my mark. Mark."

Over the speakers, the *Rain*'s chief engineer echoed her from the engine-rooms, "Emerging from Void-transit."

The resultant discontinuity passed over the ship, making Arekhon shudder. He wondered what sort of dreams the off-watch sleepers were having. Then the grey mist outside the heavy windows turned to blackness lit by glitter and spangles.

"Stars showing," said Elaeli, reciting her own part of the checklist. "Checking position against calculated."

"Negative scan on light-speed modulated frequencies," added the crewmember at the *Rain*'s communications board. "No one's talking. We're alone out here."

sus-Mevyan scowled. "There should be some noise," she said. "Pilot-Principal—light off the star-chart. Let me see Garrod's Star."

"Star-chart up." Another console glowed to life, and the familiar chart arose in the air above it. sus-Mevyan stepped over to it, and Elaeli joined her. The two of them gazed at the chart for a moment without saying anything.

Then sus-Mevyan said, "Pilot-Principal—show the *Rain*'s distance from Eraasi, based on inertial."

"*Rain-on-Dark-Water* reference up."

A bright red sigil appeared on the chart, in the middle of the dark area beyond the Edge. The mark was halfway between the white glow of Garrod's Star and the green-yellow-black mottling of Eraasi. "Not quite halfway," Captain sus-Mevyan said. "And we've already expended half our fuel, less our exploration and safety margins."

She paused. "Pilot-Principal, lay in a return track to Eraasi."

"Captain," said Arekhon, in a low, urgent voice. "We've come this far—"

"I will not endanger this ship and its crew by taking it on another blind jump to nowhere."

"Half the fuel is enough to get us where we're going," Arekhon said. "And we still have the exploration and safety reserves. We can get fuel at Garrod's Star if we have to."

"How?" sus-Mevyan demanded.

He pointed to the glowing white dot. "The marker. It says that this star is a class one system, which means abundant resources, refined and available. It's bigger and brighter than anything else on the chart."

sus-Mevyan looked unconvinced. "The plans for this voyage were based on—what? Old charts interpreted by an obsolete house-mind? If they're wrong—starvation is a dreadful way to die."

"We have luck. The Circle has seen to it."

"Only a fool trusts to luck alone," sus-Mevyan told him. "Do you take me for a fool?"

Elaeli looked up from the star-chart and touched sus-Mevyan lightly on the arm. "Captain," she said. "A word with you in private?"

Arekhon stood silent as Elaeli and the captain withdrew into the passage outside the bridge. He was glad, he supposed, that Ela had not come to his cabin, or he to hers, since the voyage began. She would never have dared to take his part otherwise, even though a ship's pilot-principal had the right to give the captain advice on such matters.

A few minutes later Elaeli and sus-Mevyan returned. The Captain looked noncommittal as always. Elaeli, walking a pace behind her, carefully avoided looking in Arekhon's direction when the Captain asked him, "You're certain about the fuel at the far end?"

"I am," Arekhon said firmly.

sus-Mevyan gazed out at the jeweled darkness for a long time. Finally she said, "Pilot-Principal, shape course for Garrod's Star. And prepare a message drone for release on a homebound course. Give the fleet all our survey data from this emergence. Whatever happens, we've already put more new space on the charts than any ship in the past hundred years."

It had taken Kerin Feyal several months to finish making all of his visits; the meeting with Theledau syn-Grevi sus-Radal had been the last. Such things, as he had been at pains to explain to the League of Unallied Shippers when they requested his assistance as a go-between, could not be hurried. Hurry made one conspicuous, and to become conspicuous, under such circumstances, would be fatal.

Feyal had, accordingly, contrived—in chance encounters, or in the odd minutes of boring civic occasions—and when the last of his word was done, he returned to the League offices in downtown Hanilat feeling pleased with the results. The great lords, one by one, had received him cordially, heard him out, and promised him nothing. And all of them, he was certain, had gone instantly into consultations with their closest associates, and begun issuing orders.

The atmosphere within the fleet-families these days was un-

settled and suspicious, though no one could say with assurance
what was the reason. Outside the families one heard more and
more the murmuring of discontent and a desire for change.
The League of Unallied Shippers, Feyal thought, had every
reason to be happy with his work.

His contact within the League, Seyo Hannet, was waiting
for him in the second-floor office suite, leaning against the
wall by the brewing urn and drinking red *uffa* from a paper
cup. The suite was empty except for the two men; the
League's clerks and data-workers would not be coming in for
another hour yet. Hannet preferred this time of day for their
meetings, as did Feyal—lower-tier personnel might not know
or care about the League's true long-term goals, but they had
been known to gossip with people who did. The fewer people
who could tie the League's public face with its private one,
the better for everybody.

"How did this one go, Ker?" Hannet asked.

"As we expected." Feyal took a cup from the dispenser and
drew himself some of the cheap, strong red, noting as he did
so that there was a sealed envelope lying atop the urn. "Theledau didn't say anything, but he took the bait."

"You're certain?"

"He couldn't afford not to. He was the last one . . . and if
the fleet-families were suspicious of each other before, they're
probably twice as suspicious now."

Hannet smiled. "Oh, they are. You've done excellent work,
Ker—and the League is not ungrateful." He glanced over at
the envelope as he spoke, and nodded slightly.

"It was my pleasure," Feyal insisted. He picked up the envelope without looking at it and slipped it into one of the
pockets of his rambling-jacket. "I don't want to rush this conversation, but I do have to go soon. Half a dozen families are
convinced that I'm going to be spending the next month or so
at a country house-party, and I mustn't disappoint the agents
they've got following me."

"Were you followed here?" Hannet asked.

"Of course."

"Then I think I'll wait until you're well away before I go.
No point in coming so far only to have them connect us now.

You'll be hearing from the League again soon anyway—this game has only begun."

"Until the next round, then." Feyal drained the rest of his *uffa* and tossed the cup into the trash. Then he headed back down to the street where his groundcar waited.

Hannet remained behind, nursing his cup of red and counting quietly to himself. Feyal would be coming out onto the street . . . standing at the door of his groundcar . . . settling in behind the controls . . . and activating the engine. . . .

Now.

The sound of the explosion reached even the back room on the second floor where the League of Unallied Shippers had its offices.

Hannet toasted the late Feyal with the dregs of his *uffa*. "Our apologies, Ker—but your spectacular demise will definitely cause talk among the fleet-families."

XXVIII:

AREKHON LEFT the bridge while Elaeli and sus-Mevyan were going over the finer points of the next transit and drop-out. He thought of returning to his cabin, but knew that he wouldn't be able to sleep. The last few minutes had been too unsettling for that. They had committed the ship—*no,* he told himself, *be honest; you have committed the ship*—to completing the outbound leg of her journey without a known source of fuel for the return.

He wondered if he should call together the members of the Circle for a working, but decided against it. The time for a working would come later, when the vessel prepared to emerge from the Void for the second time. In the end, for lack of any place better to go, he went to the small observation chamber that also served as a wardroom for the ship's officers. Nobody was there, and the steel shutters were down and locked, but the big copper *uffa* pot still had hot drink in it—the pale kind, but better than nothing.

He filled a mug and sat down to drink it. Before he had quite finished, however, the door to the observation deck opened and admitted Iulan Vai. She was dressed in her usual off-duty clothes, plain black without decoration—much like her on-duty clothes, except that their fabric and cut paid somewhat more attention to matters of style.

"I felt the drop-out," she said. "How was it?"

"Uneventful." He took a last swallow of the *uffa* and set the mug down on a side table. "Except that the distance calculations were off."

"Badly?"

"Bad enough—we don't have enough fuel left to get home with what's on board. We'll be picking up more when we reach Garrod's Star."

"If there's any there."

"There will be. Garrod wouldn't have marked the star for us otherwise."

"It's a big risk for Captain sus-Mevyan to take on your say-so." She paused. "What did the Pilot-Principal have to say about it?"

Arekhon picked up his abandoned mug and looked into the bottom of it . . . still empty. He stood up and drifted back over to the *uffa* pot, where he could busy himself pulling another round.

"She advised in favor of going on."

"Because she thought it was a good idea?" Vai asked. "Or because you did?"

With his back turned, he couldn't see Vai's face. Her voice didn't sound angry, though; just coolly interested in a piece of information. It would have been better, he thought, if she'd been angry.

He kept his attention on the burnished copper side of the *uffa* pot. If he moved slightly, he could see Vai's reflection in the red-brown metal. As far as he could tell, she hadn't moved, and her posture was as uninflected as her voice.

"Why do you ask?"

"She was your lover while you were apprenticed," Vai said. A statement of fact, not an accusation. "And afterward, from time to time."

"Yes," he said. There was no point in denying it; shipboard rumor would give him the lie if he tried. "What does that have to do—"

"Would it make her advise against her better judgment?"

"For my sake? Not likely."

He thought he heard a faint snort of what might have been laughter. "You underestimate yourself, if you think that no one would."

"Elaeli Inadi syn-Peledaen"—he gave Vai Ela's full name, for emphasis, though he didn't turn back around—"intends to run the whole fleet some day, and she's willing to take risks to get there. Maybe she's a bit more willing to gamble on my good luck than a stranger would be, I don't know. But nothing more than that."

"So our lives rest on your luck and her judgment."

"And the Captain's choice. sus-Mevyan would know the fleet gossip as well as you do."

She didn't answer. He saw her reflected image move away from the polished copper of the *uffa* pot, and turned, finally, to keep her in view.

"Vai—!" he said.

But the door was already shutting itself behind her, and she was gone.

He stood for a moment looking at the closed door, then collapsed into one of the empty chairs and rubbed his face wearily with both hands. That had not gone well . . . foolish, to think that he could have both Vai and Elaeli in his life at the same time, and not face the consequences.

If he went back to his cabin now, he wouldn't sleep. Meditation, in his current frame of mind, didn't appeal to him, though he knew that it should. He might as well stay here in the observation chamber, and wait out the hours until ship's morning. He closed his eyes and let himself go wandering among the isolated landscapes of his waking dreams, until sleep came to him at last where he sat.

Garrod stood in the center of his room at the villa belonging to Mestra Adina Therras. The pack he had brought with him from Eraasi lay on the polished stone floor at his feet. He wore a fur-trimmed robe around his shoulders, red cloth with a gold stitchery pattern—the first cold snap of winter had come that morning, with frost on the ground outside, and the Mestra hadn't wanted her visiting foreigner to suffer from the chill.

The ceiling of his room was a dome of clear glass. *Like a*

north-country devotional, he thought, although his hosts didn't know what one of those was. They knew he studied the stars—Hujerie had spoken of his observations, taken every night during their trek from the occupied hinterland to the relative safety of Raske-by-the-Sea—and so had given him a room they thought he would find congenial.

These Entiborans were a thoughtful people, for all that they wasted their energy on warfare and refused to cultivate their world's *eiran* as they should. It would be hard to leave.

Still, leave he must. His observations were done. He knew where this world was, and he could show others the way. The star-lords would send out their merchant fleets along the path that he had marked for them, and the lives of Hujerie and Saral and Minnin and Mestra Adina and all the others would never be the same again.

Or perhaps—he paused, with one hand at the collar of his robe—perhaps it would be Eraasi that would change irrevocably. The worlds on this side of the gap already had space flight, and already had their own network of trading partners. Even Garrod's rough list of locally-known worlds, culled from idle talk and indirect questioning, had more names on it than there were open planets on the far side of the interstellar gap. And the Entiborans' knowledge of the physical universe, and their manipulation of its structures, was beyond anything that he could do or had seen done at home.

Perhaps it would be better for Eraasi if he never mentioned what he had seen or where he had gone.

He took off the robe and hung it over the back of a chair, as if he would return soon. He felt sorry for his friends, the new ones he had made; they would wonder what had become of him. Perhaps there would be a search, and the suspicion of foul play. He hoped that nobody here would suffer any indignities as a result.

He put on the Eraasian clothing that he had worn when he first came to this world. His notes on Entibor's location were already sealed away, encrypted and hidden inside the metal frame of his pack. Once he returned to Eraasi he would find another place for them—one from which only he could retrieve them—and he would leave them there until he decided what it was that he should do.

He could already foresee spending a month or more in meditation to determine if this was a secret he could share. It would be easy enough just to go home and tell the Circle that he had been wrong, that they were alone in the universe. No one would ever know that he had lied.

No one except him. And if the *eiran* were already drawing Entibor and Eraasi closer together, keeping them apart might require more luck than even his Circle would be able to give.

He shrugged his pack onto his back and set out. The grey mist of the Void encompassed him, chilling him after the warmth of his room, and tendrils of fog floated up around his feet. He fixed his Circle in his mind, and set out walking.

The road between Eraasi and Entibor was a long one, but the way back would be easier than the journey out. The homeworld was marked out clearly in the Void; it was the beginning and the end-point of all his other journeys, and the journeys of the Void-walkers who had come before him. He'd needed a Great Working and the luck of his Circle to find a habitable world so far away from Eraasi. His own luck should be enough to take him back.

The first part of the walk was uneventful, though in the Void the creatures of a mind's nightmares could take on shape to strike against the unwary. Imagination placed monsters in the fog—monsters which Garrod forced himself to not think of, lest his thoughts call them to being. Nothing rose out of the fog to menace him.

Thoughts of monsters gave way to other thoughts as the cold sapped his strength and the barren mist wrapped itself about him. He pondered yet again the wisdom of telling his Circle what he had learned of the worlds beyond the Farther Edge. The people of Eraasi, and the star-lords in particular, would be less than pleased to find out that they were not, in fact, the richest and most sophisticated in the galaxy.

He had almost decided that ignorance might not be so bad when, between one step and another, an icy pain shot upward through his legs, and a deep rumbling sound filled the grey non-substance of the Void. At the same time he felt the sudden nearness of his Circle, though Demaizen Old Hall was half a galaxy and a different order of reality away.

Called by my thought? he asked himself. *Or another illusion of the Void?*

A moment later he felt a jab of awareness—*They are here!*—and twisted again to follow it to its source, taking himself through the particular angle that separated the Void from all places and all times. The physical universe rushed back in, and he found himself standing at a juncture in a labyrinth of cold steel halls lit by tubed lighting. A placard set at eye level on one of the metal panels warned him—in Eraasian script— of Critical Controls Beneath.

He was aboard one of the star-lords' vessels, then. Something must have gone wrong at the Hall, to bring him out of the Void so far from his goal. He would have to find the ship's bridge and announce his arrival. He was known to the fleet-families; they would recognize Garrod the Explorer and put him in touch with his Circle.

No, he thought, as the nearness of the Demaizen Circle struck at him again. This time he knew what the feeling meant, though he didn't yet understand how it had happened.

The Circle is already aboard.

He changed direction, heading away from the ship's bridge. He would find his Circle first, and determine what had gone amiss in his absence—why he could sense Arekhon's personality in the mix of impressions from the Mages aboard, but not Yuvaen's. Had the Great Working demanded so much from them? And if it had, then what were they doing here?

So it was that he came to the vessel's observation room, its steel shutters closed against the unsettling presence of the nothingness outside, and saw the Third of his Circle asleep on a chair, head tilted back, looking careworn even in repose.

Garrod took a seat facing the sleeper, and waited for him to wake.

Arekhon woke with a start, realizing as he did so that he was no longer alone in the observation chamber.

"Vai?" he said uncertainly.

"No."

His eyes snapped open at the sound of the other's voice. "Garrod! But—"

He caught himself before he could say more. The Garrod

who sat in the chair opposite him was not the aged and incapable man who had returned to Demaizen Old Hall from his
journey through the Void. In appearance this Garrod was
scarcely older than he had appeared at the start of the great
working, and his eyes under their heavy brows were penetrating and alert.

*In the Void, all places and times are one . . . he is here now,
because he is not yet there then. . . .*

Garrod broke the silence at last. "What are you doing here,
'Rekhe? Why aren't you at the Hall?" He paused. "And what
day and year is this?"

"Fifth Cedras, 1126," Arekhon told him. *He knows that
something isn't right, that he isn't where he intended to be.*
"A lot of things happened after you left."

Garrod's eyebrows twitched. "I can see that. Do you care
to be more specific?"

"You went into the Void, and you returned," Arekhon said,
choosing his words carefully. How much of Garrod's future
the First of Demaizen needed to know, or should know, was
nothing Arekhon wanted to decide in a hurry. For now, caution
was best. "Then we set out—using the information you gave
us—to find a world beyond the Edge."

The First of Demaizen, unfortunately, had never been an
easy man to divert from his purpose. "There are things about
this," Garrod said, "that you are not telling me. I didn't return,
not until now. Perhaps you were hoaxed—"

"By whom?" demanded Arekhon, giving up on subtlety.
Garrod syn-Aigal was First of the Circle; let him decide for
himself what was best. "We didn't lose contact with you
throughout the working, and whoever—or whatever—we
brought back at the end certainly looked like you. But you
were old, and quite mad."

"What a pleasant future to look forward to . . . you said you
had a destination?"

"Yes."

"I need to see it," Garrod said.

"Now?"

"If possible."

Arekhon sighed. Elaeli might still be on the *Rain*'s bridge,
and by this time someone had undoubtedly told her about his

argument with Iulan Vai. Sound on shipboard carried in odd ways, and no conversation was ever truly private.

My life wasn't full enough of excitement. I had to do this to myself. Maybe Garrod will distract her.

"Come with me, then," he said to the First, "and I'll show you."

Garrod followed Arekhon out of the observation chamber. The access way outside was empty, a narrow passage spiraling wormlike beneath the ship's hull—metal underfoot, and lit with amber-tinged lamps. Arekhon led the way without saying anything. Garrod, a pace or two behind him, had time to reflect upon their brief exchange a few minutes earlier.

"We," the younger man had said when he spoke of the Circle, not giving anyone's names, as if both the right and the burden of decision belonged to him. Garrod knew what that meant.

"Yuva is dead, isn't he?"

Arekhon nodded. "In the working. Bringing you back was a struggle. It almost took me as well. But you were with us before it came to that."

"*Not* me. Or, not me as I am. When I left . . . where I was, I came here."

Arekhon didn't answer, and they stumped along the spiral way for a while in silence. Finally Garrod said, "Where is Yuva now?"

"At Demaizen," Arekhon said. "Kiefen and Delath are still there, and Serazao; they'll take proper care of the grave-offerings."

"Good," said Garrod, and didn't speak again until they reached the ship's bridge.

His appearance there—a stranger, whom nobody had seen come aboard with the rest of the crew—caused a flurry of gasps and murmurings. A young fleet-apprentice, looking nervous and self-important, scurried off, probably to rouse the Captain. Garrod ignored the commotion and followed Arekhon to the station of the Pilot-Principal, a curly-haired young woman whose quick sidelong glance in their direction caused the Second's cheeks to go briefly red.

"Pull up the chart," Arekhon said. He was pretending for

some reason that the glance had never happened; under other circumstances, Garrod might have been amused.

The Pilot-Principal had her eyes fixed on the console now. "Chart up."

She touched a key, and the air above the station console began to take on form. The sparkling lights of the Eraasian homeworlds showed their curves and lines and probabilities. Beyond them stretched the blank gap of the empty space beyond the Edge, with a red ship-sigil in the midst of it marking the vessel's last known position. On the far side of the gap, a marker shone with a golden-white light.

Arekhon pointed at it. "That one."

"How much time to arrival?" Garrod asked.

"Some months," said the Pilot-Principal. She seemed to find it a relief to address Garrod instead of his Second, even though Garrod was a stranger and an interloper aboard the ship. "Wait a moment, and I'll work out the exact time."

"Not necessary," said Garrod. "I know that world. I suppose that you are prepared for your arrival?"

The Pilot-Principal regarded him with a straightforward gaze. "Is the world as rich as the marker says?"

"Yes." *And maybe when they learn about us,* Garrod thought, *they won't buy Eraasi and all its holdings out of cash in hand. Maybe they'll take their practice at warmaking and conquer us instead.* "Richer than any we've seen."

Footsteps sounded, and the door to the bridge opened. It was the Captain, with the fleet-apprentice trailing behind her.

"Captain sus-Mevyan," said Garrod, glad that the Captain was one of the handful of sus-Peledaen officers whom he knew by sight.

And sus-Mevyan, it seemed, remembered him. "Garrod syn-Aigal!" she exclaimed. "What are you doing, appearing in the middle of nowhere like this? sus-Khalgath told me you were . . . indisposed, on Eraasi."

"I seem to have recovered," Garrod said. He nodded toward the chart. "I need to know—have we gone too far to turn back?"

"We don't have enough fuel for a return," the Captain said. "We're working off the reserves, and hoping that the new world, when we find it, has fuel that we can use."

Too late to turn back now, thought Garrod, with a sigh. Aloud, he said only, "Very well. Beginning tomorrow I shall teach a course on the languages and customs of the planet known as Entibor. All hands are invited to participate."

XXIX: Year 1128 E. R.
Eraasian Space: sus-Peledaen Orbital Station
Entiboran Space: sus-Peledaen ship RAIN-ON-DARK-WATER
Ildaon: Beshkip

ATELTH SUS-KHALGATH had not grown any fonder of visits to high orbit since the departure of *Rain-on-Dark-Water* for the worlds beyond the Edge. Once again, however, obligation and family honor had conspired to bring him there. The head of the most powerful fleet-family on Eraasi could not ignore the completion of his own new-made orbital station, especially not when the station's design—like *Rain*'s—was the first new development in over a generation.

Natelth's grandfather had established the specialized construction cradles for guardships like *Ribbon-of-Starlight*, making the sus-Peledaen convoy system safer and more efficient than the unescorted ships belonging to all the other families. Natelth had gone further. He had made orbital space itself secure. The new station had an outer shell proof against any ship-mounted weapons that might be brought against it; and it had guns of its own, heavier and more hungry for energy than anything that could be mounted on shipboard.

Natelth had been reluctant, originally, to take such an unprecedented step. Resources turned away from ships and trade almost never brought in enough new wealth to justify the expenditure. When his agents reported that all of the other fleet-families were building warships, however, he could no longer justify holding back.

So far, those other warships were only a distant threat. He didn't know of any families who had them besides his own sus-Peledaen, and Natelth at least had promised himself not to use them unless absolutely necessary. Nevertheless—he would have failed in his duty to the family, if he didn't protect it against the day that might come.

The new station's inauguration into active service, at the end of many months of work, had required speeches and ceremonies honoring everyone from the designer-in-chief to the lowliest of the gun crews. Even the station's *aiketen* and the crewmembers that tended its house-mind had received their due: Isayana sus-Khalgath herself had come up with Natelth to inspect the former and thank the latter. Finally everything was done, and Natelth was able to retire with his sister for a private dinner in the station's guest quarters.

As soon as the door closed behind them, Isa kicked off her shoes with a sigh of relief. "At least that's over. And the station's kitchen will do all right—I instructed that node personally."

"Decent ingredients are still going to cost the world," Natelth grumbled. "Port-city prices plus the cost of transport up to orbit . . . sometimes I wonder if Thel sus-Radal is circulating rumors of warships purely to bankrupt me. It's exactly the sort of underhanded trick that moon-worshiping malefactor would try."

An *aiketh* floated up to Natelth's elbow. "A message, from the family's agent-in-place on Ayarat."

Isa frowned at the quasi-organic. "Can't this wait until after dinner?"

"Might as well get it over with," Natelth said. "I'll take it now."

The *aiketh* hummed and clicked for a few seconds, and extruded a slip of paper. Natelth thanked it absently, his eyes already scanning the lines of type.

The report was brief. The sus-Peledaen tradeship *Mirror-of-the-Sun*, burdened with a consignment of engine-control assemblies, was overdue at Ildaon, and now the sus-Dariv ship *Garland-of-Sweet-Branches* had arrived on Ildaon herself, selling on the auction market a set of engine-control assemblies. Typical of an after-boarding action—the sus-Dariv had been pirates since before it was respectable.

But the *Garland* didn't have the usual log notation showing that the assemblies had been taken by means of honorable boarding and skill. The sus-Dariv were denying that they'd ever encountered the *Mirror* at all. And that was definitely against all custom.

"Will there be a return message?" inquired the *aiketh*.

"Yes," Natelth said. "Return message as follows: 'Check to see what else you can learn. Ensure that no other possible source for engine-control assemblies exists other than my ship. And confirm lack of log entries.'"

A red light glowed briefly inside the *aiketh*'s upper shell. "Return message transmitted."

The quasi-organic floated away. Natelth watched it, frowning.

Isa gave him a curious look. "What was the problem?"

"A spot of trouble out near Ildaon," he replied. "Probably nothing. But it might be a good excuse to send out one of the new warships—get some use out of them and give the crews some practice. And show some people that we aren't the family that they should be playing games with."

"You aren't planning to do anything rash, are you?"

"No, not at all," Natelth said. "Just a little show of force, and strict orders not to fire unless fired upon."

"That's all right, then," Isa said. "As long as nobody else shoots first."

The towers of the Zealous Endeavor Manufacturing Company rose above Beshkip like the fingers of a hand thrust up through the earth. The hour was grey morning, just at dawn shift change. The loaders were backed to the docks and the workers just done with breakfast were going to their places on the line, while those they had replaced headed to the showers and locker rooms in preparation for the journey homeward.

In a small conference room on an upper floor, decorated with models of sea-ships and star-ships inside polished glass cases, two highly-placed conspirators met with their offworld agent Seyo Hannet at an unusually early meeting. The owners and the top-level executives of the Zealous Endeavor, who spent their days on the next floor up, were not yet in the building offices. Syrs Kammen and Riet could met with Hannet undetected, then proceed to their own offices for an early start to the day.

"Is everyone here who was involved in the original planning?" Seyo asked. "My report may be complex, and I'd rather not repeat it for latecomers."

"Jaf Otnal is at a conference on Ildaon," Kammen said. "He was the only other planner from this office. We can summarize your report for him when he gets back."

"Only you three?" said Hannet. "Excellent. The fewer who know, the better. And both of you, I presume, have been discreet? No written notes, no confidences to lovers?"

"We all know better than that," Kammen said. "No one lasts long in business who can't keep his own counsel."

"Better and better." Hannet paused and sniffed, as if repressing a sneeze, and rubbed the back of his hand across his nose. Then he stood and walked past Riet to check the outer door. It was locked. He returned to his place at the conference table and stacked his papers in order before continuing. "You asked to be brought up to date on how our plan progresses. The pieces, in fact, arc falling into place as scheduled. The fleet-families have been seduced into a pointless building program—pointless, at least, unless they use their new weapons against each other. The hook has been baited, set, and now—"

Kammen struggled against a yawn, then gave in and covered it with his hand.

"Do I bore you, Syr Kammen?" Hannet asked. "You *did* ask for a full report."

"No, no," Kammen said. "A late night and an early morning, that's all."

"Very well." Hannet stacked his papers again and continued. "The plan has succeeded so far, in that the ships have been built, and the trap has been sprung to set them at one another's throats. For the next phase—"

Riet's head nodded forward. He caught himself, raising his head and his eyes, then he nodded forward again. A snore rattled in his throat. Kammen resisted for a moment longer, then slid sideways to the floor, snoring also.

"—for the next phase, this," Hannet said.

He picked up his papers from the table and returned them to his case. From the same case he brought out a thin tool chest. He opened an access panel on the wall beside one of the glass cases and clipped a small yellow cylinder across a pair of electrical leads.

After replacing the panel, he unlocked the outer door and stepped out into the hall, then locked the door again behind him. In the elevator going down, he pulled a pair of filter plugs out of his nose, sneezed heartily, and put the plugs into a pocket envelope. He stowed the envelope in his case next to the tool chest.

In the lower lobby, where the data workers and the junior executives stood in lines to buy hot morning-bread from the kiosk vendors, Hannet walked slowly to the door, only one more businessman in a business-filled sea. As he walked through the outer doors to the ground-shuttle stop, he heard the first faint clanging of the security alarm, and the annunciator proclaiming "Fire . . . fire . . . fire. . . ."

The shuttle that took him to the center of town passed emergency equipment rushing in the opposite direction. He ate breakfast at his hotel, and lunch at the space port, while awaiting departure. The afternoon newscasts told of the tragic fire at Zealous Endeavor. It had started in the electrical wiring near the top of the executive tower. Several had been injured, and two had died, a pair of mid-upper-level executives overcome by smoke inhalation.

"Painless," Seyo whispered. He paused before boarding his shuttle to orbit to send a coded message. Even if it had been sent in the clear, the meaning would have been obscure to anyone but the intended recipient. It read, in whole, "As requested."

If *Rain-on-Dark-Water*'s first passage through the Void had felt interminable, the second—though it was, in fact, no shorter—seemed to pass with frightening speed.

Everyone aboard knew that the *Rain*'s safe return to Eraasi depended upon acquiring fuel from the new world they were inexorably approaching. Garrod syn-Aigal's unexpected appearance on board ship brought reassuring news of civilization and trade awaiting them, but the news did not stay reassuring for long. There was too much to be learned—language, customs, local politics, all of it alien and confusing—and Garrod showed no mercy in his instruction.

"This isn't one of our lost homeworlds waiting to be found," he said again and again. "This is a place that does not know anything about us, and we do not know them. What you learn here may mean your lives, later."

By the time *Rain* finished her second transit and emerged into realspace, most of the ship's officers and some of her crew had at least a smattering of the language, and a few had managed to achieve a fluency equal to Garrod's own.

Pilot-Principal Elaeli Inadi was one of those few. She was pleased that her regular duties required her to be present on *Rain*'s bridge at the time of the dropout. If anything from the new world came over the ship's communications system, she would be able to hear and interpret it for herself, without needing to ask anyone for the meaning.

There was a time, she knew, when she would have gone to Arekhon sus-Khalgath for something like that. That was before she had seen him for the first time in the company of his fellow-Mages. She understood, then, how tightly the members of a Circle were bound together—and why Arekhon had felt compelled to opt out of the fleet-family for good.

It's not that I don't trust him any longer, she thought uneasily. *Not really. But he thinks about the Circle first, and not the ship.*

He was on the bridge now, along with Garrod; the two Mages were standing out of the way against the rear bulkhead. Elaeli glanced in their direction—*looks like they don't want to hear somebody else's version of the dropout, either*—then went back to waiting for the Captain's word.

sus-Mevyan said, "Stand by," and Elaeli, her eyes on the screen showing the ship-mind's running calculations, replied, "Dropout in five, Captain . . . on my mark. Mark."

The familiar shiver of discontinuity rippled through her, coursing along the interface between body and mind, and the grey opalescence of the Void transformed itself into ordinary darkness outside the bridge windows.

Captain sus-Mevyan clicked on the speaker to the engineering compartment. "Fuel status?"

"Almost flat," came the reply. "We can do some in-system work—maybe one jump if there's another star nearby—but we're not going home again on what we have."

"We knew that." She turned back to the bridge team. "Anything on the electromagnetic bands?"

The crewmember at the communications board looked up from his bank of screens and readouts. "I'm showing something. Not natural, but if it's modulated I don't know how."

"Get me a direction on it anyway," sus-Mevyan ordered. She turned to Elaeli. "Pilot-Principal Inadi, get me a posit and drop a buoy here—wherever 'here' is—so I can find my way back to this point if I need to."

"We're working on it, Captain," said Elaeli. Her hands played over the command switches at her station. "Buoy's away . . . if we could have a look at the chart . . . that's good. Looks like we're right on top of our target."

Once again, the air above her station sculpted itself into an abstract map of space-time done in colored light. The red sigil marking the inertial location of *Rain-on-Dark-Water* had moved since the previous dropout; it was now superimposed upon the glowing white dot that marked the position of Garrod's Star.

"Sure looks that way," agreed sus-Mevyan. One of the ship's apprentices pressed a mug of hot *uffa* into the Captain's hand without being asked, and she took a swig without looking at it. "Let's see if there's any correlation between those blobs on the chart and what's really out here."

"Working," said Elaeli again. "It may take some time; the ship-mind is still assimilating new data. Do you think we should start transmitting ourselves while we wait—let the locals know we're here?"

sus-Mevyan shook her head. "Not right now. While we're waiting, pop off another drone to let the family know we made it this far."

"Preparing drone for send-off." Elaeli glanced over at the

communications board. A crash of white noise came from the speaker.

"Lots of signal, Captain," the communications specialist said, after silence had been restored. "Artificial radiation all over the EM spectrum. Everything seems to come from the same bearing."

"I didn't come this far just to lurk," sus-Mevyan said. "Turn toward the source. Pilot-Principal, what do you have out that way?"

Elaeli checked the data from the *Rain*'s realspace sensors. "One star, close."

"There's our target," said the Captain. "Lay in a microjump to the system. It's time to knock on the door and see who answers."

XXX: Year 1128 E. R.
Beyond the Farther Edge: sus-Peledaen ship *Rain-on-Dark-Water*

AREKHON WATCHED the *Rain*'s officers conferring over the chart and the ship-mind readouts. Intent on their work, they seemed oblivious to the two Mages who shared the bridge with them. He took advantage of their concentration to exchange a quiet word or two with Garrod.

"You said that Entibor and most of the other worlds on this side of the gap were engaged in constant low-level warfare."

Garrod nodded. "It's their greatest—perhaps their only—weakness."

"I see. So what happens when we show up in their space, looking like a very large target that no one can identify as friendly? How do you know that the local inhabitants aren't going to kill us on sight?"

"Because I survive," Garrod said. His voice held a note of grim humor. "You said yourself that I was—and so, presumably, that I will live to be—a great deal older when you left Eraasi."

"That's reassurance, of a sort," Arekhon conceded. His attention was only half on Garrod; over by the star-chart, the conference had ended.

"We have a course for transit," Elaeli told the Captain. "It won't put us into orbit around Entibor's primary, but we'll be close—and we'll have some fuel left for maneuvers in normal space."

"Can we make orbit?" asked sus-Mevyan.

"Engineering says not if we want to leave it again. We haven't got enough fuel to escape from planetary gravity."

"I see." sus-Mevyan turned. "Master Garrod—"

"Yes?"

"Tell me how to contact these people. What kind of light-speed comms are they using?"

"I'm afraid I don't know, Captain," Garrod said. "I know that they have such things, but I never discussed the matter with one of their technicians."

"Help me out," the Captain said. "Did you hear a phrase—frequency modulation, amplitude modulation, phase modulation—anything?"

"If I did, I do not recall."

"Wonderful. We can't talk to them. How certain are you that these people have fuel we can use, and that we'll be able to buy or trade for it?"

"Not certain at all," Garrod said. "When I tell you that the same word for 'fuel' is used to speak of what propels deep-water ships and low-altitude flyers as well as what moves the vessels that go between the stars, you will perhaps understand why—but these people do have trade with other worlds, and starships of many types. So I would say that the likelihood of finding what we need is acceptably high."

The corners of sus-Mevyan's mouth turned down. "That's still not as reassuring as I'd like. But we don't have much choice. Pilot-Principal, make the jump."

"Working."

"What is your intention, Captain?" Garrod asked.

"With everything else we lack, I must act with honor. Treat these people as I would wish to be treated, act as I would hope one of theirs would act if our situations were reversed and they were coming into Eraasian space. Give them a display of shiphandling that will show them—since without communications we have no words—that we have come to this world as their equals, and not as paupers who can only ask for charity and have no power to give anything back in return."

She turned to the bridge windows, and to the distant stars. Arekhon braced himself for the crossing of the border between the Void and reality. This time the transit would be a brief one—they were very close to Entibor's star—and he would need to use the time well.

He spoke quietly to Garrod. "We're going to need luck for this. I think it's time to gather the Circle."

The older Mage frowned slightly. "Working to affect the course of a transit isn't a good idea. The forces are too similar—"

"Not for the transit," Arekhon said. "For the chase-and-boarding afterward. Captain sus-Mevyan intends to take an Entiboran ship, to show our friendly intention."

Garrod paused. "I never heard of such a custom among them. Though I will admit I dealt mostly with their politicians, and not with those of their people who ventured into space."

"Good shiphandling has got to be a universal." Arekhon said. He paused. "Besides, if we do find out that the Entiborans' fuel won't work for the *Rain,* one of their ships may have to take us home. But sus-Mevyan wants to show them that she's an equal, first—she'd never agree to putting the fleet-family into a subservient position—and making an intercept is one way to do it."

Garrod said nothing for what felt to Arekhon like a long time. Then he said, "You acted as the First of Demaizen from the time the great working ended until I came to the ship. Do you want the Circle again?"

Arekhon braced his shoulders against the cold metal of the bulkhead behind him. "I'm not trying to take your position away from you, Lord Garrod—"

"But you have opinions on what should be done."

"Yes."

"Are you certain of them?"

"Not certain," said Arekhon. "But . . ."

"Another reason that you should take the Circle," Garrod said. "Seconds don't have doubts. Firsts do."

"Being named Third was an honor. Being Second came to me through the working. I never aspired to be anything more."

"This is not about your ambition," Garrod said. "It is about the working, and the good of the voyage. I ask you again, will you take the Circle?"

Arekhon drew a deep breath. "For the good of the working . . . yes."

Elaeli was so immersed in watching the calculations for the transit that she scarcely noticed when the two Mages left the bridge. Short transits, with their fine adjustments of time and distance, put a greater call on the resources of the ship-mind than did the longer passages. Nobody wanted to be on the rare unlucky ship that never returned from a routine jump. Mostly they were never found, but the disaster of 1114 and the meteor shower over Ramsit were remembered all too well in the fleet.

This time, when *Rain-on-Dark-Water* came out of the Void, the ship was close enough to the Entiboran system that Garrod's Star was the brightest object visible in the field outside the *Rain*'s bridge windows. Elaeli made certain that the calculations were transferred to the star map, and readied another message drone for the fleet. The next Eraasian ship to make the transit would not have to travel blind—if there was ever another Eraasian ship to visit this world.

Which there would not be, unless *Rain* and her crew could obtain—and obtain soon—the means to go home. Hunting in normal space took fuel, too.

"How far?" sus Mevyan asked.

"Middle-space," Elaeli replied. "Eight months of realspace thrust to the primary."

"We don't have eight months' food. And we don't have eight months' fuel."

"Normally I'd recommend another micro-jump," Elaeli said. "We're about the range for in- to out-system shipping lines, for interstellar distances. No gravity bobbles for the run to jump, close to a micro-piloting situation."

Captain sus-Mevyan was standing by the bridge windows, looking out at the starfield as though she could find with the naked eye what the *Rain*'s sensors were waiting to report. "Get me a scan of near space," she ordered. "Tell me who else is out there. If there's another ship, I want to know it."

The communications specialist was already working his panel intently. "Intermittent raw carrier, no signal."

"Hail them anyway. Do you have a position on any of them?"

"I'll get running fixes soon. I've got up-Doppler on a couple. I'll work those first."

"Work them," said sus-Mevyan. "Pilot-Principal—"

"Standing by to calculate intercepts," said Elaeli. "How shall I set the fuel consumption parameters?"

"Give me as much speed and maneuverability as you and engineering together can squeeze out," sus-Mevyan ordered. "Meanwhile, I don't want any surprises. Muster the boarding party and have them stand by at the sally lock. When I arrive at Garrod's Star, I want to give them as much honor as we possibly can before we have to start asking for favors."

The members of the Circle aboard *Rain-on-Dark-Water* assembled in the meditation chamber in response to Arekhon's summons. Narin Iyal looked calm and alert—standing with her feet braced apart, gripping her staff just as she might have done while watching for bad weather from the deck of a Veredden fishing trawler. Ty, on the other hand, had a bright-eyed, excited look that didn't augur well for his steadiness later. More than any of the other Mages, Ty had made friends among the *Rain*'s crewmembers; and worry, Arekhon knew, made a powerful distraction. Vai, of course, remained as quiet and self-contained as always—Arekhon supposed that witnessing a great working within hours of joining a Circle would leave one unimpressed by anything less.

They were all of them well-practiced, he reflected. As the door closed, they moved without needing consultation into the white circle on the black enameled deckplates. None of them appeared startled when Garrod took the place meant for the Circle's newest member, or for a visitor, and Arekhon spoke the words to begin the working.

"*Rain-on-Dark-Water* has come safely out of the Void," he told them, "and now the difficult part of our journey begins. Unless we take a ship, we won't have the fuel to get home. It's time for us to join in meditation and see to it that the *eiran* are brought together where they're most needed."

No more words were necessary. The Mages knelt on the deckplates with their staves before them within easy reach.

Arekhon let his mind slip into the passive, half-thinking state where the *eiran* appeared most clearly.

One piece of good fortune we've had already, he thought. *We came out near other ships, and there's luck all over.*

He studied the silvery *eiran,* trying to determine which ones were the most suited to the Circle's purpose, and which ones made the strongest connections to *Rain-on-Dark-Water.* His task was made more complex by the wild disarray of the cords as though no one on this side of the interstellar gap had ever bothered to cultivate and untangle them. Distinguishing between one cord and another, and following them back to their sources, took concentration.

That one . . . there. Or the other one, close by . . .

No. Wait.

"Ty," he said.

No answer for a moment, while Ty brought his mind back from whatever places he went to search for the *eiran.* Then he said, " 'Rekhe . . . Lord Arekhon?"

"Go stand with your friends, at the sally lock."

"Yes, lord." Ty rose obediently, but his voice sounded startled and a bit hurt. "Are you dismissing me from the Circle?"

"No," Arekhon said. "I want you to take the Circle with you. The *eiran* here—you've seen them. We need to hold fast to our own if we're going to make luck for anyone at all. Take the *eiran* of the boarding party and weave them into ours. When the time comes, we'll work the luck for everyone."

Elaeli felt drops of moisture springing out on her forehead and the back of her neck.

Nerves, she thought, as she huddled with the *Rain's* communications specialist over the displays of first one station and then the other. *By the time this is all done I'm going to look like a wet mop.*

She had good reason for tension. A normal-space interception was the most complex and delicate set of maneuvers that a vessel like the *Rain* would ever undertake. The ship-mind integrated realtime data as fast as it could, but interpreting its recommendations about course and speed—and about what the other ship would do in the face of pursuit—called heavily upon the luck and good judgment of the Pilot-Principal.

The first set of reccos came up on Elaeli's screen, a double-handful of them, ranged from near to far. She pursed her lips in a silent whistle.

No wonder we haven't aroused anybody's suspicions yet! This place is as crowded as the city lake on a hot day.

She discarded all but a couple of the ship-mind's recommendations as too distant for practical purposes. Even the quick Void-transits necessary to close the gap would use up more of their precious fuel reserves than she wanted to risk. The Captain was the sort to call for fast moves and lots of power at the end of the chase.

If we have it, Elaeli thought.

"Two targets in normal-space pursuit range," she said aloud. "Intercepts possible."

"What kind of range?" sus-Mevyan demanded.

Elaeli glanced down at the numbers on her display, working to translate the specifics listed there into the kind of useful abstractions that the captain wanted.

I wish there were some kind of display for this, like the star charts.

"Close range for target number one," she said at last. "One hour approximately. And the other . . . at least eight times that. The close one's faster, though."

Captain sus-Mevyan gazed out at the darkness beyond the bridge windows as if she could see something out there besides the stars. If she was sweating, Elaeli couldn't tell.

"Set course for match and intercept on target number one," the Captain said at last.

Elaeli let out her breath and began giving commands. "All engines on line," she reported when she was finished.

"Course and tracking laid on."

"Lock on, lock confirmed."

"Commence approach run."

Then came the long wait. The *Rain*'s great engines pushed harder and harder, and Elaeli watched the readouts for the target ship and for their own pursuit. The gap narrowed, increment by increment, while Elaeli sweated and Captain sus-Mevyan stood motionless at the bridge window. The closer they could get before the target ship became suspicious, the better . . . Elaeli stiffened and hissed through her front teeth in frustration.

"The target's spotted us, Captain," she reported. "They're putting on speed."

The captain touched a switch on the bulkhead next to the bridge windows. "Engineering, this is the bridge. Give me more power."

"We're at max already, Captain," came the reply over the bridge speakers. "We can't push it any harder."

Elaeli had her gaze fixed on the display. "Target still accelerating."

"Use the maneuvering jets," sus-Mevyan ordered. "See if we can add some side velocity change into the equation."

"Captain, I'm seeing up-Doppler," said Elaeli a few minutes later. "She's pulling away from us."

"Get me another target," sus-Mevyan said. "We haven't got many chances here, people—let's make the most of them."

Elaeli studied the ship-mind's list of recommendations. "Given the speed we already have on us, we can set up an intercept course for target number two without a lot of extra maneuvering."

"Do so," said sus-Mevyan. "Reset grapnels from optimum range to max theoretical. Shoot as soon as they're in range."

"Changing course to intercept," Elaeli said. "Readying grapnels."

And the waiting began again.

XXXI: Year 1128 E. R.
Beyond the Farther Edge: sus-Peledaen ship *Rain-on-Dark-Water*

T Y MADE his way through the labyrinthine coils of the ship's passages to the sally port. He had seen the area before; as one of the Mages on board, he could go anywhere, and people would assume he was on important Circle business and let him pass. He'd taken advantage of the freedom, and of the time in the Void, to explore the *Rain* thoroughly—making up, he supposed, for that long-denied classroom trip from his days at the Port Street Home.

If they could see me now, he thought as he entered the muster bay. The boarding party waited, drawn up in three ranks. They looked ominous and alien in their black plastic hardmasks and dark coats, and the pikes they carried gleamed in the artificial light.

On an upper platform deck around three sides of the chamber the stations and readouts of the fighting bridge glowed violet and amber. A couple of officers were already on duty on that level, talking in hushed voices to each other and to the audio pickups for the main bridge.

A masked and armored figure detached itself from the front rank of the boarding party and approached Ty. "What are you doing down here?"

Ty recognized the voice and gait of Izar, one of the *Rain*'s senior crew members—not a particular friend of his, but no enemy. "The Circle has joined to work the luck," he said. "Lord Arekhon told me to go with the boarding party."

Izar's posture relaxed. "That's all right, then. Stand over there in the rear rank with Spiru and Kalan. Did Lord Arekhon say whether he wanted you armored up or not?"

Ty shook his head. "Just that I should be here."

"It's your choice, then."

"I'll stick with what I'm used to," Ty said after a moment's thought, and went to join the crewmembers Izar had pointed out to him. Kalan was from off-Eraasi, the first such person that Ty had ever known on a day-to-day basis, but Spiru was Hanilat born and bred, with the Port Street accent strong in his voice.

"Ty," he said. "Come to wish us luck?"

"More or less. The Circle loves you so much they sent me down here to hold onto this end of the working."

"Fuel's that tight?" Spiru's face was only a featureless blur on the other side of the black hardmask, but his voice sounded tenser than before.

Kalan—he worked in engineering, Ty remembered, and would know—said, "Believe it."

"We're being tested," Spiru said, after a brief silence. "To see if we're worthy of being the first ones to make contact beyond the Edge."

Ty thought about that idea for a while. The muster bay was quiet, except for the sounds of circulating air and thrumming engines and the occasional murmur of nervous voices.

"Why?" he said finally. "The fleet-families have contacted new worlds before. I remember they opened up Ninglin while I was still in school."

"I'm from Ninglin," Kalan said. "I remember the celebration after we made contact with the lost brethren. The parties lasted for months."

"That was different," said Spiru. "The people on Ninglin and the other homeworlds were like us—like enough, anyhow. The Mages in their Circles had talked with ours. Has anyone from this side of the Edge ever talked with a Circle, Ty?"

"No," Ty admitted. "But Garrod says they're more of our

lost brethren all the same. And he certainly has talked with them."

"And a damned good thing, too," Izar cut in. The older crew member had come up unexpectedly behind Ty and the others. "When the sally port opens, keep your mind on the words Lord Garrod taught us: 'Comrade,' 'friend,' 'we surrender.' The last thing we need is for somebody to get carried away and ruin our chances for a civilized exchange."

"Captain," Elaeli said. "We have a solid contact on target number two."

sus-Mevyan had not moved from the bridge window during the long wait, as though by watching she could make one of the host of stars resolve into the ship they hunted. Before the chase was done, they would have visual contact—would come near enough, in spite of the other's evasions, to grapple and close and make an entry. The maneuvers of a chase-and-board required a skilled and daring shiphandler with a well-built ship. The *Rain* was the newest, sharpest vessel in the sus-Peledaen fleet; Elaeli could only hope that she had the necessary skill and daring.

"Get me a position in front of him," the Captain said. "Match speed if you can, but do not decelerate."

"Course laid in," Elaeli said. "Tracking."

Her voice rasped as she said it; tension had left her mouth feeling dry and papery. She caught the eye of the fleet-apprentice—the boy looked as tired as she felt—and held up her empty mug for more *uffa*. "The fuel reserves are yellowing out fast; we can expect to start seeing degraded performance before we finish mating with the target."

"How close are we going to come?" asked sus-Mevyan.

Elaeli squinted at the readouts on her station. "Unless he does something unexpected, it looks like grapnel range."

sus-Mevyan flicked on the audio pickup. "Tell the boarding party to stand ready on station. And prepare the rapid-entry system—there's no reason to think that the target's airlocks will be standardized to ours."

The communications specialist looked up from his station. "What message should I prepare for the target ship?"

"Use their language—the one Lord Garrod taught us—and

try every kind of modulation you can get out of the boards. Say that we're in need of fuel, and ready to yield our cargo in exchange for it."

"That's all?"

"Let's get the negotiations going first," said sus-Mevyan. "We can't yield anything until we've made contact."

The fleet-apprentice returned with Elaeli's fresh mug of *uffa*. Elaeli took it, gave the apprentice a smile of thanks, and began to sip at the steaming liquid. Time was crawling again. She watched the readouts at her station because they changed visibly, if slowly, while the starfield outside the bridge windows did not.

"What happens if we can't use their fuel?" the fleet-apprentice whispered nervously to Elaeli—but sus-Mevyan was the one who answered.

"Then we offer our cargo in return for a safe passage to the nearest inhabited planet, and settle down to long and productive lives as natives of these benighted parts."

"The Mages—"

"—will walk home to Eraasi if they can. But I wouldn't count on seeing another ship come back."

The fleet-apprentice didn't ask any more questions, and for a while longer there was silence. Then a muttered exclamation from the communications specialist drew Elaeli's attention away from the purple and amber lights on her display panel. She looked up, and saw what had to be the *Rain*'s second contact, now a bright light amid the starfield and steadily growing brighter.

He's coming on fast.

Elaeli felt a cold apprehension in the pit of her stomach— a sensation that had less to do with the chase at hand than with a future that she couldn't completely grasp. She wondered if this was what 'Rekhe felt like when he saw the *eiran* and tried to work with them.

And this is our slow *target. What kind of engine systems do these people have, anyway? Better than ours, it looks like. If their pilot's any good at evading boarders, this isn't going to work.*

She put her thoughts aside and concentrated on the chase. Now that the target was visible, it was starting to take on shape. Another few minutes, and it was recognizably a starship.

"Get the grapnels ready," said sus-Mevyan.

"Rigged and standing by," Elaeli said. "Awaiting your orders, Captain."

"Put the grapnel release on automatic. Extreme range."

"Range approaching extreme," Elaeli said. "Four, three, two—"

The communications specialist broke in. "No answer to our signals!"

"Grapnels away."

Metal hit against metal and the positive contact light illuminated on the bridge as the grapnels locked on. Even after Elaeli's efforts to match course and velocity, the impact was enough to jar everybody's neck and make the *uffa*-pot totter on its brass legs. The *Rain*'s engines roared under the sudden increase in their burden.

"Contact," said Elaeli.

sus-Mevyan drew a deep breath. "Boarding party away."

Arekhon had lost track of the passage of time.

Always, for him, the places he went in his mind to seek the luck and work the *eiran* seemed to lie outside the normal sequence of hours and minutes, or even of weeks and days. He knew that the others of the Circle—*his* Circle, now—were with him, but in the country of his mind, as usual, he was alone. What that meant, and what the others saw at these times, he couldn't tell.

Long before the start of the working, Garrod had warned them of how things stood in this part of space: "Seek luck, rather than order. Luck you may have a chance to find, but not order, no matter how hard you look for it. The people here believe that tending the *eiran* is wrong."

Arekhon had wondered what Garrod meant—would have thought that he was lying, except that Garrod never lied—until he saw the landscape to which he had come for this working.

He stood amid mountains, massive granite outcroppings of cracked rock overgrown with brush. The few isolated trees, when he came near them, proved ready to fall, all of them rotting in place where they had grown. Nowhere did he see any evidence of proper care.

Garrod had spoken truly. This country was dangerous in itself. The ground was pocked with holes and pitfalls waiting for the pressure of an unready foot; the bushes along the cliff-edges had roots too shallow to support a grasping hand. Except for the familiar life-strands of his fellows in the Circle, he saw no *eiran* running through it—and of the luck that had seemed to crowd the universe earlier, he saw nothing at all.

If we can't find the luck that's native here, he thought, *we'll have to make it for ourselves.*

He dropped out of the visionary world far enough to see the *Rain*'s meditation chamber—a pale and wavery image, like a painting on thin cloth, of Narin and Vai and Garrod kneeling at the other points of the circle, overlaid with an image of Ty standing with the boarders in the muster bay. The Circle's combined *eiran* ran from one image to the other, but the cords were pale and thin.

Arekhon rose to his feet. "The luck needs to be made stronger," he said. "Who will match me in the working?"

One of the kneeling Mages stood to meet him.

"I will," said Iulan Vai, and struck the first blow as she spoke.

XXXII: Year 1128 E. R.

Beyond the Farther Edge: sus-Peledaen ship *RAIN-ON-DARK-WATER*

Unknown Entiboran Ship

TY FELT the deck plates shudder beneath his feet. "What—?"

"It's the grapnels," said Spiru. "They've caught."

Kalan added, "If you've got any luck for us, now's the time to pass it along."

"Luck . . ." Ty put his hands over his eyes to shut out the lights and distractions of the muster bay. The Circle's *eiran* ran somewhere nearby—he felt them, like cables running through the bulkheads, or through the steel of the deck. But the cables weren't strong enough; there wasn't enough power coming through them to give the boarding party what they needed. Not yet—

"Ty?" asked Kalan nervously.

"Luck," he repeated. "We've begun a working. Soon there will be luck."

The *Rain* shuddered again as he spoke.

"Positive hull contact," said Spiru. "We'll be going across any minute now."

At the same time, Izar shouted, "Fast deploy boarding tunnel! Let's move, people!

Ty heard a metallic groaning followed by a heavy *clunk*. That had to be the tunnel, fastening on and settling into position . . . the *eiran* extended in that direction, stretching out toward the other ship.

"Are you coming, or not?" Spiru demanded. "Because we're going to be moving out in another couple of seconds."

"Luck," said Ty for a third time. The cords of his own *eiran* were part of the Circle's larger cable, and where he went, the working would follow. "Yes, I'm coming."

He took his hands from his eyes in time to see the first two ranks of boarders swinging into the open mouth of the tunnel at a trot. Spiru and Kalan entered with the third rank a few seconds later, and Ty was with them. The tunnel was dark, lit only by amber battle-lanterns, and the hatch at the far end had no shape to it that Ty understood. The boarders drew up in their ranks again before it, temporarily thwarted.

"It's an airlock," said Kalan. "No external controls, though—somebody must have skimped on the design. Now they're going to lose the whole thing."

"I sure hope they're ready for this," Spiru said nervously. "If the inner door on their side isn't closed, we're all going to get sent to the star-road by the wind."

"Stand by to blow the door," ordered Izar a moment later, and a crewmember whose voice Ty didn't recognize said, "Door coming up."

A brief, silent flash of light came from the hatch, Ty felt a shivering in the soles of his feet, and the hatch was open. A puff of air flowed out from the newly opened space, bringing with it tiny fragments of plastic and metal floating in a cloud of smoke.

"What do you see?" Izar demanded.

"We've got light," said the crewmember who had spoken earlier. "And the inner door is still intact."

"Right. Formation, in the lock. Overpressure the tunnel from our side."

The boarding party moved forward again and took station inside the lock. They stood in three ranks, their pikes grounded, with each crew member positioned half an arm's length from the people to either side and a full arm's length from the person in front.

"They can't say we didn't do them right and honor," Spiru commented under his breath as Izar and another crew member huddled over the controls of the inner door.

Kalan said something in reply, but Ty didn't catch the words. He was concentrating on the work going on up ahead of them. That inner door had to open soon, or else the boarding party would force it open with more of the white explosive. Ty was fairly certain that this would not be good—either for the *Rain* or for the ship they were trying to board.

Luck, he thought. *The luck of the Circle, coming through me to the door and convincing it to open. Opening it . . . now.*

Lights came on above the inner door, a row of them, one at a time. Red . . . red . . . red . . . red . . . green. Izar stepped forward, pike at the challenge position. And the door slid open.

Light poured out of the opening—boiling, hot-colored light that wrapped itself around Izar and the whole front rank behind him, burning and blackening whatever it touched. The air was full of the smells of ozone and cooking meat.

Ty lay where he had fallen, half under Spiru and Kalan where they had thrown themselves down as the first rank of boarders fell.

Garrod was right, he thought, as he drew a choking breath. *There is no order on this side of the gap. Only pure, untouched chaos. Evil.*

The weight on top of him lessened; he pushed himself up with his hands until he could look ahead. Spiru and Kalan were crouching like sprinters, their pikes in their hands.

"They shouldn't have done that," Spiru said. His voice sounded quavery and unnatural behind the dark plastic of his hardmask.

"No," said Kalan. "Ty—are you with us?"

No order, only chaos. "Yes."

"Then on three, on my count, we're going in."

The curving flank of the Entiboran ship filled the bridge windows and blocked out the stars.

The vessel's white-metal hull, blank except for a dull black row of unfamiliar symbols, gave no indication of what might be happening inside. Elaeli and the others on the *Rain's* bridge listened to the reports coming over the audio pickup from the muster bay, and tried to force them into making sense.

It shouldn't be taking this long, she thought. Her fists clenched as she struggled to keep up at least the semblance of a fitting demeanor. She was the pilot, the one whom even the Captain depended upon to bring *Rain-on-Dark-Water* safely into the proper place at the proper distance. It would not do for her to become disturbed.

I put us alongside them clean and smooth. . . . I swear we didn't even scratch the enamel once the grapnels locked on . . . they should have opened up smiling by now.

Captain sus-Mevyan was talking over the audio pickup with the officers on the muster bay auxiliary bridge. "What's the holdup down there?"

"Somebody didn't get the word, looks like," came the reply. "Our boarding party had to blow the outer lock."

"That's a dead waste of some pretty maneuvering . . . are we in yet?"

"Door's opening—I can see "

There was a sudden noise, a crescendo of volume and pitch underlaid by a deep hum. The link dropped.

"What *was* that?" demanded sus-Mevyan into the silence that followed. "Communications, get me the muster bay. I want to know what happened, and I want to know it now."

The audio pickup crackled back to life. "Muster bay here, captain. Whatever hit us, hit us bad—we've lost contact with the boarding party. Nothing and nobody coming back."

"Send a runner down. Let me know what's happening."

The *Rain* gave a sudden, violent shudder. The sensation reminded Elaeli unpleasantly of the throes of a wounded animal.

Energy weapons, she thought, with a sense of outrage. *They're hitting us with energy weapons.*

"Lost communications with engaged-side forward engineering," reported the communications specialist. He was pale and sweating, but his voice was calm. Another shudder ran through the ship. "Loss of pressure alarm forward."

The fleet-apprentice who had brought Elaeli her *uffa* not long before swallowed hard and said, "What's going on?" in a voice that didn't quite squeak.

"They're cheating," Elaeli told him under her breath.

The communications specialist was still relaying bad news to sus-Mevyan. "No communications with the boarding party, no communications with engineering. Repair parties report hull breached."

"Muster standby boarding party."

"Interior communications are all down, Captain."

sus-Mevyan's features hardened. "Bridge crew, secure your stations. Send runners. All hands, muster in the boarding tunnel. Lock all air-tight doors."

Arekhon stood in a desolate landscape where blue-grey storm clouds gathered above the peaks and threw the upper slopes into shadow. A cold wind blew down off the highlands to scour the valley below.

He was not alone this time; Vai was with him, partner and adversary in the dance of their working. It had been a long while since he had last tested himself so much, moving at full speed and full strength without holding back—not the crushing, relentless onslaught of a great working, driven by the need for enormous amounts of sheer power, but something far more delicate and complex. They were building an intention, he and Vai, weaving the *eiran* into a sturdy network through the speed and grace of the blows they struck and blocked and struck again.

Vai wore a Mage's black robes, here in Arekhon's dream-landscape as well as in the physical world that their bodies still inhabited. She brought her staff around in a snapping blow, and the loose cloth fluttered and swirled around her like wings. Arekhon blocked the blow as it came in, the staves meeting with a resonant percussive outcry of wood against wood. He heard Vai laugh out loud from sheer delight.

Their staves were glowing golden and violet, drawing lines of dazzling color against the dark green of the mountainside and the dark grey of the lowering sky. The *eiran* wove in and out among them, shining like polished metal, making a pattern strong enough to capture the wild luck of the universe and direct it according to their desire. One of the threads had enough power to pull others toward it, and to draw on the luck that Arekhon and Vai were calling up between them.

Ty, Arekhon thought. Once recognized, the younger Mage's touch was unmistakable. And Ty was—was—

With the boarding party.

Here in the world of his own mind, Arekhon found that the idea of a boarding party was a hollow one—barely a word, with almost nothing behind it to provide a referent. But Ty himself, through his presence in the working, remained vivid and familiar. The luck that the intention had gathered belonged with him.

Ty.

Arekhon feinted at Vai's head, then struck low, aiming for her leg just above the knee.

With the boarding party.

Vai ignored his feint and moved to block the leg blow coming in. Their staves let loose fiery cascades of sparks in gold and violet, and the sound of wood striking against wood echoed off the mountainsides like thunder.

Luck.

Shadowy figures moved among the fallen in the darkened airlock of the Entiboran ship. They paced along the line where the front rank of *Rain-on-Dark-Water*'s boarding party had stood, pausing at each of the dark shapes lying crumpled on the deck.

Flashes of light blazed down out of the shadows' hands. Sometimes the fallen bodies twitched, other times not. Then the shadows moved on.

Ty's heart pounded. He crouched between Spiru and Kalan, ready to rise and rush forward on Kalan's word. The wooden grip of his staff felt slick and sweaty in his hand. He remembered, like a glimpse of something from long ago, Delath syn-Arvedan's practice of wrapping the grip with soft leather—he'd once thought of trying something like that himself but had never done so. Now he wished he had.

The dark figures were coming closer, were almost within reach . . . *luck,* thought Ty, *luck that they not notice us . . . luck that they are slow this time with their mysterious fires. . . .*

"One," whispered Kalan beside him. "Two. Three."

Ty pushed himself to his feet and surged forward. Kalan and Spiru were running beside him, with their pikes in their hands and poised to strike. More from instinct than thought, he reached out to grab the wild luck that spun out around all three of them like streamers in the wind.

His staff glowed with luck and power, a hot, incandescent green like the color of life itself, brighter even than the flames the dark figures carried in their hands. When the light from his staff struck the dark ones, they halted for an instant—in fear, or in amazement, or in some kind of recognition, Ty never knew—and that instant was their undoing.

Kalan yelled and slammed his pike into the nearest shadow. Spiru thrust at another, and Ty struck out at that one as it fell.

In the viridian glare from his staff, Ty saw that he had brought down a human-shaped pressure-suited figure, holding a weapon of some kind in its hand. He kicked the weapon aside, out of reach of the two fallen bodies—not that either of them would be reaching for it, he thought. They were bleeding too much where the steel pikes had pierced and cut them.

Ty left them behind and sprinted to catch up with Spiru and Kalan, already moving deeper into the mazy tunnels of the opposing spacecraft. Spiru glanced back over his shoulder as Ty rejoined them.

"Nice bit there with the staff. Can you do it again?"

"I don't know. Wild luck . . . it changes."

"Doesn't matter," said Kalan, and hefted his pike. The steel tip had blood on it, blood as red as any that ever flowed on Eraasi or Ninglin or Ildaon. "If they want a fight, they'll have one."

They came to a junction of two passageways. Kalan was in the lead. He paused and looked back at Ty and Spiru.

"Which way's forward, do you think?"

Spiru shrugged. "Don't know. Pick one."

Luck flared suddenly, a pattern of clear silver to draw the mind and the eye—

"That way," said Ty, pointing.

The other two followed his gesture in time to see a man come around the bend in the passage. He wasn't wearing a pressure suit at all. Spiru and Kalan thrust and slashed at once, Kalan's pike coming over Spiru's shoulder, and more blood sprayed against the bulkheads as the man went down.

The three surviving boarders from *Rain-on-Dark-Water* left him behind as they had left his companions in the airlock, and ran onward in the direction that Ty had chosen for them.

XXXIII: Year 1128 E. R.
Beyond the Farther Edge: sus-Peledaen ship *RAIN-ON-DARK-WATER*
Unknown Entiboran Ship

Elaeli had never performed an emergency shutdown of the pilot's station, except in drill. She knew the procedures—had practiced them, because in theory even the best ship might someday turn unfortunate and fall prey to mechanical disaster or to criminal intent—but such things did not happen in the sus-Peledaen fleet.

Only now they have. Lucky, lucky me, to get to see the day.

She worked as fast as she could, pulling boards and disconnecting power cables with hands that she didn't dare let shake or fumble, watching the screens go blank and the readouts die. The rest of the bridge was already dim and shadowed. Outside the bridge windows, the white bulk of the Entiboran ship shone with the reflected light of Garrod's Star.

Captain sus-Mevyan stood at her shoulder, watching. "Are you done, Pilot-Principal?"

"Almost, Captain." Elaeli pulled out the backup data-wafers for the updated star charts and sealed them into the inner pocket of her uniform tunic. "There. That's the last of it."

"Good. Let's go."

They hastened through the passages to the muster bay, their

footsteps echoing in the unnatural quiet. The floor of the bay was crowded with members of the *Rain*'s crew, some of them armed with boarding pikes but most of them carrying nothing but what they'd had in their hands when the order came.

Elaeli tried to spot 'Rekhe and the other Mages amid the crowd, but no one in the muster bay wore robes or carried a staff. The Circle's absence both worried and heartened her. She didn't want Arekhon sus-Khalgath to die lost and forgotten on an abandoned ship, and she didn't want him to die for the Circle, either—but if the Mages hadn't given up working to bring the luck to *Rain-on-Dark-Water,* then some of the people aboard her might yet make it back home.

The muster bay's auxiliary bridge held most of the *Rain*'s officers. Elaeli and Captain sus-Mevyan climbed the narrow metal staircase to join them.

"What's our situation?" the Captain asked the Chief Engineer as soon as she reached the upper level. "How soon can we effect repairs?"

"Looks bad, Captain," said the Chief Engineer. Elaeli felt a surge of sympathy for him. He'd already worked miracles to give sus-Mevyan the engine power she'd needed for the chase and interception, and now he had nothing more to give. "Our fuel's flat, and we're holed and leaking atmosphere fore and aft."

If his news discouraged Captain sus-Mevyan, she gave no sign. "What you're trying to say is that we aren't going home in this vessel."

The Chief Engineer nodded wearily. "That's about the shape of it."

"Fine." sus-Mevyan turned away from the consoles of the auxiliary bridge and pointed down across the muster bay at the open mouth of the boarding tunnel. "Then we're going home in that one."

The three survivors of *Rain-on-Dark-Water*'s boarding party stood outside a closed air-tight door.

"I think this is the way to the bridge," Kalan said.

Ty looked at him. "What makes you think that?"

"Just guessing," said Spiru. "We found the galley and we

found crew berthing, and there wasn't anyone in either of those places."

Kalan tried the heavy lever-arm that should have opened the door. "I think it's locked, though."

"Don't worry about it," said Ty. There was still luck in the universe—patterned and focused, the product of the Circle's labors. He seized on it and directed it into his staff. Then he touched the lock.

Metallic noises came from inside the door. The lever-arm moved down and back up again. With a final groan, the door cracked open.

"There," Ty said. "We can go in. If this is the bridge, maybe there's somebody on it who'll give us a chance to surrender properly before we have to kill them."

"I sure hope so," said Kalan, and kicked the door open so hard that it slammed against the limit of its hinges. The *Rain*'s boarding party—what was left of it—leaped onto the bridge through the widening gap.

Ty saw a room full of consoles and displays, and a person in drab clothing standing at the central point. She had an audio pickup link in one hand and what looked like a weapon in the other, and she was raising her hand to fire.

Spiru was in the lead; he brought the butt of his pike around and knocked the weapon out of her grip.

It clattered and spun across the deck. The woman jumped for it, but Kalan moved faster and threw himself on top of her, bearing her down under his weight.

"We surrender," he said breathlessly. "Surrender . . . surrender . . . ah, *lasreno! Het lasreno!*"

She kept on struggling. Spiru pointed the tip of his boarding pike at her head.

"Comrade, friend," he said. *"Idesten . . ."*

The woman spat out a string of angry words and redoubled her efforts at escape. Ty stepped forward, groping in his mind for more of the phrases that Garrod had taught them.

" 'We-are-honored-to-meet-you,' " he rattled off in rote Entiboran. " 'We-come-to-make-a-trade.' "

After a moment the woman started to laugh. It was hysteria, not mirth; she didn't stop laughing until after Kalan had tied her hands with the belt of his uniform, and her feet with

Spiru's. Then the laughter turned to weeping, and then to silence.

Ty drew a deep breath. "Now what do we do?"

"We wait for the Captain," Kalan told him. "And we let the Captain figure it out."

The airlock at the far end of the boarding tunnel was a slaughterhouse.

Elaeli smelled the extent of the carnage even before her eyes took it all in: Blood and filth and cooked meat and melted plastic mixed together into a foul, malodorous slurry. Bile rose in her throat, and she swallowed it back down.

She was the Pilot-Principal; she was syn-Peledaen; she was supposed to set an example for the fleet-apprentices and the ordinary crew. If Captain sus-Mevyan could walk through the ranks of burned bodies, struck down where they stood and lying where they had fallen, then Elaeli Inadi could follow her.

It wasn't hard to figure out which way to go. Two of the bodies in the airlock hadn't burned; they'd been hacked apart with boarding pikes, and the blood that ran out of the cuts and slashes in their pressure suits had covered the deck with a wash of sticky red. The bloody prints of boot soles led away from the puddle into the depths of the ship.

Elaeli didn't want to look at her own feet. She let sus-Mevyan set the course. They came to a place where two passages crossed, but—Elaeli fought down an impulse toward manic, inappropriate laughter—the *Rain*'s boarders had considerately left them another body to mark the trail, and even more blood.

No pressure suit this time, and the man's face was untouched. He looked scared and surprised, and distressingly ordinary in spite of the wounds that had killed him.

An alien from beyond the Edge, she thought. *And if he wasn't dead I could invite him home to dinner and nobody would even blink. Arekhon was right; the Sundering isn't a legend after all.*

The realization sobered her. She was just as glad that the blood-trail she and the Captain followed didn't lead to any more bodies. They hit a couple of dead ends—empty com-

partments full of bunks and kitchenware—before coming to
the ship's main control room and the survivors of the boarding
party: Two of the *Rain*'s crewmembers, their hardmasks and
armored jackets smoke-stained and streaked with red, and one
of Arekhon's Mages in long black robes gone stiff with blood
at the hem.

The two crewmembers took off their hardmasks as the Captain approached. sus-Mevyan looked at them, her mouth
bracketed by hard lines and her face revealing nothing.

"Spiru and Kalan and"—the cold eyes paused for a moment
on the young Mage before lighting briefly in recognition—
"Ty. Are there prisoners?"

"Yes, Captain." Kalan pointed toward a bound figure
slumped against the far bulkhead. "That one."

"Are there any others?"

"No, Captain." Kalan's voice wavered. Elaeli realized that
he was close to breaking down. "Should we have—"

"You did well," said sus-Mevyan firmly. She stepped over
to the control panels, but was careful not to touch them. A
chair was bolted to the deck on the right-hand side of the
compartment, and she sat in it. "Now we have to go on. Let's
get a temporary lock rigged, and start salvaging the *Rain*. I'm
going to need the charts, the communications rig, and as much
else as we can carry and will fit."

Kalan looked relieved to have something more to do. "Aye,
Captain."

"And fetch Lord Garrod. I need him here."

The working was over.

Arekhon knelt, exhausted, on the deck of the meditation
chamber, waiting for his head to clear. Vai leaned against the
bulkhead a few feet away, breathing hard. The working had
been a strong one, building to a great rush of focused power,
and Arekhon felt a faint surprise that it hadn't gone so far as
to call for a life. He was tired, and bruised in a number of
places, but in spite of everything he had come out of the experience without serious injury.

He pushed himself back onto his feet and looked over at
Vai. Her black hair was slicked into flattened tendrils against
her cheeks and forehead, and when she lifted her hand to wipe

away the sweat, the sleeve of her robe fell back enough to show a discolored welt above her wrist. Except for that, she was as uninjured as he was.

Narin and Garrod remained on the perimeter of the circle. The working hadn't called on them to do anything more than steady the pattern; odd, again, seeing that the luck had been so strong.

Unless I misdirected it, Arekhon thought. *Unless I only thought we'd made enough luck . . .*

"The engines have stopped," said Narin. "Is that good or bad?"

"Not good, usually," he said, coming back from his worries with an effort. His voice sounded hoarse, and his throat felt sore and scratchy. "In our case, it probably means that we're out of fuel. Which is why we did the working in the first place."

Vai shoved herself away from the wall and came over to join him. "I suppose one of us should go see what's up."

"We should all go," he said. "We're finished anyway."

Before anyone could reply, a frantic hammering came at the locked door of the meditation chamber, and a voice shouted something urgent but unintelligible on the other side. Narin sprang to the door, working the lock mechanism and pulling the door open before the shouting and the pounding stopped.

Ty stood on the threshold, one fist upraised to strike again at the metal door as it swung inward. He rushed—almost fell, in his haste—headlong into the meditation chamber, and dropped to his knees in front of Arekhon. The younger Mage's face was greyish-pale underneath a mask of soot and perspiration, and his pupils were wide and black.

He drew a ragged, shuddering breath. "Lord Arekhon—"

"Ty?" Arekhon reached down to take Ty by the arms and help him back to his feet. One touch was enough for him to feel how Ty was shaking. "What's wrong?"

"The Captain." Ty swallowed. "She wants Lord Garrod on the bridge of the other ship. Right now."

"Then we should go there. Can you show us the way?"

Ty nodded jerkily. "It's . . . not hard to find."

"Good." Arekhon summoned Vai and Narin with a glance,

and Garrod with a quick but respectful inclination of his head in the direction of the door. "Let's go."

Outside the meditation chamber, *Rain-on-Dark-Water* was silent, the narrow passages lit only by dim amber lights. Garrod strode on ahead of the other Mages, his dark robes billowing. Arekhon didn't try to stop him—Garrod might not be the First of the Circle any longer, but neither was he truly one of Arekhon's Mages to command. The Captain had asked for him by name; if she wanted the rank and not the man, they would soon find out.

Meanwhile, Arekhon had Ty to deal with. The younger Mage hadn't said anything since the Circle left the meditation chamber, and Arekhon was beginning to feel worried all over again. He drew closer to Ty and spoke to him in what he hoped was a nonthreatening voice.

"What happened? Was the interception successful?"

"Yes. They . . . we . . . used the boarding tunnel." Ty stopped, wet his lips, and started again. "The other end didn't open."

"I see."

Arekhon let the matter drop. Pushing for details right now wasn't going to make Ty any happier—and if Captain sus-Mevyan had summoned Garrod to the bridge of the Entiboran ship, that meant the *Rain*'s boarding party had made their way past the obstacle one way or another.

The muster bay, when they reached it, was empty—even the fighting bridge on the upper level. Displays that should have been glowing were dark and empty, like eye sockets, and the entrance to the boarding tunnel was a gaping black mouth.

Ty pointed. "In there."

"Yes," Arekhon said. "The tunnel. But you'll have to show us how to find the bridge."

"I don't . . . yes, Lord Arekhon."

Garrod was already striding ahead into the dark opening. Arekhon paused for a moment on the edge of the shadows, fighting down a resurgence of his own earlier apprehension. Something, somewhere, had gone wrong; otherwise Ty wouldn't be in the state he was in, and Captain sus-Mevyan wouldn't have sent him as a runner to pull Garrod away from his Circle in the middle of a working.

"This is not good." Vai's words came out in a tight undertone. "Do you smell it?"

He *had* caught the smell—had thought, until she spoke, that it was an artifact of his own mind, a physical cue to match his unspoken concern. But it was real. Real, and horrible, and tied without question to the working that he and his Mages had done.

Slowly, with a great reluctance, he went into the tunnel, and down it to the airlock at the far end.

XXXIV: Year 1128 E. R.
Beyond the Farther Edge: Unknown Entiboran Ship sus-Peledaen ship *Rain-on-Dark-Water*
Ildaon: Country House of Elek Griat

ELAELI WATCHED the instrument console on the bridge of the Entiboran ship and wished she knew what it was telling her. The console had a varied array of lights and switches and small flat screens with symbols displayed in them, and she found it at once alien and teasingly familiar.

I could make this work, she thought. *Just give me some time with the manuals and a decent translator. . . .*

She glanced over at the prisoner, tied up with a pair of uniform belts and huddled out of the way against a bulkhead. The woman didn't look disposed to be helpful. Elaeli turned her attention back to the rest of the bridge.

Captain sus-Mevyan sat in the chair by the instrument console, looking across it at a rank of larger flatscreen displays mounted on the opposite bulkhead. The image of *Rain-on-Dark-Water* filled all the displays: A different angle in each screen, and in all of them an ominous dark presence, a black hunting bird with a prize in its talons.

"We've done it," sus-Mevyan mused aloud. "Done *something,* at any rate. I wish I knew what."

Elaeli tried to frame an answer, but was saved from the need to reply by the arrival of Garrod syn-Aigal.

Garrod spoke to the Captain. "I understand you've given the order to abandon ship."

"Yes," said sus-Mevyan. "We're too severely damaged to live, and we don't have the fuel to go anywhere even if we weren't damaged. We appreciate what you've done with regard to luck and all that, but right now we need something else."

She gestured toward the bound woman. "We have a prisoner, it seems, in spite of our best hopes for a fair fight and a willing exchange, and we'd like you to explain to her what happened. Maybe persuade her to help us with getting everything sorted out."

"I'll try," Garrod said. He turned to the prisoner and spoke in the Entiboran language he had labored to teach the *Rain*'s officers and crew. "Good morning, honored lady."

Her reply was long, and too rapidly colloquial for Elaeli to follow. As soon as the outburst was over, she returned to silence and sullen glowering.

"What did she say?" the Captain asked.

Garrod shook his head slowly. "I didn't catch absolutely everything," he said. "But the gist was that she believes we practice some amazing sexual customs, that our foodstuffs are things of wonder, that our immediate forebears were of a different species than ourselves, and that—were the worlds orderly—our lives would prove both brief and miserable."

sus-Mevyan didn't look amused. "Tell her that I'm just thrilled, too. But what's done is done, and if we work together we can all live a bit longer in a bit less misery."

Garrod spoke to the woman again. Her reply this time was shorter. He turned back to the Captain and said, "I never did have time to explain about Entiboran religious beliefs, I'm afraid. Some of them involve malignant spirits who guard an afterlife of eternal torment."

"Let's discuss that some other time. The ship—"

"Her exact words, Captain, were: 'Going to hell would be a pleasure if it meant I could watch you fry.' There are a couple of other concepts there I should explain; linguistically, the form of 'you' she used encompassed not just me, but all persons present in this place other than herself—"

sus-Mevyan regarded the prisoner with what might have been respect, or the recognition of a kindred spirit. "The short version, Lord Garrod."

"The short version of her reply is 'no.'"

"Thank you," said the Captain. "Tell her that we will treat her with all honor, as we are guests aboard her ship. And after that, help me find something—anything—that will show us how to run this vessel. Logbooks, records, instruction manuals—whatever will help us get back home."

She swivelled her chair around to look at Elaeli. "Meanwhile, Pilot-Principal—get someone to fetch an *uffa* pot from *Rain-on-Dark-Water* and rig it to run."

"We still don't know what kind of power they're using over here," Elaeli protested. "If it's incompatible, all we're going to get for our trouble is a lot of blue smoke and a dead pot."

"I know," said the Captain. "But we've got to test the Entiborans' power systems eventually. I'd sooner blow out the *uffa* pot right now than the ship-mind later."

Summer was well advanced on Ildaon's southern hemisphere. The days were long and warm, and the weather remained fair. The political atmosphere was likewise pleasantly calm, at least on-planet—though news from off-world spoke obliquely of trouble brewing out in space, with clashes occurring between Ildaonese mercantile interests and the Eraasian fleet-families. Jaf Otnal, once again on holiday with his friend and mentor Elek Griat, remembered a breakfast-table conversation of some years back, and smiled to think that those early efforts had at last begun to bear fruit.

On this day at Griat's country house, the sun cast dappling shadows on the grass among the trees, and the sky was high, cloudless, and blue. Jaf was lounging on the second-floor portico, overlooking the western lawn, when he noticed, high above, coming from west to east, a series of parallel clouds. Very high, they seemed, and perfectly aligned east-and-west. The forward edges of the clouds—they looked almost like points—were all of a level, as if the clouds were high aircraft flying in formation. But what formation could extend from horizon to horizon, north to south? Their passing seemed to take forever, but it was in fact only a matter of minutes before the line of clouds had passed across the western horizon. A second sweep of cloud appeared, following the first, if anything lower and heavier.

Then, from beyond the western horizon, a dark mist arose, and the light of the falling sun went blood red. The darkness rose, and rose, and grew darker.

The clouds were passing overhead more frequently now, and were closer together, more densely packed.

"Elek!" Jaf called. There was a shaky note in his voice that he couldn't help. He had grown up and gone to school on this world, before leaving it to follow his ambitions elsewhere, and he had never seen or learned of any weather like that which he now saw. "I think you ought to come outside and look at this."

Elek emerged from the country house's interior in response to Jaf's outcry. Jaf pointed in silence to the strange clouds passing overhead. Elek paused a moment on the portico, then turned back inside and came out again a moment later, holding his contra-cithara. He sat on the bare stones of the upper portico, and began to play a haunting tune.

"What is it?" Jaf asked. His friend's reaction had filled him with a sudden nameless apprehension—and still he had no idea what kind of weather the strange cloud formations might portend.

"We will see, presently," Elek replied, and resumed his music.

Jaf continued looking out in the direction of the sunset. The darkness beyond the western horizon was mixed now with light, like sparks leaping upward, and Jaf was able to feel a trembling under his feet, like a distant earthquake.

The darkness came nearer. A sound came with it, faint at first, almost too deep to hear. It grew louder. The base of the darkness came into view—highlighted with fire—and the tips of another set of clouds smashed into it. Pillars of earth, miles high perhaps, fountained up. The sound was delayed, but it came—fifty miles, perhaps, and growing closer.

And now Jaf understood.

Someone was attacking Ildaon from space, wave after wave of rocks, flung from the deep vacuum, falling through the atmosphere and smashing to the ground. Where they struck, the energy converted to heat. They struck sparks like a hammer on the forge. The sound was loud, drowning out the steady music of Elek's contra-cithara, crashing, silent, then another, louder, closer crash. Jaf could see the flames now of a firestorm. All coming nearer.

"This isn't what I intended!" he shouted. "I didn't mean this at all!"

Elek did not answer, but continued to play until the leading edge of the bombardment struck. The darkness passed over them and continued to the east. Where Griat's country house had formerly stood, only sterilized and cratered earth remained.

Arekhon was alone aboard *Rain-on-Dark-Water.* The ship was becoming progressively less habitable and more dangerous; before long the air and gravity systems would fail, and even the amber battle-lanterns would wink out, leaving the vessel to the cold and the dark.

Work parties had already come and gone, transferring as much of the *Rain*'s gear as they could to the Entiboran ship—stripping Arekhon's cabin along with the other public and private spaces aboard. Arekhon hadn't gone with them when they left. He supposed that eventually he would have to go back into the boarding tunnel, and through the broken airlock where the dead of Eraasi and Entibor had lain together in burning and blood.

Eventually, but not yet.

Instead he wandered through the winding, intertwined spaces and passageways of *Rain-on-Dark-Water,* oppressed by the weight of responsibility for something that he had intended but never—in its final outcome—envisioned. His black robes kept him from feeling the worst of the increasing chill in the ship's air, but the low-light reflections he glimpsed in dark glass or burnished metal made him look like a drifting, sable-clad ghost.

One of the homeless ones, he thought. *Like those two Entiborans dead in the airlock.*

The *Rain*'s crew members would be properly remembered—by their shipmates, if by no one else—but Arekhon's thoughts kept returning to the strangers who had also died. Would anyone care for them enough to tend the altars and make the memorial offerings, or would they go unnourished by honor and remembrance until they forgot their names and remembered only a hatred for everything that lived?

The people on this side of the interstellar gap didn't believe in caring for the *eiran;* Garrod had said so. No reason, to think that they knew anything about how to honor their dead.

Someone else, then, would have to do it for them. There were no candles on board *Rain-on-Dark-Water,* and neither flowers nor wine. Everything had been taken away—almost everything.

He went back to the empty muster bay. There, standing in the amber-lit shadows, he took out the clasp knife he had carried, in fleet uniform and out of it, ever since his prentice-voyage. The engraving on the metal case had worn some in the intervening years, but he could still read the lettering: "sus-Dariv's *Path-Lined-with-Flowers.*" He unfolded the knife and slashed the blade across the heel of his left hand.

Blood rose up and flowed freely in the track of the knife. He held out his hand and let the red liquid fall in steady droplets to the deck in front of the boarding tunnel.

I don't know your names, he thought, *but I do this for you. So you are not forgotten.*

He was still standing there when the fleet-apprentice from the *Rain* came looking for him.

"Lord Arekhon!" The apprentice came up to him at a run, slowing abruptly at the sight of the knife and his dripping hand. "Lord Arekhon—what is this?"

"An offering," Arekhon said. "There's no wine, so this will have to do."

The apprentice glanced down at the small puddle of blood that had already collected. Reluctantly, he held out his own hand. "Should I—"

"No. I don't think you need to. Save it for our own people, if things come to that." Arekhon looked about for something to staunch the bleeding, and ended up pressing a fold of his robe against the cut. "What is it you wanted me for in the first place?"

The apprentice reached into the inner pocket of his tunic.

"We found this in the forward cabin on the other ship."

This was an envelope, stiff and heavy, with a name written across the front: *Arekhon Khreseio sus-Khalgath sus-Peledaen,* in Garrod's strong, flowing script. Arekhon took the envelope, ignoring the stab of pain from his wounded hand, and used the point of his knife to work open the flap.

"Where in the forward cabin?" he asked.

"That's the strange part," the apprentice said. "It was in the strongbox, the one that we needed torches to open. None of us had ever been in there before."

"Ah." Arekhon reached inside the envelope and pulled out a sheet of paper. It was stiffer than any he was accustomed to, with a peculiar metallic sheen, but the handwriting on the paper, like that on the envelope, was Garrod's.

Arekhon—I have placed a copy of this letter aboard the Entiboran vessel that we will someday capture, with instructions that it not be opened. Once it is in your hands, you should use this vessel's "return home" navigational setting to bring yourself to the planet Entibor.

There you will take an orbit that the ship's charts will identify as standard orbit GG-12. Should anyone local question you, tell them that Grand Councillor Demazze commands it. I will send a vessel to convey you, Syr Inadi the pilot, and my younger self to the planet's surface. I do remember that this ship's primary external lock sustained heavy damage in the boarding action, so the courier that I send to meet you will be prepared to deal with it.

I know that I will die mad. Though I have reconciled myself to the prospect, I am in no haste to encounter the day. Therefore, do not tell my younger self that you have received this message. Nothing good, I am certain, could possibly come from such foreknowing.

(signed) Garrod syn-Aigal sus-Demaizen .

Arekhon slipped the letter back into the envelope. His name across the front of the envelope was smeared with blood from his cut hand, and he'd left red fingerprints on the letter as well.

"You never watched me read this," he said to the fleet-apprentice. "And you have no idea what was in it. In fact, you aren't interested in knowing what was in it. And if you're in the habit of talking in your sleep, you're going to tape your mouth shut at bedtime. Do you understand?"

The apprentice nodded. "Yes, Lord Arekhon. I understand."

"Good. Now go. Tell Captain sus-Mevyan that I will be coming back aboard directly."

The apprentice took a few steps backward, turned, and all but ran into the boarding tunnel. After he was gone, Arekhon dropped the clasp knife from *Path-Lined-with-Flowers* into the puddle of drying blood.

"Leave us in peace," he whispered. "We never meant the harm that we did."

XXXV: YEAR 1128 E. R.
ENTIBORAN SPACE: *SWIFT PASSAGE*
FREIGHT CARRIER
NUMBER FORTY-TWO
ERAASI: HANJLAT

T HE NAME of the Entiboran ship, Arekhon learned, was *Swift Passage Freight Carrier Number Forty-two*. He wondered what her builders had been thinking of, to give her a name like that, where any luck that came to it would have to be shared with forty-one sisters. Or maybe more ... there was no telling when a forty-third might show up, or a hundredth.

All the removable contents of *Rain-on-Dark-Water* had been brought on board *Forty-two*, and room had been found for all the *Rain*'s surviving crew members. It was a tight fit, even with the reduction in numbers; *Forty-two* was as large as the Eraasian ship, but she ran with a fraction of the crew. Most of her extra space went to engines and cargo, and to mechanical devices that did the work of the missing people.

"They've got some kind of double-engine system," Elaeli told him, soon after he came aboard. "One set for normal space and another for the Void ... that's how they get their speed, it looks like. The chief engineer is in love; he thinks we can retool the orbital yards to make something like that for ourselves and outrun every fleet-family in the homeworlds. If we can get a prototype home with us, that is."

"Getting home is going to be a problem," Arekhon agreed. He leaned wearily against a bulkhead in the space that until recently had served as *Forty-two*'s galley and dining hall and recreation space combined. Now it held rows of sleepsacks and bedrolls, most of them occupied by exhausted, slumbering bodies. "Have you figured out how to make our charts talk to their ship-minds yet?"

Elaeli ran her hands through her hair. " 'Rekhe, we haven't even figured out what makes their ship-minds work! Everything we've taken a peek at is inorganic, like the junk they used to make on Ayarat before they started buying good-quality components from us instead. You might as well try to hook up a side of meat to a sledgehammer—you'd get better results and you wouldn't ruin the meat."

"How about manual input?"

"Sure. Ten, fifteen years from now, when Garrod's finished translating all of their manuals into Eraasian so we can understand them, and all our data into their lingo so we can punch it in. But hey, we've got the time."

She closed her eyes and drew a deep, shaky breath. "I'm sorry, 'Rekhe. It's just . . . I'm tired, and I don't know what we're going to do, short of calling on some of these strangers for help and getting ourselves hauled in for salvage. Us, the pride of the fleet!"

"We're not quite that desperate," Arekhon said. "At least, I don't think so."

He thought about the letter from *Forty-two*'s strongbox. Somebody on Entibor was expecting them—had even prepared the way for their arrival—somebody who claimed to be Garrod himself. Arekhon wished he knew whether he believed in the letter or not. The Garrod who had joined the Circle at the midpoint of the *Rain*'s journey had never mentioned planning such a thing, and the Garrod who had come back after the working had been incapable of speech or thought.

Sighing, Arekhon pushed himself away from the bulkhead. "I've got some work waiting to be taken care of," he said to Elaeli, and went off to ask the prisoner about *Forty-two*'s Return Home navigational setting.

He found Iulan Vai standing guard outside the berthing compartment that was serving as a cell—it was locked, but there was no way of telling if the prisoner had access to some kind of emergency override. Vai had changed out of her Circle robes and was back in her plain black tunic and trousers. Her eyes had dark smudges under them, and like everyone else Arekhon had seen recently, she looked tired.

"I need to talk with the prisoner," Arekhon said. "This is important."

"Give me a minute, then." Vai wrestled with the unfamiliar lock mechanism until the door swung open. "There. Go on in. If she tries to throttle you or something, give a yell and I'll come charging to the rescue."

The prisoner didn't look to be up for throttling anybody at the moment. She lay on the cabin's single bunk, hands flat beside her on the mattress, gazing up at the metal plates of the overhead. The arrival of a visitor brought no reaction on her part.

Arekhon pulled up the compartment's only chair and sat in it. Then, speaking to the air somewhere above the bunk, he said in halting, careful Entiboran, "Who do you think we are?"

"Pirates," she said. Her voice was a dull monotone, but the words were slow and clear. "Criminals. Thieves. Murderers. Scum and degraded *seglinry* . . . "

"Yes. Where do you suppose we are from?"

"Does it matter? From Galcen or Khesat or farther, what difference does it make to me?"

"No one has told you?" he said. "We come from farther even than that." Even though the place names she had given were unfamiliar to him, he hoped he was not lying. He waited for a reaction; when she said nothing, he went on. "Do you know about the gap between the stars—the dead plane, where there are no worlds?"

"No. I don't care."

"You should," he told her. "There are people on the far side of that gap, and we're them."

This time she did react, turning her head on the pillow and regarding him with angry grey eyes. "Go back, then. And take your murdering ways with you."

"We're trying," he said. "There's nothing we want to do more. We came for trade, did you know that? All we wanted to do was trade."

"You have a strange way of going about it."

"I'm sorry. We'll go back as soon as we can. But first I need to learn about the Return Home navigational setting."

She gave a harsh laugh. "The Return Home will ·take us straight back to Entibor. Once you get arrive, you'll be torn limb from limb and hair from hair. We don't like pirates."

"I thought you'd approve," said Arekhon. "But I want to use it anyway."

"Why should I trust murdering scum *eru tarraquin lindeleos lindela latanque* . . ." The invective trailed off into a string of terms that Garrod hadn't bothered to include in his instructional vocabulary, or perhaps didn't know himself.

"You will not need to trust anyone," Arekhon said. "But my Captain trusts me, and I will trust you."

Her eyes were puzzled now, instead of angry. "I don't understand."

"A simple matter. I will trust you to press the Return Home setting, rather than the self-destruct."

"Your ships have a self-destruct?"

He nodded. "Sometimes they damage themselves in chase-and-boarding, and it's better to destroy them than to leave them adrift for salvage. We'll be disposing of the *Rain* that way tomorrow—would you like to watch?"

A flicker of vindictive interest crossed the prisoner's face, the first reaction that she had shown other than dull anger. "To· see your pirate ship destroyed, yes."

"Then I'll arrange for you to be on the bridge with us tomorrow," he said. "You can watch everything."

Seyo Hannet had returned to Eraasi full of the satisfaction that comes from a piece of work neatly done. Now that a plausible amount of time had elapsed, he sat at a secured communications line in the Hanilat office of the League of Unallied Shippers and made ready to tackle the next item on his list.

He had already tied off one set of inconvenient loose ends at his employer's behest. The people on the Ayaratan end of the conspiracy, with the exception of Jaf Otnal, had always been lukewarm in pursuit of its goals, as well as—in Hannet's private opinion—insufficiently ruthless. With the game moving into a more active phase, the Ayaratans had known too much for safety.

Their demise was only fair, was Hannet's opinion. Those who were unwilling to take risks and act vigorously in a project's early stages should not expect to see a reward at the end of it.

The next job was different. Some people were dangerous because of what they knew and whom they might tell; others were dangerous in and of themselves. Like knives, once those had done their cutting they had to be put away. Those who made luck could also destroy it, if their minds should change . . . but not even a luck-bringer could survive in the face of overwhelming force.

It was better, Hannet decided, not to inform Felan Diasul about this stage of the plan in advance. Family loyalty might prove stronger than ambition, in a direct contest between the two; and there was no point in forcing Diasul into a choice while he still had useful contributions to make to the greater project. How to carry out the present agenda, though . . . Hannet's fingers tapped out quick, disjointed rhythms on the desktop while his mind considered methods and alternatives.

A stanza from an old song came to him, weaving through his thoughts on a fragment of music: *O tell me should I slay this one, or should I slay them all, or should I take you from this place and burn this cursèd hall?*

He stopped tapping and called up the desk's address book instead. A quick access code later, he was scanning the entries in a select roster.

That one—a mercenary outfit belonging to a prominent fleet-family, recently formed and now on training maneuvers in the hinterlands north and west of Hanilat. They would get a change in orders, for a live-fire exercise, coupled with an infusion of cash sufficient to quell any doubts in their minds about the ethical grey areas in what they were hired to do.

Hannet circled an area on a map of the Wide Hills district, labeled it "Free Fire," and sealed it in a courier envelope along with a bearer bond convertible to securities anywhere, with no questions asked. He rang for a messenger, then turned his attention to the other matters.

Some hours later he heard—on a communications channel

which he should not have been able to monitor—of how a ship of the sus-Peledaen, in response to certain atrocities committed in deep space, had struck against selected sites on the planet Ildaon. Hannet wondered if his employers had been among the multitude of casualties. After a few minutes' thought, he dismissed the question as irrelevant.

By the time the shuttles and relays that allowed for communication between the worlds were able to bring him an answer, the current phase of operations would be long over.

The members of the Circle were quartered together in one of *Forty-two*'s pressurized cargo bays, surrounded by crates and containers marked in strange alphabets. Narin snored; Ty had nightmares; and the Entiboran night-cycle was shorter than the one the fleet-families used. Arekhon slept poorly, and woke up feeling disoriented and oppressed.

For an instant he couldn't remember where he was, or why he should be in such heavy spirits. Then he remembered. He was aboard an alien ship, on the far side of the Edge from home, and today they were going to set free the *Rain*.

After putting on clean clothes, the best ones he had with him, and finding the nearest *uffa* pot, he felt somewhat better. An hour after ship's-rising, he went to the prisoner's cabin where Garrod, this time, was keeping watch.

"I promised her she could watch the self-destruct," Arekhon said. "I'll send down an apprentice from the bridge when everything's ready."

Garrod raised his eyebrows. "What does the Captain have to say about that idea?"

"She agreed when I told her it would raise the prisoner's spirits." Arekhon felt uneasy about keeping back part of the truth, but the letter that he still carried on his person, sealed in the inside pocket of his tunic, had been specific. Garrod should not know.

Arekhon continued on to the *Forty-two*'s bridge, where others of the crew—Elaeli and the Captain among them—were already watching the bank of flatscreens. In all of the displays the looming shape of *Rain-on-Dark-Water*, tied to the Entiboran ship by its boarding tunnel, hung black and silent. It wasn't as good a view as would have been afforded at this range by proper bridge windows, but it was impressive nevertheless.

"Is it time yet?" he asked.

"Everything's in place and armed," sus-Mevyan said. She turned to the fleet-apprentice. "You can send for the prisoner now."

The apprentice hurried off, and returned a few minutes later with Garrod and the prisoner. The Entiboran was glum and silent; she regarded the *Rain*'s hovering, enscreened image with undisguised hostility. Arekhon gave her a polite nod of greeting, but she didn't respond.

Captain sus-Mevyan frowned at the unfamiliar console for a moment, then stabbed at one of the switches. Her action was rewarded by the faint crackle of an open communications line.

"Is everybody clear?" she asked.

The voice of the Chief Engineer came over the line. "All clear and ready, Captain."

"Stand by to blow explosive bolts. Execute."

The boarding tunnel fell clear and the two vessels separated.

"Stand by to fire distancing rockets. Execute."

A twinkle of light exploded along the side of the *Rain* nearest them. In ponderous silence, the black ship drifted away, changing shape as it receded into the distance—from a flattened sphere to a disk to a pinpoint of light, shining at them in multiple images in the flatscreen displays.

Captain sus-Mevyan looked over at Arekhon. "You're from the inner family. Would you do her the honor of giving the final word?"

Arekhon thought of protesting that he had no place in the fleet any longer, that he'd opted out of the family well before leaving Eraasi, but he knew that the legalities didn't matter. He was a sus-Peledaen of the senior line—he had never denied his family or his ancestors—and he had used that position unashamedly to bring this voyage about. He stepped up to the console, into the range of the audio pickup.

"She was sus-Peledaen's *Rain-on-Dark-Water,*" he said. "Now we release her from the family's service and set her free." The bridge was silent; he could hear the sound of his own breathing grow ragged for a moment before it steadied and he was able to continue. "Stand by to fire demo charges. Execute."

A moment passed. The pinpoint of light grew larger. Like a bubble of metal with a yellow flame at its core it expanded. The flame faded to red, then went out. The bubble grew too faint to see.

"There," Arekhon said to the prisoner. "You have seen; now, please, take us back to your world."

"With pleasure," she said. "And I hope they kill the lot of you."

XXXVI: Year 1128 E. R.
Eraasi: Demaizen Old Hall
Entiboran Space, Standard
Orbit GG-12: *Swift*
Passage Freight Carrier
Number Forty-Two
Octagon Diamond

SUMMERTIME AT Demaizen Old Hall brought changeable weather. The sun that day had shone through most of the morning, but by mid-afternoon the sky had clouded over. Serazao cut sprigs of flowering tartgrass and put them in Garrod's room, to give it cheer and a pleasant scent and color. Garrod's state had not altered since coming back from the Void, though his body had dwindled through lack of action. Delath exercised him, moving his arms, helping him walk, but accomplished little more than slowing his steady decay.

Kief had been restless all day, walking to the door, then back to the workroom, scanning the empty hills. 'Rekhe and the rest of the Circle had been gone for over three years—far longer than anyone had anticipated, almost the limit of their supplies of fuel. Kief thought about the travelers often, remembering them in his workings and his private intentions, and feared for them, perhaps, more than did either Delath or Serazao. It was the fault of his stargazer's training, he told himself, the cost of too much knowledge.

All the news these days was disturbing: Stories about the

star-lords building warfleets, and men fighting battles in far off places. The Hall had everything it needed, either from the supplies in the pantry, or from the gardens; when Delath said that they shouldn't go into town unless it became absolutely necessary, Kief and Serazao agreed. Kief remembered his brother in his workings, and asked the others to keep his intentions in mind as well, but even that much effort seemed pointless and tending to nothing.

Toward evening the sun dipped below the edge of the clouds, casting golden light on the peaks of the roof and adding a luster to the deep green of the trees along the walk. Kief was standing under the archway of the main door when he heard a growling sound coming from the distant highway. At first it seemed a like a far-off echo of thunder, though the clouds were wrong for a thunderstorm, but it kept up too long.

I don't like this, not even a little, he thought.

He backed up, turned, and walked into the hall, not quite running. He found Del in the kitchen, making soup—not as good as Narin's, but good enough with condensed stock from the pantry and fresh vegetables from the garden.

Del looked up from chopping lorchen stalks and regarded Kief with a worried expression. "What's the problem?"

"Something bad is coming. I can feel it."

"I meditated today," Del said thoughtfully. "I didn't see anything like that. Only the patterns, growing brighter."

Kief shrugged. "I'm worrying too much, maybe. It's probably just the weather."

"Or maybe not." It was Serazao, just entering from the upper hall. "Garrod's been restless all day too. Sometimes I think he's on the verge of coming out of it and talking to me—I know he wants to talk. He's asleep now, though, so I thought I'd slip away."

The sun dipped behind the low clouds, and the kitchen grew darker. Rain began to patter against the windows.

"Ah," said Kief. "It was the weather. That's all."

The Void-transit was a short one this time, barely long enough for the faint queasiness of transition to subside before it was time for emergence. When they came out, the displays on the bridge showed images of a marbled, temperate globe:

A tracery of clouds; glittering ice caps; wide blue oceans and brown-and-green continents.

The crew of sus-Peledaen's *Rain-on-Dark-Water*, now of *Forty-two,* watched the new world grow closer. The Entiboran ship put itself into high orbit with the same efficiency as it had taken itself through the Void, and began transmitting a signal. Arekhon, waiting on *Forty-two*'s bridge with Captain sus-Mevyan, hoped that the signal wasn't a pre-set message giving somebody orders to shoot them on sight.

Enough time passed for Arekhon to stop worrying about an armed attack and begin worrying instead about being ignored. Finally, the communications link crackled open, and a faint voice began speaking in Entiboran. Arekhon moved closer to the console, straining both mind and hearing to make sense of the alien, signal-distorted words.

"Swift Passage Freight Carrier Number Forty-two, this is Inspace Control. State the nature of your emergency."

Arekhon glanced over at Captain sus-Mevyan. At her curt nod of permission, he spoke to the audio pickup. "We have assumed standard orbit GG-12"—at least, if GG-12 was the orbit set into the Return Home—"by the command of Grand Councillor Demazze."

There was a brief pause. *"Swift Passage Freight Carrier Number Forty-two,* we have received your message. Please stand by for instructions."

The link crackled shut. The wait that followed lasted long enough for Arekhon to start getting nervous again. Then the link came back on.

"Swift Passage Freight Carrier Number Forty-two, prepare to transfer your crew to deep-space passenger vessel *Octagon Diamond.* Previously designated personnel will remain aboard *Forty-two* and await a shuttle to the surface."

sus-Mevyan looked at Arekhon curiously. " 'Previously designated personnel'?" she asked as soon as the link had closed. "Who are they?"

"Lord Garrod," he said. "Pilot-Principal Inadi. And me. For negotiations, I suppose—we're about the only ones who speak the language well enough to hold a conversation."

"That mysterious letter of yours again?"

He nodded. "I don't understand it either. But we've tried doing things our own way and gotten nowhere."

Octagon Diamond was enormous. *Forty-two* was pocket-sized by comparison. Not even the lost *Rain-on-Dark-Water* had been so big.

Transfer to the *Diamond,* accordingly, was slow and cumbersome. The tunnel connecting *Forty-two* with the larger ship was a flexible zero-gravity tube; pressure-suited crew members, towing their bundles of personal effects, made the awkward journey along its length in a long, floating line.

Once the transfer was completed, the *Octagon Diamond* disconnected from *Forty-two* and assumed an orbit not far away—at least, not far away as things went in space. The three Eraasians still aboard *Forty-two* donned their pressure suits and waited for the promised shuttle.

Elaeli was carrying the helmet of her suit in the crook of one arm. She ran her free hand through her hair. "You know, I hope we're not doing something really stupid."

"So do I," Arekhon said. "But I don't think we have much choice. We're a long way from home in an unfamiliar ship, and if these people take offense and decide to stop us we may never get back."

"Have you seen the *eiran* here?" Garrod asked.

"I haven't had the time for a proper meditation," he admitted. In the aftermath of the bloody takeover of *Forty-two,* he'd also lacked the inclination. That would have to change soon, he supposed. "Or the opportunity, with the ship so crowded."

"You should make the opportunity," Garrod said. "Someone, somewhere near here, is taking the lines in hand. There is order—not much of it, I grant you—coming out of all this chaos."

"Our mysterious friend, do you think?" asked Elaeli.

"Mysterious, certainly. And powerful, if he has ships like the *Diamond* at his disposal to give away. Friendly . . ."

Arekhon shrugged. "Who knows? So far, at least, he doesn't seem to wish us ill."

A hooting sound over the ship's audio broke into their conversation—*Forty-two*'s warning that the shuttle was making ready to approach the lock. Arekhon put on his helmet and sealed his pressure suit for the transfer.

No need this time for a clumsy swim through a transfer tube; the shuttle turned out to be small enough to mate with the outer port directly. Changing ships was a matter of climbing a ladder that extended itself from *Forty-two*'s transfer lock into that of the shuttle—more of the automatic machinery that had made it possible to run the ship with such a small crew.

The shuttle itself was scarcely more than a passenger pod, unenhanced by local gravity or any other amenities. The main compartment held several objects which Arekhon recognized as acceleration couches, though of unfamiliar design. He took the nearest one, and indicated to Garrod and Elaeli that they should make their choice of the others.

Forty-two's ladder retracted, and the hatch cycled shut. The sound of another hatch opening somewhere inside the shuttle made Arekhon look around, and he saw that two men—two people, at any rate—had emerged from the forward compartment. They wore tight, quilted blue livery over all of their bodies, from boots to gloves, and helmets like round, mirrored blue globes.

Moving easily in the zero gravity, they approached the couches and adjusted the webbing that secured Arekhon and the other two passengers on their couches. Again, the purpose of the webbing was obvious, but the design was not like that of the homeworlds: Couches here had a central strap running down the center of the occupant's body, with webbing stretching to either side at the shoulder, chest, hips, thighs, and ankles. When all of the webbing was in place, the passengers were effectively immobilized.

If somebody wanted to do us harm, Arekhon reflected, *here and now would be an excellent opportunity. No need to take any action; just leave the inconvenient visitors tied up on the couches and go away.*

The two Entiborans returned to the forward compartment, and Arekhon heard the mechanical sound of the closing hatch. Then all at once the bottom dropped out, and Arekhon felt his stomach heading for his windpipe as the shuttle accelerated downward. *They're in a hurry,* he thought, as the blood rushed to his head and his vision blurred. *And they don't believe in coddling the passengers.*

Abruptly the pressure reversed, so that he felt many times heavier than his natural weight, and a low moaning vibration filled the craft, even through the padding and restraints. Side forces pressed him first one way against the restraining ties and then the other. The motion ceased and the weight became even, not the artificial pull of a ship in space, but real planet-bound gravity.

The lights flickered once, then returned, burning more brightly and evenly than before. Silence replaced the sounds of motors and engines, and even the hum of the ventilators.

The door sounded a moment later, and the two blue-clad Entiborans returned to help the three passengers out of their couches. The Entiborans didn't speak, but indicated by signs and gestures that it was now possible to remove the pressure suits, though they made no move to take off their own.

Arekhon unsuited and sat up, rubbing his shoulders to return the circulation to them. Opposite the lock where *Rain-on-Dark-Water*'s crew had debarked, a section of the shuttle's deck had swung down to form a ramp. Beyond the ramp, external lights glowed—not the natural light of a star, but the artificial light of electricity flowing through carbon rods. It was hard to tell from within the shuttle, but Arekhon thought that it was night outside.

The two Entiborans withdrew again to the forward compartment, still without speaking. Garrod swung his legs over the side of his couch and nodded toward the lowered ramp.

"The message seems fairly clear," he said. "We go that way. I can already vouch for the gravity and atmosphere being well within homeworld tolerance."

The ground at the bottom of the ramp was black and hard and wet. The light came from spotlights mounted on tall poles. Beyond the protecting overhang of the vessel, a heavy rain was slanting down, the falling drops turning golden in the artificial light. A figure was approaching, a tall man silhouetted against the spotlights' glare.

When the man arrived, Arekhon saw that he wore a rain garment of some kind, a sleeveless rectangle of green fabric worn surcoat-wise, with a hood in the center enclosing his face and yellow hair. In one hand he carried a walking-staff almost as tall as he was; with the other, he held out to the travelers three packets made of the same slick cloth as his surcoat. Unfolded, the packets proved to be rainwear similar to his own.

Elaeli smiled at the man as she pulled on her surcoat and drew up the hood. "Thank you," she said in the local tongue. "I hate getting my hair wet."

"I am Master Lenset, aide to Councillor Demazze," the man said in the same language. "I ask that you follow me."

XXXVII: Year 1128 E. R.
Entiboran Space, Standard Orbit GG-12: *Octagon Diamond*
Entibor: Secure Landing Zone
Eraasi: Demaizen Old Hall

ULAN VAI sat cross-legged on her bunk aboard *Octagon Diamond*, writing a message. The *Diamond* was a luxurious ship by Eraasian standards—maybe by the standards of this side of the galaxy as well; Vai didn't know—and for the first time since leaving Hanilat she wasn't sharing quarters with anyone but herself.

It made some things a great deal easier.

SUS-PELEDAEN SHIP *RAIN-ON-DARK-WATER* LOST, she tapped out on the tiny keys of her message pad. CREW AND CIRCLE RETURNING IN SHIP OF LOCAL MAKE. RECOMMEND PREPARING SHIPYARDS FOR EXTENSIVE CHANGES IN ENGINE CONSTRUCTION TECHNIQUES. SEE ATTACHED COPY OF SUS-PELEDAEN ENGINEER'S PRELIMINARY REPORT AND DIAGRAMS.

Vai was proud of that attached copy. Acquiring it—in the midst of the worry about disposing of the *Rain*, and then about *Forty-two*'s auto-controlled transit to Entibor—had taken all of her old skills and some of her new ones, and she had enjoyed herself a great deal. It was good to know that taking up Magery hadn't ruined her touch.

Getting the report back to Theledau sus-Radal was going to

be easy by comparison. Captain sus-Mevyan had brought all of the *Rain*'s message-drones across to the *Diamond*, which meant that Vai could hide her report in the general clutter of information.

A drone was mostly data storage with a Void-capable engine, and it would backtrack along the *Rain*'s trail of navigational beacons at speeds a manned vessel couldn't match. News of the *Rain*'s adventures would reach the sus-Peledaen shipyards well before the *Diamond* appeared in Eraasian space.

And thanks to her efforts, the news would reach the sus-Radal yards as well. She wondered if Natelth sus-Khalgath talked family business with his younger brother any more, and what Arekhon would say if he found out that she had told Theledau sus-Radal about *Forty-two*'s engines.

Worry about that when you get home, she told herself. *Meanwhile . . . a private cabin makes a lot of things easier.*

The guide led Arekhon, Garrod, and Elaeli across the rain-swept landing area to an armored metal doorway let into the side of a hill. The doorway swung outward, admitting them to the anteroom of what was clearly an extensive underground complex.

The room was paneled in wood, with non-structural but still impressive rib-groined vaults overhead, and dim but pleasant lighting. Soft carpets covered the floor beneath their feet, though from its coldness and lack of give Arekhon thought that the surface under the carpet might be stone rather than wood. The guide led them through the antechamber and down a long corridor, without bothering to turn aside for any of the closed doors along the paneled walls.

They came at last to an open doorway, and passed through it into what Arekhon guessed was a reception hall of some sort, a long narrow room furnished with a number of alcoves and conversational nooks. Its high ceiling was painted with heroic scenes in bright colors, showing foreshortened figures ascending into a mass of clouds and bright light.

Something to honor the ancestors, Arekhon thought, then shook his head. *For all you know, it could be favorite pictures from a children's bedtime storybook. These people are not like us.*

"Wait here for my lord Demazze," their guide said, and, bowing, departed through one of the room's side-arches.

They waited. Arekhon felt uncomfortably conscious of his wet surcoat shedding rainwater onto the carpet. Elaeli was craning her neck to look at the ceiling. Garrod, meanwhile, stood in the center of the room with his arms folded across his chest, seemingly unintimidated by their reception and the elegant decor.

Maybe he saw more impressive stuff than this all the time when he was here before, Arekhon thought. *Or else he's a better actor than I'll ever be.*

A fanfare sounded over an unseen speaker—the notes had the tinny, remote quality of a synthesized recording—and a man entered the room through a sliding doorway that had been concealed in the paneling. He was tall and solidly broad-shouldered, with a heavy shock of grey hair and a close-trimmed, iron-grey beard.

Arekhon recognized him at once. The letter aboard *Forty-two* had not lied; this was Garrod syn-Aigal sus-Demaizen, as Arekhon and Narin had pulled him out of the Void at the end of the great working.

Arekhon looked at him closely. *Is he already mad, I wonder? His letter was certainly strange enough.*

But the Councillor's eyes, while brighter and holding more suppressed excitement than Arekhon found comforting, were at the moment sane.

"I'm Councillor Demazze," the newcomer said. "No need for introductions—I know all three of you very well. I've been waiting for you to show up for years now; I'd begun to think I might have made an error when I did the initial calculations, but it was all so long ago I couldn't remember."

"You *know* us?" Elaeli asked. "How?"

Garrod was regarding the Councillor with suspicion. Demazze's lined and weathered face was not the one that he was accustomed to seeing in the mirror, but Arekhon didn't expect the difference to puzzle him much longer. And yet the Councillor himself had set up this meeting . . . Arekhon wished he knew what was going on.

"You came through the Void?" Garrod asked.

"Of course," said the Councillor. "But we don't have time to compare notes. The political situation is terribly tense right now—Hegemony troops all around, and the Meteunese—but everything will work out, I'm certain of it, if we can just get all the papers signed in time . . ."

Elaeli said, "Papers?"

Demazze waved a hand. "Diplomatic credentials. For you especially; the nation-state that I judge to be most receptive to the idea of open trade has a matrilineal succession, and I've had enormous trouble getting the current ruler to regard me as anything more than an impractical scholar. Perhaps you may have better luck."

"I don't want to be an ambassador," said Elaeli. "I'm a shiphandler who wants to be Fleet-Captain someday."

"A laudable ambition—but if you would do an old man a favor and go through the portfolio over there on the side table . . ."

"Humor him, Pilot-Principal," Garrod said curtly.

Elaeli glanced from Garrod to Arekhon, who nodded. She moved off in the direction of the alcove the Councillor had indicated. Garrod, eyebrows bristling, turned back to Demazze.

"What in the world are you up to, Councillor?" he demanded. " 'Diplomatic credentials,' indeed!"

Demazze smiled. "What in the world, exactly. You and I, Lord sus-Demaizen, we know how to organize and run a planetary government based on recognized family structures. It seems natural to us. But these poor benighted heathens don't have a clue. They're stuck in the political thinking of a millennium ago. We're going to have to change all that, if you want your dream of a single galaxy to have a chance."

"You *are* mad," said Garrod.

"No," said Demazze. "Not yet."

As he spoke, red lights began to blink above all the doorways. A moment later, all the lights in the room went out.

"The Hegemony," said Demazze quietly in the darkness. "Or perhaps the Meteunese. I never knew which."

Arekhon felt the tug of *eiran* coming into place and drawing a pattern tight. Loss and separation, striving and exile . . .

"Elaeli!" he shouted, but his cry was lost in a deep, rumbling crash of falling stone and metal as the ceiling collapsed.

At Demaizen, the wind began to rise. Kief went to the kitchen window and looked out at the night.

Something about the way the rain dashed against the windows—fitful bursts, fast and hard, followed by a few minutes or seconds of quiet, then the hard dashing rain again—made him edgy and restless. Delath and Serazao didn't seem to be affected by it; Del was absorbed in skimming the fat off the soup, and 'Zao was half-asleep at the kitchen table, nodding over her mug of *uffa*.

"Listen," said Kief. "Did you hear something?"

Del laid aside the spoon. "You check in back. I'll go around to the front and see if anything's wrong out there."

Kief started for the back door—the old servants' entrance, from the days when the Hall had servants—and stopped again when 'Zao blinked, tilted her head to catch the sound, and said, "No. It came from upstairs."

She was right. Kief could hear the sound distinctly now: Footsteps—slow, shuffling footsteps—moving along the hallway outside the kitchen. 'Zao, pale and trembling, half-rose from her chair, her eyes lit with sudden hope.

Garrod—thin, haggard, but moving of his own volition, walking—stood in the kitchen door and reached out his hand to support himself on the frame. A bolt of lightning struck nearby, the flash intense, the noise instantaneous. It limned Garrod with an intense blue-white light.

"Where is my staff?" he asked, his voice husky and low. "Did I leave it on Entibor?"

"Lord Garrod," Delath began, starting toward him. "You've been unwell for a long time, and we—"

Garrod opened his mouth to speak again—but nothing came out of his mouth, nothing but blood and bone fragments, and he pitched forward, thrown by the force of the projectiles hitting him from behind. He fell into Delath's arms, and his weight bore them both down to the floor.

The doorway behind him was full of men carrying automatic weapons. Their leader pointed a handgun down and emptied the magazine into Del and Garrod, then calmly re-

loaded while the others flowed around him into the kitchen.
The pot of soup fell over on the stove and sent up a cloud of
foul-smelling steam. Serazao raised her staff, the fire of her
wrath blazing, and lunged with a scream of fury at the nearest
soldier. He shot her down before she could close half the distance. She collapsed to the floor and did not move.

Kief—still unseen in the shadows of the rear entryway—
stood motionless with shock. But not for long. Serazao had
died with the fire of the universe running through her; he took
her energy into himself before it could escape, and turned it
outward again in a burst of crimson, killing wrath.

The man who had shot Serazao died where he stood, his
weapon clattering from his hand and blood spurting from his
eyes. Kief stepped out into the center of the kitchen. His staff
was in his hand, and blazing with a pure red fire.

The men who had brought death into the room were all dead
themselves, blood mixed with clear fluid pouring from their
ears and noses. But far off, he heard more voices shouting
orders: "Spread out! Search the buildings and the grounds! No
survivors!"

Kief walked out of the kitchen and into the main part of the
Hall. His mind raced along the pathways of power. He saw
the betrayal—the illusions and lies that lay beneath the carnage—and none of the men who saw him that night lived to
speak of what they saw.

Outside in the rain, a dark line of vehicles waited on the
circular gravel drive. Kief recognized them from their pictures:
Armored groundcars, designed to fight for one faction against
another—brother against brother—in the growing unpleasant-
ness. They were an abomination. He laid his hand on the first
one as he passed. The fuel and ammunition inside it exploded,
drowning the screams of the men trapped in the blazing hulk.

"City against city," Kief repeated aloud, as one vehicle after
another exploded and lit up the night with fire. "Brother
against brother."

And all at once he knew. He left the Hall behind him and
started walking toward Hanilat. His way was lit by the flames
that rose from the burning Hall, but he did not turn to see, not
even when the roof collapsed and the rain fell inside the blackened walls.

XXXVIII: Year 1128 E. R. Entibor: Secure Landing Zone

ELAELI WAS riffling through the contents of the portfolio—it was all paperwork in Entiboran, and she was most certainly not going to sign anything she hadn't read, regardless of who Lord Garrod thought she should be humoring—when the lights went out and the ceiling crashed down.

I'm alive, was her first coherent thought after the noises stopped. She felt like she ought to be panicking, but other things were claiming her attention first. She'd have to panic later, when she had more time.

She still had the Councillor's portfolio clasped against her chest with her left hand—*all that paperwork probably saved my life; if I hadn't come over here to look at it, I'd be lying under a pile of rubble right now, instead of standing on my own two feet*—so she reached out with her right hand toward where she thought the wall ought to be. Her fingers met the coolness of polished wood; she maintained the contact and shuffled forward toward the room where her companions had been waiting.

The wall ended with the carved molding of the doorway.

The air around her was thick with plaster dust and a faint smell of smoke.

Fire? she thought, and strained her eyes apprehensively for a glimpse of flame in the darkness. Instead, she saw a faint glow coming from somewhere ahead and above. Not the ruddy color of firelight, but a cool, steady green. She felt a wash of relief so strong it made her dizzy. One of the Mages, at least, was still alive.

She felt her way forward. The light was coming through a tiny gap, somewhere in the room ahead. Rubble slid and shifted under her feet. She stumbled, caught her balance, and went on, until she came to what had been the center of the room and could go no farther. The way was blocked by two metal beams angling downward, half-buried in blocks and slabs of stone. The green light shone through the gap.

"Who's there?" she called out.

"Elaeli?" Arekhon's voice, shaken but clear.

" 'Rekhe! What happened? Are you all right?"

"I'm fine. I think there's fighting going on, and we're in it."

Elaeli tried to imagine fighting on a scale that could destroy mountains. "No wonder that ship shot at us. They thought we were enemies."

The light grew brighter. Arekhon was coming closer, his feet crunching on the broken stone.

"Elaeli, listen," he said. He spoke in an undertone, as if he were afraid that someone might overhear. "Councillor Demazze has some kind of plan involving you. He wants to use you in a political scheme of his own."

She could hear rocks clicking and scraping as Arekhon spoke, and the green light bobbed and wavered. He was pulling at the rubble on his side—trying to dig through to her. She wondered if he had to dig one-handed, and keep the other hand on his staff as long as he wanted light.

Inconvenient, she thought—she was effectively one-handed herself, as long as she was clutching the Councillor's portfolio, but she couldn't bring herself to discard the papers that might have saved her life. *But better than the dark.*

Thinking about the papers reminded her that Arekhon had not been standing in the room alone. " 'Rekhe, where *is* Councillor Demazze? Where's Garrod?"

"I don't know," he said breathlessly. "I can't find either of them. Maybe they're buried under all this junk."

More scrambling sounds came from the other side of the pile of rubble, and a rock clattered down the pile of debris with a noise like breaking porcelain. Elaeli heard heavy breathing, followed by a faint curse and more clattering. Finally Arekhon gave a heavy sigh.

"It's no use," he said. "There's too much rock, and it's too heavy for me to move. I'm sorry."

She heard the scuffle of boots on stone as he moved closer to the gap in the rubble. She put her hand into the gap as far as she could, until she felt his fingers brush against hers.

"It's not your fault," she said. "Just don't go away."

A shaft of light, yellow-white and artificial, cut through the darkness of the buried reception hall. Elaeli heard voices shouting back and forth in Entiboran, and the sound of clattering feet.

"Arekhon!" she called out through the gap in the rubble. "Someone's coming on this side. If they have tools for digging, we can both get free."

She felt Arekhon's hand straining again to touch her own. "Be careful," he said. "This was a deliberate attack, not an accident. Not all the people here will be our friends—if any of them ever were."

The noises were coming closer. Another minute, and liveried men with hand-lights and drawn weapons burst into the room. The beams from their lights danced about the room, picking out bits of broken wood and jagged concrete, and here and there a gaudy slab of painted ceiling.

"Here she is!" one of the men called out. A light stopped its random motion and shone directly in Elaeli's face. "It looks like her, all right."

Another one of the men stepped forward. He wore different livery and insignia than the others, and she supposed that he was their leader. "Come, my lady," he said. "Councillor Demazze ordered us to keep you safe."

"Wait," she said in her best Entiboran, and pointed at the rubble. "My friend is there on the other side. All that is blocking the way."

"Come with us now," the leader said. "We cannot delay."

"What about my friend?"

"We will do what we can for him once you are safe," the leader said. "Meteunese troops are already in the building. Come, now."

He gestured two of the others forward. They took Elaeli by the arms on both sides, pulling her respectfully but firmly away from the gap in the wall, until she couldn't touch Arekhon's hand any longer.

"Let me go!" she shouted. She tried to wrench free of her rescuers, but their grip, while courteous, was determined. " 'Rekhe! Do something!"

"Go with them, Ela," he called through the gap in the rubble as the men bore her away. "Demazze knows what this is about. Let him keep you safe."

"What about you, 'Rekhe? What about you?"

"Don't worry about me." The glow from his staff was gone, driven away by the blaze of hand-lights, and the touch of his hand was just a memory. He was only a voice, rapidly fading behind her into the dark. "I'll find you again, I promise. No matter how long it takes."

Garrod had never quite trusted the Councillor, and his mind was primed to recognize a trap. When the lights died, he threw himself to the floor and rolled toward the wall where another of the side tables stood. He was under the table before he could quite recall how he got there. A second later, the ceiling collapsed.

Not a trap, he thought. Memories of his first weeks on Entibor came back to him, bringing images of war machines and cities in flame. *An attack.*

But thanks to his suspicions, he remained alive; the next problem would be getting to the open air. He inched to his right along the wall in the silence and dark until he bumped into a doorway. He pushed the door open with his extended hand, waited to see if someone lurked outside, then belly-crawled on through. The air on the other side was moving, which was good.

A passage stretched out before him. He cautiously made his way along it, keeping close to the perfumed carpet. Up and out, those were his goals. After he was away from the scene of the action, he could collect his thoughts and try to determine what had happened and how best to act.

Far away, he heard the muffled sound of small arms. Ground troops were in the building, and they were engaging other ground troops. Not a good sign.

He moved as quickly and as quietly as he could. Two turnings and a flight of stairs later he found a lighted passageway. At last he dared to stand and run. The passage turned and branched again. Each time he chose the path that led away from the sounds of fighting.

He heard a shout from behind, and running feet. Garrod sprinted, rounded a corner, and came to a dead end and another door. He yanked it open and plunged on through, then slammed the door shut and locked it behind him.

His new refuge was square and empty—and devoid of doors and windows. Shelves and boxes on three of its four sides suggested that its primary function was as a storage locker for cleaning supplies. There would only be one way out of here, and he didn't know if he was prepared to take it. Alone, without a Circle to back him . . .

He had scarcely controlled his breathing before running feet arrived outside. The door rattled, and a voice shouted "Open up!" with a Meteunese growl to the accent.

Garrod said nothing, and did not move to unlock the flimsy barrier. A projectile weapon stuttered outside, throwing slugs through the door to spatter against the far wall. Garrod threw himself face down to the floor.

The door couldn't take much more. In a moment they'd be through. If these combat troops were anything like those he'd encountered before, the first thing into the room would be a grenade. He drew a breath, caught at the *eiran,* and twisted himself to leave the material world and enter the Void.

Cold grey mist billowed around him as he rose to his feet. Now he was in a place where his enemies could not follow, but where could he go? He reached out for his Second—no. His Second was gone, and he had no Circle. No anchor. He closed his eyes and began walking in the direction that his inner feeling said was best. When at last the chill of the Void was replaced by a warmth that spoke of friends and home, he stepped back into the world and opened his eyes.

He stood in his glass-domed observatory in the villa of Mestra Adina, and the red, fur-tipped robe lay over the chair where he had placed it only a moment before.

A soft knock sounded on the door. Garrod walked over to it, opened it. Hujerie stood outside.

"Ah, Garrod, my friend," the old scholar said. "Mestra Adina has guests tonight, and begs you to join her and them for supper."

"With great pleasure," Garrod said. "Allow me a moment to freshen myself. I shall attend the Mestra presently."

Elaeli was gone, carried off against her will into the darkness.

Garrod—Councillor Demazze—had plans for her, Arekhon told himself. *He had a reason for telling his people to keep her safe. Once I'm out of here, if I can find his reason I can find her.*

First, though, he had to get out himself. He rekindled the light of his staff and entered the maze of passageways that opened off of the reception hall. For some time he wandered, following the *eiran* of the place—pale and untended though they were—until they took him from the inhabited areas into the rough-walled spaces beyond the shell of the underground complex.

The air here smelled of wet stone, but its faint motion, almost too slight for notice, gave him reassurance. The *eiran* led him further out into the natural cavern that housed the complex, drawing him on a path that—though it grew rougher and narrower as it went—tended steadily upward. Higher and higher he went, until he reached a place where the air smelled of damp earth rather than stone, and the warm water dripping down came not from broken pipes or from hidden underground watercourses, but from natural rain.

He let the glow from his staff illuminate the tunnel overhead, and soon found the source of the fresh rainfall. The *eiran* had guided him well: The gap was low enough for him to reach, and wide enough to take his body. He boosted himself into the opening and scrambled upward.

A last tight squeeze, and he squirmed out of the crack in the hillside into the night air. The slope onto which he had emerged was soaked by the driving rain and cratered by—he assumed—the same kind of powerful blows that had brought down the ceiling of the reception hall. From the noise the attack was still going on; he took shelter in the lee of a boulder that had been uprooted and shattered by the impact.

He crouched there for a while, watching streams of colored fire tracing across the sky and listening to the sound of explosions. Then, still keeping himself low, he began working away from the sounds and lights, over the crest line, until he put the bulk of the hillside between him and the fighting.

On the flat ground at the base of the hill, he saw the field where he had landed with Garrod and Elaeli only a short time before. The entrance—or at least, *one* entrance—to the underground complex had lain on that side of the hill. Perhaps that was where Elaeli had been taken. Carefully, using all of the skill he possessed in being unnoticed by others, exerting his force of will to overcome their own suspicions, he passed down the slope.

The field was silent and mostly dark. The shuttle still waited, ramp down on the hard black earth, but the pole-mounted lights that had shone so starkly before were all dead now. A flash of light from a distant explosion showed him the way to the heavy, armor-plated door, and he took the rest of the distance at a run.

The door was open, but only onto darkness. He stepped across the threshold and called light into his staff.

"Elaeli?"

"Go back to your ship."

The words were Eraasian; the voice was that of Demazze's aide who had guided the companions earlier. Master Lenset was standing between Arekhon and the passageway into the complex's lower depths. The attack had not left him unmarked—his rain-surcoat was ripped and mudstained, and his yellow hair was clotted with blood and earth.

"Where is Elaeli?" Arekhon demanded in Entiboran. "The young woman who came with me?"

"Go back to your ship." Lenset didn't move, or change languages in response. "You must return to Eraasi to finish the working."

"Not without Elaeli. Men took her—did they come this way?"

"Go back to your ship. You must return to Eraasi to finish the working."

"No." Arekhon strode over to confront the fair-haired man directly, gripping him by the shoulder with his free hand and shaking him hard. *What—happened—to—Elaeli?*

To his horror, the man's head jerked and lolled sidewise with the motion. The limp wet flesh of the earlobe brushed across Arekhon's knuckles as the head swayed back and forth, making him cry out and snatch his hand away.

With a wet, crunching sound, the head righted itself on the broken neck.

"Arekhon, you fool," it said, and the accent and cadences of its speech were those of Garrod sus-Demaizen. "She is as safe as I could make her. Safer than you are. Get to your ship and go."

Arekhon stood his ground. "I have to find Elaeli—I promised, when the men took her away."

"The great working isn't complete." The dead man's eyes focused on Arekhon's face, and for an instant it seemed as if Garrod himself stood before him. "Leave it half-finished, and the galaxy will learn that there are worse things than the Sundering."

"Then come back yourself and finish it!"

"I did come back. You brought me out of the Void through your own efforts. *Are* bringing me, even now. And left me behind, mad, on Eraasi." A wet laugh gurgled in the broken throat. "You'll get no more help from Garrod sus-Demaizen. He's dead."

With that, all intelligence vanished from the corpse's staring eyes, and its voice became a flat, wheezing monotone. "Go back to your ship. You must return to Eraasi to finish the working. Go back to your ship. . . ."

Arekhon backed away, toward the open door. He didn't turn around and put the dead man behind him until he had stepped back over the threshold into the night.

The rain was still falling. He looked out across the darkened field. The lowered ramp of the waiting shuttle, lit by the reflected glow of the ship's interior lights, made a paler spot in the darkness.

I gave my word to Elaeli, he thought. *But I gave myself to the working first.*

How many more promises will I have to break before it's done?

A line of ruddy explosions flared down the hill, then crossed the landing zone—missing the shuttle, though not by much. He sprinted across the blackened concrete and up the ramp. Before the echoes of his footsteps died, the ramp was lifting.

No one emerged from the forward cabin to strap him in. He flung himself onto the nearest couch, pulling the straps across his body and fumbling them closed as best he could, scant seconds before the roaring and shaking started and liftoff pushed him down into the cushions like the pressure of a giant hand.

The acceleration went on for a long time before it eased. The shuttle pilots were spending as little time as possible on getting rid of their inconvenient passenger. Perhaps, Arekhon thought bitterly, they too had made Garrod sus-Demaizen a promise that they now regretted having to keep.

Eventually, he felt the tug of magnetic seals taking their grip, and heard the clanks and thuds of one craft matching with another. When the door cycled open, he left his couch and passed through the joined locks into the *Diamond*'s receiving bay.

Captain sus-Mevyan was waiting for him. "What happened to Lord Garrod?" she asked. "And Pilot-Principal Inadi?"

"Gone," Arekhon told her. "Both gone. Nothing is left but the working."

XXXIX: Year 1128 E. R.
Space: *OCTAGON DIAMOND*
Eraasi: House of the Diasul

CAPTAIN SUS-MEVYAN took *Octagon Diamond* out of orbit the next ship's-morning—out of orbit, but not yet into the Void. The surviving crew members of *Rain-on-Dark-Water* might have been given a new ship by their unknown benefactor, but the gift had not included lessons in its use.

"I want us a long way out before we try making a run for the Void," sus-Mevyan told Arekhon during their conference on the bridge just before departure. "I don't intend to pay back our benefactor for his kindness by turning the *Diamond* into a meteor and hitting the planet with it."

"I'm not sure the Councillor intended to be kind," Arekhon said. "He had his own agenda all along; if his enemies hadn't struck first, he might have mentioned how he planned to use us to further it. But not everyone down below is our friend, and we may have inherited some powerful enemies."

"Another reason to take the *Diamond* out deeper. As long as we're in orbit, anyone can figure out where we're going to be." sus-Mevyan turned to the young officer at the pilot's console. "Pilot-Ancillary, you are now Pilot-Principal, acting.

Make me a course out of orbit to a location where you can comfortably calculate the path to Eraasi."

"Working," said the new Pilot-Principal. His station had the salvaged navigational gear from *Rain-on-Dark-Water* lashed into place on improvised racks that had been fastened to the main console with cords and cable tape. The connection to ship's power appeared to be functional, although the tangled nest of wires made Arekhon think, unhappily, of how much Elaeli would have disapproved of the chaos . . . and how much she would have resented letting her ancillary have all the labor, and the glory, of dealing with it.

Arekhon leaned against the bulkhead of the unfamiliar bridge for a while, watching the pilot's calculations without saying anything. Then he pushed himself away and headed aft.

He made his way through oddly angled passageways, the bulkheads glowing with polished brass and the decks tiled with a resilient material. The pipes and lines of the interior controls and power conduction were all exposed, not concealed within the bulkheads, overheads, and decks, and they were all neatly stenciled with what he presumed were words and numbers of identification.

The *Diamond* had more room inside her than any spacecraft Arekhon had ever encountered, and the sus-Peledaen cargo ships were some of the largest in the homeworlds. He knew from talking with Captain sus-Mevyan that the vessel had guns and engines like those on the abandoned *Forty-two*, only of much greater power, but minimal cargo space. She was a guardship, then, or something like one, though she had a subtly alien quality about her—an unaccustomed angularity to her internal layout; dimensions always a few inches too great or too small; everything dyed or painted with odd colors in unsettling hues—persistent reminders that the *Diamond* had been built by other hands for other minds.

Arekhon had a separate cabin assigned to him; he knew its compartment number in the Entiboran script that Garrod had taught him, and Captain sus-Mevyan had provided him with a sketch map of the ship's interior. His personal effects, or what remained of them after being twice transferred from one ship to another, already awaited him in the cabin, but he himself had gone directly from the *Diamond*'s entry bay to the conference with sus-Mevyan on the bridge.

It took him several minutes of wandering, therefore, to find the cabin, and several more to work out the lock on the door. Iulan Vai emerged from her own quarters shortly before he was finished; the idea that she now lived almost adjacent to him was a disturbing one. She stopped a little distance off and watched him. He could feel her curiosity pressing against him like hands in the dark, and turned his face away.

"What happened down there?" she asked. "You look dreadful."

The door opened. He stepped inside, and heard Vai's footsteps following, then pausing on the threshold before he could close the door. With a sigh, he moved aside and let her enter. She was trim and sleek as always, her plain black clothes only serving to accentuate a form at once rounded and compactly muscular. Arekhon found himself resenting, nevertheless, the fact that she was not Elaeli Inadi.

That was no way for the First of a Circle to think about a valued and active member. He suppressed the resentment and gestured her to the cabin's single—and oddly contoured—chair before himself dropping wearily onto the bunk.

"What happened?" he said. "We lost Garrod and Elaeli, that's what happened."

"How?"

He explained, at first in brief sketchy sentences, then in longer and more painful ones. Vai listened to the whole story, shaking her head when he was done.

"I mistrust our so-called friend Demazze," she said. "He may have arranged for that attack himself."

"I don't think so. But he would have known that it was coming." Arekhon hesitated and then went on. "I haven't told sus-Mevyan this, but—Councillor Demazze was Garrod syn-Aigal sus-Demaizen."

"How? Garrod was with us on the ship all along."

"At the same time as he was a madman back on Eraasi," Arekhon pointed out. "The Void connects times as well as places, and Garrod was a master at walking between them."

"But was Councilor Demazze as mad as Garrod became—will become—whatever?"

"I hope not," Arekhon said. "For Elaeli's sake, I hope not. Garrod believes—believed—that this world, that *all* the worlds on this side of the interstellar gap are too strong for us. They would swallow up the homeworlds and not even need to chew. He wanted to—to subvert them, somehow, and Elaeli was a part of that plan."

"It would help," Vai said, "if we knew what his plan was."

There was no answering that; Arekhon dropped his head into his hands and sighed. After a while he spoke without looking up. "Has the Circle found any place at all on this ship that's fit for us to meet in?"

"One or two. But there's another matter that needs to be settled first."

"What kind of matter?"

"The prisoner," Vai said. "We both know that sus-Mevyan isn't planning to let her go. And I'm not sure that I blame the Captain for it, either."

Arekhon lifted his head and saw that Vai was serious. "Haven't we done enough harm already?" he asked. "We crippled her ship, we killed her friends—and now we're going to make her finish her life among strangers?"

"We may have to," Vai said. "She knows—"

"—what? That we aren't from Entibor and don't speak her language? There are dozens of planets like that on this side of the galaxy."

"But none—as far as they know—on the other side of the interstellar gap. *That's* the killer, 'Rekhe. How long will it take these people to send out an expedition, in their fast ships with the big guns, once they know there's something waiting on the other side for them to find?"

"I don't know." Arekhon felt deeply and inexpressibly weary, both in body and mind; he wanted nothing so much as to dim the cabin lights, collapse onto the unyielding mattress in his bunk, and sleep for a long time without dreaming. But there would be no chance of that for a while yet. "We began this journey intending to bring the galaxy back together, not tear it further apart . . . do you think anybody is going to believe that, five hundred years from now?"

"It doesn't matter if they don't," Vai said. "The prisoner's coming with us—sus-Mevyan's already made up her mind—

but will she be with us as an enemy, or as an unfortunate guest?"

Arekhon gave a short laugh. "That's the prisoner's decision, isn't it? We certainly haven't given her much cause to like us so far."

"No . . . but if she's going to make any sort of life for herself on Eraasi, she's going to need friends, or at least allies. I believe the Circle should think hard about trying to fill that need."

"Have you foreseen a reason for it?" Arekhon regarded Vai curiously; he hadn't thought of her as having the prophetic gift. "Or is this only your personal opinion?"

"Call it opinion based on experience," Vai said. "She's going to have to trust somebody eventually, or else go mad. Better she trust us, I think, than trust the sus-Peledaen."

Arekhon felt a brief stirring of anger—or what would have been anger, if he hadn't been too tired to feel anything more than a kind of sullen irritability. "Are you saying that the fleet-family isn't honest?"

"I'm saying that the Circle doesn't owe the family any special loyalty, and might be a better friend to the prisoner because of it." Vai paused. "sus-Mevyan hasn't been worried about the prisoner's welfare. You have. That's the difference."

A rumbling engine-pulse came through the deckplates, and Arekhon felt a brief catch of pressure as the *Diamond* accelerated. "Captain's lifting from orbit," he said, grateful for the interruption. "She was talking about finding a safe place to calculate the transit."

"How long is that likely to take?"

"As long as it needs to," he said. "Tracing a back-course is easier than making a blind transit, but the navigator's working off of a makeshift console that scares me just to think of it."

"The prisoner could be helpful with that, if she wanted to be," Vai pointed out.

"If we gave her a reason not to wish all of us dead, you mean."

"You said it, I didn't."

Arekhon sighed and unfolded himself from the bunk. "Summon Ty and Narin; we need to find the prisoner and talk honestly with her."

* * *

Kief walked the night away, and all the day, while the hot anger in him chilled, and towering fury built with every step. In the end he came to his brother's house, and flung open the door. Felan Diasul exclaimed in horror at the staff burning in Kief's hand.

He walked through the doors, and no electronics could keep him out. The *aiketen* tried to prevent him, for he had been removed from their access lists, but he strode past them, and left them broken. At last, he stood at the door of his brother's office, and the wind smashed in the windows. It blew the door open amid a swirl of paper, a splinter of shards, and a shower of sparks as the viewscreens and the datadesks went nonfunctional.

A man was sitting facing the desk. As the door fell he rose, turning, and pulled a weapon from inside his clothing.

Kief saw him and knew him, in sudden images that flashed through his mind like electric shocks or bolts of lightning: *Men expiring in flame and smoke in an office tower . . . ships exploding in the deeps of space . . . Garrod and Del and Serazao, struck down by this man's order and lying in their life's blood on the floor of the Hall.*

The first priority was the weapon. Kief held out his hand, allowing the fire from his staff to leap across, arcing to the metal in the weapon's grip.

Flames played around the handgun, and the charges stored inside it exploded in a rippling thunder. The fire continued back, running along the veins in the man's arms, bursting through the skin, charring the clothing, tracing out the hidden pathways in the flesh. The man fell to his knees, his left hand grasping his right arm above the elbow as the fire spurted like burning fuses up his right arm toward his shoulder. When the tongues of flames met his left hand, the fire jumped across and the veins started burning in his left arm, reaching toward his heart.

Kief stayed with him, forcing the burn, feeling it as the man felt it—hot at first, then cold, like a stream of ice water, numbing him. He saw himself with the man's eyes, a figure in the door like death, outlined with a pulsing glow of light too bright to look at directly.

The man felt a tickle in his nose. It was incongruous. The fire was tracing up his arms—he could smell the hair, the meat, the cloth, all burning—and the smoke tickled. Then the smell was gone, and he sneezed. What came out was writhing, like animated white seeds. Maggots. Running from his face. Then his vision went dark, the cold reached his shoulders and spread across his chest. He could feel the maggots writhing across his face, filling his mouth as they tumbled from his nasal passages down his throat. He couldn't breathe. Then the darkness, cold, and pain rose and took him. He didn't feel himself slump to the floor.

Kief stood unmoving, as the man who had been Seyo Hannet of the League of Unallied Shippers turned from a living man to a decayed corpse—all dried skin, smoke-blackened, stretched across brittle bones—in scarcely a minute. Then he turned to where his brother stood appalled in the doorway.

"Through action or inaction," he said, "and it matters not greatly to me which one it may have been, you have hindered the greatest working this galaxy has ever known."

He stepped forward, and placed his left hand over his unresisting brother's face. "Now I take back what I gave at your desire. I take your luck—all of it—from you, from your associates, and from all who share your goals."

The staff in Kief's right hand glowed with a twisting fire, more brilliant even than the fire that had consumed the men in the kitchen of Demaizen Old Hall, and the wood consumed, twisting like a serpent. His hand blistered, and still he drew luck, and held the power within himself until the taking was done.

Then he left his brother's house and the family altars, and never came back again to the Diasul.

The Circle found the prisoner under guard in the ship's laundry—at least, the Entiboran script on the compartment label said it was the ship's laundry, and the stacks of neatly folded sheets and blankets appeared to confirm the label's assertion. The prisoner sat on the deck against one of the machines, clutching her ankles with her hands, her chin on her knees. She looked up when the four members of the Circle came in, her grey-blue eyes sullen and mistrustful.

Arekhon approached her—not too closely, for fear of alarming her—and went down on one knee. "My lady," he said in careful Entiboran, "we need your help."

Her reply started with a verb and ended with a noun, neither of which Arekhon knew. He supposed that the intent was rude. He marshaled all of his grammar and vocabulary and tried again. "My friends and I are members of a—" he grasped for words "—meditation group. We do not wish to dishonor your ancestors. Please help keep us from falling into error."

Her reply this time was only a single word. Arekhon slogged on. "The Captain is unwilling to let you go, and we don't have the authority to set you free—you can be sure that if the situation were otherwise, I would do so. But I can offer you an observer's place in our group."

She looked directly at him for the first time. "Will I have to believe what you believe?"

"No," he said. "Only what you yourself see and hear. In the meantime, are you familiar with this kind of ship?"

"Not particularly. Some."

"Then can you help me find the paint locker?"

She stared at him. "The *what?* Why do you need it?"

This was a test, Arekhon knew. He would have to answer fully and honestly, or the prisoner wouldn't trust him. And having Ty on the bridge capturing her hadn't helped that any.

"We need to make ourselves a black deck with a white circle on it," he told her. "To aid in meditation, as a symbol of unity. Unity is important to us. That's why we're here. The universe is divided, and Garrod wanted to make it one."

Her mouth twisted. "You've done a fine job of that so far, haven't you? Listen, this ship has evacuation pods, in case of accident or injury to the ship. Put me in one of those and set me adrift."

"Can you guarantee that someone will find you in time? It's a bad way to die, otherwise."

He could see her wanting to lie to him, but in the end she shook her head and said, "There's a transponder—but without a distress call from the *Diamond,* nobody's going to be listening for it. It's a gamble I'm willing to take."

"Joining with us is so intolerable? Let us show you what we do, first, and then you can decide."

"If you insist. But don't think I'm going to change my mind."

"Very well," said Arekhon. "Watch and learn. But whatever happens, please don't interfere."

At his nod, the four Mages of the Circle knelt close together facing inward, knees touching knees and staffs held up before them. Arekhon closed his eyes and turned his vision inward, to the place where the lines of life and luck took shape and were transformed.

And the *eiran* were there. With barbs and hooks and razor edges, twisting like worms and striking with their cut and broken ends like snakes. He reached out a hand and took one of the *eiran*. It lifted him from his feet and snapped him about like a man riding a fire hose. He seized the silver-white line with both hands and held on.

The line pitched and bucked. He could feel his hands cramping, and his sides growing bruised as the other *eiran* struck and flailed against them. No scenery came to fill the picture around him, only the stark black and silver of the place, telling him that no choices save victory or death awaited. No greys, no colors—and, more importantly, no long view. Only what lay close at hand.

The line seemed to be tiring, like a live thing that had struggled against its captor too long. It sank down, its motion slowed. He pulled it toward another line—*I hope it's the right one. Is connecting two unrelated lines of life and luck worse than leaving them broken?*

Doing nothing was worse. It was doing nothing that had brought the universe to its current state, and he could not in good conscience do nothing. He pulled the lines together, and watched the lines meld, a slightly darkened seam filling in and glowing brightly.

"I know you," a voice said. The accent was strange; he couldn't easily place it. "I know you now."

It was the prisoner. She was gazing at the Circle with wide, dark-pupiled eyes. "You are Adepts," she said. "I have never heard of Adepts working together. But I know you."

" 'Adepts,' " said Arekhon. The word had an unfamiliar ring to it; Garrod had never covered it in his language instruction. "Are they good people?"

The prisoner shrugged. "Many say no. Whenever something bad happens, they are blamed."

"What do you say?"

"My brother is one," she replied. "And I think—if I could talk with him—that he would tell me that I need to go with you."

XL: YEAR 1130 E. R.
SPACE: *OCTAGON DIAMOND*

THE *DIAMOND* made the journey back across the interstellar gap in a single transit. The acting Pilot-Principal, with Arekhon's help as translator, had succeeded in converting *Rain-on-Dark-Water*'s chart data into a format that the *Diamond*'s ship-mind could use. He didn't want to compound his chances of error by making two jumps instead of one. The prisoner had helped also—teaching the use of the *Diamond*'s controls, and the art of communicating with the ship-mind—though she spoke more to Arekhon and the Circle than she did to the *Rain*'s regular crew.

Arekhon, for his part, had learned the prisoner's name by now, or at least as much of it as she was willing to share with her captors: She called herself Karilen, Karil for short, and if she had a family name she did not choose to give it. Nor did she ever volunteer the names of her shipmates who had died on board *Forty-two*.

The transit this time was a quick one. The *Diamond*'s dual-engine system—one set, huge and powerful, for maneuvering in normal space, and the other, compact and fuel-efficient, for pushing the ship through the Void—took them across the gap at a pace Arekhon would not have believed when he left Eraasi aboard *Rain-on-Dark-Water.*

Captain sus-Mevyan summoned him to the *Diamond*'s bridge for the emergence into homeworlds space, and requested the prisoner's attendance as well. "The Pilot-Principal thinks that Eraasi is somewhere around here," said the fleet-apprentice who brought the message. "The Captain wants a luck-bringer on hand in case he's mistaken."

"Fair enough," said Arekhon. "If the Pilot-Principal and I figured the emergence point wrong, our names will go up on the family tablets a lot earlier than we'd planned."

Karil, frowning, asked, "Is the danger really that serious?"

"Almost," he told her. They spoke in the Entiboran language—his fluency in that tongue had increased markedly with practice, and he told himself it was for the sake of translating the *Diamond*'s logs and instruction manuals. "Our charts and yours don't interface very well. And none of us have taken a ship like this one through the Void before. That's where you come in. If anything goes wrong, you're the expert."

She gave a short laugh. "Not that much of an expert. What I don't know about starship engines could fill an entire book."

"You know more than the rest of us," Arekhon said.

He didn't add that if the *Diamond* were lost or damaged, Karil's hope of escaping back to her own people went with it. He knew that the Entiboran hadn't given up on the idea—it showed in countless small things, like the names she didn't speak—but he didn't see any point in bringing up the subject in front of the fleet-apprentice, who might understand more Entiboran than he let on. The reticence said something, Arekhon supposed, about his own changing allegiances. The capture of *Forty-two* had altered his relationship with the sus-Peledaen fleet in ways that formal severance from the line had not; losing Elaeli had increased his sense of isolation even further.

In the company of Karil and the fleet-apprentice, he went up through the *Diamond*'s narrow, sharply angled passageways to the bridge compartment. sus-Mevyan was waiting there, poised just behind the pilot's station like a predatory bird.

Arekhon gave her a polite bow. "You requested my presence?"

"Yes, Lord Arekhon," the Captain said. "Now that you're here, we can proceed." She raised her voice slightly to reach the *Diamond*'s audio pickups. "Stand by for dropout."

"Dropout on time," echoed the Pilot-Principal. His voice was tight—and no wonder; this was a test of his abilities, and the price of failure was more than usually high. "Stand by, on my mark. Mark."

"Emerging from Void-transit," said the voice of the ship's engineer over the audio. A shiver of discontinuity passed through the bridge, and the bank of flat-screen monitors that had been unlit and empty clicked on and started glowing into life.

"Checking position," said the Pilot-Principal. Several minutes of tense silence followed before his shoulders relaxed a bit and he said, "We're inside homeworlds space, Captain. A bit off where we wanted to be, but I should be able to refine our accuracy before the next transit."

"Excellent," the Captain said. "See if you can take us to a safe port. It doesn't have to be Eraasi—any world will do, as long as the family has contacts there."

The communications specialist broke in, saying, "Something odd, Captain. Old message traffic, but it's showing a profile I don't recall seeing before."

"Never mind that," said Karil, in the badly-accented Eraasian she had been learning from the Circle. Everyone on the bridge turned to stare at her. In the company of the *Rain*'s regular crewmembers she normally kept silent unless directly addressed, and even then maintained her distance. She was pointing at a flashing red light on one of the bridge consoles. "You need go faster *now*. Someone coming at you, intercept course, hitting you with scan."

"Engineering!" snapped sus-Mevyan over the audio link. "Increase normal-space speed by twenty-five percent." She turned back to Karil. "You'd better be right. How did you know about the intercept?"

Karil ignored the captain and looked at Arekhon. "*Diamond* has sensors—can detect scan," she told him. She switched briefly to her own language. "It's why we didn't expect you to attack; you hadn't scanned us first."

She glanced over at the console—the red light was still flashing—and switched back to Eraasian. "Not going fast enough."

sus-Mevyan's lips tightened. "We're already going as fast as I feel is prudent."

"Ship like this has speed," Karil said. She folded her arms. "Don't listen if don't want to."

The communications specialist broke in before the Captain could react. "I'm getting another odd signal. Very high frequency, showing up-Doppler."

"Other ship throwing things at you," Karil said. A second red light beside the first began to blink, and a buzzer sounded. Karil pointed to another button. "I you, I push that."

"What does it do?" Arekhon asked. He repeated the question in Entiboran—this was no time for nuances to get lost in a linguistic haze.

"Automatic close-in defense system," said Karil, in the same language. "It should handle your homing missiles."

Arekhon translated rapidly. sus-Mevyan frowned.

" 'Should?' "

Karil shrugged. "Might. Nothing perfect, this universe."

"Oh, very well," the Captain said. "Pilot-Principal, set the switch. And increase speed another twenty-five percent."

"Lost the signal," the communications specialist said a moment later, and the second red light stopped blinking. A moment later the voice of the engineering officer came over the bridge audio.

"Captain, we just took a number of micrometeorite hits all along the starboard side. Some small leaks, but the plugging and patching teams are out. No major problems."

" 'Micrometeorites'?" Karil asked Arekhon quietly. She stumbled a little over the pronunciation; the word wasn't one that they'd had cause to use before.

"Tiny little rocks," he explained in Entiboran. "They show up some places, orbiting stars."

"Ah," said Karil. "Micrometeorites. Not this time; those were fragments from the missile. Listen, Arekhon . . . I've learned enough from you during the last few months to know that your people don't do this 'war' thing like we do. But I think while you were away from home, somebody figured out the concept."

The transit to Eraasi was short, only a few hours in duration. Arekhon spent the time in the jury-rigged meditation chamber, fretting about the ship—the homeworlds ship—that had fired on the *Diamond* without so much as a query first.

The rest of the Circle shared his apprehension. Ty sat on the deck at the edge of the white-painted area, hugging his updrawn knees and rocking back and forth. Arekhon suspected that he was reliving the capture of *Forty-two*. Ty had recovered from his shock, for the most part, during the transit from Entibor, but an attack on their own ship could easily have brought the memories rushing back.

After a while Arekhon caught his eye; the young Mage stopped rocking and said, "Shouldn't we do at least a small working for the emergence at Eraasi? I mean, if things have gotten so bad they're *shooting* at people . . ."

"If the Captain requests it," said Arekhon. "But she appears to have the situation in hand."

Narin sat on the borrowed storage crate that served to hold the Circle's robes and candles and practice staves, sharpening her knife on a pocket whetstone. Arekhon remembered her using the same knife to fillet silverlings in the kitchen at Demaizen, the day that he brought home the sus-Peledaen charts.

"I wouldn't do a working right now unless I had to," she said. "There's no telling who else is pulling on the *eiran*, or what they're pulling for."

"The real question," said Iulan Vai, "is whether that was a one-time problem, an outlaw ship of some kind—"

"With homing missiles?" Arekhon said. "The families wouldn't let technology like that go rogue."

Vai shook her head. ".You'd be surprised what the big industrial companies on Ayarat and Ildaon were trying to buy, not too long before we left Hanilat."

"How would you know?" Ty asked.

"Let's just say I had a professional interest," Vai said, and went on, "whether it was an outlaw ship of some kind, or whether it belonged to one of the fleets."

"Better outlaws," Arekhon said, "than that. The homeworlds have changed since we left, and I don't think they've changed for the better."

The door-buzzer outside the meditation chamber sounded as he spoke; he nodded to Vai, who was closest, and she toggled the entry switch. The door unlocked itself with a heavy metallic click, and swung inward enough to admit the same fleet-apprentice who had brought sus-Mevyan's summons before.

"The Captain requests that Lord Arekhon sus-Khalgath come to the bridge for the emergence at Eraasi," the apprentice said.

So, Arekhon reflected, Captain sus-Mevyan felt as worried as he did about the state of affairs in the homeworlds. She feared trouble, coming back from her long voyage with one ship lost and another, stranger one serving in its place, and she wanted Arekhon—prime instigator of the voyage, First of the ship's Circle, brother to the head of the sus-Peledaen—on hand to speak for her if it became necessary.

"I'm on my way." Arekhon stepped past the fleet-apprentice, and started for the *Diamond*'s bridge. To his surprise, Iulan Vai followed him out into the passageway and matched her pace to his.

"I think I'd better come along for this," she said.

He looked at her curiously. "What for?"

"Insurance," she said. "I used to know a lot of people—the sort who don't care if they're talking to Lord Somebody sus-Somebody-else—"

"The sort who might have gotten their hands on misplaced fleet-family technology?"

"You could say that. And a few of them owe me favors I never bothered to call in."

The shiver of transition passed over them before Arekhon could frame a reply. When they reached the *Diamond*'s bridge, the bright star that was Eraasi's sun shone at them from the *Diamond*'s multiple flat screen monitors. Captain sus-Mevyan was pacing back and forth in front of the array; she met Arekhon's arrival with a curt nod.

"Good—you're here. Communications—I need to talk with the sus-Peledaen. Give me whatever you can."

"Got it, Captain." The communications specialist sat in a

tangle of wires connecting the *Rain*'s salvaged ID transponder and crypto gear to the *Diamond*'s comm panel. Arekhon had helped with the translations for that job as well; it had been easier than patching together the navigational systems, even if the result wasn't particularly elegant.

"Very well. Let me know the instant someone answers up." sus-Mevyan scowled at the array of flat-screen monitors. "I'd give almost anything for decent bridge windows—these screens are nothing more than annoying. What happens if we lose power?"

"Getting a reply, faint," the communications specialist reported. "syn-Avran syn-Peledaen, calling us. Wants us to present a positive identification." He listened to his headset for a moment longer. "They seem to be concerned that our present configuration doesn't match what's on record for the ship with this transponder."

"Let me talk with him," Arekhon said. "I know the man."

"Do so," Captain sus-Mevyan said. "Output on open speakers."

Arekhon moved into range of the audio pickup. "Captain syn-Avran, this is Arekhon Khreseio sus-Khalgath sus-Peledaen. Do you recall when I was with you on the *Ribbon* for my apprentice voyage? I was one of those two apprentices who brought back news about sus-Dariv's *Path-Lined-With-Flowers* lifting from Ildaon—we picked up some *leind'r* out of it."

"Understand Arekhon Khreseio sus-Khalgath sus-Peledaen," the reply came back. "What was the name of your particular friend on that voyage?"

A reasonable request, Arekhon reflected. Anyone could give his name, and the matter of the *Path* could have been found in the *Ribbon*'s logs. A cautious man like syn-Avran would want corroborating details. . . . "Elaeli Inadi," he said. "You'll find her on the family rolls as Inadi syn-Peledaen these days, with my name down as sponsor."

There was silence for a while. Then syn-Avran's voice came over the speaker again. "Elaeli Inadi syn-Peledaen is listed as Pilot-Principal for *Rain-on-Dark-Water*. Put her on."

Arekhon closed his eyes tightly for a moment and drew a deep breath. "I regret to inform the fleet-family that Inadi syn-

Peledaen was a . . . casualty . . . on the voyage. Unable to comply."

"Stop your engines. You're entering sus-Peledaen controlled space."

"May I, Captain?" Vai said, before sus-Mevyan could speak.

"If you think you can help, go ahead."

Vai moved into audio pickup range. "Captain syn-Avran," she said. "This is Iulan Vai. If you've got *Rain-on-Dark-Water*'s crew list there, you'll see that I'm listed with the ship's Circle. Do you recall the last time we met, on the corner of Port and Lily Streets in Hanilat? I handed you an envelope, you handed me one. Do you want me to embarrass you all over the system by telling you what was in both of those envelopes, in the clear, on a common frequency?"

There was another pause, this one not so long as before. "ID check complete, *Rain-on-Dark-Water*. I intend to escort you to orbit."

Captain sus-Mevyan took Vai's place by the audio pickup. "Thank you for your assistance, Captain. We accept with gratitude. It's been a long trip. Request you pass to Lord sus-Peledaen that I'd like to report to him in person as soon as possible."

"I'll pass that along." The carrier wave clicked off.

"What was in those envelopes?" the Captain asked Vai.

"Dirty laundry," Vai said. "And enough soap to make it all clean again."

The captain raised an eyebrow but made no further comment. "Shape course for Eraasi," she said to the Pilot-Principal.

"Ahead slow. And switch off that close-in weapons system. I don't want to shoot any of my friends."

XLI: Year 1130 E. R.
Eraasi: *Octagon Diamond*
Hanilat Starport

OCTAGON DIAMOND hung in orbit over Eraasi. There was no cradle in the yards, Arekhon knew, that was large enough to take her, and like the lost *Rain-on-Dark-Water,* she had never been intended to touch ground. She could only wait; but she did not have to wait for long.

"Shuttle inbound," the communications specialist reported as soon as the orbit had stabilized. "And a message: Lord Natelth is pleased to welcome us back from our historic voyage. Captain sus-Mevyan, the First of the ship's Circle, and our honored guest are invited to dine with him tonight in Hanilat."

By "honored guest," Arekhon supposed, his brother meant the prisoner. He hoped that the invitation meant Natelth was inclined to look to the worlds beyond the gap as potential friends and allies, but nothing he had seen so far in the homeworlds had given him cause to feel sanguine about the possibility.

He was not, apparently, the only one to harbor doubts. Captain sus-Mevyan wore her most formal fleet livery for the evening's dinner, in spite of the fact that the sus-Peledaen shuttle had to dock with the *Diamond* by means of a boarding tube, necessitating an awkward zero-gravity scramble from the larger ship to the smaller. Arekhon, after considerable thought, had chosen to wear his most formal working robes, as a reminder to Natelth that the Circles were not the fleet, and that he belonged to the Circles. Nor would it hurt for the head of the sus-Peledaen to be reminded exactly whose agency had made the voyage of discovery possible.

The prisoner had presented difficulties. sus-Mevyan had offered Karil a set of fleet livery—trousers and tunic of blue piped with sus-Peledaen crimson—but she had refused them. Her own clothing, such of it as had been transferred from *Forty-two* before leaving Entibor, was worn and strictly utilitarian. Narin had to use the sharp point of her knife to rip away the crimson flashes and piping from the fleet livery, leaving it a plain nobody's-color blue, before Karil would agree to wear it.

The three of them, sus-Mevyan and Arekhon and Karil, made a silent, uneasy party aboard the shuttle to the planet's surface. The dimensions and angles of the Eraasian ship, instead of reassuring Arekhon with their familiarity, felt disturbingly alien after the time he had spent aboard *Octagon Diamond*. The shuttle's captain and crew all wore sidearms, another new thing in his experience: Not symbolic weapons like the boarding pikes, but heavy projectile weapons meant to kill from a distance.

He saw that sus-Mevyan was also taking in the sidearms. The Captain's expression, which had not been cheerful before, darkened even further, but she said nothing. If the Captain had dreamed of better things for her homecoming than this, she wasn't going to embarrass herself by admitting it.

The shuttle landed, and the crew escorted them to a waiting groundcar. Arekhon supposed that all the men and women in sus-Peledaen livery were meant to show Natelth's respect; but he couldn't help thinking of them as an armed guard. The groundcar had thick tinted windows, so that nobody watching it go past would be able to tell who was inside, and it whisked them through the streets of Hanilat without stopping for signs or signals.

Another oddity, Arekhon thought. Natelth hadn't thought

before that the sus-Peledaen were above the law. That they *were* the law, sometimes . . . but never above it.

The sus-Peledaen town house where he had grown up looked much the same as it always had, at least from the outside. But when the door swung open, it wasn't one of Isayana's hand-crafted *aiketen* waiting inside to welcome them, but yet another armed man in fleet livery.

"Dinner will be ready shortly," he said. "Meanwhile, Lord Natelth wishes to see you in his study."

The three from the *Diamond* followed him up the stairs. Arekhon felt the give of the carpet underfoot and the cool slickness of the polished darkwood banister beneath his hand, and remembered how he had come up the same stairs, once upon a time, for the purpose of talking his brother out of the fleet-family's confidential charts. He wondered if Natelth remembered the occasion as well.

The study looked much as it had during that previous visit, except that there were two more chairs, and the glass in the bay window was thick and tinted like the windows of the groundcar. The *uffa*-pot stood on its tripod legs in the center of the low table, with crystal glasses surrounding it, and Natelth stood with his back to the table, looking out of the window.

He didn't speak until after the door guard had left. Then he turned and spoke to Captain sus-Mevyan, without bothering with a formal greeting.

"So. Your message-drones preceded you, and the family's builders and stargazers have been doing wondrous things with what you have already given them. But what you say about a multitude of worlds on the far side of the gap disturbs me; I don't know if that is good news, or bad. You were there, Captain—tell me what you say."

"Mixed, I think," the Captain said. "Lord Garrod—who is lost—himself had grave misgivings about what he had done. It's true that the far-side worlds can build starships faster and more powerful than any I've ever heard of, with ship-minds of unusual construction and weapons that make ours seem pitiful. But they have no idea that any worlds lie beyond the interstellar gap, and unity, as we have it, is unknown to them. And more—we were able to bring back with us a native of that world, who can translate all the *Diamond*'s papers and textfiles, and explain its workings."

She gestured to indicate Karil. The Entiboran caught Arekhon's eye and murmured in her own language, "What is she saying to him about me?"

"She says that you can be a translator and a teacher for his people."

"Hunh. Does he plan to give me a choice?"

"Probably not. We can talk about it later."

The quiet exchange in Entiboran had caught Natelth's ear, and Arekhon saw a moment of suspicion cross his brother's features. It vanished as Natelth came forward to clasp him in a warm embrace.

" 'Rekhe, it's good to have you back safe again. Isa's been working over the kitchen's instructions ever since word came that your ship was in orbit—she doesn't trust the far-siders' ship-kitchens, she says. I think she believes you've been starving."

"For lack of red *uffa* and *neiath* jam, most certainly," Arekhon said. "Otherwise . . . I do well enough. All the same, it's good to be home."

"Excuse me, my lord," Captain sus-Mevyan broke in. "But we've been out of touch for quite a while, and have returned to find things changed from what they were. How shall I explain the difference to my crew?"

"There is no explanation," Natelth said, "except that somehow we must have offended the gods and the ancestors beyond all forgiveness. The old customs that kept peace between the star-lords have been broken, and the ties of trade and obligation that bound together the homeworlds have come undone. The unity you spoke of is a thing of the past."

"Someone's going to have to restore it, then," said sus-Mevyan bluntly. "Because I tell you truthfully, my lord, it's the only advantage we've got."

"I don't like it," Narin said.

Iulan Vai looked at her. "Don't like what?"

The three remaining Mages of the *Diamond*'s Circle had gathered in their meditation chamber after the shuttle's departure. Their withdrawal had gone unnoticed, as far as Vai knew, in the general excitement of making orbit and renewing direct contact with the sus-Peledaen. She had long since determined that the chamber was both without spy-holes—either accidental or deliberately constructed—and free of electronic eavesdroppers, and she rechecked it frequently; it was as safe a place for private conversation as any aboard ship.

"Don't like having 'Rekhe down in Hanilat while we're stuck up here," Narin said. The Veredden woman had a long strip of the scarlet piping from Karil's despised fleet-livery, and her square brown hands worked with it as she spoke, tying and untying complex knots. "If he runs into trouble, we'll never know until it's too late."

"He's going to dinner with his own brother," Ty protested. "What kind of trouble could he run into that way?"

Vai suppressed an urge to smile. Ty was the youngest of the Demaizen Mages, and sometimes it showed. "His brother is also the head of the sus-Peledaen fleet-family—which appears to be claiming this part of space, though I'd like to know how—and Natelth might have ideas about keeping things like the new ship-knowledge private to the family."

" 'Rekhe's brother has trouble understanding that the fleet doesn't own Circles like it owns ships," Narin said. The strip of red piping twisted and knotted under her hands. "I'm afraid he may try to claim us for the fleet as well."

"That would start trouble, all right," Ty said, after a moment's thought. "Arekhon wouldn't like it."

Narin began unpicking the latest knot with the point of her knife. "As long as we're on board the *Diamond,* the fleet has us, whatever Lord Arekhon likes or doesn't like about it."

"Then we have to get off the *Diamond,*" Ty said.

"It's not so easy as all that," Vai told him. "Notice how few people they've actually let down to the surface so far—the Captain, the First, and the prisoner, and all three of them sent straight to Natelth."

"Maybe we should ask—"

"No." The knot came undone, and Narin slid her knife back into its sheath. "If we ask the sus-Peledaen for a shuttle to the surface, they'll have to refuse. And then they'll know what we want to do."

"So we don't ask," Vai said. This was a problem whose

solution she understood. "We tell them. And we don't tell them the truth, either. We tell them a lie, and make sure it's a big enough lie that they'll want to believe it . . . that Garrod spoke to us through the Void, maybe, with an urgent message for Lord Arekhon."

"They'll never believe it long enough to send up a shuttle," Ty said. "No matter what we tell them."

"We're Mages," said Narin. She tucked the red piping away inside her jacket and unclipped the staff from her belt. "If we work the *eiran* properly, the sus-Peledaen will believe us for as long as we need them to."

Dinner was worse than the conversation in the study had been. Isayana had done prodigies of instruction in the kitchen, and the food served up by the *aiketen* was everything that Arekhon could have hoped for—*neiath* jam and all.

Nevertheless, he found himself having to feign an appetite. The changes he had witnessed since returning to the homeworlds, and sus-Mevyan's words to Natelth, combined to fill him with a sense of oppressive dread. The voyage they had all undertaken with such great hopes and such high aspirations—what could be nobler and more audacious than striving to bring together an entire sundered galaxy?—had ended in nothing but corrupted endeavor and growing darkness.

Natelth and sus-Mevyan spoke together for most of the meal. Natelth asked an occasional question about the far side of the interstellar gap, but only to clarify things he'd already learned from the message-drones. The rest of the talk was all about the current state of affairs on Eraasi, and why somebody had seen fit to fire a missile at the *Diamond* on her way past Ayarat.

"Sus-Radal, most likely," Natelth said. "They're born pirates, those people, and they hold a lot of trade routes on the edges of homeworlds space."

"You'll have to take care of them someday," said sus-Mevyan. "Maybe sooner than someday, if things are as bad as you say."

"They're that bad. But the sus-Radal are too strong for me to hit them now. Let somebody else try it and get broken first."

Arekhon had been translating under his breath for Karil's

benefit—there was no point in keeping the prisoner in the dark, and she understood enough of their language by now to follow the drift of the conversation anyway—and Natelth's remarks appeared to startle her much less than they did him. She caught his change of expression, shrugged, and said in Entiboran, "Politics. You'll get used to it."

In the same language, he said, "I shouldn't be having to get used to it. Things were never like this before."

Isayana looked at him with concern from her end of the table. "Is there something wrong, 'Rekhe? I hope the menu isn't displeasing to our guest."

"It's fine, Isa," he said. "She was asking me about the jam—I told her it was my favorite when I was a boy."

He hadn't lied to Isayana before, outside of the usual minor evasions of childhood; that he did so now, by instinct, disturbed him. Isayana would never use his private opinions against him—he trusted her implicitly on that—but she would pass them on to Natelth. And Arekhon was not quite willing, any longer, to trust his brother.

The meal ended with sweetened tartgrass sorbet in fluted wafer cups. Natelth, smiling graciously, offered the three from the *Diamond* hospitality for the night—"we still have a great deal to talk about in the morning"—and sus-Mevyan accepted for all of them before Arekhon could demur. Isayana took sus-Mevyan and Karil away with her to the guest rooms; Arekhon, pleading weariness, made his escape before Natelth could draw him into a conversation, and settled down for the night in his old bedroom on the top floor.

The room had changed very little since he had last slept there. Somebody—Isayana, probably, or one of her *aiketen*—had put most of the toys and models away out of sight, although enough of his favorites remained that the walls and the shelves weren't bare; and *Ribbon-of-Starlight,* his last-built and favorite, still hung suspended from the ceiling on thin, invisible strings. The *aiketen* had left a night robe and a sleep-shirt on the foot of the bed. He changed into the shirt, leaving his black Circle garments folded on the chair beside the bed, and lay down for the night.

XLII: Year 1130 E. R.
Eraasi: Hanilat Starport
Entibor: Villa of Mestra Adina
Therras

A REKHON HADN'T expected to get much rest, but
the familiar surroundings of his childhood lulled
him into sleep despite his uneasiness. It was past midnight by
the bedside clock when the sound of footsteps crossing the
threshold brought him suddenly awake. He sat up, reaching
for his staff, but drew back his hand when he saw that the
prowler was Captain sus-Mevyan. She was barefoot, and wore
a guest-robe like the one at the foot of his bed.

"Captain," he said warily.

In the faint glow from the clock, he could see her lips twitch
in a brief, wry smile. "Relax, sus-Khalgath. I'm only here to
talk."

He relaxed, as ordered, but only a little. "Talk, then."

She moved his folded clothes to the foot of the bed and sat
down on the chair. "To make it brief: If you intend to break
away completely from your brother and the sus-Peledaen—
and I could see the thought in your face, while Lord Natelth
and I talked—then do it tonight."

"Why tonight?"

Again she gave him the half-smile. "Because tonight you're

in your brother's house, and if you leave from here it's his problem. But if you wait until you're back on the *Diamond* to have second thoughts about working with the fleet, then—if Lord Natelth's conversation tomorrow goes the way I think it will—I'm going to have to stop you."

"Then why speak to me about it now?"

"Three reasons," she said, "and three reasons are enough to make me decide to act. The first reason is that I'm not such a fool as to think that seizing you and putting you in detention will make your brother feel grateful to me, regardless of what he would do to me if I failed. And the second reason is that I'm definitely not such a fool as to want what stopping you would do to my luck."

"What's the third reason?"

"Gratitude," she said. "This voyage has done well for me, sus-Khalgath—the *Diamond* outweighs *Rain-on-Dark-Water* in your brother's eyes, and I have a chance at a new ship in the fighting fleet he's building. Lord Natelth is a determined man; he'll have peace again in the homeworlds if he has to rule them himself to do it, and a captain who throws in with him now can rise high and go far."

"We—the Circle—didn't do any of this for the sake of your advancement, Captain. Or for the sake of the sus-Peledaen." He sighed. "We wanted to restore the galaxy . . . and now it seems that everything we've done since we started has only broken it further into pieces."

"All you Mages think too much," sus-Mevyan said. She stood up again and moved toward the door. "I'll leave you now, sus-Khalgath . . . sleep well."

She padded out of the room, and her footsteps diminished into silence.

Arekhon waited for several minutes until he was certain that the upstairs was quiet once again. Then he got out of bed and dressed himself in the Circle robes he had worn earlier—the dark folds would blend into the shadows, which was an unanticipated advantage—and stepped out into the hall.

Moving quietly, he made his way to the second-best guest bedroom. sus-Mevyan might still be awake, but she would not be expecting him to come this way—the Captain had glimpsed his growing alienation, earlier that evening, but he didn't think even she understood how far it had already gone. The door to the second-best room was locked from the outside, but the lock answered to his hand without complaint; he was a Mage, after all, and a member of the family.

The door swung open without sound, as he knew it would. Isayana would never allow squeaky hinges in a mechanism under her control. Inside the room, Karil stood at the window overlooking the back garden. Arekhon saw at a glance that she was still fully dressed, and that the bed had not been slept in.

"You could probably get out that way if you wanted to," he said, in a low voice that wouldn't carry outside the room. "The back wall isn't too high to climb. But you'd do better coming with me instead."

Karil didn't turn around. "Why would going with you be any better?"

"Because I won't imprison you and force you to speak against your own people—as you're afraid that my brother will."

She turned, then, and looked at him. Her eyes were pale in the shaft of moonlight coming in through the window. "You know him. Would he?"

"If you'd asked me before I crossed the interstellar gap, I would have said no. But everything has changed since then."

"Where are you going?"

"Away from Hanilat. To a place where my brother doesn't have any authority. I'll think about what to do next when we get there." He paused. "Are you coming?"

"Yes."

"Good. Let's go."

After dinner was over at Mestra Adina's, Garrod returned to his chamber and once again began calculating the days and years.

He understood now that for him, there would be no return to the homeworlds—at least, not while he still had the mind to know it—and he didn't dare try walking through the Void again, not when each attempt brought him to a worse position than he had started from. If he wanted to continue his work he would have to do it from here.

If he wanted to continue.

For a moment, sitting at his desk amid his logs and printouts and pages of scratched-out numbers, Garrod felt the future's madness already pressing against the edges of his mind. He didn't know any longer what he should want—the survival of the homeworlds, the reunification of the galaxy, or just a peaceful existence for himself in this place to which the tangled *eiran* had apparently bound him.

But there would be no peace. He knew too much of the future already to hope for that. Entibor was bound to a wheel of political rivalry and civil war, and there was no one on the planet who cared to work the *eiran* on its behalf.

He laughed aloud, a sound that shocked him with its bitterness. How should he expect the people of Entibor to work the *eiran* when they had been cast into darkness by the stroke of the Sundering? The people of this world had departed so far from a true understanding of the universe that a man like Master Drey of the Cazdel Guildhouse—whom Garrod had come to respect, and with whom he had corresponded on a regular basis ever since they had first met—could deny that the *eiran* even existed.

And Drey at least, thought Garrod, *is one who would be able to work the* eiran *if he wanted to.*

Garrod allowed himself a moment of fantasy, letting his imagination picture an Entibor nourished and protected by its Circles, growing into a world pre-eminent on this side of the interstellar gap, a fit ally and trading partner for Eraasi and the homeworlds. Then he sighed and let the vision go. There would be no Circles on Entibor, and no partnership. The first ship from Eraasi would find a world once again devouring itself in internecine warfare, and possessing ships and weapons more powerful than any the homeworlds knew.

He forced himself to put aside despair and take account of his resources. He had a patron in Mestra Adina Therras, and he had the beginnings of a network of friends in the community of savants like Hujerie and Master Drey. And he had—even alone—the ability to work the *eiran* for his own benefit. He had scorned to do so on Eraasi, but Eraasi was not here.

No one working alone is powerful enough to change the

future, Garrod thought. *But with luck, and the help of friends, I can hope to be ready to meet it.*

Arekhon led the way down the hall of the guest wing. There was a back staircase in the sus-Peledaen town house, a relic of the long-ago days before *aiketen* replaced living servants. He had come and gone that way when he was a boy, to avoid getting stopped and trapped in polite conversation with Isa's friends or Natelth's business associates, all of whom used the much grander, and carpeted, stairway in the front. Now—with any luck—he could use the back stairway to avoid meeting the armed man in sus-Peledaen livery who had admitted them that afternoon.

The door to the back stairs was made of the same papered-over wooden panels as the rest of the hall. He found the latch quickly, working by feel, and swung the door open.

Still no creaks . . . good. Beckoning Karil to follow him, he stepped into the darkness and shut the door.

"Can't you make a light?" Karil's voice whispered.

"I don't want to draw anyone's attention. Count the steps instead—there's twelve between this floor and the second—five and seven with a landing in between them—and the same between the second and the first."

He heard her mumbling under her breath all the way to the first floor, where the stairs opened into the kitchen. He stepped out of the stairwell and into the kitchen proper—and froze when a crimson light blinked at him from the darkness.

"Lord Arekhon," it said. "Are you not sleeping well?"

He relaxed and suppressed an urge to laugh. It was only another of the household *aiketen,* going about its rounds.

"I was restless," he said. "So I came down to the kitchen, like I used to do in the old days."

The *aiketh* blinked again, four times on a slow count, communing with its links and records.

"The house-mind remembers," it said. "Will you need anything?"

"No, thank you," he said, and the *aiketh* drifted off toward the downstairs front. As soon as it was gone, he gestured Karil to come forward out of the stairwell.

"The delivery entrance is this way," he said.

Arekhon led the way across the kitchen to the rear entry. The door to the outside was locked, and as soon as he touched it he knew that opening it would trigger an alarm as well. Isa's work, of course; his sister would never have let an outsider touch the house-mind.

She'd never thought to make her systems proof against him, either. He could see the luck of the house where it touched the lock and the alarm, like a silvery network threaded through with his sister's unmistakable presence. It was the work of scarcely a moment to tug at the lines gently and pull them into a new pattern, one that would let him pass and bid the alarm be silent.

He opened the door.

The motion of the door swinging open must have alerted the guard at the rear entrance. The lurking figure came up out of the shadows between the trash bins before Arekhon could get his staff into his hand.

"High time you showed up," said Iulan Vai. "I was about to go in after you."

XLIII: Year 1130 E. R.
Eraasi: Hanilat Starport

Ty AND Narin were waiting with a rented ground-car at the Five Street transit hub. They'd parked the car in the shadows at the far end of the lot from the kiosk—Ty, lounging at the steering yoke with his hair combed forward over his ears, looked like a Port Street native ready for a joyride. Narin was only a dark figure in the obscurity of the back seat. She swung open the rear door as Arekhon approached.

"We thought you might be needing us," she said. "So we summoned ourselves. The car was Vai's idea, though."

Arekhon gestured at Karil to take the seat beside Narin. Once the Entiboran was safely within, he turned back to Vai with one hand still on the top of the open door and said, "They'll be able to trace you through the account slips."

Vai shrugged. "Renting a groundcar's not illegal. I didn't use my real name when I signed for it anyway."

"Your real name's going to be on the account when they cross-check it."

She chuckled, a surprisingly warm sound in the shadowy parking lot. "No, it isn't. And I didn't put down Demaizen for the drop-off point, either. You *were* planning on going to De-maizen, weren't you?"

"Where else?" Arekhon said. The silent, stealthy escape from the town house had left him feeling fretful and pettish, with other, darker feelings waiting beyond that to have their turn with him. "There's nothing left for me in Hanilat, and even less than nothing in the fleet. I'm out of options."

"You could walk the Void, like Garrod—" Narin cut in.

"If I did, I'd have to leave the rest of you behind. And we've had more than enough of that already."

"Then you need a ship."

"Natelth gave me one ship. I don't think he's likely to give me another."

"There's a chance that I can find a ship for you," Vai said. Her expression, in the light of the groundcar's reading lamps, was thoughtful. "But it may take a while. I'll join you at De-maizen as soon as I have news."

Natelth went to bed after dinner feeling considerably more pleased with the universe than when he'd gotten up that morning. 'Rekhe's venture beyond the Edge might not have charted any useful trade routes—in these uncertain times the distances were too far for profit, and the fuel requirements were too high—but the ship *Octagon Diamond* was a prize beyond all estimation. Natelth had read the reports sent back on sus-Mevyan's message-drones, that told of the *Diamond*'s powerful engines and her complex inorganic ship-mind, her delicate sensor array and heavy, crushing guns. She was more advanced, in many ways, than the ships of the sus-Peledaen; but not so advanced that the orbital yards couldn't copy her.

He hadn't yet thanked his brother properly, Natelth reflected as he drifted off into sleep. Because 'Rekhe had done well by the family, even if he'd had to leave their altars in order to do it—with a whole fleet of warships like the *Diamond*, a man could restore order to the homeworlds, then go on to deal from a position of strength with the strange, rich planets across the gap.

He was dreaming of stars falling on the lawn of the back garden like blossoms after a windstorm—an oddly cheerful dream, considering the image—when the household's primary *aiketh* awakened him.

"Lord Natelth." The synthesized voice held a distinct note of urgency.

The field of drifted stars vanished into the mists of dream. Natelth groaned and pushed himself up onto one elbow. "What is it?"

"There is a situation that requires your input."

"Explain."

The red light inside the *aiketh*'s plastic shell blinked on, then off again. "The house-mind on the orbital station reports that the members of the Demaizen Circle who remained aboard *Octagon Diamond* have effected an unauthorized departure. A check in response of personnel from *Octagon Diamond* now in this building brings word from the unit assigned to housekeeping in the guest wing that the special guest's room is now unlocked, and that the room is empty."

Natelth rose and put on his night-robe. "Show me," he said. "Instruct one of the *aiketen* to fetch Isayana as well."

He followed the *aiketh* down the hallway to the guest wing. Outside the windows, the sky was beginning to turn pinkish-grey. In the faint light, he saw that one of the bedroom doors was standing a little ajar. He crossed over the threshold and stepped inside.

As the *aiketh* had told him, the room was empty. The pillows and coverlet on the bed were unwrinkled—as if no one had slept there, or even sat for a moment or two on the edge of the mattress—and the sleep shirt and night-robe lay untouched where the housekeeping unit had placed them. The window was shut; the guest had left, unmistakably, through the unlocked and open door.

"Search the house and grounds," Natelth ordered. "And summon the housekeeping unit. At once."

The *aiketh* blinked and flashed. "The housekeeping unit is currently in transit to this point. Lady Isayana comes with it."

Natelth waited impatiently for the unit and his sister to arrive. He hoped that Isa wasn't going to be difficult about questioning the household *aiketen*—she had instructed all of them, and many of the specialized units were of her personal design and assembly. She would shield them from trouble if she could.

The housekeeping unit and Natelth's sister came into the room together. Isa had responded to the summons without bothering to robe herself; she still wore her long nightgown and bed socks, and her hair hung down over her left shoulder in a thick, loose braid. The housekeeping *aiketh* floated close by her, and her right hand rested—*protectively?* Natelth wondered, *or proprietorially?*—on the top of the unit's domed plastic shell.

She took in the empty room and the unused bed, then looked down at the *aiketh* beside her. "This unit tells me that our special guest is missing."

"Gone out through an open door," Natelth said. "Which should have been locked."

Isa shook her head. "It was locked when our guest retired. I instructed the house-mind myself."

The primary *aiketh* blinked crimson. "Units involved in active searching report that the special guest is not inside the house or the back garden, and the house-mind reports that no one has effected egress since it sealed off the house for the night. One of the housekeeping units"—it paused, and the *aiketh* hovering next to Isayana flickered rapidly in response to the acknowledgment—"now reports that Lord Arekhon's room is likewise empty. The house-mind correlates with an entry in the housekeeping night-log, that Lord Arekhon was active in the kitchen area at the second hour."

Natelth looked at Isa sharply. "Could 'Rekhe have opened this door?"

"We never took him off the list," Isa said. "But why would he—?"

"The reason doesn't matter," Natelth said. He felt the beginnings of a deep, cold anger stirring inside his chest. "What about the main doors front and back? Those were newly instructed since *Rain-on-Dark-Water* left for the Edge. Could Arekhon have opened either one of them without setting off the alarms?"

Isa pulled on her braid, frowning thoughtfully. "I'd bet good money against anybody else in Hanilat being able to do it . . . but not against 'Rekhe. He's a clever one; he knows how I think better than almost anyone else on Eraasi; and he's a Mage. What I don't understand is why he took our guest along with him."

"I suspect that he felt some kind of obligation," said Captain sus-Mevyan's voice from the open door. The *Diamond*'s Captain was an early riser, and already had on her fleet livery. She glanced about the empty room. "But as you said yourself, he's a Mage. They don't think like the rest of us."

"It makes no difference," said Natelth. The anger was fully roused now, and running through his veins like an icy current. "He's left us, and taken a valuable resource with him. The situation will have to be . . . dealt with . . . before he does anything to make it worse."

Vai didn't take long to get from Five Street to the avenue where the sus-Radal townhouse stood. Once there, she waited for some time in the shadows of an adjoining building, as she had waited earlier outside the sus-Peledaen delivery entrance, to make certain that she had arrived unobserved.

Things had changed with the sus-Radal since her last visit. She marked a watcher—whose, she couldn't tell—keeping tabs from across the street. The rear entrance had its watcher also, but a less observant one; and the palmscan lock on the door still answered to the touch of Vai's hand.

The moon was rising as she slipped into the quiet house. She'd always preferred the night hours for her dealings with Theledau sus-Radal, when she could find him alone in his own place, under the watchful eye of the moon. The room at the top of the house was unlocked, as usual. The other members of Thel's household were Hanilat-bred, but he'd always left the moonroom open in case anyone should feel drawn into a proper reverence.

Vai didn't feel any reverence to speak of, but she did feel gratitude that her former employer hadn't abandoned his ideals completely. She seated herself on one of the side-benches set against the wall and waited again, this time until Theledau himself arrived.

He came into the room and made a brief obeisance to the moon, visible in its first quarter just below the apex of the crystal dome. Like everything else Vai had encountered since the *Diamond*'s return, Thel had changed: Even by the pale light of the quarter moon she could see that his black hair had wide streaks of grey, and his face was marked by deep new lines of care and worry. He noticed her almost at once, however, and his abstracted expression changed to one of genuine delight.

"Syr Vai," he said. "I'd heard that sus-Peledaen's ship was home at last, but I hadn't expected to see you down from orbit quite so soon."

"I took leave," she said. "Very informally."

Thel nodded. "Are you planning on going back?"

"I don't think so."

"Ah. The question then is, what news do you have for me?"

"You read my reports," Vai began. "Off of the sus-Peledaen message-drones."

"Yes. Excellent material. The sus-Peledaen have been incorporating the new technologies into their ships for some months already—"

"We noticed," said Vai. "Someone shot at us on our way in."

"Natelth sus-Khalgath isn't a trusting man, and his captains follow his lead. But our ships, at least, knew what to expect—thanks to you. The fleet-family owes you a debt, Iulan."

"And I have a request," Vai said at once. "So we're well matched."

The opening had been deliberate, she was sure. Theledau wasn't stupid enough to bind himself to a debt by accident, and he had to suspect that she'd come to ask a favor—news alone would have arrived through other channels. Vai felt a moment of relief. She hadn't liked the idea of trying to wheedle Thel out of a ship, no matter how much 'Rekhe and the Circle might need one, but the delicate weighing of favors and obligations was another matter, and she was used to that.

"What is it that you need?" said Thel. "If it's within my power—and within reason, of course—then it's yours."

"I need a ship," Vai said. "Void-capable, long-range, small crew. Surface-to-orbit, if you can."

Thel regarded her thoughtfully. "A ship is within my power, certainly. But within reason? Convince me, Syr Vai."

"I won't mention the message-drones," she said; "you know

about those already. But the sus-Peledaen also have the vessel *Octagon Diamond*—a fully-functioning source of more technical information than could possibly have been encoded into a drone—and they have an honored guest from the *Diamond*'s homeworld to assist them in learning their way around."

She paused, and allowed herself to smile. "Or at least they used to have one. She's with the Demaizen Circle now, and the Circle intends to keep her. Is that news worth a ship, do you think?"

"It might be," Thel conceded. "But if you've stolen something that Natelth sus-Khalgath thought was his, a ship may not be enough to save you. Not an ordinary ship, at any rate."

Vai studied Thel's expression carefully. She knew a counter-offer when she heard one coming, and she wondered what this one would be. At least she could be sure that Thel was bargaining with her in good faith; he wouldn't insult the moon overhead by doing otherwise.

"You've got an extraordinary ship?"

"A prototype," he said. "Incorporating the material from your drone reports. We didn't waste time upgrading older vessels . . . leave *that* to the sus-Peledaen! . . . we made a full-size working model instead. Armed and armored, with a range that should take you from Eraasi to—what was the name of the *Diamond*'s planet again—?"

"Entibor."

"Eraasi to Entibor without needing to steal another ship at the far end. And if you've crossed Natelth sus-Khalgath, Entibor's barely far enough from the homeworlds to be safe."

XLIV: Year 1130 E. R.
Eraasi: Demaizen Old Hall
Hanilat Starport
sus-Radal Experimental Shipbuilding
Facility

THE DRIVE from Hanilat to Demaizen was a long one. Arekhon sat moodily watching the road ahead unroll in the light of the groundcar's driving beams. The other passengers were equally silent. After a while, the Hanilat suburbs fell away behind them, and they turned onto the Long Ridge Highway heading north and west toward Demaizen.

Arekhon roused himself enough to ask, "Did you call ahead to let them know we were coming?"

"Now *that*," Ty said, "somebody would have been able to trace. Sorry."

"It's all right," Arekhon said, and went back to watching the road. Eventually—it was late, and the afternoon and evening spent in his family's house had been emotionally wearing—he fell asleep.

When he woke, the sky was pearly-grey and the eastern horizon was a line of golden light. Ty had made good time; they'd passed over the Long Ridge and into the rolling fields of grain interspersed with open pasture land that marked the Wide Hills district. Arekhon felt his bleak mood lightening.

More than the fleet or Hanilat, Demaizen was home, and now he was returning to it.

"About another half hour," he said. "They'll be starting breakfast soon."

Now the familiar landmarks were coming into view: The long rise of land steadily climbing, the curve of highway around the shoulder of the slope, the stone gate that marked the turn-off onto the private road.

Karil, in the back seat of the groundcar, spoke for the first time since leaving the house in Hanilat—the words were Eraasian, so he knew she meant them to be understood by everyone. "Is pretty here, in the not-city."

" 'Countryside,' " he said. "Yes."

The road grew steeper. Engine growling, the groundcar took the sharp curve into the stone cut, and shifted into a lower gear for the final ascent.

"They've let the home fields go wild," Narin observed, looking out at the tall grass waving above the walls of the cut. "Garrod would have words to say about that, if he knew."

Then they emerged from the cut to see Demaizen Old Hall on the crest of the hill, backlit by the rising sun, and shock closed Arekhon's throat so that he couldn't answer.

The Hall was a burnt-out shell: Its stone walls were black with carbon, and its distinctive many-chimneyed roofline had fallen away into rubble. Weeds grew inside the hollow interior, and light shone through the empty spaces that had once held windows. Outside on the drive stood a row of metal hulks, blackened but with streaks of rust running down the sides.

Ty braked the groundcar to a sudden stop. His hands on the yoke and gearshift moved into position for the sharp, three-cornered turn that would send the vehicle speeding back the way it had come.

"No," said Arekhon. His mouth was dry, and the word came in a hoarse whisper. "Keep going."

"Whatever you say."

Ty put the groundcar back into motion. The gravel drive crunched under its wheels as he took it slowly past the row of burnt-out armored vehicles. He gave the hulks as wide a berth as possible—though it was obvious, as he drove past, that they had been long deserted.

The flames that had devoured the Old Hall had scarcely touched the outbuildings. The garage still had a roof and most of its exterior walls, although the door had been ripped open and left hanging from its hinges. Ty backed the rented ground-car inside and cut the engine.

"Now what?" he said.

Arekhon unstrapped his safety webbing and got out. "Now we go see what happened."

Natelth left the guest wing while Isayana was still quizzing the house-mind, through the *aiketen*, about the breach in her security instructions. "I'll take breakfast in my study," he told her as he departed.

Such a change in the morning routine—combined with the need to provide hospitality for Captain sus-Mevyan, who as the Captain of *Octagon Diamond* was in truth and not merely in circumlocution an honored guest—would keep Isa busy for at least an hour. He needed the time. If Isa found out what he intended to do, she would try to stop him, and she might succeed. He needed Isayana, both for her management of the household and for her skill in the complex work of instructing the *aiketen* and ship-minds of the sus-Peledaen fleet. And Isa's fondness for their younger brother exceeded all reason.

Once it's done I can blame it on somebody else, Natelth told himself. Still in his belted night-robe, he strode into his study and locked the door behind him. *The sus-Radal, maybe, or the sus-Dariv. Isa may not believe it, but she'll know better than to ask for the truth.*

At his desk, he picked up the voice-comm handset and pressed the numbers for a certain code sequence, one of a handful that he trusted only to his own memory. Friends—such few as he dared to have—and family could be reached by codes kept in the house-mind's archives, and the desk itself would remember the codes of his business associates. A de-termined investigator, such as Isayana, could persuade the house-mind or the desktop to give up its secrets; but Natelth himself was not such easy game.

The signal at the other end of the line stopped abruptly, and a sleep-heavy voice grumbled, "What do you want?"

Natelth spoke a code phrase—another item he hadn't entrusted to the household quasi-organics.

The voice on the other end of the line changed, as though the speaker had been jerked into complete wakefulness. "We're standing by, my lord. Do you have specific instructions?"

"Yes," Natelth said. "I want you to assemble your personnel and go at once to Demaizen Old Hall in the Wide Hills District."

"Yes, my lord." The voice paused. "You do know that the Old Hall, um, burned down last year in a tragic accident?"

"I'm quite aware of that. Nevertheless, I want you to go there."

The Demaizen Circle had been 'Rekhe's other home; if he had left the family and the fleet, there was no more likely place for him to go. And where he went, his Mages would follow. Natelth pulled open his desk's central drawer and extracted several pictures, which he fed one at a time to the desk's scanner.

"You are receiving images for all people currently at the Hall except one; she does not have an image on file. She is also an honored guest of the sus-Peledaen, and whatever happens she must come to no harm. In fact, you could look upon your job as a rescue mission—she doesn't speak our language well, and I'm afraid that her present company might mislead her, or work to cause her some injury."

"Don't touch anyone we haven't got a picture for," the voice said. "Got it. And bring the extra back with us."

"Crudely put," Natelth said, "but there you have it. One other thing—"

"Yes, my lord?"

"Extreme measures may not prove necessary. Don't act until you hear the confirmation signal."

"Yes, my lord."

"Enough for now—I'm delaying you. I look forward to hearing your report."

He clicked off the transmission. After a moment he pressed another code-sequence.

"This is sus-Khalgath sus-Peledaen," he said, as soon as the signal ended. "I need to speak with your First."

* * *

The sus-Radal's prototype ship had been built in secret, but the vessel's surface-to-orbit design meant that the work could be carried out on-planet rather than in one of the orbital yards. The yards were rife with bribery and espionage—as Vai knew from experience—and they leaked information like water out of a basket. Theledau had opted for a simpler, old-fashioned method of securing the fleet-family's new construction: He had built his shipyard and factory complex on an island in one of the remote far northern lakes.

Vai made the journey by flyer from Hanilat, leaving the city not long after dawn. By late afternoon she had crossed the mountain barrier between the fertile upland plains and the deep subarctic forest. The land below her was mapped, but mostly from orbital observation; the tribal peoples who lived there were said to make the fishers of Veredde look progressive, and the practices of their Mage-Circles were not those of the modern world.

She reached the island near the close of day. From the air, the factory complex looked like an ordinary shipyard for building and repairing small surface-to-orbit craft, like the shuttles that moved cargo to and from the lumbering, space-bound transports. Vai gave Thel—or the advisor who had persuaded him—full credit for a clever idea. Every fleet-family built shuttles. If Theledau syn-Grevi sus-Radal chose to build his on a desolate island in the back of beyond . . . well, he was a moon-worshiping northerner himself, and nobody would be surprised to see him taking care of his home-people now and again.

The codes that Theledau had supplied allowed her to land the flyer at the edge of the shipyard's main field, and brought a family representative hurrying out to meet her. He wore a quilted jacket in spite of the summer season; Vai, who had left subtropical Hanilat dressed for the weather there, was relieved when his first action was to present her with a similar jacket of her own.

"Visitors from down below always need something warmer," he explained, as they made their way across the open, windswept field toward a collection of low wooden buildings. "It's even worse in the wintertime, believe me. You said you have papers from Theledau syn-Grevi?"

"That's right," Vai said. They entered the nearest of the wooden buildings, which turned out to be a construction office full of bulky office-minds and drafting-*aiketen*, with plans and printouts pinned to the walls and spread out on the tables. She pulled Theledau's note to the shipyard from her tunic pocket. "He sends you this, over his signature and seal, and says— this part isn't in writing—not to worry, she'll have a fleet of sisters before you're done."

The representative looked over the papers, and looked at Vai. "So you're the one who's going to take the *Daughter* away." He handed the note back to her. "You're acting as your own pilot, it says here. You might want to reconsider that part—this isn't an atmospheric flyer we're talking about."

"The information I have says the *Daughter* answers to the same basic orbit-to-atmosphere commands as a fleet-family shuttle," Vai said. "And I'm qualified to pilot one of those."

"This is all for some scheme of Lord Theledau's that I'm never going to hear the whole story about, isn't it?" The representative shook his head glumly. "Oh, well. Working up here, we never hear anything anyhow."

"And nobody hears anything about you," Vai said. "Which is the whole point. At least now you know that the family appreciates what you're doing and has faith in your work."

"We live to serve," said the representative. "How soon do you need the *Daughter* to be ready?"

"The sooner the better," said Vai. "Right now would be ideal."

"Natelth had to have known about this," Arekhon said, when they had completed a circuit of the outer walls and found nothing but charred timbers and blackened stone. "No matter who did it, Natelth would have found out afterward. But he never spoke a word of it to me."

Ty said, "Maybe he was afraid that if he did, you'd ask him why he let it happen."

"He wanted to keep you in Hanilat," Narin said. Her square, brown face showed no emotion, neither shock nor grief nor anything else. "And he knew that once you heard about Demaizen, you would be gone."

"So what became of Garrod?" said Ty. "The Garrod we left behind, I mean? Is he gone too?"

Arekhon drew a deep breath. "We'll have to go inside and look."

He went up the stone steps of the Old Hall and entered through the gap where the great front doors had hung. One of them still stood partway ajar; the other lay face-up on the ground inside the ruin. The hall's interior was mostly level, with partly-burned beams protruding from the surface. The grand staircase had been made of stone, and a portion of it still led upward, giving access a second floor that no longer existed.

They found calcined bones lying throughout the wreckage, but none that they could identify until they came to the area that had once been the kitchen. There, among the many, they recognized Delath's remains by the nearby silver grip and end-cap of his staff. Another skeleton, much smaller, also had the fittings of a staff lying amid the jumbled bones.

Narin went down on one knee to touch a finger to the charred wood. "Serazao."

"There's still one staff missing," Arekhon said.

Ty nodded. "Kief's. I wonder why."

"Sometimes things happen and you never know the reason," Narin told him. "That's how life works."

"Not for us," said Arekhon. The coldness that had been with him since coming to Eraasi was back, changed now into a bleak resolve. "We're Mages. We can learn the reason."

Karil asked, "How?"

"Come with me," he said.

He led the way through the ruin to the open, fire-blackened space that had once been the meditation chamber. Without needing to be told further, the other Mages joined him to form a circle, kneeling on the burned-over ground with their staves lying before them.

Karil hung back—something in her, Arekhon suspected, still thought that Magery was an unnatural act. He beckoned for the Entiboran to come closer.

"Keep watch," he said. "If anyone comes, let me know."

She nodded and moved away toward the entrance to the Hall. Arekhon watched her go, then turned back to his Circle.

"Now," he said, and allowed himself to slip away from the material present to the place where the *eiran* themselves had weight and form . . .

. . . it was the place of broken stone, again and always as it had been since the start of Garrod's working.

He looked for the *eiran*, and found them at last, high above him and out of his reach, all torn, the broken ends snapping one way and another as if a hard wind blew them. Through the gaps in the shattered weaving he could see the stars in a night sky. As he watched, the *eiran* turned from silver to blood-red.

"Who did this?" he shouted into the silence. "Who?"

No answer came. Instead the stars began to fall, rushing down out of the sky, straight toward him. Then he realized that the stars were not falling—that instead he was moving toward them at titanic speed. They zoomed past him on every side like streaks of light. He passed through the ragged network of the *eiran* and out into the Void.

He stood on a grey hillside surrounded by fog, his staff blazing in his hand. He looked behind him, and saw a woman bundled in white wool, her face obscured by the folds of cloth.

"You promised to come back," the woman said. She spoke with Elaeli's voice, and the hand that reached out to him and touched his shoulder was Elaeli's also, though it was cold. "You have to cross the gap, if you want to mend what was broken."

XLV: Year 1130 E. R.
Eraasi: Demaizen Old Hall

THE HAND on Arekhon's shoulder grasped more tightly, and shook him hard. He opened his eyes and saw that night had fallen over the ruins of the Old Hall, and that the hand on his shoulder belonged to Karil.

"Someone's coming," she hissed in his ear. "Wake up. You asked me to wake you if anyone came. Wake up."

He took his staff and rose from his knees. "Thank you. You did right."

"What about the others? Should I wake them up too?"

"Yes. But quietly, and tell them to stay back."

He left Karil struggling to rouse Narin from a deep meditative trance, and went out to the broken doors of the Hall. There he saw that the Entiboran woman had spoken the truth. A man was coming on foot up the long drive, his progress marked by the red glow of the staff in his hand. The man's posture and gait were familiar: Even before he drew near enough for the light to illuminate his features, Arekhon recognized the lanky, gangling frame of Kiefen Diasul.

I wanted to know why Kief wasn't dead like all the others, Arekhon thought. *And it looks like he's come here himself to tell me.*

Kief passed by the line of empty, burnt-out vehicles and climbed the steps to the doorway. Arekhon moved forward to meet him, and the two men embraced.

" 'Rekhe," Kief said. "You were gone for too long—I believed that the *Rain* was lost."

"The distance across the interstellar gap was greater than we expected," Arekhon said. He gestured toward the empty walls. "What happened here?"

"Treachery," Kief said. His voice was harsh, and heavy with old anger. Arekhon saw the lines of it marking his face in the red light from his staff. "There's more than enough of it to go around in these degraded times."

"What became of Garrod?"

"Dead, like the others."

"You spoke of treachery," Arekhon said. The memory of Natelth's silence was painful in his mind, and the thought of Kief's staff, absent from the burning. *Don't say it was your word that betrayed them, or his money that paid. . . .* "Whose?"

Kief laughed, a bitter choking noise that was more like a sob. "Mine," he said, "though I didn't know it until too late. He used me—"

"Natelth?"

"No," said Kief. His voice was still ragged. "It wasn't *your* brother who asked the Mages for luck, and it wasn't *your* brother who twisted the luck he got until it snapped and took the Circle with it. It was mine."

Relief surged through Arekhon; he felt ashamed of it, in the face of Kief's pain and regret. "The guilt is your brother's, then, and not yours."

"His—and I broke him for it, 'Rekhe, when I knew! I took back all the luck I had ever given him, and all the luck he had, and the luck of all the *eiran* he had ever touched . . . in my anger I took everything. And there's no way to give it back."

He spoke truth. In the darkness of the ruined Hall, Arekhon saw the webs and skeins of the *eiran* wrapped around Kief's entire body like chains—more luck than one man could spend in a dozen lifetimes, and all of it stained with blood. His heart ached for Kief, trapped in the *eiran*'s knots and coils.

"Our Circle is smaller than it was," Arekhon said, "but it isn't broken. We can take your brother's luck and use it to finish the working."

"No." Kief's features were set and implacable. "Garrod's working was a disaster from the beginning, and I won't waste luck on repairing it. I have another Circle now. Come to us as First, if you like—but Demaizen is dead."

"Demaizen lives, and so does Garrod's working." Arekhon thought of the Circle's *eiran* as he had seen them in his meditation, stretching away and out of sight amid the stars. *You have to cross the gap,* the woman had told him, *if you want to mend what was broken.* "I can't join your Circle—not even as First. There's no place left for me in the homeworlds."

"I know you, 'Rekhe. You think you can finish a working that killed the greatest Magelord of both our lifetimes. You'll betray your blood and your ancestors for the sake of your own pride."

"I don't think either one of us is going to convince the other," Arekhon said. He felt an overwhelming rush of sadness and futility. "We should part friends while we still can."

"You're right on that, at least. Good-bye, 'Rekhe."

They embraced again on the steps of the broken Hall. Then Kief let go and moved back. At the foot of the steps he dodged to the right and flattened himself to the ground.

At that moment a twinkle of lights sparkled among the overgrown hedges two hundred yards away. Arekhon felt a burning pain in his side. He fell backward, his knees no longer supporting him, and collapsed across the threshold. A hand, wet and dark with blood, swam into his view, and he realized it was his—his hand, his blood.

A rushing sound filled his ears, and even above the intense pain he felt the floating sensation that meant his body was going into shock. *I can't die here,* he thought as the rushing sound grew louder and his vision darkened. *I have to cross the gap and finish the working.*

At the edges of his clouded sight, the *eiran* started to glow.

Narin stood on the cliff above the harbor at Amisket. For all her years of absence, she hadn't fully understood how much she'd missed the Veredden fishing port until she returned there at last in her mind's interior world. Always, with Demaizen, she had used traditional imagery of ordered parks and gardens, drawn from the common training of all Mages, or—for her private intentions—images of water and the open sea. But never a real place until now, when her quest for understanding brought her home to the town for which she had saved the fishing fleet, and broken her Circle doing it.

She stood on the windswept headland, looking down at the harbor and wondering what her mind—or the universe—was trying to tell her, until a hand on her shoulder brought her abruptly out of her meditative trance. The woman Karil's voice hissed in her ear.

"Wake! One comes—Arekhon says to wake!"

Narin opened her eyes and saw that the daylight had come and gone since she began her meditation. The grey of early morning had left the sky, and the ruins of the Hall were wrapped in the full darkness of another night. Karil had moved on, and was busy rousing Ty; Narin left her to it and stood up, her staff in her hand.

Moving as quietly as she could, she reached the shadows behind the broken doors just in time to see Kief Diasul bid Arekhon farewell and then step away. An instant later, weapons fire opened up in flashes of light from the shelter of the overgrown hedges, and Arekhon fell backward across the threshold of the Hall.

There was no time for thought. Narin threw herself forward to grab Arekhon by his shoulders and pull him away from the door, sliding his limp body across the ash and rubble. A moment later Ty and Karil arrived, crawling on their elbows and knees. Karil took one look at Arekhon and began tearing away his clothing to expose the dark, ugly wounds where the projectiles had struck. She drew a hissing breath inward between her teeth.

"Is bad." As she spoke, the Entiboran woman pulled off the fleet-livery tunic she'd worn since leaving the *Diamond* and rolled the fabric into a bulky pad. She pressed the makeshift dressing against the wound in Arekhon's side. "Help me please here yes?"

"Yes," Narin said. With her knife—the same one she's used to cut the crimson trim from Karil's livery only the day before—she began slashing at the sturdy fabric of Arekhon's formal robes, first a wide band of cloth to make a second pad for his chest, then narrower strips to tie both of the pads into place. "You were here when it started. What happened with Kief, and who *are* those other people?"

Karil wiped her bloodstained hands on the trousers of her fleet-livery and shrugged. "They talk," she said. "Whatever they want, he says no. Stupid. Dead soon now, bleeding like that."

"Maybe I should try talking with them this time," Narin said. She felt responsibility for the Circle settling onto her shoulders like a heavy weight. "Now that 'Rekhe's wounded—"

"I don't think they're interested in conversation," Ty said. He had crawled forward to peer out around the edge of the doorjamb. His voice was higher than usual, but at the same time curiously flat. He'd sounded the same way, Narin suddenly remembered, after the fighting when the *Rain* captured *Forty-two*. "I see at least a dozen of them out there."

"Too many," said Karil. "We all die soon, not just him."

"Not if we can find shelter for long enough to work undisturbed," Narin said.

"The basement," Ty said. "If it survived the fire, there's a way down to the basement behind what's left of the grand staircase. And if the medical *aiketen* are still intact—"

"—then 'Rekhe's got a chance at living," Narin said, "and we've got a place to hide. Let's go."

Arekhon stood in the midst of the desolate and rocky place from his meditations, and the *eiran* glowed around him like a web of polished silver. He could see the pattern clearly now, the true pattern of the great working that Garrod syn-Aigal had barely started, and that had fallen into his own hands. From one side of the galaxy to the other the working stretched, and from age to age, and its beauty was enough to make him shake with awe.

All this is mine to finish . . . and I'm not worthy.

Weakness swept over him, forcing him to his knees. He braced himself with one hand to keep from collapsing further; the jagged rocks cut into the flesh of his palm.

Unworthy, he thought again.

Unworthy and dying, the fading of his strength here in the nonmaterial world only an image of his body's collapse. He wanted to weep, for the glory of the pattern that stretched out overhead, and that was destined to remain unfinished.

My fault. I didn't have the time.

A voice spoke out of the dark behind him. "You can have the time, if you want it."

Arekhon tried to turn around to see who had spoken, but felt the speaker's hands on his shoulders pressing him back down. He moistened his dry lips. "How?"

"You've seen the pattern of the working. Your life is woven into it, and its energy and yours are one. When the end comes, you will know."

XLVI: Year 1130 E. R.
Eraasi: sus-Radal Experimental Shipbuilding Facility
Demaizen Old Hall

THE SUS-RADAL prototype ship waited underneath a closed construction dome, larger than the domes for the cargo shuttles but looking no different on the outside. An orbital observer might conclude from the visual evidence that the sus-Radal were building a new generation of heavier transports—and Iulan Vai would have put money on Theledau circulating rumors to that effect—but would have no clue to what actually lay under the dome's retractable roof.

"She's a wonder," Vai said to the family representative. "I hope Theledau makes you outer-family at least for this. You've earned it."

Night's-Beautiful-Daughter, to give her the honor of her full name, was a curving wing-shape in nonreflective black, almost twice the size of a sus-Radal cargo shuttle. Most of that extra volume would be given over to the double power system that the family's engineers had copied—extrapolated, really—from the reports Vai herself had smuggled out on the sus-Peledaen drones. Some of it, though, would be the ship's guns, more technology stolen from the sus-Peledaen reports. The ship's main hatch stood open, with a short ramp leading to the floor of the dome.

Vai frowned. "She's going to burn this whole place down when she lifts."

"Not the *Daughter*," said the representative. "The counter-force units will push her clear before the thrusters fire."

Vai tried to envision a unit strong enough to hold up a starship. "More sus-Peledaen stuff?"

"Ours, actually. The reports from *Octagon Diamond* and *Forty-two* provided some help when it came to the implementation, but the basic research was already done."

"The things nobody tells me . . . you're sure the *Daughter* will answer to shuttle commands?"

The representative nodded. "As long as you stick to the basic sequences, the ship-mind will handle everything else."

"Good," said Vai. She looked again at the sleek black lines of the ship, and squared her shoulders. "If she's ready as she stands, there's no point in delaying matters any longer. You've been a great help to me, and if luck stays with me I'll speak well of you in Hanilat."

She went up the ramp to the main lock. The controls there matched the sus-Radal standard. It took her only a few moments to close and seal the hatch behind her. The ship's internal layout was similar to that of a fleet shuttle; she found the main control room more or less where she expected it to be, and was pleased to see that the family's designers had given the *Daughter* a proper window and not just a bank of monitor screens.

Vai settled herself into the pilot-principal's chair, strapped down the safety webbing, and hit the first control in the standard lift sequence.

The ship's main power plant came on line with a muted roar, followed by a low grumbling sound that—after a few seconds—she recognized as belonging to the ship's counter-force unit. The tiny units that lifted Eraasi's mobile *aiketen* gave off a faint hum that, multiplied several thousand times, was the same noise as the one she heard now. Outside the windows, the roof of the construction dome started rolling back, at the same time as the *Daughter* began steadily rising.

The edge of the open dome slid downward past the windows and out of sight, and the grumbling noise of the counterforce unit grew louder and more labored. Just as Vai thought that the counterforce unit could lift the ship no further, the console beeped at her and she pressed the second control in the basic sequence. The engines roared, and she felt herself pressed back against the padded chair with a long steady pressure.

Standard lift procedure for a sus-Peledaen shuttle went to low orbit as soon as possible; Vai was relieved to see that the *Daughter*'s command sequence did the same. Safe at the end of gravity's tether, with nothing but the dark of space outside the cockpit windows, she could rest for a moment and consider where she was going. Hanilat was her first thought, where there was a proper spaceport and where she had last spoken with 'Rekhe and the Circle.

Then, in memory, she heard herself saying that she would meet them at Demaizen—and knew, as soon as she remembered it, that the time to do so was now.

Ty helped Narin and Karil move Arekhon's limp body away from the broken doors of the Hall and over to the alcove behind what remained of the grand staircase. They were almost there when a trio of explosions sounded behind them—for Ty, the sound brought back a sudden memory of standing sweaty-palmed in the *Rain*'s muster bay, waiting for Izar to blow the lock.

"What was that?" he asked.

Karil said something in her native language—identifying the things that had exploded, he supposed—and added, "For stunning. They come in soon."

"We'll be gone by then," said Narin. "Here's the way down."

The darkness that surrounded them lit up briefly with the glow of her staff. She touched the staff to the door tucked away behind the staircase, and the slab of charred wood swung in and open. A rush of moldy-smelling air came out. Narrow metal steps led down into the basement.

Ty glanced back in the direction from which they had half-carried, half-dragged the wounded Arekhon. The marks of their progress showed plainly wherever the starlight and the magelight touched. "They won't have much trouble figuring out where we went."

"It's all we've got," Narin said. "Let's go."

They went down the stairs into the basement, supporting 'Rekhe awkwardly all the way. The lower reaches of the Hall were cold and dark, and water dripped from a distant place. The sound of the falling drops echoed loudly in the passage. Ty couldn't rid himself of memories of the fighting aboard *Forty-two,* and finally gave up the effort.

"You and Karil take him from here," he said. "We'll be followed. I'll slow them down until you can find the *aiketen.*"

Narin didn't argue with him. He would have found her agreement frightening if he hadn't already gone beyond fear, back to the corridors of *Forty-two* and the smells of blood and ionized air. The two women took over supporting Arekhon's body—Narin at his head, with her still-glowing staff tucked through her belt, and Karil at his feet—and headed off down the narrow passageway. They turned the first corner and vanished from sight, leaving Ty by himself in the dark.

He didn't have much time. But he knew the layout of Demaizen Old Hall almost as well as he'd known the Port Street Foundling Home. Two long steps took him into a side-room that the Circle, like the sus-Demaizen before them, had used for long-term storage of things they didn't need but didn't want to throw away—old clothes, boxes of books, children's dolls and broken toys. Ty faded back around a corner, into the shelter of a pile of bundled papercopy magazines.

Voices sounded at the top of the stairs, two men having some kind of whispered conference. Trying to decide who went first, Ty guessed. Then came a metallic clink followed by a pair of crashing explosions. His ears rang, and powder from the ceiling sifted down like flour on his face and hair. After a few more seconds, a light slanted down across the darkness outside the open door. Someone was coming with a hand torch.

Ty couldn't hear the footsteps—he still couldn't hear anything over the loud roaring that filled his ears—but the light was getting closer. He reached around the corner, found cloth under his fingers, grasped, and pulled.

The attacker had been an excellent fighter with his projectile weapons and his explosives, but Ty had trained long and hard at close-in fighting with a wooden staff. Without pause—almost without thinking—Ty struck against a vulnerable point on the man's neck, then swept the other end of his staff into the man's nose, crushing the sinuses. The man fell and lay still.

Ty bent and flicked off the dead man's hand torch—he didn't need it, and there was no point in helping anyone outside who did. The man's projectile weapon had fallen to the floor only a little further away; still stooping, Ty picked it up and curled his own hand around the metal grip.

He knew about such weapons from entertainments and the news, though he had never had an opportunity to use one before. The feel of the releasing studs under his fingers reminded him of what he needed to do next. He stepped into the hall, pointed the weapon toward the stairway, and fired until the device stopped bucking in his grip.

Still holding the empty weapon, he faded back down the dark passage. He shut and locked the doors behind him whenever he could, hoping to slow down the marauders by that much at least, until he came to the portion of the basement that housed the Circle's infirmary. One glance told him that the medical gear, with its self-contained power units and standby shutdown mode, had survived the fire intact. Arekhon lay on the main infirmary table, his pale skin bathed in the eerie blue glow of the low-power lights, while the *aiketen* worked over him. Narin and Karil stood watching nearby.

"How's he doing?" Ty asked. His ears still hurt, and he couldn't tell whether he was speaking too softly or too loud.

"Garrod didn't believe in buying cheap equipment," Narin said. "He'll make it."

Karil shook her head glumly. "No use mending him . . . we all die soon."

As if to underscore her words, another explosion rattled the room and knocked down more dust from the ceiling, making a dim layer of haze in the blue light. On the worktable, Arekhon coughed twice, a faint dry sound, and tried to sit up.

"Help me." His voice came out in a papery whisper. "The working isn't finished. We can't stop until it's done."

The silver cords overlaid the dim infirmary with a network of light. Arekhon saw the pattern in them. It was a only a reflection, or a shadow, of the single pattern he had seen in the nonmaterial world, but carrying out the lesser pattern would further the greater.

He pushed himself up into a sitting position—he was surprised at the effort it cost him, even now that the *aiketen* had completed their work—and swung his feet off the table onto the floor. His head spun as he stood, and the network of silver cords whirled about him.

"We have to finish the working," he insisted. "There's no other way."

A muffled explosion sounded in the basement outside the infirmary, and the floor vibrated. Arekhon, still dizzy from standing up, swayed a little on his feet. Narin reached out a hand to steady him.

Ty said, "There's only one door left, and then they'll be in here."

"The root cellar," Narin said. "If they don't know about it, we've got a chance."

The *eiran* flared with dazzling silver as she spoke. Arekhon said, "Yes."

They left the infirmary in a group, with only the blue worklights from the room behind them for illumination on the way. Arekhon leaned on Karil for support—he'd lost a great deal of blood, he knew, and most of his strength along with it. What he had left, he would need for the working.

The Entiboran woman spoke to him under her breath in her native language. "What is this 'root cellar' that she says we're going to?"

"A storehouse for keeping vegetables through the winter," Arekhon said in the same tongue. "From before there was electricity at the Hall. This is the back way into it, for when nobody wanted to go out into bad weather."

The entrance to the root cellar lay behind a deep closet lined with empty wooden shelves. It had never been intended as a secret passage, only as a convenience for the domestic staff, but if the men behind them didn't know the Hall's interior layout they would be unlikely to guess its existence in a hurry. The entire back of the closet—shelves and all—pivoted when Narin shoved on it, and they edged through the opening into a stone-lined tunnel.

Ty pushed the wall back into place. They were walking

down the narrow tunnel by the light of Narin's staff. Arekhon, still light-headed from his injuries and from the medicines the *aiketen* had pumped into him, saw the *eiran* running through the tunnel in cords thick and twisted together like cables made of silver wire. The strength of the cable reassured him: They were going in the right direction for the final pattern.

Another door, and they were standing in the root cellar itself, a deep, square chamber cut out of the earth, full of bins and flat, traylike shelves for storing bulbs and tubers over the winter. A half-dozen stone steps led up to the heavy wooden cellar door. Narin beckoned to Ty, and the two Mages together heaved its dead weight open.

The creaking noise sounded enormously loud in the silence, but when no explosions or projectile fire came at them in response, Narin gestured again. The remnants of the Demaizen Circle climbed up the cellar steps and out into the open air.

Kief Diasul was waiting for them in the darkness outside the root cellar, his staff ready in his hand.

Arekhon heard Narin swear under her breath in the Veredden dialect. "I should have known you'd remember about the root cellar," she said.

Arekhon moved away from Karil's supporting arm. "Don't worry," he told Narin. His staff was still with him, clipped to his belt; he unfastened it and brought it up to guard. The familiar deep violet glow appeared in answer to his will. "It's all right."

" 'Rekhe," said Narin, "you're just barely back in one piece. You can't—"

"I'm the First of our Circle," Arekhon said. The pattern was coming clear to him again, like a great and overarching network. "And what we do now is part of the working. Kief— will you match me?"

"I tell you again," Kief said, "it can't be mended. But for the sake of Demaizen"—he brought his staff to guard in turn, and its faint red glow became a solid bar of vivid crimson light—"we'll make one last attempt. And let it be as the universe wills."

XLVII: Year 1130 E. R.
Eraasi: NIGHT'S-BEAUTIFUL-DAUGHTER
Demaizen Old Hall
Hanilat Starport
sus-Radal Experimental Shipbuilding Facility

V AI BROUGHT *Night's-Beautiful-Daughter* down from low orbit into Eraasi's atmosphere.

She knew the surface coordinates for Demaizen Old Hall, both from her first journey to the Hall in a rented flyer and from her later tampering with the local communications system and power grid. Now she used the *Daughter*'s console keypad to enter the remembered figures. With those, and with the information from the ship's sensors and internal status boards—and if the prototype ship-mind continued accepting the sus-Radal shuttle commands—she ought to be able to plot herself a basic course.

So far, the black, winglike ship had handled smoothly, al though Vai hadn't asked the *Daughter* to do anything that might fall outside the scope of normal shuttle maneuvers. She knew from her talk with the family representative that the ship was capable of a great deal more—but she herself was only a novice pilot compared to the fleet experts. 'Rekhe needed a spaceship, and she had found him one; it wouldn't do for her to damage it through ignorance or recklessness on the way to give it to him.

The ship-mind finished its calculations, and Vai entered the commands for the new course. The *Daughter* headed into Eraasi's night side and began a long, steady descent.

The sky above remained as dark as before, and the marauders had not yet finished their search of the unburned basement area, but Arekhon had been fighting with Kief Diasul for what already felt like hours. Exhaustion, adrenaline, and the heightened awareness of the working all combined to stretch out his sense of time until the minutes and seconds were as taut-drawn as the *eiran* whose silver network patterned the night.

He struck; and Kief met the blow with his own staff so that the wood shivered in their hands and the combined red and violet of their staves flared up in a many-colored dazzle. Then Kief slid in with a head blow that would have sent Arekhon reeling if he hadn't managed to drag his staff upward in time to block. This time the impact sent a wave of pain through the newly-repaired tissues of his chest and side.

Pain and blood fed into the working. The glowing staves dripped with light, shedding sparks like logs in a hot fire.

This was not like the working with Yuvaen—that one had been fast and brutal, an outpouring of raw energy strong enough to break down space and time and drag Garrod syn-Aigal home. This was deliberate and careful, almost a dance, releasing life and energy in precise amounts to draw the pattern tighter strand by strand.

Arekhon kept in his mind the completed pattern as he had seen it in the nonmaterial world: A tapestry in silver thread, wide enough to cover the galaxy from one side to another. The design here was rougher, and scarcely a corner of the greater work—

—*but every move we make brings it closer to the true pattern.* A fierce joy burned in him at the thought.

"Look around you!" he shouted at Kief, heedless of a barely-turned grazing blow that drew a line of pain across the muscle of his thigh. "You were wrong—the working *can* be mended!"

"Yes." Kief stepped back and let his staff hang loosely from his hand. His voice was hoarse and sad. "But there's not enough time left for us to mend it. They've found you again,

'Rekhe, and this time there's no place where you can go for shelter."

Arekhon cried out in wordless frustration. He could hear the footsteps himself now—heavy-footed ones thundering up the passage into the root cellar, stealthy ones working their way around the sides of the burned-out building—and he knew that Kief spoke the truth. There was no time left for careful, measured work, only for a final intention: A last desperate giving of all his energies when the projectiles struck.

And die in the hope that someone will take up the work again, he thought, and readied himself for the end. *Any moment now—*

But the *eiran* refused to fade. Instead they flared still brighter, until he thought that the design of the true pattern would burn itself permanently into his sight, and a huge roaring sounded in the sky overhead.

A black shape larger than any three of the Hall's outbuildings came thundering down out of the night like some great, dark-feathered bird of prey, and hovered above them on a column of bright blue light. It spat a fiery beam at the open mouth of the cellar, and more beams into the grass and hedges to either side. Then, with all the footsteps silenced, it settled gently to the ground and became a black spaceship of unfamiliar design, wreathed around with cords and threads and tendrils of luck.

In Hanilat Starport, the noon sun shone in through the bay window of Natelth's study, adding a lustrous sheen to the polished wood of the chairs and table, and highlighting the blues and crimsons in the carpet. Natelth had been working at his desk, with only brief moments of respite, since the morning of the day before. The unsettled state of public affairs—and the fleet-family's new ventures in shipbuilding and weapons design—demanded long hours from everyone.

So, at least, Natelth would have told Isayana, if she had ventured into the study to ask.

He was not surprised, in the beginning, when no messages came from the first person with whom he had spoken over the voice-comm. The journey to what remained of Demaizen Old Hall would have taken some time, especially if his contact had any specialized equipment to deal with. Natelth had made a point of not inquiring about methods; provided that the desired result was obtained, he was willing to leave the details to an expert in the business at hand.

As noon came, then evening, then midnight, and no word came, Natelth's tension increased. He took lunch and dinner in his study, scarcely tasting the kitchen's excellent sunbuck stew and home-made bread. The bread had been one of Arekhon's favorites, especially spread with *neiath* jam; Isayana had instructed the house to make a fresh supply of the jam only two days ago. The kitchen added a small crock of jam to the tray one of the *aiketen* brought up in response to his summons, but he sent the crock back to storage unopened.

He slept that night at his desk. If he left the study and went to his bedroom, he might run into Isayana along the way, and she would ask him what he was doing about 'Rekhe. But the expert whom he had sent to Demaizen never called, and Kiefen Diasul walked into his study unannounced at noon the next day.

Natelth wondered what the Mage had done to the *aiketen* and the house-mind, not to mention the liveried guard, but he didn't ask. Arekhon could have slipped past all of them without ruffling a hair, on his own head or the guard's, and Kief had trained with the same Master.

He gestured at Kief to take the empty chair, but the Mage shook his head.

"There's not much to say. I'll stand."

"As you will," said Natelth. "Is the honored guest safely in custody?"

"No." The Mage laughed. "And you can ask about your hired killers as much as you like—they're all dead."

Natelth half-rose from his chair, the cold anger rising again like the incoming tide. "You did this. You let them get away."

"No," said Kief again. "I did just what you asked me— offered your brother one more chance, then gave the signal."

"What happened?"

Kief Diasul smiled. "The Circle didn't choose to go quietly, and your killers forgot that death only lends strength to a working. They died themselves when the ship came down out of the sky."

" 'The ship came down. . . .' Are you mad?"

"Not mad," said Kief. "Just very unlucky. Your brother is gone, sus-Khalgath . . . escaped, vanished, taken elsewhere by the strength of the working, and your honored guest has gone with him."

Natelth let his breath out slowly. "The ship—*whose* ship?—what happened to it? And where is my brother now?"

"No names were ever spoken. The ship came, and it went away again. And your brother is . . . I don't know. Alive, I'm certain. But a long way away."

"Not far enough," said Natelth. He stood and walked into the center of the room. "House-mind!"

The synthesized voice came over the room's hidden speakers. "Yes, Lord Natelth?"

"Listen and record. The name of Arekhon Khreseio sus-Khalgath sus-Peledaen is erased from the family records. It appears on no tablet, no plaque, no scroll. His name is cursed in the homeworlds, and his luck is severed from ours forever. Do you hear?"

"Yes," said the voice of the house-mind. If there was regret in it, Natelth thought, it was only his own imagination. "I hear and record."

The evening sky over the sus-Radal's northern construction site rippled with the colors of an auroral display. *Night's-Beautiful-Daughter* stood on the hard ground of the landing field, hatch open and ramp down. The remaining members of the Demaizen Mage-Circle stood close together in the lee of the *Daughter*'s matte-black side, sheltering from the raw chill of the wind.

Arekhon pulled his quilted jacket tighter around his shoulders. He was still tired and drained after the fight with Kief Diasul, and the cold bit into his bones.

"You two go ahead and strap down in crew berthing," he said to Narin and Ty. "And Karil can take the Pilot-Principal's chair. There's no point in all of us standing around and freezing."

"You'll be along soon?" Narin asked. "You're still wobbly from that patch-job the *aiketen* did on you, and if you get a chill—"

"I'll be fine," he said. "Go on."

They went into the ship, leaving Arekhon alone except for Iulan Vai.

"So," she said. "This is where we part ways."

"You're sure you won't come with us?"

"I'm sure. I had to make a lot of promises to get this ship, and I can't keep them unless I stay behind." She gave an unsteady laugh. "Think of me once in a while, and wish me luck."

"All the luck in the world," he promised. "In whatever you do. You're a part of the great working, now and forever."

She put a hand on either side of his face, palms warm against his cold skin, and pulled his head down and kissed him. "Goodbye, 'Rekhe. And be happy, if you can."

Vai turned and departed. Arekhon stood watching until she reached the lighted buildings at the edge of the field, but she didn't look back. When she was gone, he went up the ramp and cycled the hatch shut behind him.

A few minutes later, the engines began to rumble, and a column of blue light slowly raised the vessel above the hard-packed ground. Fire blossomed as the main thrusters roared into life, and *Night's-Beautiful-Daughter*, named in reverence to the moon, left Eraasi for her place among the stars.

Epilogue

THE ENCLOSED porch of the summer house looked out over a wooded slope leading down to the open fields below. The Mestra liked to take out her deskpad and sit there in pleasant weather, going over correspondence and paperwork. There was more and more of it these days. The Meteunese war had ended in a stalemate, but everyone expected the fighting to start again soon. The loose coalition of smaller states that occupied the continental heartland needed a voice—someone to negotiate on their behalf with larger, more belligerent powers—and Elaeli Inadi meant to have the position for herself. She hadn't intended to be a politician, except to make her way up the sus-Peledaen family ladder, but she was never going to make it to fleet-captain now. Speaker for the Central Quarter would have to do.

She had not been grateful when the troopers of Councillor Demazze pulled her out of the rubble in the late Councillor's underground retreat. None of her pleading had convinced them to turn back and pull Arekhon from the wreckage as well, and she suspected, then and ever afterward, that they had received specific instructions to the contrary.

The Councillor had been specific enough in all other things. Within a week the troopers, still acting on Demazze's orders, had escorted her to a safe house in the neutral state of Lille pont. She herself, according to the troopers, was not Lillepontan, but a refugee from Immering: A wealthy and well-born refugee, from a district already twice broken by war. Councillor Demazze's portfolio, which Elaeli had brought with her out of the wreckage, contained enough records to substantiate her claim, and a duplicate file—somebody hadn't believed in taking chances—waited for her in Lillepont.

She had not yet at that point given up hope. Only a few

days had passed, and the crew of *Rain-on-Dark-Water* would need a while to familiarize themselves with the controls of *Octagon Diamond*. Using the name that the Councillor's false records had given her, she contacted Entiboran Inspace Control.

The starship that had waited in orbit GG-12, she learned when she enquired, had left normal space a week before.

Councillor Demazze was never seen again. General opinion held that he had died in the fighting at his retreat, though when the complex was excavated several months later no body that could be identified as his was ever found.

Elaeli was not surprised. She had lost the capacity for that particular emotion, as for most others; they had died in the rubble of Demazze's underground reception hall. She never knew what the Councillor had truly intended for her to do: Lay the groundwork for an Eraasian trade mission to Entibor, protect the homeworlds from discovery, or simply to survive. 'Rekhe had spoken of bringing together the galaxy, but 'Rekhe was gone. In the weeks after *Octagon Diamond*'s departure Elaeli considered what she had been given—rank, wealth, and troops once belonging to Councillor Demazze but now, by his final orders, loyal to her—and chose for herself.

The voice of her majordomo at the summer house broke into her thoughts. "Mestra Elela, there is a message for you on the private link."

She set her deskpad aside for later and went to the alcove holding the secure line she used for important political conversations. "Elela Rosselin," she said into the audio pickup. By now the alias—another construction of Demazze's—seemed almost as familiar as the long-unheard syllables of her true Eraasian name. "And you are—"

"Entiboran Inspace Control," the caller said. "According to our files, you expressed a wish to be notified if certain events took place."

"Yes," she said, though in truth she had all but forgotten making the request.

"Then it is my pleasure to inform you, Mestra, that an unregistered ship has come from deep space to assume Standard Orbit GG-12."

"Her name?" Elaeli was glad that the representative of Inspace Control could not see her face; she'd gotten a local reputation for icy, unwavering calm, and one look at her now would destroy that image forever.

"She calls herself *Night's-Beautiful-Daughter*"—the representative's voice stumbled over the unfamiliar Eraasian syllables—"and her pilot claims to be a survivor of *Swift Passage Freight Carrier Number Forty-two.*"

"Thank you," she said, "I won't forget your help. If you could do one thing further—"

"Whatever the Mestra wishes."

She paused, gathering her thoughts. "Keep the ship's people away from military intelligence and the gossip lines," she said, once she was able to speak without fear that her voice would break or quiver. "And bring them straight to me. Do this discreetly, and you can count on my gratitude."

She closed the communications link and returned to the porch, where she stood for a long time looking outward at the clear blue promise of the sky. She had been wrong, she thought; it seemed that she had not lost the capacity for strong and distracting emotions after all. Especially hope.

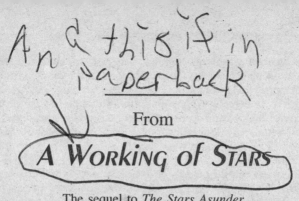

And this if in paperback

From

A Working of Stars

The sequel to *The Stars Asunder*
Coming from Tor in early 2001

ON A world not his own, in a life he had never anticipated, Arekhon sus-Khalgath lay dreaming, and knew that he dreamed.

In his dream he knelt in the meditation chamber of the starship *Night's-Beautiful-Daughter*, where he had not gone in his waking body for over a dozen years. His staff, a cubit and a half of black wood bound with silver, lay on the deck in front of him, and all around him the *Daughter* vibrated with the urgency of her passage through the Void.

Arekhon wondered what he was meant to do. Had he only now begun his meditation, here inside his dream, or had he just ended it? He couldn't remember; but somewhere outside the chamber, an alarm began to sound.

He picked up his staff in his right hand and got to his feet. Outside the chamber, the alarm bell continued its steady, pulse-note chime. He found the door and opened it, and stepped through—not into the harsh illumination of a starship's passageway, but into the Old Hall at Demaizen, and the warm golden light of an autumn afternoon.

He had walked through the Old Hall in dreams often enough

before, in the years since the Demaizen Mage-Circle had split apart in fire and blood, but never as now, with the weight of knowledge bearing down hard upon him. In these rooms, he had grown from a sus-Peledaen fleet-apprentice with a knack for seeing the *eiran* and making luck, to a working Mage in Lord Garrod's Circle—and now he came back to them with the sound of the *Daughter*'s alarm bell following him wherever he went.

Sometimes in his dreams he saw the Mages of Demaizen as he had known them before. On those nights he sparred with Delath or Serazao in the long gallery, or talked of space and stars with Kiefin Diasul, though in the waking world both Del and 'Zao were dead, and Kief had gone years ago to another Circle. Tonight, though, was different. Instead of Delath or Serazao, the dream gave him Iulan Vai.

Vai—the last-come member of the Circle, who had brought *Night's-Beautiful-Daughter* from the sus-Radal to save the Demaizen Mages from utter destruction, then stayed behind on Eraasi to repay the debt. He found her in the long gallery, with its tall, westward-facing windows and its racks of exercise mats and limber practice staves. She hadn't changed since the last time he saw her in the flesh. Under the touch of the afternoon sun, her dark hair still glinted with rusty-brown highlights, and she still clothed her compact frame in tunic and leggings of ordinary black.

"Iule," he said—though she had always refused the forms of affection, even with those who might have had a claim to use them. "What are you doing here?"

"Looking for you," she said. Outside the long gallery, somewhere in the rooms—and the life—that he had left behind him, the sound of the *Daughter*'s alarm changed from a bell-note to a strident metallic wail. "You have to leave now. It's almost time."

He awoke into darkness; the hour was well past moonset, so that the starlit rectangle of his bedroom window took a long minute to resolve into a patch of gray against the black. The furniture—bed, nightstand, chair, desk—took a little longer to emerge from the undifferentiated night. When he could distinguish the outline of the half-open closet door, over on the far side of the room, he got out of bed and began to dress.

His clothes were on the chair where he had laid them out before retiring: Garments of local cut, but made in the plain black and white he had always preferred. He'd never grown accustomed to the colors of this world, its alien dyestuffs and yet more alien aesthetics; after a while he had given up trying. He put on shirt and trousers and a loose jacket, then hesitated a moment before pulling on his boots. Stocking feet would have been quieter, but far less dignified. Arekhon had nothing against suffering embarrassment in a good cause, but he had no desire to suffer it unnecessarily.

The lower floors of the building were silent and empty. In the town houses of Arekhon's childhood, the night hours had belonged to the *aiketen*, the constructed intelligences in their metal shells; it had been impossible for anyone to move about in secret without first subverting the quasi-organic servitors. They didn't have *aiketen* here on this side of the interstellar gap. The men and women who did what should have been a construct's labor—and who worked late and rose early—slept in a warren of small rooms high up under the mansion's eaves.

No one lived on the bottom floor except for Arekhon. He was, at least nominally, a scholar-savant under the Mestra's patronage, and entitled to maintain private chambers elsewhere at her expense. But those closest to the Mestra knew him— by face if not by name—as the man responsible for House Rosselin's domestic security, and they would expect to find such a one keeping his quarters under the Mestra's roof.

The stairs ascending from the mansion's lower level were dark and narrow. Arekhon went up them with the familiarity of long practice, and up the next set of stairs as well. These were wider, and lit by a nightglow in a niche halfway along. The door at the top answered to a palmprint scan; Arekhon was one of the people it recognized. He placed his right hand against the pad and the lock clicked open.

He passed through one darkened room, noting the dim shapes of chairs and cabinets and pieces of unobjectionable art, all unchanged since his last visit, and through another, this one a private office similarly unaltered, before he came to another door with a palmprint scan. Again he touched the pad, and, when the lock answered, opened the door.

Elaeli was awake, though it took him a moment to spot her in the unlighted room. She wore a loose bed-robe of dark fabric, and—standing as she did a little to one side of the window—seemed at first like a part of the curtain that had been drawn aside. She looked around as he entered.

" 'Rekhe," she said. "I was just wishing I dared to go looking for you. I couldn't sleep."

He crossed over to where she stood, and put an arm around her, so that she could lean her head against his shoulder. "I'm here now."

"I miss you when you're away downstairs."

"This is the city," he said. "If I stay in your rooms for the whole night, the servants will know, and if the servants know, the scandal-rags will have it by nightfall."

"Damn the scandal-rags." She sounded tired, worn down with waiting for sleep that hadn't come. "Fourteen years I've been here, 'Rekhe, and I still don't understand this place."

"Don't try. Just ride the luck, and trust it to carry you in the right direction." Which it would do, Arekhon reflected; he had expended considerable energy over the years in working the *eiran* for this world, and for Elaeli Inadi syn-Peledaen. The threads of his own luck were tangled and untended by comparison. He would probably come to regret that one of these days, but not yet.

She made a disgruntled noise. "The Provost of Elicond is coming here tomorrow. For three weeks."

"Will that be long enough, do you think?"

"It's all he's going to get. This year, anyway. He's that eager to make a gene-link with House Rosselin, he can try again next year. As soon as he's out of the way, I'm going to the country and staying there. . . . Will you come with me?"

"Yes," said Arekhon. Elaeli's summer cottage was isolated enough that the scandal-rags didn't bother with it—at least not for something as commonplace as bedroom gossip. Arekhon thought of the pleasure of waking beside Elaeli in the morning sunlight, and sighed.

You have to leave now, the woman in his dream had told him. *It's almost time.*

He did not think that she had been speaking of the house in An-Jemayne.

* * *

Azeri sus-Dariv had been attending her family's annual business conclave every year since she'd reached her sixteenth birthday—old enough to enroll as a fleet-apprentice if she so desired, or to leave her family's altars and train with the Mages, though not of age to hold a family commission or Circle membership. Azeri didn't want to be either a fleet officer or a Mage; since she had to study something until she reached her majority, she claimed to be an aspiring merchant-administrator. In that guise she went to the meetings and observed her family's internal politics in action, and found them dead boring.

Almost a decade later, she still hadn't changed her opinion. Not even holding this year's meeting in the private conference areas of the Court of Two Colors, Hanilat's most exclusive hostelry and dining-place, could make Azeri feel more than a passing interest in the matters at hand. Some years she'd lasted as long as the full week; this year she gave up trying on the fifth day.

She remembered the moment clearly afterward. She'd been at the late afternoon snacks-and-*uffa* break in the Court's Grand Reception Hall, where the working members of the sus-Dariv, the men and women upon whom the inner family relied for support, stood about in gossiping clusters on the black and white tessellated floor that gave the Court its name. Tables on the long side of the room held trays of food—small sausages wrapped in flaky pastry, grilled miniature vegetables on wooden skewers, cubes of hard white cheese and slices of neiath fruit drizzled with bittersweet syrup—flanked by giant copper urns full of both red and pale uffa.

The pair of outer-family administrators with whom she'd been working all afternoon—first generation syn-Dariv by adoption, which meant they were ambitious up-and-comers—had been talking about differential rank and compensation scales for the last half-hour. The conversation seemed to press down upon her like a pillow, vast and formless and smothering. What was she doing here, anyway? She'd missed this month's theatre-arts group meeting already—

She caught sight of her first cousin Herinath filling a crystal mug with *uffa* at the nearest urn. With a skill honed over years of family conclaves, she detached herself from the two syn-Dariv and bore down upon her cousin.

"Herin!" she exclaimed, as soon as she came within earshot. "This is the first time I've seen you, this whole session—have you been avoiding me?"

"Not on purpose," he said. He added, "I didn't get here until today, as it happens."

"Lucky for you. Where were you all that time?"

He filled a mug with pale *uffa* and handed it to her. He knew her tastes well enough to omit asking for her preference, which was handy if a bit unsettling when she considered that they'd never been particularly close. "Here and there," he said. "Studying."

"Studying what?"

"Private security forces, mostly," he said. "And how they're being integrated into different family structures."

"Ah." That was the main issue facing this evening's open session; it had depressed her a little that more people hadn't been talking about the problem earlier. "How are they being integrated?"

"As a general rule?" He drained the last of his mug of *uffa* and filled it again. "Badly. Either they're not exploited well enough or they're a danger to the family that supposedly controls them."

"I suppose that means you're going to vote against establishing a sus-Dariv strike team," she said.

He nodded. "The odds of it working as intended aren't very good."

"I suppose not . . . look, Herin, will you take my proxy for that vote when it comes up? If I don't get out of here soon I'm going to suffocate."

"Of course," he said. She set down her mug and searched through her folder of conference materials until she found a pen and a slip of paper with which to write up the formal authorization. He tucked the finished note inside his shirt. That done, Azeri gave Herin her thanks and a smile of farewell, then began working her way through the crowd to the door.

His cousin 'Zeri, Herinath decided some hours later, was quite a bit smarter than she looked. She'd made a neat escape from a largely pointless evening, not-to mention the remainder of the afternoon working sessions, while at the same time ensuring that her vote was counted on the only issue of any actual importance. The folded paper with her authorization on it crackled stiffly inside his jacket as he made his way to the banquet hall from a roundtable seminar on kinship parity. He didn't have any interest in the subject—he was one of the Hayerit sus-Dariv, and high enough in the inner family that the work he did was not done for rank or recognition—but he'd attended the seminar out of a sense of duty.

A flicker of motion caught at the corner of his eye just outside the leather-covered double doors that led from the conference area to the banquet hall. He looked in the direction of the anomaly, only to have it vanish; a second later, it was teasing at him again. This time he was more careful, using his peripheral vision to watch the thing, whatever it was. He was rewarded with a glimpse of what looked like pale, glowing thread, that sometimes trailed on the black-and-white patterned carpet and sometimes appeared to float in the air above it.

Very odd, Herin thought. People who worked in the Mage Circles spoke of the *eiran* as looking like silvery thread; but he had never been a Mage, or even trained for one. He wasn't supposed to be seeing the *eiran* for the first time at a business conference in Hanilat.

But now that he'd spotted it, the glowing line wouldn't go away. It curled and snaked about, twisting in and out among sus-Dariv and syn-Dariv alike. Herin was seized by the thought that it must be trying to find him, personally, by some kind of touch. Before he could think better of his action, he stepped around a knot of gossiping life-sciences savants and let the questing silver thread wrap itself whiplike around his ankle.

Something like an electric shock passed through him with the contact. This was luck, all right—strong and real, the pulsing current of life itself. Next to it, the furnishings of the Court of the Two Colors, and the chattering crowd outside the banquet hall, seemed diminished and pale, like objects from a lesser order of existence. He marked how the thread of the *eiran* wound away from him, through the room and out the farther door, and felt it pulling at him to follow.

This is definitely something new, he thought. And because Herinath Hayerit sus-Dariv was an inquisitive man by nature as well as by profession, he gave in to the urge and let the silver cord draw him away from the banquet hall.

The *eiran* led Herinath away from the private areas of the Court of the Two Colors, and down to the pavement level. He let the silver thread draw him, unresisting, through the heavy glass doors and past the gatekeeper-*aiketh,* and from there out onto the street. Night had fallen outside, and the glowing thread stood out against the darkness like a line of silver fire. Herin wondered if any of the passers-by hurrying along to their transit connections or their evening appointments also saw the *eiran* as he did—or was that beckoning silver thread intended for him alone?

He followed it across High Port Street, weaving in and out of the vehicular traffic and through the press of pedestrians on the other side. There, in the shelter of a recessed doorway, the *eiran* left him, dissipating like fog and taking its strange compulsion away with it into the night.

That was certainly peculiar, he thought, in the instant remaining before the world as he had known it came to an end.

There was a noise—an enormous, unexpected noise—and the whole Court of Two Colors swayed as if struck by a giant fist. The right-hand side of the building, the side holding the grand ballroom, collapsed downward. Dust rose in a vast cloud, water spurted from broken mains, electricity sparked from severed cables. The high-velocity shockwave touched and killed everyone in its path, as far out as the middle of High Port Street.

The left wing, where the public restaurant and the guest-rooms were, swayed and canted but did not collapse and—judging strictly from its effects—the shockwave was more attenuated there. After the explosion, silence fell; though it could have been merely a temporary deafness. Tongues of fire began to lick at the wreckage. Emergency vehicles with lights and sirens—all the power of a city come to deal with a hurt—arrived soon after that.

Herin watched, unscathed. All that he could think of, beyond the fact that the *eiran* for some reason wanted him alive, was that somebody else definitely wanted all of his family dead.

Azeri sus-Dariv yawned and stretched her way out of a sound and dreamless sleep, then sat up in bed and raised her voice for the benefit of the house-mind.

"Kitchen! Fix me some toast and red *uffa*."

The kitchen's synthesized voice came back to her. "I hear."

She rose and made her way down the hall to the necessarium. After a session of hot mist followed by a cooling waterfall had coaxed her the rest of the way to wakefulness, she put on a light morning-gown and thin-soled slippers and went to have her breakfast.

The late morning sun shone in through the half-curtained windows of the apartment's outer room. Azeri sat down in the high-backed woven wood chair where she usually took her meals, just as the *aiketh* floated in carrying a tray. The servitor construct—a quasi-organic node of the house-mind, encased in a roughly cylindrical shell of metal and plastic—hovered on its counterforce unit a handspan or so above the green and yellow carpet.

"As you required," the *aiketh* said.

"Excellent," said Azeri, after the *aiketh* had unfolded the legs of the tray to make a table. "You may go."

The *aiketh* floated off. Azeri applied herself to the toast and *uffa*. She was not quite halfway through the meal when the entrance monitor chimed an alert and spoke.

"Fas Treosi is here with urgent news, and requests admittance."

She felt a stirring of curiosity. Had the conclave actually decided something noteworthy, after all? "Let Syr Treosi come in."

She heard the door opening, and a moment later Treosi appeared: An elderly gentleman, the very image of a respectable legalist, his coat and trousers of sober gray a silent reproach to her own informal dress.

"My apologies for being so late in breakfasting," she said to him, and gestured toward the woven wood guest chair. "Please join me for *uffa*, at least."

"I don't want to trouble you," Treosi began.

But the *aiketh* was already bringing up another tray, this one bearing a cup and saucer, and placing it beside his chair. Then the servitor took the pot of *uffa* from Azeri's tray and filled Treosi's cup with the steaming red liquid.

"You see," Azeri said lightly, "it's no trouble for me at all. Now, Syr Treosi what brings you to my door, of all places, so early in the midmorning? Has some unforeseen disaster cut down all the senior family and left no one standing besides me?"

To her astonishment—followed, a heartbeat later, by the slow crawl of increasing fear—Fas Treosi's face went pale. "Yes," he said. "You are Azeri sus Dariv, the last of the family's senior line and the only holder of the true name left alive."

"Explain," she said. She knew better, seeing Treosi's face, than to ask if this was a joke. "Please."

"An incendiary device," Treosi said. "During the late meetings . . . somebody must have known who would be there. If you hadn't chosen to leave early . . ."

"Yes," said Azeri. She'd meant to look in on her theatre-arts group, but the conclave had left her feeling dull and out of sorts. She'd gone home instead, to read a journal article called "Civic Turmoil and Public Art: A Window of Opportunity?" and play solitaire against the house-mind. Pure slackness on her part—Cousin Herinath would have said so, and only half in jest—but she was alive because of it, and he was dead.

"Somebody else had to have missed the late meetings," she said, in desperation. "Great-uncle Dariyein—he wasn't there at all that I remember. Somebody said he hadn't been feeling very well."

"Apparently not," said Treosi. "His household *aiketen* found him dead this morning."

"Killed?"

Treosi gave a minute shrug. "Without further examination, who can say? If you want to order—"

"What would be the point?" She set down the cup she'd been holding ever since Treosi made his first, bald announcement. "He's gone. So are the rest of them. Anybody left is away with the fleet. We have to call the convoy home and sort things out."

"I'm sorry," said Treosi. He was shaking his head, and his expression had not lightened. "I didn't get the chance to finish telling you—"

She had been cold; she was growing colder. "Finish it, Syr Treosi. What else happened last night?"

"The trading fleet is lost."

"What! How?"

"Pirates, out beyond Ruisi. The guard and attack ships were destroyed, the cargo haulers boarded and left empty. *Path-Lined-with-Flowers* brought the word in just before midnight."

"I see." Piracy had always been a key element of the game of trade as the fleet-families played it, but seldom piracy so complete and so disastrous. "Did the *Path* recognize any insignia or fleet-livery?"

"Black only," said Treosi. "And the boarders never unmasked."

"Against all custom," Azeri said. She laced her hands together in her lap, hidden under the breakfast tray so that Treosi would not see them shaking. "Tell me something, if you can—"

"Of course."

"The incendiary device. Did it go off before or after the *Path* came into orbit?"

"After."

"I understand," she said. The timing was too exact for anything but luck, and not the luck of the sus-Dariv, either. She clasped her hands even more tightly under the shelter of the lacquered tray. "It would have been more convenient for everybody if I had stayed at the meeting. I was never intended to be head of the family."

"If I may offer a suggestion—"

"Please."

"The outer family and the junior lines are still relatively intact despite the losses of the past few hours. Your wisest course would be to approach one of the syn-Dariv, or perhaps the Hayerit—I can make a few recommendations, if you don't actually have a preference—with an offer of contractual alliance."

"I don't think so," she said.

"You have to do something," Treosi protested. "Soon, before other families notice the absence of control and move to devour you."

"Someone is devouring us already," she pointed out. "Our fleet is weaponless, our senior line is destroyed . . . if I were to find a capable man and make him head of the sus-Dariv in every important respect, with his line to be senior after I'm gone—that's the kind of agreement you were thinking of, wasn't it?—how long do you think the rest of the fleet-family would last?"

"But what else is there to do?"

She had shocked him, Azeri could tell; he hadn't thought that she would reject the idea. She wondered briefly which of the ambitious junior families had seized the moment, in the midst of flame and consternation, and solicited Treosi's ear.

It didn't matter. Somebody had made the sus-Dariv into a target—somebody who could command secret operatives in Hanilat, and a fleet of raiders in deep space, and a Circle powerful enough to break the luck of a entire fleet-family—and before long the carrion eaters would be closing in. The only safety lay in attaching the sus-Dariv to another family, one strong enough to keep all the lesser predators at bay.

The sus-Radal or the sus-Peledaen, Azeri thought, while Syr Treosi was still remonstrating with her across the breakfast tray. *It has to be one or the other of them . . . and one or the other of them blew up the meeting and destroyed our fleet. Nobody else is strong enough.*

"Go to Natelth sus-Peledaen," she said. "Tell him that the head of the sus-Dariv wishes to speak with him on a matter concerning our two families."